Empower

I0667188

Publishing

Watch for These Titles
from Louise Gore Sayre-David

John Steel: The Man and the Legend
Green Sea Plantation
The Land Darkens
Springs Gift of Light
The Turbulence and the Struggle

and *Empower Publishing*

The Winds Grow Gentle

She Heard a Whippoorwill Series:
Book Five

By

Louise Gore Sayre-David

Empower Publishing
Winston-Salem

Empower

Publishing

Empower Publishing
PO Box 26701
Winston-Salem, NC 27114

This book is a work of fiction. The events and opinions related in this work are entirely the creation and opinion of the author and do not represent the opinions or thoughts of the publisher. All individuals described are the author's interpretation of history and creative imagination.

First Empower Publishing Books edition published
February, 2020
Empower Publishing, Feather Pen, and all production design are trademarks.

For information regarding bulk purchases of this book, digital purchase and special discounts, please contact the publisher at empowerpublishing2015@gmail.com

Cover design by Pan Morelli

Manufactured in the United States of America
ISBN 978-1-63066-500-5

Dedicated in loving memory to the sweet spirit of my oldest sister Mary Doretha Gore Hinson.

—Louise Gore Sayre-David

Chapter One

Autumn fell and the season was soft, and it was to mark another event in this turbulent year—though a happy one—which resulted into such pleasure for everyone who became associated with it that for several years to come it nearly came to be an annual occurrence. Tom Green came to Green Sea! It had taken Tom five years to patch up and replace what the ravages of War had done to his fruit farm and finally make good the promise he had made to Luke that day they had been reunited in Jeb Stuart's Cavalry division.

Betsy and the nine-year-old Luke, Luke's namesake, accompanied Tom. And, Tom's visit was to bring back something that had been missing at Green Sea a great deal of time, lately—laughter. In addition, that same exhilarating echoing Roar of Toms appeared to rekindle over that certain spark that tragedy had near about smothered out, seeming to douse everything at Green Sea with a lively tonic that brought a spirited bounce to the whole Plantation from the moment of his arrival to the hour of his departure.

The Greens came to South Carolina by train. Luke, allowing of the three-year-old Carr to accompany him inside the carriage, while granting Doss the pleasure of guiding it with jailor perched proudly on the outside driver's seat beside Doss, met Tom and his family at the Depot in Charleston. The meeting between the two friends was moving for each, almost bringing tears. But both were quickly to repress emotion and greet the others. Tom picking up Carr with a hearty, "Hello there big boy" and swinging him in the air much to Carr's displeasure because it was Carr's notion that he was much too grownup to be thrown high above this lusty stranger's head as if he were a baby, while Luke turned to give his attention to the other members of the Green family.

"Betsy," said Luke, beaming, as he bent forward and kissed the still pretty woman who had never seen him as a stranger on the cheek while he closed his hands around hers, "you can't imagine my pleasure at seeing you again it's been too long, dear."

1

"It certainly has, Luke," Betsy cheerfully replied, "but let's hope it won't be this long anymore between visits."

"I'll second that wholeheartedly," agreed Luke, turning to extend a warm greeting and his hand as well to the plump round face blonde youngster standing beside her. As young Luke Green's hand met Luke's in a surprising firm grip despite its smallness and he saw the flashing affable grin on The boy's face that was so remarkably like that of Tom's, he was certain that had Tom and Betsy Green been nowhere around he would still have recognized the boy any place. Luke Green was the spitting image of his father.

The excitement finally eased up in the midst of seeing to the Green's baggage and the barrel of apples that Tom had aboard, too. The apples were the most select that came from the noted Green Orchards and, once the barrel had been firmly secured on the back of the carriage, the baggage secured on the top between the guardrails; and all the passengers aboard, the somewhat loaded carriage set out for Green Sea.

If Eliza had been a little solicitous over her role as hostess, wondering about the things the Greens favored and those they did not wanting everything to be right and proper for these longtime friends of Luke's but strangers to her, it was all to dissipate the instant she saw the exuberant Tom Green sweeping across the space between her and him with the animation of a brush fire.

She was in the kitchen endeavoring to effect the finishing touch to an already perfected table when she heard the front door open and Luke call eagerly, Eliza darling, they're here!"

Swiftly, she jerked off the white starched apron that was protecting the front of her best and choice house dress—a turquoise—blue sateen with white collar and cuffs, throwing it upon a chair. One hand went flying to her head to give her hair which was dressed attractive but simple a pat while the other hand was quickly smoothing the lines of her dress. Then, with her face flushing and nervously drawing upon a deep breath, she raced for the parlor where she found Luke ushering his last guest through the door and closing it.

Luke hurriedly stepped to her side and even before he could finish saying, as he proudly draped an arm around Eliza slender waist, "well, Tom, here she is! Eliza dear, my good friend, Tom Green, his wife Betsy, and their son, Luke," Tom Green was already exclaiming, "My stars, Luke, she's just as pretty as you always lead me to believe!"

Sending a devilish wink toward Betsy he went on mischievously grinning, "Honeybunch, no wonder this scamp was in such a hurry to leave us, ready to brave blizzards again, endure sore feet and everything else in order to reach Green Sea, "making his way to grasp Eliza's outstretched hand which he began to pump vigorously.

And, for the first time in months, Eliza began to feel a lifting of heart. She felt as though she could almost see currents of high-flying enthusiasm radiating from Tom Greens body and began to respond immediately to the fervent way in which he appeared to meet every aspect of life he encountered—even meeting strangers, seeing plainly that she had been foolish; indeed, in worrying that there would be distant moments between her and the Greens.

Setting her eyes directly to the dancing light her gaze met in those of Tom's, Eliza said, as she somewhat amusingly thought that Tom Green's zestful personality just night loosen every nail and board in the modest small house before he left, "Mr. Green, my sincerest wish for years has finally been granted. It makes me very happy to welcome you and Mrs. Green and your son, Luke, to Green Sea, at last."

"The pleasure is ours and I thank you, but listen," Tom laughed, "none of that Mr. and Mrs. stuff, please!"

"Very well, then, Tom and Betsy," laughed Eliza, as she disengaged her hand From Tom's and turned to Betsy, embracing her, "Betsy, I've always felt that Luke's lucky day was that Christmas morning that Providence guided him to walk into the warmth of yours and Tom's home.

"I feel the gift that was awaiting him there, the beauty and goodness of your hearts, was one of the most beautiful gifts he could've come by. I shall always be grateful to you both."

"Thank you, Eliza, but Tom and I feel we were the fortunate ones that day. Not only did Luke enlighten our Christmas holiday in more ways than one that year, but his friendship has been a source of joy over the years since then and especially to Tom who looks upon Luke as being that brother he never had."

"Sugarplum, you couldn't have expressed my sentiments any better. However, Eliza dear," Tom guffawed once more, "I must straighten out one detail concerning that particular Christmas Day. It was more like Luke crawling and stumbling into our home rather than walking, that is to say, what time I wasn't half carrying him!"

"Tom!" objected Betsy, rather demurely

Betsy need not have feared though that Eliza felt put out. She was catching on fast to Tom Green's witticism. Never batting an eye, she retorted, "just so he got there, Tom, and what a blessing you have such strong arms!" while Tom roared with laughter with Luke joining in, turned her smile upon young Luke Green, telling him, "Luke, I hope you'll enjoy visiting us here at Green Sea as much as we're going to enjoy having you."

Eliza was almost started at the patterned heavier between father and son as Luke Green's tiny hand shot out toward her as unhesitant and self-assertive as his father, flashing her that same grin, replying, "Thank you kindly, ma'am, I like Green Sea already."

During Luke Green's response to Eliza, Tom and Luke's mirth had quieted down while both had looked and listened, experiencing an entirely different like feeling—Luke, a song of gladness running through him in seeing at long last that what he feared had been destroyed In Eliza by Frank Drakston, was finally showing signs of being revived again. Giving silent thanks, he inquired of her, "Eliza dear, is dinner about ready? The train was some minutes late and it's not the shortest road I know of between here and Charleston. I wouldn't be surprised if all the rest aren't suffering the same pangs of hunger that I am."

"Everything's ready, Luke, all I have to do is take it from the stove to the table. While I do that, why don't you show our guests their room?" she suggested. "They may want to freshen up a bit." she started for the kitchen but turned back. "Oh, I'm sorry the baby has missed all this, but she's already eaten and fallen asleep. Luke, you might do something else if you will. Those telltale candy streaks on Carr's face and hands needs to be washed off before he comes to the table. Apparently, someone found the time to visit the candy store again," she chided him, but quite sweet-tempered as she moved on toward the kitchen.

Seeing the Green's strained expression, Luke smiled and quickly explained, "She's on to my candy buying spree again. She believes too many sweets will cause the children to lose their teeth too early in life."

"You know," replied Tom thoughtfully, tugging at his chin, "come to think of it, I'll go along with your little lady's philosophy any day, bearing on that idea."

Smirking, Luke quipped, "oh, you would, would you?" slapping Tom on the shoulder, "Come on, let's hurry, I think she's having fried chicken!"

"You bet!" grinned Tom, giving Luke a whack back in return, "Now, I'll gladly go along with your idea, friend!"

Betsy smiled at the two men's give-and-take buffoonery, shaking her head, as Luke gestured for everybody to follow him.

Tom Green's decision to pay his first visit to Green Sea that fall could not have been any more perfectly timed on every account. It had been geared to harmonize with Luke's harvest schedule, that is, what harvest was left to attend to. Added to all the rest of Luke and Eliza's woeful ordeals that year, there had been an almost total crop failure at Green Sea. It had not come about by any less effort from Luke or anybody else on the plantation. In truth, it seemed everybody had worked harder than ever. But, by the last of July, it was clear that drought had ruined the tobacco and corn crop and the cotton appeared to be slated for the same. When the rain had finally commenced to fall, it had come too late and had been too plentiful to bring the cotton through to a successful harvest. Cotton required dry, warm days for its pods to burst wide and full with the white, fluffy product, not wet and dampness day after day. Due to the drought the cotton crop had fallen way short, anyhow, and now it seemed a vast amount of its product would mold and decay on the stalk before it could be picked.

The ill-suited weather tapered off at last though and the damaged cotton was picked and baled and hauled to market, the final yield proving it had hardly been worth the effort. The only crop that had been planted at Green Sea that year that appeared to have come along where near that of former years, were the sweet potatoes. And, Luke was not rushing to get this crop out of the ground, though the task had been started the day Tom's letter arrived. There was always ample time to dig the potatoes and bank them before cold weather set in.

Through late summer and early fall when it had been manifested the crops had failed, Luke's gaze would often stray to the house foundation that he had started so eagerly and had seen so much trouble over and feel nothing but despair. He knew now that the mansion he had envisioned rising upon it in a few years, the dream that he had harbored since that March day when he and Eliza had sat on the kitchen steps, had suffered a severe setback. Sometimes, looking at summers trailing vines and weeds that had flourished so lavishly in the abundant supply of water the heavens had seen fit to pour forth for days on end, Luke would come near to feel as though Frank Drakston's ghost were hovering close by, laughing at him from the grave. He was well aware this was morbid; thinking however and kept his destructive thoughts to himself. He made every attempt to present an optimistic front to Eliza, and, most the time, he had been successful in pulling it off, or at least he felt he had.

Luke did take heart that it looked as though no one would be suffering from hunger at Green Sea while waiting and working toward another harvest. It appeared there would still be plenty of sweet potatoes. There were several hogs to butcher. Eliza had raised a lot of fryers that spring and summer, so it looked like they would be eating the usual Sunday chicken dinners and sometimes through the weekdays, too. In addition, there would be eggs to eat as well as sell at O'Henry's store to buy items that were not raised or made on the plantation. The fruit trees had born a fair supply of fruit, enough for their own use and the hands, also. A lot of canning had been done, fruit and vegetables alike. Due to Doss' diligent care, pouring gallons of water at the most crucial time, the garden had done all right, too. But, as for cash, there was not going to be enough money to even last until Christmas, not one dollar to spare for the smallest luxury. And moreover, it was clear the essentials another crop would demand, the cash to buy them would have to be obtained through a loan at the cooper's bank against the crop before it was ever planted and brought to harvest.

Thus, it was little wonder that Luke, even though he was thrilled to hear from Tom, had opened Tom's letter with a despondent heart. Even so, within seconds, his worries began to seem less important as he ran his eyes down the first page of Tom Green's letter—the unique way that Tom had of handling his words stirrings that ever prevailing amusement. When he turned to the second page his worries suddenly became lost altogether as the words began to impart facts and suggestions that moved him to exclaim excitedly, from where he was dropped down at the kitchen table reading the letter that Eliza had handed him as he came through the kitchen "Eliza dear! Tom's coming to Green Sea! It's true, Tom, Betsy, and Luke! Tom's bringing them too!"

The news startled Eliza, understandingly so, because Tom had been writing in most every letter for as long as five years that someday he was paying a visit to Green Sea. With an incredulous look spreading across her face, she turned from the stove where she had begun to dish up dinner, inquiring, "You mean to say Tom Green's finally going to pay a visit to Green Sea rather than continuing to promise you, that he was still rolling the thought in his mind, so he's so often put it?"

"That's what he's written and next week at that!" Luke's lifted voice rang, his greedy gaze hurrying on down the page, adding excitedly as he read on, "And, he wants to go to Sandy Cove Beach while he's here if it can be arranged, says he wants to do some surf fishing and give Betsy and Luke a chance to see the ocean!"

"They've never seen the ocean?" That was hard for Eliza to comprehend, too, having always had the Atlantic Ocean so near her doorstep.

"I guess not," replied Luke, finally reaching the last line of Tom's letter which had not been in keeping with his former ones—the same repeated promise that someday he was coming to Green Sea. It appeared that "someday" had arrived.

Folding the letter and laying it down on the table beside his plate as Eliza was setting the last dish of food down, Luke exclaimed again, his expression seeming to travel far from where he was seated, "I can't believe it! I guess though I shouldn't have had doubts that Tom would come through sometime. He's not the type to say something that he doesn't believe in. After he came into Jeb's cavalry, he and I used to sit around the campfire at night, with Sam Sweeney's bongo thumping resounding from Stuart's headquarters in the distance and discuss thousands of subjects it seemed, and one was our hope of going surf fishing together someday. Then, all too soon, there were no more lively discussions with Tom, or, as for that matter, anyone else for a long time. The Yankees stopped all that." His expression hardened for a moment.

"You hold a special feeling in your heart for Tom, don't you, Luke?" Eliza said as she sat down at last with him and the children.

"Well, I suppose so, or I've either fallen victim to that firsthand quality that Tom has and that one so seldom sees. You'll understand what I mean once you've met him. He seems to make every moment in life count, whether it's good or bad. It's almost literally impossible to feel down in the man's presence."

And, you've been down a lot lately, thought Eliza, as Luke dropped his head and began to say the blessing, a blessing that she was to observe was recited in a more stimulating peal than others of late had been.

Notwithstanding Luke's presumption that he had carried through with presenting a fair semblance of naturalness when it came to being himself where Eliza was concerned, she had been and still was far from being deceived. She knew and felt his despair—his deep disappointment, too, over the crops not having yield at least an average sum. The prayer of thanks had been repeated and she began to help the children with their plates. Having gotten them settled, she then served herself. But all her moves were being performed automatically for her scrutiny of Luke was holding most of her attention.

While Eliza observed Luke now eating his dinner in silence, his thoughts obviously turned to other matters other than his worries since his having read Tom's letter, she noticed something else that Tom's letter seemed to have affected. Those lines that she had begun to see of late in Luke's still handsome face appeared to have relaxed somewhat—those premature marks that the strained years had put on Luke—something that pained her dreadfully to acknowledge but again something she forced herself to recognize as anything but undisputed fact. Suddenly however, seeing how Tom's letter had lifted much of the gloom from Luke's face and thinking about the Green's pending visit and Tom's desire to go surf fishing, she found her own thoughts straying far beyond the kitchen table, becoming lost in time—a yesteryear when she had gone to Sandy Cove Beach most every autumn on a happy holiday outing with her parents and brothers and most often the Drakston's and Wilton's, too. From the time she could remember and on throughout her girlhood, the fresh, natural wonders of Sandy Cove had provided a part of the happiness she had known in her growing up years.

Sandy Cove Beach, the awesome and restless Atlantic Ocean beating a continuous roll of turbulent, eruptive waves upon its mirror smooth strand which at low tide stretched well to a quarter-mile wide, lay about twenty-five miles direct east of Green Sea. Starting somewhere near late August or early September, the fishing season at Sandy Cove began and continued on to the onset of cold weather. The first of these tasty species to come flocking in near the foaming surf were the mullets, to be followed soon after by various other types of fish that were as equally delicious as the mullets were. At times, schools of fish could be seen swimming so plentiful in the mountainous building waves they came near to resembling bees gathered on a beehive, seeming to be driven toward shore by instinct as the salmon is instinctively driven to abandon its habitual waters of the northern oceans and head toward the Columbia River where its fate awaits it.

Save this particular time of year when the fishermen came to Sandy Cove, the beach lay uninhabited—an ancient relic totally unspoiled by man—a good portion of its pearl—white sandy earth having yet to cushion man's footsteps. For miles and miles its hard-packed strand stretched as far as the eye could see, an unbroken shoreline as level and glistening as a sharpened knife blade. Pinned there by distant time and looking nearabout as flowerlike and lustrous as snow white gardenias pinned on a dress, giant, towering sand dunes laced the Atlantic's skirt and entire surrounding land as methodically and splendidly as a ship's speeded sails, adding another wonder to this natural haven.

There were the sea gulls, dipping low over the washing waves. There were the wild oats and wire grass bent to the wind. There was the bothersome sandbur, too. There were also the jewel-colored seashells and Eliza saw it all now and herself as well as she once had been, running along Sandy Cove's strand with Phil and Nat, their bare feet splashing through the rolling waves. And, of course, when the Drakston's and Wilton's had joined the outing, there had been Martha and Caroline to play with, too. And, yes, Frank also; that is, those few times when Frank had finally gotten bored from sitting in the wagon by himself. She had climbed and rolled down the sand dunes. Gathered seashells. She had watched the fishermen jump inside the longboat and go sailing out over the rocking waves to drop the fish nets when the schools of fish were sighted, and later, she had feasted on fresh fired mullet, sitting beside a campfire with her plate in her lap. She had seen the full moon rise from the darkened ocean and had thought at the time, that it looked just like a big sunny egg lying in the cook's iron skillet. She had quietly sat on her father's knees and listened to stories the grownups told about the past, mainly the fight by the colonists for independence and most of its sayings that had been handed down from her Great Grandfather Matthew. Then, as the firelight flickered in the star-studded night and the stories continued to roll, the sandman finally won the game he had played with her eyelids since nightfall. And, what seemed like minutes later to her, her mother was gently shaking her shoulder where she slept in the covered wagon, telling her it was time to rise for breakfast and once again her eyes opened to meet the beginning of what she knew was going to be another marvelous camping day at Sandy Cove.

Season following season, the entire Carson family had gone to Sandy Cove Beach. Then, all of a sudden it seemed; the annual outing came to an end. Time played a big part in altering the holiday; however, bringing it to cease. Phil and Nat reached the age where they much preferred to go courting alone rather than spend what they came to look upon as a dull week at the beach if, to Phil's good fortune, Caroline Wilton was along. Phil seemed to think Miss Amelia Wilton hovered more closely around her daughter at the beach than anywhere else. Of course, he had kept his views strictly between her, Nat and himself! Perhaps Miss Amelia had had her point, something the younger people were unable to see at the time. Certainly, Caroline, Martha, and herself as well had reached the age, too, where it would not have been very ladylike had they suddenly thrown caution to the wind and gone tumbling down a sand dune with their skirts flying up, way over their heads. To allow even a mere peek of one's petticoat to show was a disgrace not to mention the disgraceful horror of having one's pantalets exposed! Anyhow, she, her brothers, and friends alike had all found much to their dismay and seemingly rather suddenly at that one day, that there was a wide expanse between what was acceptable as a child and that in being a grown-up. What had been perfectly permissible then, once they all reached maturity, the same innocent behavior would have ruined their reputation for all time.

Nonetheless, she thought the main factor that had brought about the ceasing of the holiday outing had been the coming of so many tragic and unfortunate happenings in the family, her mother's illness and sudden death: and even though there was one happy interim, which had been her marriage to Luke, to a certain degree it had been clouded by the shattering news of war so soon after. Through the war years when Luke and the others had gone away, she had hardly thought about Sandy Cove much less contemplated the idea of going there. After the war it seemed as if the absence of so many faces had not been enough to dampen one's day, there were the burdens and hardship, too, curbing any notion that one may have held to go away for a few days of relaxation. When the fishing season had resumed after the war, Doss or some the others, with Luke going along a few times, had made a quick trip to the beach to purchase fresh seafood; that is to say, when there was money to spare for it.

Well, there was going to be very little money this fall and certainly none to spare for an outing. Still, one had to be realistic, recognize the aspects of the situation for what they were. The Greens were practically on their way to Green Sea. Tom Green had expressed his wish to go surf fishing and give his family a chance to see the ocean. The harvest was almost over. Luke could surely spare a number of idle days. He was going to have to play host to Tom Green anyway. Thus, what better time to revive a long-lost holiday, start the annual custom again with her own children? They were just the age to begin to enjoy the water, to love Sandy Cove as she once had loved it. She would speak to Luke about it. Plans had to be made and quickly at that. The two larger wagons would have to be covered and provisioned. Oh, she hoped Luke would like the idea and not think she had suddenly gone daft! On second thought, perhaps it may be wiser to feel out Luke's views on the matter first, refrain from showing too much excitement. She desired him to favor the idea as much as she did, not say yes just because he thought it would please her.

Making an attempt to keep that tingling eagerness that was suddenly running through her out of her voice, Eliza asked rather gingerly, feeling her words were slicing the silence much too loudly in-spite of all, "Luke, how long do you suppose the Greens will be visiting us?"

Deep in his rambling thoughts her abrupt question started Luke. Quickly looking up from his plate as he paused his fork of food, he said, "I'm sorry, sweetheart, what did you say? I guess Tom's letter has my mind in a flutter."

She repeated the question. Her emotion was more controlled.

"I really have no idea, dear," Luke replied. "Two weeks at the very least I should think since Tom wants to go to the beach. Going there will take up a good part of his time—he stopped, eyeing her for a moment. "Sweetheart," he went on to tell her, "I hope you won't start wearing yourself down in preparation for Tom and Betsy's visit and concerning yourself in regard to entertaining them. I can assure you they're both quite ordinary. They'll expect no frills or, as for that matter, won't want any. They live as we've been forced to live here at Green Sea since the war, simple. Now, I don't mean to imply they're country bumpkins, nothing of the sort. Tom may not affect the social graces of some I've seen and heard, but that doesn't mean his restrained because he can't. He's a well-bred gentleman and from what I can gather a rather prosperous one at that. As for Betsy, there's only one way to describe her, a gracious and pretty lady. Anyway, I don't want you worrying about the Greens. Take my word for it, you'll enjoy their company." He pushed the loaded fork on into his mouth, feeling a sudden pessimism that his last words had not carried. As much as he wanted to see Tom and his family, would that, too, sour as everything else had seemed to do this year, he thought, bringing more strain upon him in being there, than pleasure?

"Oh, I didn't mean anything like that, Luke," Eliza quickly assured, seeing her question had given him the wrong impression. "Tom's letter set my mind thinking about the beach. I was wondering how it was going to be arranged that Betsy and Luke see the ocean. If they go along with you and Tom when you go surf fishing, that's going to require some planning on your part. The beach is a good distance form here, probably farther away than Tom realizes, and Betsy surely can't rough it as you men no doubt would if she were not along."

His mind easing considerably, Luke thoughtfully paused his fork again. "You're right," he agreed. "They'll surely go along with us and that aspect does change the situation. I guess that's why Tom mentioned the fishing and their wish to see the ocean in his letter. He's giving me time to work out the details before they arrive." He shoved the mouthful of food on toward his mouth and lifted his coffee cup. "I'll have to get busy and outfit one the larger wagons, so it'll be ready to go when they are here, I suppose."

"It looks that way," she said, cutting her eye across the table, suddenly feeling piqued that he appeared to have nothing on his mind but outfitting the wagon as he took a big gulp of coffee and resumed the working of his fork. Even so, as she still continued to cut her eye at him, all of a sudden, she saw him stop eating altogether and life his head toward her, studying her Immediately, she withdrew her glance and turned all her attention on the baby, pretending to be concerned that Jane Anne had not fully cleaned her plate which was not unusual.

However, if Luke were on to her eyes artful dodge and her concern over the baby's normal habit, there was no sign of it in his voice as he said, "Eliza dear, why couldn't you go to the beach, too? If Betsy Green goes, I surely can't see any call for your staying home. You seem to have finally gained back your normal strength lately, and actually, I think the trip and setting a different pace for a change would be enjoyable to all of us. We could take the children. They'd love wading in the water, the weather is still warm enough. What do you think? Couldn't we all go?"

"I don't see why not," she told him, her annoyance softening toward him for his slowness in asking her but making an attempt at the same time to affect a trivial air about her. Nevertheless, in spite of herself, she was suddenly forced to drop her head lower toward her plate to keep him from seeing the cattish smile that was curving her mouth.

She was too late. He saw it and something else, too, that he had not detected until then, her eagerness to go with him—an entity in her behavior that had not surfaced for such a long while. He reached across the table and tilted her chin, seeing the clever smile leave her face in the look that passed between them—space that was suddenly hanging heavy with bittersweet memories.

Finally, she said, "Sometimes, it may take a few minutes, Luke, but you've always read me like a book."

'Not lately, I haven't been able to, my darling,' he thought, but he said instead, "So, that was your motive all along in asking about the length of time the Greens would be here?" A tender smile covered his face.

"Something like that," she promptly confessed, and before he hardly knew what had taken place, she had jumped up and run around the table, plopping herself down on his lap. After rattling off one dozen or more things she wanted to do such as baking a batch of tea cakes for the children to munch on, explaining this was one the things her mother used to do when the Carson's went to Sandy Cove while Luke sat and listened—almost breathless lost in her freshly found lightness, she went on to make a suggestion of her own, "Luke, let's make this a real holiday. It's been so long since we've had one. Why not invite Martha and Bruce and their children to go along, too? Martha and I were reminiscing only a few days ago about those outings at Sandy Cove when we were growing up. I think they'd love to go. Of course, after the Greens arrive, we'll give them time to rest and visit here at Green Sea for a few days. But, in the meantime, Bruce could also be outfitting and stocking their wagon, too."

Near bursting at the seams by now at her apparent readiness to have done with grief, wounds, and hurt feelings and meet the present and tomorrow in its prospective, Luke almost shouted, "Why, that's a wonderful idea! Bruce would go fishing on Christmas morning if he thought he could get by Martha, whether the weather suited or not. Yes, we'll ask them and by gosh, we'll have us an outing this fall regardless of any sign there's going to be a meager pocketbook at Green Sea in the months ahead of us!"

"Well, meager harvest, meager pocketbook, or meager whatever, you deserve to take a holiday, Luke, if anyone ever has."

"What about yourself, darling?" He asked, beginning to nuzzle over and around her ear lobes, "You never seem to get out of this house anymore."

"Stop that, Luke!" She coquettishly giggled, ignoring his remark. "You're tickling me!"

"Is that all?" He teased, becoming all agog at seeing this mannerism in her surfacing again—something that had ever enraptured him and even more so after he had learned that underneath it there lay an intense simmering passion just waiting to be brought to its fiery height. Far too long he had waited and worried, wondering if its absence was going to be permanent.

"Well—maybe not!" She admitted, fanning his passion for her more wildly with each word as she snuggled closer to his chest and went on to tell him quite demurely, "But, there are the children, you know. Carr's still eating and even though he appears to be preoccupied and the baby; also, I don't think it would be very wise of us to leave them alone with all this glassware, china, knives and forks at their disposal, do you?" Now say if they were napping—" Her voice stopped in a most alluring whisper.

"Ugh," Luke groaned, "You've made your point, darling, and at my expense too, if I may add." Playfully tweaking both her ear lobes again, he grinned, "Now, before I become any more miserable than I am, Mrs. Heyward, would you be so kindly as to remove yourself from my lap so that my mind might have a chance to shift to other things; for example, something like making a move toward all those plans we've just made and getting back to digging potatoes, too?"

He need not have feared she would have stayed within reach of his hands any longer. She had already sailed off his lap before his last words had fallen, clapping both Hands

He stood up; his grin still wide. "You'd better run," he quipped again, turning toward a wooden peg on the wall beside the kitchen door which held his hat. "I have you know my mind's still lurking in the direction of that bedroom in there rather than toward that potato field."

In regard to making love to her, he was affecting a far lighter manner than what the actual facts of the situation constituted and was much more serious than what he would as leave Eliza not detect. Assuredly, he had made love to her several times since that dire day they had gone to Drakston Hall and he had learned Frank had raped her. But it had not been the same. Not on his part but hers. He had not mentioned it to her, nor did he have any intention of doing so because he was almost positive that his behavior that day had had more to do with it than anything else.

Even though the news had totally shattered his nerves that day— to the point that he thought he could have finished Frank Drakston off before he did go without feeling a quiver of emotion, he had bitterly regretted a thousand times over that he had behaved toward Eliza in the manner he had. No, concerning their lovemaking, she had not turned from him. Neither, by the same token, had she turned to him— something she had not hesitated in doing all through their marriage. Moreover, since that awful day—his mind would ever vision it as such, she had seemed cool in the matter of their love-making, at times almost impassive in his arms and, to him, what made the situation seem even worse was the fact that he sensed she strove to overcome this phlegmatic reaction as much as he endeavored and desired to bring her out of it.

Besieged with his own contrition, it had taken Eliza's absence by his side during Frank's funeral to bring Luke around to properly collecting his thoughts. He began to see how deeply she had been affected by Frank's death, the wounds and scars Frank had left for her to carry and recognized his own behavior had been too blunt considering the circumstances involved. As he witnessed the covering of Frank Drakston's grave, lending a supporting arm to his grieving widow, Luke silently vowed he would bury his grievances with Frank Drakston and when he reached home he would try to make it all up to Eliza—his distant behavior toward her everything—before it came to making a lasting impact upon her. And, from the moment of their meeting in the field when he had returned from Frank's funeral, he had done just that, not verbally because it was too painful a thing and too sensitive a subject for him to discuss, but by his actions. Even so, in regard to their physical relationship, it had appeared for months that he had come to his decision too late, until now. He was certain had the moment been opportune in their behalf, deeply regretting it was not, her cool responses of late would have melted altogether in her pronounced warmth; and that sweet ecstasy that had been theirs to delight in would have been recaptured once again.

Nevertheless, Luke strained his mind to forget what might have been, still effecting a light mood—continuing to send her a wide smile as he waved her aside and grabbed his hat form the wall and stepped through the kitchen door. As he went on across the porch and down the back steps, heading back toward his many continual chores and obligations, the wonder of Eliza obviously warming in his embrace again moved him with a degree of buoyancy he had not felt for some time.

It was Indian summer when Tom and his family arrived at Green Sea—weather that blazed in a kaleidoscopically leaned landscape under azure-blue skies—days that were so radiantly skirted they seemed as though they were truly waltzing to autumn's song as the brilliant colors whirled and danced—rustling to nature's floor. The weather held, one bright day following another save a few brisk days while the party was at Sandy Cove which only made for more suitable fishing weather, bringing the fish swimming to shore in profusion.

Later, in the afternoon on the day of Tom's arrival, after his hearty dinner had settled somewhat and hoping he was not being too insolent in regard to the women for mentioning it, he expressed his wish to see the lands of Green Sea that he had longed to view for so many years "By all means, Tom," Luke agreed, pleased to have a chance to visit with his old friend in private. "I would've suggested it myself but thought you might be a little too worn from that long train ride."

"It'll take more than riding on a train to jade me," declared Tom, fastening a squinting eye upon Luke. "You should know, my friend, that if I'd had any soft spots and if I may add that goes for you, too, they all vanished serving under J.E.B. Stuart. After riding with General Jeb, a saddle hardly poses any more hardship for me than if I were sitting in a rocking chair."

"Well, in that case," laughed Luke, "Come on and we'll saddle up."

They jumped up and headed for the stables, leaving Eliza and Betsy harmoniously chatting away as though they had ever been old friends.

As Luke had been awed when he first cast his eyes upon the vast flat fields of Green Sea, Tom was likewise even though many acres still lay fallow those five years after the war. They had ridden for a good while, covering a good portion of the plantation which was under cultivation til their route was finally taking them past the cemetery. Their conversation had hardly paused until now when Tom slowed his mount and silently stared, appearing to rest his gaze on the two newer tall marble tombs.

"The Carson family plot," Luke volunteered to Tom's questioning expression.

"I take it, that one of those tombs is where Mr. Carson finally laid Nat to rest," said Tom, rather somberly, seeming to want to linger.

"Yes, Mr. Carson brought his body back in sixty-five and buried him there beside his mother." Aware that Tom had met Nat through his own friendship with Tom and, that later on for a short while Nat had actually served as Tom's company commander with Tom always speaking highly of Nat, Luke hastened to ask, "Would you like to stop for a few minutes, Tom?"

"Yes, I would," Tom replied, quite resolutely

They pulled their mounts up beside the high lacy wrought iron enclosure, dismounted and looped the horse's reins through the sturdy grillwork. They followed the fence for a short distance and as Luke lifted the heavy bolt and let the tall gate swing aside, Tom said, "I don't suppose Mr. Carson ever did find out what happened to his other son?"

"Not even a faint trace," Luke replied, as they went on through the gate and up the slight hill toward the big elm tree whose bright graceful limbs were swaying softly over the two costly markers. "It's as though Phil never lived at all except to those of whom knew him."

"That's too bad," Tom said, as they reached the marble pillar that marked Nat's grave. "It's painful to know, but I would think it would be still worse not to know. There were so many. too many, and most in their prime

"Yeah," Luke muttered, reaching for his hat and lowering his head along with Tom who had suddenly ceased his words and was standing in reverend silence, holding his own hat clutched against his chest with both hands. Thus, for some few minutes they stood, each in common silent prayer, the gentle falling of elm leaves stirring the only sound around them.

Presently, they raise their heads and put their hats back on. They walked back down the hill and through the gate. Luke dropped the iron bolt in place. They reached their horses and remounted. Neither had said another word. Both appeared as though they were giving the voice of a third party the courtesy of uninterruption—the easy, lazy drawl of the invisible young man with the slow but positive smile who seemed to be riding along with them.

"I've got a surprise waiting for you just beyond those cabins over there," Luke finally said, pointing across the field toward the old slave cabins which were mostly empty now, saving a few that were stored with junk and those that were occupied by the tenants.

"You don't say?" Questioned Tom, his face lightening, as his head came up to follow Luke's gaze.

"Well, I think it'll surprise you," grinned Luke, turning his head back to face Tom. "But, I hope you won't think I've overplayed my hand in coming up with the idea."

"I can't imagine what it is," Tom replied, his mind hammering away at trying to guess what Luke had waiting beyond the cabins.

"It's at the old carpenter shop," hinted Luke, "If that will help any," taking delight in seeing Tom ransacking his brains in growing puzzlement.

"Well, I know you too well to think you're going to give your surprise away before the proper moment. So, how about us rushing it up a bit?" Hooted Tom, setting his mount's pace to a fast gallop.

Luke followed suit, gaining just a fraction on Tom as they belted down the lane between the two rows of cabins, reining his mare in near two large covered Conestoga wagons setting side by side in front of the carpenter shop where a grinning Doss was applying the finishing touch to the already snug, neat canvas tops.

Stopping his own mount, Tom's eyes appeared to grow wider and wider in amazement as he croaked, "Well, I never! Fancy that!"

Luke jumped to the ground, beaming, "You did say you wanted to go fishing, didn't you?

Tom caught on, touched that Luke would put forth this much effort to please a guest.

"Well, yes, I did, but I didn't mean for you to go to all this trouble, friend."

"Who says I did it for you?" chided Luke.

"What!" Spluttered Tom completely baffled; frowning as he failed to grasp Luke's slam.

"Oh, come on down from off that horse and have a look," shrieked Luke, shaking with laughter at seeing that he had left Tom blank, "I did

18

it for Betsy, Eliza, and the Children! You could've rough it old coot!"

Trying to keep a straight face, Tom said, as he crawled down from his mount's back, "So help me, Heyward, I'm going to pay you back and in the nearing future at that! Covered wagons, indeed! I feel like a fool!"

Luke slapped him on the back. "Oh, don't take it so hard, Tom, I'm just one ahead of you. No, seriously, most of this was Eliza's idea. Since Betsy and Luke have never seen the ocean, we decided to make a real holiday out of it, of course after you've visited here at Green Sea for a while."

"No, they've never been to the beach and it was most thoughtful of both of you to go to all this effort in planning that they do. I sure appreciate it, Luke."

"Don't mention it. The pleasure is ours. Eliza's family used to go most every fall and stay a whole week. She hasn't gone for years so we thought it would be a good time to revive the custom with our own children. We've asked Bruce and his family, you remember me speaking so often about them, to go along also. Bruce is busy now preparing his own wagon; therefore, they'll be three wagons plus Doss with a smaller one which will carry feed for the horses and other supplies."

"Just like the pioneers blazing the western trails," retorted Tom, swinging back fast to his usual blustery self, and I'm certain with no finer looking wagons than these." He leaped inside to have a closer look. Luke followed him. After a moment's keen scrutiny, Tom added, "Why, Betsy's going to be bedazzled by all this. Those women are going to be as comfortable as if they were riding in a rocking chair."

"Well, if they're not," Luke quipped again, "it won't be from the absence of having one aboard. I plan to put one in each wagon!"

"Not one bit surprised," voiced Tom with a shrug, but the delighted glow in his eyes belied his manner. "When it comes to organizing things, and that goes for credit and honor, too, no Grand Duke or the most capable of leaders could bypass you, Heyward, if Tom Green does say so." During the time they spent together in the war, Tom began addressing Luke by his last

name mostly. Although Luke never let on to Tom that he gave it one thought, Luke had a suspicion that the name had reminded Tom of his young son too much, at the time. Anyway, the habit had appeared to stick with Tom.

Even though he had meant every word of his commendable statement, Tom was not slow in observing that it had had a total reverse effect upon Luke than what he had expected. Seriously, with all light gone from his face, Luke was saying, "I fear you're much too generous with your praise, Tom, though I've tried to make the wagons as comfortable as I suppose they can be made, and I hope Betsy and Eliza, too, will not find the trip too rough and will enjoy it."

"Oh, they will! Don't worry about that!" Tom quickly put in.

"Tom, I almost lost Eliza last December." This simple statement referring to Eliza's illness, which was not all his words carried by a long shot, was as much as Luke Heyward could bring himself to say in the matter of the worst personal problems that had ever beset him—Eliza's illness, the revelations that day returning from Drakston Hall, everything. When it came to his personal life and his relationship with his wife, Luke reserved that for no one's ears save what little he had said to Seth Roalf in regard to Eliza having another baby; and, for the most part, this held true regarding his anxieties and burdens, too.

"I know, and I regret that I couldn't have been closer at hand to give you what support I could," said Tom. Then, after a moment pause while Tom observed that Luke's dark expression was continuing to linger, he cheerfully went on to boost, "But, she certainly looks and seems to be in excellent health now."

"Yes," Luke agreed, "I'm grateful to say, just recently, she does appear to have regained her general well-being. Even so, it's been a rough year on her and me, too. On top of everything else this year—" Tom began to wonder besides Eliza's illness what the "everything" consisted of but naturally did not voice his interest—"I've had an almost total crop failure as far as laying one dollar aside for the future. Frankly, Tom, I don't mind telling you, sometimes I feel as though I've been a complete failure in regard to my wife, my children, and this entire plantation."

Tom was certain there was more involved than the two things that Luke had revealed and was positive again that he had never seen his friend any more serious, realizing it was not the time to mince words even if he were also aware that he was chancing the effect of what he was going to say when he rapped, "You're talking nonsense, Luke Heyward! You've failed nobody or anything, you're not of that mold. Personally, and I mean no disrespect to anybody when I say this, it's my opinion in regard to this plantation, had it not been for your effort and the devotion and effort of that little lady you married, Green Sea would've gone under long ago. Have you ever thought of that? You and your wife have saved this plantation from the clench of those Yankee carpetbaggers as well as all other adversaries. You've had a crop failure, so what? Everybody that grubs in the ground for a living, suffers one every so often, I know I have, even though most of my grubbing is on top of the ground since I make my living growing apple trees which requires my crawling around in branches and up and down stepladders. But it amounts to the same thing. Stop putting yourself down! I know you want to get that mansion built back, but don't despair and become obsessed by desperation just because you've been forced to let it lay for a while. You'll build it, but, in the meantime, you're going to have to allow for those reversals." Tom stopped on a note of anxiety. Seeing that Luke's dark expression remained unchanged, he thought he had said enough. For a moment, while Tom's lecture made its way into the door of Luke's sound reasoning, both men were held captive in a wave of tenseness with Tom suddenly feeling he had blown his friendship with Luke just as a wide smile broke the gloom on Luke's face and he gave Tom a hard plop on the shoulder, saying, "I guess I needed that, thanks!"

"I guess you did," grinned Tom, still a little fearful he had said too much and admitted it, "For a few seconds there I was thinking maybe I'd already wore out my welcome."

"Not a chance, Tom Green," replied Luke. "Come on, Eliza's probably got supper waiting."

"Heyward," Tom called, jumping down after Luke from the wagon.

"Yeah?" said Luke, turning to face Tom.

"Don't forget to send me an invitation to your first ball when you get that mansion built. I want to help break it in, tame that new floor with those old kickers of mine to every confounded tune."

Luke stuck his hand out. "Let's shake on it," he said" One among the first invitations going out will be headed for the post office in Ashville.

In the brightening rays of a golden sunrise in the latter part of that same week, the outing party setting out for Sandy Cove Beach was climbing upon the wagons at Green Sea. Everybody was scrambling around taking his or her designed place. It had been settled upon that Bruce and Martha would lead with the first wagon. The Greens would occupy the second wagon. Luke and Eliza would take the third position with Doss following behind them in the smaller wagon which was carrying drinking water, feed for the horses, and a few other essentials.

Except for the baby, Jane Anne, who was settling down happily on her mother's lap where Eliza had taken her seat on the driver's bench of their wagon, the other children began to clamor and plead to ride along together. Tom, ever inclined to see that a child or anyone else around him was made happy, backed up the children's pleas. He quickly pointed out that his center wagon would be the most appropriate, of course, if the other parents consented, telling Luke, "That way, Luke, you could help me keep an eye on them."

Luke and Bruce both nodded in agreement and told the children to hop inside Tom's wagon and to be sure and mind what "Mr. Green" told them. Thus, the children merrily piled inside, Luke Green, Maggie and Laura Randolph, and Carr all sitting side by side in the back of the wagon with their short legs dangling down and Tom Green could not have been happier surrounded by their numerous laughs and gleeful shrieks along the way—oftentimes joining in that resounding peal of his floating to the other wagons along with that of Maggie Randolph and Luke Green, both of who were near the same age, as they would go suddenly leaping from the wagon and give one another a merry chase around the entire small caravan. Jailor, the hound dog, save those brief respites when he chose to rest his legs inside his master's wagon, trotted and frisked in and out between the four wagons, never failing to be right at the heels of the running children, barking as though he were on the fresh track of game.

"Enough to make anyone within hearing distance think the war may have started again," Luke said, as he turned to Eliza and shook his head. "Well, at any rate, Tom seems to be taking it all in stride and having fun besides."

"If his laughter is any sign," said Eliza," I wonder about Betsy though."

"Don't fret, she's doing fine as long as she's beside Tom Green. In any event, I would think her nerves would've become well-preserved against Tom's sportive and exuberant nature by this time anyway, wouldn't you?" He said, as he shot a rather sportive wink of his own at her.

"I suppose so," smiled Eliza. "But I am glad to see, for the sake of

Betsy's nerves, that Carr and Laura appears to be fairly quiet and contented, sitting where they started out at. Still, four shrieking children plus a grown-up is quite a lot to ask of anybody even though their nerves may be in a good state of preservation and their nature the most temperate."

Luke chuckled and shook his head again, ever amused at the way his wife put things.

Nonetheless, the next fall, strong preserved nerves or whatever, there were additional voices to shriek and holler, additional legs to run and jump additional skinned knees to soothe and bandage up, additional fights and disagreements to settle when Seth Roalf Jr, Bill Cooper, Whit, and Stuart Drakston were to join the annual outing.

On this day; however, as the bright, warm sun journeyed along through its clear blue path, the wagons carrying the vacation party continued to roll along with it, covering a good many miles. Even so, by midafternoon, it was apparent the beach would not be reached till way past dark. Hence, rather than rush the horses and still be forced to make camp in the dark of night, Luke suggested that the group camp overnight in a hickory grove a few miles ahead. Eliza had told him about the grove, a place her family had camped at several times in former years. Everybody readily agreed, with Luke going on to point out that it would be more enjoyable, and no doubt make more of a lasting impact on Betsy and young Luke to see the Atlantic for the first time in daylight, anyhow.

They reached the hickory grove, which was still radiant, wrapped in its golden leafed blanket. The men promptly set out to gather wood and build a fire. Doss unharnessed the horses, gave them water and feed and corralled them in a small area that he had enclosed by stringing rope around several of the close spaced tree trunks.

While the women made coffee and spread supper from the generous supply of already prepared food that Eliza and Martha had brought, the men gathered more wood and kept an eye on the children, too, as they ran through the hickory grove, hunting and gathering hickory nuts which had already ripened and fallen into the bedded leaves—leaves that had banked from season to season. The women finally called supper, and everybody ate. The children's heads were falling forward before supper's remains had hardly gotten cleared away, the dishes rinsed, and everything packed inside the baskets. And, after the children had been put to bed on the cotton mattress' inside the wagons, the grownups were not long in lingering around the campfire, either. They only remained long enough for the men to smoke one pipe of tobacco. On this first night of the excursion it appeared that everybody had one thing in common, heavy eyelids.

On the next day by the lightening of dawn, camp was broken, and the wagons rolled on forward and by mid-morning had come within range of the towering white sand dunes and the sound of the roaring tide in the distance. That constant song of breaking waves in the washing surf stirred an instant excitement through the wagons—a natural wonder that was still hidden from view behind the tall white pyramids—bodies of sand which the ocean had heaped upon the ground in previous ages gone by. The wagon wheels rolled faster and in a short while gained the beach.

Before Tom could pull their wagon in alongside Bruce and Martha's which Bruce had just pulled from the deep ruts that led to the strand and parked in a cozy spot beside one of the tall sand dunes, Betsy was already standing up in the wagon crying, as she shaded her eyes from the glare of the sparkling water with her hand, "Oh, Tom, it's more than I ever imagined! Stop! I can't wait to have a good look. Let me get down so I can run with the children!" Luke and Maggie had spring from the wagon and were running past it toward the foaming waves.

"Whoa, there!" Tom promptly roared to the team and like a light sailed from the wagon seat and lifted his arms up to Betsy, exclaiming to her, as his broad grin stretched wider, "Sure thing, sugarplum, run on and have a good time! That's what we're here for!"

Having heard his mother's cry of excitement and realizing his father had stopped and let her off the wagon, Luke Green halted his pace and turned around, waiting until Betsy's feet plowing through the spilling sand could reach him. Betsy grasped Luke's hand and with it lying inside her palm and Maggie Randolph's hand in her other, she went racing on toward the breaking surf as lively and inspired as the two children who were flanking her.

Tom bolted to the back of the wagon and lifted the two smaller children down, cheerfully telling them; also, "Go on, little mites, and stretch your legs, too," standing by the wagon and watching, as Carr and Laura's small feet struggled through the hindering sand in their attempt to follow the others, until it registered on him that Luke was stalled behind him, patiently waiting for him to get moving and parked so he could do the same. One did not chance pulling a wagon in and out of that deep sandy track as one might have done had they been on a normal hard packed road.

"Sorry, Luke," bellowed Tom as he hurled himself back upon the wagon seat, "I'll be out of your way in less than no time."

Gallantly, Luke hollered back, "No rush, Tom," though he was fairly certain that Eliza had become a litter more than anxious to get moving because she had lost sight of Carr behind the tall sand dune and his instinct was suddenly being proven for she was asking, "Luke, do you see Carr?"

"No, but he's all right, darling. Betsy's with the children, and I see that Bruce and Martha are watching in that direction while they wait for us. I don't think Carr will venture near those waves, anyhow, til he's explored them awhile with his eyes."

"You're probably right. Though, just the same, I'd like to hurry and get parked so I could check on him."

"Ever the cautious mother," smiled Luke.

"I would think you have no room to talk," she shot back, playfully making a lip at him.

Tom finally got parked and Luke moved forward, settling his wagon last in line with the other two. His position was nearest to the beach though. Eliza, carrying the baby in her arms, joined Martha and they hurried on to where Betsy and the children were running along the washing surf, their glee running along with the high-pitched voiced sea gulls and the ocean's rumble.

And, from that moment on, even though the wheels of time had continued to whirl deviating the course of her life to extremes she would have scoffed off as absurd at the time, Eliza was to see the scene before her had not veered to any great degree save the faces and voices she saw and heard no more and those that she did hear and looked upon then, finding as the day wore on that the many activities which were to fill it were mostly what they had ever been at Sandy Cove.

The children were soon wading and frolicking in the rolling, breaking waves. The baby began to squirm in Eliza's arms, fussing to join her brother and the others. Eliza removed her shoes and socks and stood with her by the hand near enough to the waves so the water would wash over her feet, and it was not long before Eliza found her own weak resistance to do likewise giving way. With Martha and Betsy joining her, she hurriedly doffed her own shoes and stockings and took to the water, too. Holding Jane Anne by the hand, she used her other hand to gather her long skirt and petticoats up around her knees to protect them from the washing waves and waded into deeper water, acutely aware that she was braving society by showing her knees in public but chanced it, anyhow. Scorning conventions; also, Martha and Betsy followed suit. However, for all their daring of what society had imposed upon them, when all three women found the hems of their clothing becoming wetter and wetter, they could not gain the courage to scorn propriety any farther by raising their skirts any higher and expose the shameful sight of thigh—giving in to the dictates of fixed rule—wading to more diminishing waves.

Later, along with the others and her own children now playing around her feet, Eliza again enjoyed the adventure of hunting out the most rare and prettiest seashells among the innumerable varieties that the ocean current unceasingly laid upon the shore. Then, there was the excitement of watching Luke, Bruce and Tom wade into the surf, loaning their strength to the fishermen who a short while earlier had dropped the huge net in the schools of fish. As compensation for having helped pull the enormous bulk of flopping fish from the shallow water to the strand where the fish were subdivided between the fishermen, Luke, Bruce, and Tom, each was given a sizeable portion and for the vacation party it was back to the wagons to make camp again and delight in their sea bounty. The men quickly built a fire from the kindling that had been brought from home and the additional wood the group had gathered from the hickory grove. The fish were dressed and while the children played on a nearby sand dune Eliza, Martha and Betsy started preparing supper along with a helping hand now and then from the menfolk.

Again, there was that outdoor tempting aroma of mullet frying in a pan of lard, the pleasing johnnycake cooking in an iron griddle, the whiffy smell of coffee sifting through the air, the honey-sweet scent of sweet potatoes baking in live coals. Again, there was the coziness of sharing this unique, flavorsome meal with family and friends. Again, there was the thrill of seeing a full moon rise on the rim of a darken ocean, and the companionship of conversation that ranged from growing apples to the gripping and enthralling tales of sea—robbers and buried treasure. Even so, despite the pleasant setting and interesting talk and the absorbing storytelling, the lazy warmth of campfire soon had the children yawning and sleep-filled, finally being tucked in their beds. And, not too long afterwards, when Eliza's own body was stretched out at last beside Luke's on their makeshift bed inside the wagon and from all accounts should have fallen asleep instantly, she found to her dismay at least one hour later she was still wide awake, her tense body straining to relax against the constant churning sound of the sea and the thoughts that were steadily running through her mind.

Long ago, oh so many years ago—not so many but sometimes years that seemed like a thousand to her, she had promised Luke they would run together beside the sea. Well, here she was with Luke at Sandy Cove long years after that promise and she had been here all day and not one single minute had she had with him alone—just the two of them. She was not complaining or anything of the sort. The day had been pleasant enough for everybody, herself included. Still, the fact was, those activities that had filled every minute of this day to the brim, had been a far cry from such a personal and intimate doing as running along the strand with Luke.

Eliza gave another sigh, turning again to face Luke's back. Was Luke asleep? He was certainly still enough to be! Suddenly, her eyes grew wider. Why not make that long ago promise good now! The night was warm, glowing with a moon almost bright as day! Even if Luke was asleep and she did wake him up, it surely would not be the same as disturbing him and her knowing he had to be in the fields by sunup! Yes, by heaven! She was going to do it! They were on vacation. When morning came Luke had nothing to do save what he wished to do, neither did she. Well, in her case, a few things maybe. Anyway, why not take advantage of this tiresome insomnia!

Quickly, her head shot up from the pillow and leaning over Luke's shoulder with her mouth nearly resting on his ear while her bosom pressed rather provocatively against him, she hastily asked him in a little fluttery whisper, "Luke—Luke dear, are you asleep?"

Luke smiled. Contrary to what she had assumed, he was not asleep. Nor had he been to sleep. What's more, strange as it was, the thoughts that had been preventing his relaxing and keeping him wide awake had been very much in line with her own. The sound of the washing surf so nearby had also caused him to remember what she had told him that day beside the meadow fence when he had proposed to her, bringing him to recall, too, all the hope and delight that they had embraced; and this had moved his mind on to center upon those few intimate moments they had shared a few days earlier—that urge of passion she had stirred him to and which had yet to be assuaged. Though inert it had lain, by no means should this have indicated it had quelled to oblivion.

The truth of the matter was, the few days that had elapsed since that day, had become so taken up in preparing for the Green's nearing visit and the planned outing, and especially in Eliza's case where some of her chores had extended on 'til way after the supper dishes had been cleared away causing her to appear as though all she wanted to do was to flop down and go to sleep and for good reason once they had hit the bed, out of consideration for her he had only given her a light kiss and turned over and brushed the idea of making love to her aside. The night they had spent in the hickory grove had hardly posed any variation in manner as far as love making was concerned and this night had been no different. In fact, she had not only appeared totally exhausted again but half asleep as well, falling down upon the mattress on the floor of the wagon and giving a loud sigh along with a faintly murmured, "Goodnight, Luke, I love you, too," in reply to his tender kiss and warm remark. Moreover, in addition to her obvious languor there was another problem. Though young in years they were and sleeping in the front part of the wagon besides, their two children were still too near to them for favorable lovemaking anyway, to Luke's way of thinking.

At any rate, now surprised at her sudden switch of behavior and also curious as to what she was up to, Luke turned to face her and still wearing his slightly amused expression he softly teased, "Well, let's say if I were asleep, I'm not now. What is it, darling?"

"Luke, let's slip away and take a walk on the beach!"

"You mean now?" He whispered back, his voice on the edge of excitation at the thought of being alone with her on a moon-shrouded beach, "you want to take a walk at this hour?

"Yes," she huskily replied, "What makes the difference what time it is, I can't sleep."

"Well, neither can I, darling," he finally admitted, "and I love your suggestion, but what about our two children lying up there?

"Oh, they'll be all right," she assured, sitting up and sweeping her hand about in the blurry darkness as she added, "Where in the world did I put my skirt?"

Seeing, she meant no nonsense, Luke sat up, too, calling her attention to something else while he studied her in the veiled, thin moonlight which was seeping through the wagon's canvas cover, "But, what if they should happen to awaken, dear? They could you know and become frightened; also, since they're in strange surroundings?"

"I don't think we have to fret about that," she told him as she discovered her wide, long skirt and began to pull it up over her nightgown. "Save those times the sniffles have awaken her, the baby has always slept the night through once she goes to sleep, and considering all the effort Carr made today in keeping pace with Luke Green, I'm certain he'll know nothing else til morning, if then—" she paused, endeavoring to scrutinize him in the obscured interior. "Don't you want to go, Luke?"

"Of course, I do, darling."

"Well then, stop your worrying and get your trousers on," she said, sweeping her hand about once again. "I'm almost ready if I can find my shawl. Oh, here it is and also your trousers" she pushed the trousers toward him, suggesting, as she threw her shawl over her shoulders and picked up her shoes, "just slip them on over your nightshirt, Luke, no one's going to see us."

Suddenly, Luke was weighing the situation no longer. He had thought about Doss lying all wrapped up in his blankets only a few feet away from them. Both children loved the aged former servant and would have no fear whatever if he were close at hand to comfort them. Feeling almost giddy with relief, Luke's hand shot out for his trousers. While he quickly pulled them on, he told her," I know what I'll do, I'll ask Doss to keep his ears open and come to the children in the event they should arouse and cry out."

"As you wish, Luke," Eliza smiled. "But I'm sure they'll be fine."

"Most likely, but I think we should let Doss know we'll be gone for a while, just in case," he replied, slipping his feet in his shoes and scrambling over to where she was waiting beside the wagon's tailpiece. "Let me go first, dear, and then I'll help you down," he went on to suggest as he unfastened the canvas at the corner and leaped out. He held his arms up and swiftly Eliza was over the tail piece and falling into them, the flooding moonlight instantly sharpening her senses to the freshness of this sudden unplanned experience.

While Luke tucked the canvas back in place and stepped over to Doss' wagon and gently aroused him with the message that he and Eliza had decided to take a walk on the beach, Eliza stood beside their wagon and waited, and while she waited she looked in the direction of their apparently sleeping neighbors—so calm and quiet their wagons set— and began to feel as though somehow, the others were blowing a most opportune chance. And, when Luke turned to come back to her, she met his smile and told herself that if their neighbors preferred to sleep that was their business, but as for herself she was going to seize the present and make the most of it! After all, how many times in her life could she hope to be granted the privilege of taking a stroll with Luke on a moonlit deserted beach? Not very many in her opinion even if fortune did approve!

Eliza reached out and locked her hand with Luke's. As they started to walk away, they both stopped momentarily to observer that Doss, without anyone suggesting it, had risen from the spot where he had bedded down and was now settling himself in his blankets again under their wagon, directly where the children were sleeping over his head. Having had their minds fully rested now by this devoted move on Doss' part, hand in hand, Eliza and Luke turned again and started walking down the moon drenched shore—walking where foaming waves were gently ebbing away near their feet.

They had covered a long distance, talking as they had not talked together for a good many months, discussing various things. Though whether by coincidence or choice, all the hurt and all the tragedy and all the suffering that had transpired since they had first looked upon the other at Windsor, they let lie. And, eventually, while they talked and shared together the wonder and beauty that graced the world around them, together again, they both came to silently realize that notwithstanding all the misfortunes that had come their way they still had a good many things going for them—the blessing outweighing the pain. Thus, by coming to discover this, it brought Eliza around to feeling as though her weighted heart and her feet, too, were turning to the feather lightness of thistledown floating on a soft wind, moving her to suddenly chuckle, "I'll race you, Luke, and make that promise good that I made to you long ago, if you'll let go my hand."

He pretended it had never crossed his mind, suddenly stopping in his tracks to turn a deepening quizzical expression to her, finally saying, "That's right, Miss Carson, it seems I do recall your promising me something like that, not that you've mentioned it. Very well then, I'm certain neither the timing nor place will ever be more favorable for holding you to it." He dropped her hand and while he inclined forward with his hands resting on his knees and locks of hair falling form his cowlick onto his deep-tanned face which was creased by his wide beaming smile as he went on to add, "Make ready, here we go," she thought more handsome had he ever looked as she sprinted forward, gaining on him because he had purposely let her get an edge at the start by holding back. He allowed her to hold the lead with them running some few yards until she looked back at him over her shoulder and laughed. Then, within seconds, his long legs were abreast hers and he was scooping her up in his arms before she hardly knew what was happening.

"This isn't fair, Luke, put me down!" she breathlessly giggled.

"No, Miss Carson, the race fell to me and I shall claim the victory" he laughed, as he began carrying her away from the near washing water toward the pearl-white sand dunes towering majestically one after another along the shinning shoreline.

"All right," she giggled again. "I concede to you. Now you can put me down, I may have known your long legs would overtake mine."

"And, they did and I have no intentions of putting you down. Well, not here, anyway."

"No?" She twitted. "Then, if I may ask, what do you purpose to do with me? Surely, you're not thinking about carrying me all the way back to the wagon, I hope."

"Never mind," he replied, grinning down at her. "You did suggest that we take this walk, did you not? You did suggest that we race one another, too, did you not?"

"Well, yes, I did. But, what does that have to do with this, and just where are you taking me, anyhow?" She asked, squirming in his arms to look in the direction he was walking, seeing that they were headed toward the lofty white dunes that looked as though they may have been standing there for all time, sand that gleamed so transparently in the moonlight it could have passed for newly banked snow.

"If I'm lucky enough to find it, I'm taking you to a cozy haven which will be all our own, Mrs. Heyward," he told her as she turned her head back to gaze up at him. "A place where I'll be able to relish you to my content without being concerned with the presence of anyone else or any one thing, but us. You will agree I'm entitled to this since I won, won't you" The glittering sparks in his eyes made no mistake in revealing his intent, causing a sudden stirring of expectation to flow through her at the thought of Luke making love to her in this nondescript, seductive setting.

31

Fate's unknown hand must have been leading Luke. He spied it, a small place which had been neatly hollowed out at the base of one of the many mountainous banks that peppered the land, a place where the ocean winds over a period of time had kept chiseling away at the hard packed sand until its force had formed a somewhat snug nest-like den in which Luke now stepped and said, "Chance must be smiling, Mrs. Heyward, I think I've found just the right spot." He set her down, adding, as he brushed his hair back from his cheering features, "Take a look. Don't you think this'll do?"

She glanced about them and while a rather mirthful smile played with her pretty lips, she pertly replied, "That depends, Mr. Heyward, I would think, on how much wear and tear you have in mind! To subject its strength to too much, could collapse it on us, you know!"

"True enough, but what do you say we start putting the question to a test?" He grinned, as his hand moved to unloosen his trousers, not worried in the least that they would come to any harm because its depth was too shallow and the forming of its structure too slanting, for that.

She let the banter hang, mutely eyeing him as he slipped his trousers off and then turned to her, their eyes meeting and holding to the other's while she slowly began to unbutton her wide-spread worsted herringbone skirt at the waist and allowed it to fall to her feet. She stepped from the bulky fold of cloth, bent down and picked it up and held it out to him.

As if their minds were all one, he instantly caught the factual meaning of her silent gesture, quickly taking the skirt form her and spreading it out upon the sand. That done, he rose and while they eyed one another again, she untied the shawl draped around her shoulders and that, too, went sliding to the sand.

Now, as she stood before Luke in the luminous purity of moonlight, her lithe body shrouded in white with her heavy long hair now partly tousled and falling over her shoulders form their running along the beach while her full round breast swelled and pushed against her gown, for him the years and events between them and their wedding night fell away as though they had never been, with her becoming his virginal bride again—pure and innocent as the light that shone upon her—in his eyes the soft glow of candlelight.

As it had been for several months now, never once did Frank Drakston's mark upon her cross his mind. Overwhelmed, he groaned and scooped her up again in his arms and knelt down with her, tenderly laying her upon their chaste bed, softly telling her, "Eliza darling, you're so beautiful. I love you so." He lay down beside her and took her in his arms, one of his hands pushing her gown away so his eyes and his mouth could savor the delight of her unsullied loveliness.

And, as Luke's sensuous lips began to move over Eliza's body in a limitless exploration, she finally, after long months of frustration, let herself go and freed her mind of everything save the wantonness of their haven and Luke's tantalizing seduction—seducement that brought her to gasp cries of delight and he moved on and took her with him into that over chasm of sweetness which was no less wonderful than the first time—a rampant wave of passion that left them blissfully spent.

Silently, they lay in one another's arms, both minds once again centering on the same thought, grateful that they had recaptured this divine gift that Frank Drakston had near destroyed for them.

And again, typical for Eliza's nature, she wanted to talk about it and murmured, "Luke—I—I—" she suddenly stopped though, leaving it as it was lest she might do harm, telling herself that in all likelihood this was the main reason she had refrained from telling Luke about Frank's deed in the first place because of her fear of her own reaction in regard to their physical relationship if Luke were to find out. Everything seemed clear to her now.

Still obviously of one mind, Luke raised his head and looked down at her, telling her, "I know, darling, I know, let's not talk about it," as he began to brush his lips over her cheeks once again.

The moon had traveled a good way on its bejeweled road before the wagon was to creak again from settling bodies, causing Doss to start and listen. Then, he peered out from his blankets and cocked one eye up at the moon. With his weathered face crinkling up in a smile he rolled his head back inside his covers and remained where he was for the rest of the night!

Chapter Two

November. In the quiet of an early afternoon study hour, Lucy Randolph, sitting behind her desk inside the classroom at Drakston Hall, closed the book upon its marked page—the lesson she had just prepared—and looked longingly through the window at the still blazing landscape. In this year of 1870, fall had come later than usual and the leaves were continuing to linger on day after day in a flame of radiance as they had in another year, on another November day that season such as this it all came back to her so vividly that it seemed as if it were actually happening all over again—Nat Carson standing in a splash of sunlight that was hitting the doorway of the rooming house where she lived in Columbia, incredibly handsome in his captain's uniform that shone impeccably with its gleaming gold buttons and yellow braid. smiling rather keenly at her as she ran to meet him.

Would that memory ever become dull and vague to her? No, she thought not, Lucy told herself no matter how old she may become and especially now that fate, lot, or whatever one wished to label it had not only brought Whit Carson to her classroom as a student but had also brought him to live at Drakston Hall on permanent basis—a chance event that would never have crossed her mind in a hundred years when she had allowed Matthew and Amy Carson to adopt the baby she had borne out of her love for Nat Carson.

She would like to think that Providence had had a hand in it but somehow could not bring herself to think of Frank Drakston's tragic death had brought it all about as being a godsend, even if one turn of it had been the near about daily contact with her child again. Strange as it was even though Frank had certainly kept his all exclusive personality out of bound to others the greater part of his life, she thought had his untimely death been prolonged a little longer that he would have come to have been included among that small group who she looked upon as her most trusted friends. In a certain sense she had, anyway, and still found it hard not to think he was going to pop through the doorway most any minute, though he had been dead over six months now. Frank had truly seemed to enjoy having school there at Drakston Hall, coming in quite often to observe and check with her about supplies, though he had always cut his visits short.

34

Many people had looked on Frank Drakston as being rather eccentric and that may have been, but in her eye he was long from being anybody's fool because she was certain Frank, for one, had seen through her entire false front and had known that she was the mother of Whit Carson. Even so, with her sensing that Frank was on to her secret pose, it still had seemed to never bother her in the least. She supposed this had been due to her feeling that she and Frank had sorta been of kindred spirits in that respect, with him understanding her plight. In regard to losing one's heart, had it not been with Frank as it had been with her? Even though she was certain Frank Drakston had loved and respected his wife, she was just as certain he had never recovered from the shock of losing Eliza Carson to Luke Heyward, as she herself would never recover from the shock of Nat Carson's death, losing him for all time, too.

If she could have glimpsed even a small fraction of what she had endured, would she have been any less eager to run into Nat Carson's arms that day, giving herself to him with abandon that same afternoon? Here she was asking herself that question once again when she knew full well the answer was going to evade her as it always did. So far, regarding that matter, there seemed to be only one factor that had left her holding few doubts and apparently it was never going to be any other way with her and that was the fact she had lived a lifetime in that blissful short while she had been granted with Nat Carson.

Had Nat loved her as deeply as she had him? What an impossible question? Who could measure emotion? Had there ever been any two people whose emotions lay on the same level? She liked to think that her's and Nat's had been fairly matched at the time considering what their lovemaking had resulted in. Further, even though Nat had been an ardent lover, his tenderness with her had been so openly demonstrative that it was hard for her to entertain any question concerning his sincerity. Moreover, Nat's letters to her—letters that she would ever treasure were there to speak in furtherance of his devotion for her. Certainly, she had been aware of Nat's sewing a few wild oats in Virginia. As a matter of fact, he as much as told her himself. But he had also professed his love for her, telling her she was the only girl he truly loved and wanted for his wife, suddenly revealing he was ready to settle down, asking her if she would marry him before he left Columbia. She could near see that lopsided smile of his now as he had gone on to add he wanted to make sure she became Mrs. Nathan

Carson without delay so that, he would not have to worry about someone else coming along and snatching her away from him. Of course, she had said yes to Nat, but nothing had seemed to work in their favor. Their sudden desire to be married before he left for the battlefields again had proven to be much more difficult to carry out than said, and Nat had been forced to leave before making her his wife or anything settled on for certain, save her promise she would come to him in Virginia as quickly as he could make arrangements for her.

In regard to that aspect; however, it seemed the smiles of fortune were still inclined to turn from them. Victories commenced to be fewer and further apart for the South, putting additional hindrances in the way of her and Nat's plans and hopes. Added to the number of wives and sweethearts already in Richmond trying to keep contact with loved ones in the moving armies, war refugees by the hundreds poured into the city each day from all parts of war-torn Virginia. Thus, living conditions became dire; indeed, and anxious months began to move by and Nat could work out nothing in the way for her to join him. Nat had not known she was carrying his baby; though, until a few weeks before his death. She had deeply regretted not telling him earlier, but as time had marched on and moved into another war-struggling year, the South's manpower had become so severe making it imperative that every soldier put his nation first, she had hesitated in adding a message of that sort in her letters to him. At any rate, she did at last tell him and in the intervening time between their letters, Nat was also finally promised a room for her that was to be vacated right away. Nat's wire had come shortly after that, telling her to take the next train for Richmond, the room would be available by the time of her arrival. He had also added that he loved her and was anxiously waiting. Elated, she had wired Nat back. At last, fortune seemed to have turned their way.

Five and one half months pregnant—though it was questionable one would ever have suspected it due to her smallness and her fashionable wide-spreading skirts and flowing capes she had been happily packing when another telegram had come from a close fellow office of Nat's, who had been aware of Nat's plan to bring her to Richmond, telling her of Nat's death. The days following that telegram had been nothing but a black nightmare for her and were still somewhat hazy in her memory. She could see that her grief for Nat in addition to the anguish she suffered over her pregnancy had not liked much in driving her out of her mind. All she could seem to recall about that black period was that one deploring thought of suicide that had churned steadily in her head for days. Somehow though, she wondered now from where she gathered it, she gained the strength to rally from her dark despair, resolute to carry through and have Nat Carson's unborn baby, doing the best she could for its ever well-being from then onwards.

Having been unable to bring herself to front her parents with her disgrace, out of desperation, she had turned to the one person who she would have thought would have been the last she would have asked for help in circumstances such as that—Miss Amanda Taylor, her employer.

She was sure what had prompted her to reach this decision more than anything else, was Amanda Taylor's ever admiration for the Carson family and especially Matthew Carson. In truth, although she had never seen, nor did she have anything to back up her theory, rumors or otherwise, save the way Amanda Taylor's face lit up every time Matthew Caron's name was mentioned; she nevertheless had reason to believe that Amanda Taylor was secretly in love with Matthew Carson and had been for years. She would never forget how low and disappointed Miss Taylor had appeared the day she had learned that Matthew Carson had remarried again and had married his departed wife's sister at that.

In any case, it had been Amanda Taylor who had come to her rescue, helping her work out all details and seeming to be rather apt at it as well and more than happy to do so. It had been Amanda Taylor's suggestion that she make a journey home to Oak Grove to visit with her parents a few days and inform them she would be living permanently in Columbia and with an extra bow added here and maybe a flounce somewhere else upon her dresses, she had gone and no one had seemed to be the wiser to her pregnancy. Amanda Taylor had also taken it upon herself to spread the word at school that "Miss Randolph" would be absent from her teaching post for a few months due to extreme grief and depression over the death of her betrothed on a battlefield in Virginia, which, unfortunately, had been true enough. Upon Amanda Taylor's advice again, she left the rooming house where she had been living in Columbia and moved in with Miss Taylor, giving to her family the excuse of having better living accommodations at Miss Taylor's as an explanation for her move.

And, there in Amanda Taylor's rather modest but comfortable house, following one of the most desolate periods she had ever known and very much doubted if there could ever be any worse in store for her— come what may—Whit was born one sultry August night, in sixty-four while the moans of Nat Carson's name filled the room despite all her effort to suppress calling to him.

Amanda Taylor's maidservant and housekeeper, a buxom, very dark-skinned negress, boosted along to the task by that indomitable spirit of Miss Taylor's and who had become her own main source of companionship and comfort through those dark months, had been her only attendant. The maidservant had proven to be capable; though, and Whit was finally laid in her arms. Small he had been at birth but perfect in every way and also resembling Nat Carson even in infancy.

In early fall, she had resumed her teaching, the same fall that General William T. Sherman had begun his march to the sea—a ruinous and grievous event that made it easy enough to fabricate the truth regarding the presence of a fatherless little boy—with this especially being the cruel fact when Sherman and his invading army had reached Columbia, sweeping a wide path of destruction in its wake and leaving the city in a reign of terror. If anyone; however, had inquired in respect to Whit's progenitors or presence, she could not recall/it; for by this late day of the South's four year struggle for independence from federal rule, a displaced baby, child, or grown-up, as for that matter, presented nothing out of the common run of things. In addition, the majority of Southerners had become so crushed in spirit and burdened by the long chaos of war, one could hardly endure one's own troubles anymore much less allow their minds and curiosity to be stirred over much by someone else's.

It had pained her deeply not to be able to acknowledge Whit publicly. But, from the first, her sole aim had been to protect Nat's child from any name calling ever being stigmatized a bastard. She had not been able to bear the thought of that, and, in truth, had gone to great length not to arouse people's curiosity regarding all that was conducted at school. She had led a retired life with her baby in Miss Taylor's house to which she had withdrawn and, to her dismay and surprise too, no one had been the wiser with one year having passed and then another with Whit reaching his second birthday, she had become more concerned and anxious than ever because she had been well aware she could not continue more or less to hide Whit publicly.

However, as fate should have it, with Whit in her arms, she was rushing around a street corner on her way to purchase more thread to finish the dress she was making when suddenly she felt someone's hand lying on her arm slightly restraining her and looked up into the face of Nat's father as he exclaimed, "Lucy! Lucy Randolph! Dear, I do believe you would've passed me by entirely, so preoccupied you seem with wherever you and this little chap are hurrying to!"

She had not seen Matthew Carson since the day she had attended Nat's final burial a Green Sea. Now, in seeing him, it brought it all back—everything she had endured. She felt the sudden welling of her heart. Still, for the moment, she managed to hold on to her composure enough to tell him, "I'm so sorry, Mr. Carson, I suppose I was sorta lost in my thoughts, I didn't see you. Please forgive me."

"No apology, dear, it's not necessary," he smiled, "I'm too guilty of doing the same myself, far more often than I care to admit to. But, I'm awfully glad my eyes and mind, too, as far as that goes, were alert this time. How are you, dear? It's so nice to see you." He was observing that same haunted look about her that she had worn at Nat's final rites, and it was his opinion; also, that she looked far too frail to be dashing around street corners carrying this chubby little fellow who she had clutched tightly in her arms.

"And—likewise, Mr. Carson," she replied, her words falling in a halting low-voiced tone, "I'm—happy to see you're looking well and Mrs. Draks—"

Matthew laughed, "It's all right, dear, and don't you start apologizing for that, either, it happens all the time. Amy and I both are used to it and think nothing of it. Besides, you've never been used to addressing Amy by any other name than, Mrs. Drakston, and may continue to call her that if you wish to, neither of us would mind."

The tears were still gathering, waiting just under the surface, but Matthew Carson's ability to set one at ease with his outgoing nature gave her the strength to continue to keep them in check as she went on to say, "I am sorry, Mr. Carson. It seems I'm nothing but blunders today. Anyway, I do hope she's well, too, and I realize this is coming rather late, but I want to congratulate you both and wish you every happiness in your marriage."

"Thank you, Lucy, and I'll thank you for Amy too. Amy and I have found a wonderful happiness together. The fact is, we've just rented a house only a few blocks from here and have only gotten settled in a couple days ago. Rather than commute by train between here and home to attend to my senate duties as well as being forced to live apart the greater part of the time, we decided to make our permanent base here for the time being, which, of course, could change most any day due to the state of the South's political situation. Anyway, we were planning to call on you right away. I presume you are still residing at the same place, Amanda Taylor's residence, isn't it?"

"Y—essir, over two years now," she murmured.

"Well then, we'll surely get together right away. Amy will be anxious to see you and more than delighted when she learns that we're living so close to someone from home."

Matthew had already detected her nervousness but had thought that it and her obvious sadness, too, had been brought on because of revived memories of their last meeting. Now, however, he was not so sure that that was all she was so jittery and sad voiced about. Moreover, he was becoming plenty aware of his own creepy feeling— an uneasiness stealing over him which he was at a complete loss to understand. And, as the increasing silence began to grow between them—a silence which was full of growing tension—he found himself staring intently at the little boy in her arms, who she appeared to be endeavoring to shield her face against as she clutched him tighter and tighter to her.

With his gaze still fastened on the child's face while the lengthy moment became longer, Matthew began to wonder what was it about the little boy, a child who he had never laid his eyes on before, that had aroused this sudden keen interest on his part and at the same time, was telling himself "he could think of nothing that would explain his desire to stare, either." Thus, this being the case, it was more to ease the building tenseness than anything else—certainly not to pry—that brought him to reach for the child's hand and go on to say, "I presume this little chap who appears to be so fond of you—." Whit was gripping onto his mother as tightly as she was him. "And you him if I may add, is some of Amanda's kin folk. What's your name, fellow?"

Whit, resolute for the moment in having nothing to do with this stranger, pulled his hand away from Matthew and when he did, Matthew was to observe that Lucy let her head fall lower as she nervously bit down on her lower lip, causing him to be at another loss in searching for the answer to this side of her personality that had never been revealed to him before. After another moment's pause though to his relief she came through and murmured again in a broken voice, which was also puzzling him more and more, "Whit—ney. Tell—the gentleman your name is Whitney, darling."

Unknown to Matthew, his question and Whit's behavior, had cut Lucy severely. She could never remember having yearned so deeply for anything as she was yearning then, her love for Nat Carson included, for Whit to be known by his rightful name—Carson.

"Whitney is it. Well, that's one fine and honorable name. And, I'm certain it will ever be claimed with esteem, too, by this handsome chap, if I do say so," Matthew was cheering, because Whit had begun to give him a rather sharp eye and suddenly, to Matthew's amazement, his little mouth was crooking at the corner in a slow but positive smile— a smile that Matthew was sure he had seen before but was at a further loss to recall on who or when he had seen it.

Matthew had become so nonplused by now that even had they not still been standing in the middle of the street with traffic walking around them, he would not have waited any longer in bringing their meeting to an end; therefore, quickly suggesting, "Lucy dear, could I give you a hand with Whitney wherever you've started to. If he'll allow me, I'll be glad to carry him for you. He's obviously quite a load for you."

There was only a brief pause this time before she raised her head and looked Matthew full in the face, attempting no longer to hide her teary eyes from him.

"Y—es," she agreed, "he—he's." Her voice had finally choked and stopped altogether, as a big tear rolled down each cheek.

Fearfully alarmed now and worse still because he knew not the why and wherefore for his fear, Matthew stepped closer to Lucy and draping an arm about her, he implored, "What is it, Lucy dear? Won't you please tell me? If our meeting again, is not the reason for your sorrow, then, please, dear, do tell me what it is that's brought you this grief and let me try to comfort and help you, if I possibly can."

"It's—It's—oh, Mr. Carson," she quietly sobbed, "It's—"

"Yes, dear," prompted Matthew. "It's what? Please go on.

"It's—It's Whitney, Mr. Carson."

"Whitney?" frowned Matthew, staring at Whit again, more baffled than ever. "What about Whitney, Lucy dear?" What is it you want to tell me about Whitney?" Matthew saw she was hesitating to tell him;

41

however, dropping her head once more. Thus, rather than appear too forceful in urging her along, he tried a different approach, making another suggestion, as he let his arm fall from about her and held out his open hands, "Please, dear, do tell me what it is that's brought you this grief. I help you, if I possibly can. Give the little boy to me, Lucy dear, then maybe with your being more relaxed it'll be easier for you to tell me."

Lucy's grip on Whit grew slack and without one flinch or protest, Whit loosened his grip, too, and allowed Matthew to take him from his mother's arms, quietly settling himself down, staring somewhat curiously back and forth between the strange man who held him and his mother as they made another attempt to talk with each other.

"Now, dear," continued Matthew." What seems to be your problem in regard to this little fellow? As I've just said, I'd very much like to help you, if I possibly can."

With her head still lowered, Lucy replied, "you're so kind, Mr. Carson, and I do want to thank you for your concern, but I see no way that you could help me because it's my belief my situation could hardly be any more hopeless."

Her despairing reply unsettled Matthew even more than he already was. Still, wanting to help her, he went on pointing out to her, "Try me, dear, and see. You'll never know for sure unless you give me the opportunity."

Sensing his earnestness, Lucy held back no longer, raising a painful, tear-streaked face and telling him, while a stunned Matthew Carson had to actually steady his buckling knees to keep himself upright, "I pray, Mr. Carson, that you won't judge me too harshly or allow your memory of Nat to be any less sublime than it's ever been, but that little boy who you're holding in your arms is your own grandchild, Nat's and mine! He was born three-and-one-half months after Nat's death, here in Columbia!"

For some few moments, Matthew Carson stood speechless and looked at Lucy Randolph's pained expression, his mind racing as he was saying to himself, 'heavens and earth! I should have known! The child's smile is Nat's over when Nat was his age. In fact, his eyes— his entire facial makeup is a miniature image of Nat.' It had been the child's coloring which was identical to his mother's and apparently the only feature Whitney had inherited from Lucy, that had prevented his mind from seeing through that motivation that the child's smile had induced in him.

Still near reeling as he continued to rest his startled gaze upon her, Matthew became aware that Lucy was anxiously waiting—looking and searching for that comfort in him which he had more or less promised her—and, immediately, he let his whirling thoughts go where they would and silently started to pray that he would be granted the wisdom to make the right move and say the right words, laying his free arm once again across her shoulders as he did so, finally exclaiming, "God be praised! What you must've gone through, child!" He swiftly shifted his gaze from her face and looked around them, miraculously spying a vacant bench under a clump of trees near the sidewalk across the street and went on to tell her, "Take my arm, dear, and come with me, we must talk."

Carrying Whit in one arm and Lucy holding onto his other, Matthew forced his quivering a legs to leave the side street and proceed to move on until he had safely maneuvered them through and around the many various horse-drawn conveyances that made up the street's busy noon day traffic. Having finally reached the vacant bench, Matthew indicated for Lucy to take her seat and he took his own beside her, thankful to let his unsteady legs slump as they would, at last.

Matthew was certain he would not have been near as jarred had the young woman with her startling news sitting beside him, been someone else other than Lucy Randolph; in that, he had never viewed the relationship between her and his younger son as being anything but a mild attraction on Nat's part and a sort of adolescent knight-in-armor affection on Lucy's part. Granted, he had never thought of their relationship being one that would make for such dire consequences and was deeply regretting that he had not viewed Nat's seesawing courtship of Lucy Randolph with a more serious eye—weighed it with the same importance that he had that of Phil's and Caroline Wilton's.

As Lucy Randolph began to unfold her story to Matthew, he could see now that she had ever been nothing less than a serious-minded, remarkable young woman, certainly no giddy adolescent when it came to her strength of purpose and deep devotion in regard to his son and the child they had conceived together, to say nothing of her devout concern and respect for the Carson name as a whole. In truth, he was seeing Lucy as being one of the most enduring, self-disciplined young women he had ever known and held her hand with much compassion as she began to talk easily and openly of her relationship with his son.

While Whit toddled and played around Matthew's and Lucy's knees, she recounted to Matthew most of her relations with his son, including that brief period of happiness she and Nat shared in Columbia, their endeavor to be married, their plans—the hopes that turned to disappointments, and her dark, despairing hours as well, finally raising her drawn face to Matthew Carson and asking, "What am I going to do, Mr. Carson? When it comes to protecting my baby's name, I realize I'm nearing the end of the line. He's growing up, only a few years away from school age. This may come as an additional shock for you, but I've done none of this to protect myself. I did it for two reasons only, mainly to give me time to see if I could possibly work out something in the matter of Whitney's legitimateness, which, of course, I've failed at, and the other reason is my parents. I deplore hurting them."

"I take it then that your parents are still in the dark about all of this," said Matthew.

"In regard to Whitney, yes. The way I felt about Nat and still feel, the answer is no. Both my parents were very much aware of my love for Nat, from the beginning. I think that's why they sorta let me go my own way and especially after—after Nat's death. I'll probably tell them someday but not now. No, no one knows that Whitney is my baby except Amanda Taylor and her housekeeper and now, you."

Still shaken, Matthew regarded Lucy thoughtfully for a moment, slightly shaking his head from side to side. He made no comment; however, bearing on this further astonishing disclosure but as he reached down and took hold of Whitney's hand that was clinging to his knee, he did comment on Lucy's earlier statement, agreeing with her as he said, "yes, you're right, dear, about keeping this little fellow confined. You won't be able to do that much longer."

"I know, Mr. Carson, and it weighs on my mind day and night. I so much want to protect Whitney though from hearing any derogatory remark ever in regard to his birth. I think I'd go to any limit to prevent that. Still, I know it's, inevitable, if the situation doesn't change, and it pains me so to realize he's going to be hurt time and time again if no way, opens for me to stop what will eventually have to be revealed.

Matthew was doing his ever best to force his befuddle mind to come up with a few encouraging words at least, but he was soon to acknowledge that when it came to having even one helpful suggestion, his mind was totally blank. He turned and started to ask Lucy about one possible way out which had suddenly occurred to him—were there anyone present who she was interested in enough to marry—but as his scrutiny of her began to linger in the growing silence, he thought better of it because something about her stressed expression told him that she would be highly offended if he did, much less asking her straight out if she had any special one in mind.

As far as that went, when it came to this business of suitors or matrimony, Matthew, continuing to study Lucy sitting there with her head and shoulders drooped appearing as though she had grown bewildered and lost, too, in her searching for some solution, concluded that Lucy Randolph had not and would most likely never look upon another man again in that respect. Matthew had promptly formed the opinion then and there that Lucy felt already married—married to Nat as devoutly and lawfully as he himself was married to Amy.

Suddenly, having come to think of Amy, an idea popped in Matthew's head, bringing him to ask, "Lucy dear, had you started to attend to something that needs your attention within the next few hours?"

Lucy brought her head and shoulders up a bit, turning toward him. "No, Mr. Carson," she replied, "it was nothing important. Since I didn't have any more classes for today, I'd decided to finish some sewing and was on my way to purchase more thread, that's all."

"Good!" exclaimed Matthew as he sprang from the bench with a sudden reinforced vigor, sweeping Whitney up in his arms. "I want you to come with me, then!"

Staring at Matthew rather inquisitive as she turned her grave expression up to him, Lucy inquired, "Come with you? Where to Mr. Carson?"

"To see Amy! Amy will help us!" Matthew told her, the tone of his voice sounded as refreshed and clear as the look of green grass after a spring shower.

"To see Mrs. Draks—Mrs. Carson!" Lucy cried with alarm. "Oh, Mr. Carson, I don't think I can! Please don't ask me to do that!"

Opening her heart to Nat's father had been hard for Lucy; yet, she was convinced that had been nothing compared to the horror she was positive would be hers to endure, if she were to face the demure and dignified Amy Carson with her woes and plight. The thought of it sent a chill through Lucy.

Perceiving the very thing that Lucy feared most, Matthew was quickly to tell her, as he forced back the smile that Lucy's slip-up concerning Amy's name had brought to his face, "Now, don't fret, dear, you'll see once we face Amy, your fears have been groundless. Take my word for it, when it comes to keeping one's confidence and understanding one's problems, Amy scores with the highest. I've found that Amy has a remarkable depth of perception about her, giving her a deeper insight into a problem than most of us. It's my bet that she won't only be deeply sympathetic but not long in coming up with some solution to our problem, as well. Come on, Lucy dear, and trust me, and you'll find what I've told you is truth." Matthew held out his hand to her.

Still fearful, Lucy sat upon the bench with downcast eyes hesitating in spite of Matthew's assurance. Even so, to finally have a masculine strength to lean on, something she had yearned for so long and it being the strength of Nat's father besides, his hand so near that all she had to do was reach for it—all of it—was too much for Lucy to ignore and she found herself lingering no longer to go with him. Quickly, her eyes were lifting to his and she was rising, letting her hand find its way inside Matthew Carson's palm.

Lucy was still filled with misgivings every step of the way, even holding Matthew's hand while her heart seemed to flutter with every beat. But once she felt Amy Carson's warm, motherly arms gathering her close, her fear of Matthew's wife lapsed into a quiet ease as she realized he knew Amy rather well and sensed everything was going to be as he had said it would be.

Nevertheless, for all Lucy's abated anxiety, when they all had gotten settled down in their chairs with Matthew undertaking the burden of narrating the circumstances which had led to Lucy's being there, Lucy became quite shocked to see Amy Carson absorbing the whole story as calmly and serenely had she been listening to some fashion designer give the descriptive details of his latest fashions. And, sometime later when Matthew stalled somewhat after having covered the most important details, Lucy even though Matthew said that Amy most likely would come up with a solution, sat dumfounded and merely stared as Amy promptly said, "Matthew darling, don't be so downcast and you, too, Lucy dear. I have a solution if Lucy will agree to it that'll protect this dear little boy for life!"

"You have, Amy?" asked Matthew, appearing as astonished as Lucy in spite of his faith in Amy.

"Yes, dear, I have and it's the only possible way that I can see this child coming by its rightful name, and even that way will not eliminate keeping his true identity unexposed if he's to be protected in the manner that Lucy desires."

"What way is that Amy," inquired Matthew, amazed as ever at Amy's thinking power.

"If Lucy will give her consent, you and I, dear, will adopt Whitney, giving him the legal right to be known as a Carson, which, of course, he is!"

Matthew's mouth fell open in astonishment. So did Lucy's. Neither had given one thought to this astounding solution. All the same, as an electrifying stillness began to descend upon the group, both were to admit to themselves that Amy's proposal was; indeed, a sensible one, growing more sound to them as the hush lingered on.

Finally, Matthew asked, "You mean to say you would do that, Amy, take on the responsibility of bringing this child up, if Lucy should see fit to agree to your suggestion?"

"Yes, dear, I would and be happy to do it. You see—"Amy paused, a faint color spreading over her cheeks. "Well—you see, Matthew, I'd so hoped when we were married that maybe I was still young enough in years to give you another child, hopefully a son. Now though, I hardly think so in spite of my yearning for it—"

"Oh, Amy," Matthew broke in overwhelmed at her disclosure.

"However, dear," Amy went on to say as cool and collected as ever, that's only part of the reason for my suggestion. What I'm proposing here doesn't apply to just any child because neither of us are young in years anymore. This matter concerns a child whose bloodline is part Goodyear as well as Carson, not to mention that of his mother, the noble and honorable Randolph's and the Whitney line, too." Amy turned to Lucy, who was still staring wide-eyed at this amazing woman, going on to say, "Lucy dear, ponder my suggestion thoroughly before you settle upon anything, but try to come to your decision as quickly as possible. If Matthew and I adopt your baby, we all must see to it before he grows much older in order to prevent his becoming affected emotionally. By no means, would any of us want that to happen. There's another important reason; also. For my suggesting we act in haste. I'm thinking, if we plan the adoption very carefully, you dear, need not be separated from your baby. In fact, I would prefer it that way and I'm positive that Matthew sees it likewise.

In time, certainly, he will come to look upon Matthew and myself as a part of his life, too. Now, here's how I propose we handle it."

And, thought Lucy, as she had continued to gaze in amazement, she had gone on outlining the whole process of the adoption before she had risen from her chair again. While she and Nat's father had listened in speechless wonder, Amy Carson had outlined her amazing plan that had only taken her a few minutes to reason out. Listening to her, one would have concluded, had not one known better, she had had the plan under consideration for months instead of the short while it had taken Matthew Carson to reveal the circumstances which had raised it.

Of course, she had given her consent and as doubtable as Amy Carson's plan had been at the time, it had worked out and without too much difficulty at that.

Beginning that same day, she and Whitney had begun to practically live at the Carson residence, with her leaving him there for days after he had gotten to know them, while she went back to Miss Taylor's she had gone alone. And, the day came when she was to leave Whitney with them for always, and she had faced the remainder of her life without him. As Amy Carson had proposed, the adoption had been a slow and gradual process with her allowing the Carson's to supply most of the attention that Whitney's needs and comfort called for. In short, she had backed away and allowed the Carson's to gain first place in Whitney's affection. It had been painful to see her baby shifting the close affection that he had held for her to the Carson's. The hardest part of all though had been the day when she caught Whitney, who Matthew Carson had tagged Whit, call Amy Carson "Mommy."

Had she regretted her decision? No, in all truth, she could not say that she had because she had meant it when she had told Nat's father, she would go to most any length to protect Nat Carson's son.

She wondered why it was that she had been able to unburden her heart to Matthew Carson that day when she still had not gained the courage to tell her own parents—something she must do right away because she had come to feel—and rather strongly at that—that they should know. She thought possible all the heartache and sorrow Matthew Carson had suffered, too, had had more to do with her confiding in him than anything, doubtless bringing her to feel when chance had directed their feet toward the other that day that if anyone would understand her situation or could help her, it would be Matthew Carson. And, in all honesty, she would have to say he had yet to let her down. The same applied to Amy Carson, Still, if only Nat could have lived. Nat Carson—the only man she had ever loved or ever wanted and it would remain to be so with her for all time. She knew that now—Nat.

Lucy's engrossment with the past was brought to an abrupt end by the sudden splash of a teardrop upon the closed book, snapping her back from that dreamy world her thoughts had transported her to. Mindful now of where she was, she quickly snatched her handkerchief from the pocket of her blouse and dabbed at her eyes. Then, she feigned two or three dry coughs and blew her nose rather noisily. She were wishing she could come up with a good loud sneeze but aware she could hardly feign that, she cleared her throat once or twice and settled for one or two more thin sniffs before she finally raised her head to observe if anyone was looking at her.

Seeing that the children's heads were still bent over their readers, Lucy heaved a sigh of relief and told herself that her endeavor to feign a cold had been all for nothing. It seemed no one in the class had been observing her daydreaming after all, Lucy was glad she had not been discovered, promising herself on the spot that from then on, she would do her daydreaming someplace else besides in the presence of her pupils. Suddenly, however, she was not so sure that her self-absorption with the past or her tears had gone unnoticed. It was Whit. Even though he had his head bent over his reader, his abstracted gaze was plainly revealing that his attention was certainly not upon his lesson. Nor did she think it had been for a good while if his sly expression told her anything.

Fully knowledgeable to the fact, in those few weeks since Whit had become her pupil, that he lacked a lot when it came to measuring up in reading, Lucy started to rise from her desk and investigate the reason for his obvious disinterest. Glancing at the clock though and seeing that it was almost time for class recital, she thought better of it, telling herself that no doubt there would be another time for Whit to bear the brunt of a lecture from her. All the same, while she continued to keep her eyes on him, Whit brought his head up fast and shot a glance her way and then dropped his dead down again. Now, Lucy began to sorta reproach herself for not having gone ahead and reprimanded him regardless of the time. None the less, her self-reproach was to last only a moment or so. Whit let his head come up this time and stay up while he set his keen brown eyes direct to hers.

Then, as teacher and pupil continued to stare—studying one another—that same slow lopsided smile that Lucy had seen Nat Carson wear many times began to curve Whit's small mouth until it had finally grown into a somewhat bold and mischievous wide grin.

The likeness was too much for Lucy. Her heart pommeled wildly. Powerless to resist him, she found herself retuning Whit's grin as recklessly as he sent it while she felt a gladness lift her in a new discovery. She knew now, despite all and come what may, she and the child sitting before her still shared an immutable common spirit and it would ever remain so. Further, as Lucy passed those few silent moments of balanced accord with Whit, she came to discover something else, too. She told herself, no longer would she question that short, happy interlude she had had with Nat Carson, because she had now come to believe that Nat Carson's destiny had been sealed from the very beginning and in so being that Providence had had a hand in leaving this trace of him—his very smile planted on the sunny face of this winsome little boy—all that fate had finally seen fit to favor her with in the matter of her love for Nat Carson. She was grateful for that much though and would cherish it as she secretly cherished the child who wore it.

Certainly, she knew the day would come when Whit would leave her classroom at Drakston Hall, taking the image of Nat Carson's smile with him. Nevertheless, in knowing when he did go he would be facing the world as a Carson—carrying his true father's name—she was positive that one accomplished fact would be enough to sustain her. Besides, she would always have that memory of Nat Carson, standing in a splash of sunlight—a memory she would now be able to call to mind in all its nostalgic sweetness, without searching for that ever answer, as to why?

Lucy let her gaze leave Whit's face for an instant, straying over the other members of her class. Then, she looked at Whit again and laid a finger upon her lips, slowly shaking her head back and forth at him. Whit was sharp. He read the meaning of her actions in a flash. His chubby hand went flying to his own mouth where he firmly popped a finger likewise against his lips.

Whit was gleefully happy over this secret he shared with the appealing "Miss Lucy." He sent another smile in her direction and what made him even happier was the fact she smiled back at him again. Momentarily; however, Whit's grin was chilling fast. He could hardly believe his ears and found himself distressfully questioning the solidity of that alliance he had made with "Miss Lucy" because she was saying, as she still continued to smile at him, "Study hour is up, children, in class today. Whit, would you come to the front of the classroom, please?"

Whit's admiration and high esteem that he had ever held as long as he could remember for the charming "Miss Lucy" was growing cold, indeed. Daunted, head bent down, he picked up his reader and slowly crawled from his desk. Lifting his eyes somewhat though as he started forth and seeing that engaging smile still upon him, Whit was promptly taken in again, changing his view, instantly. His quick mind came up with the shrewd notion that "Miss Lucy" had favored him after all by calling on him to read first. He told himself, that way, he would be getting the ordeal over with and would have the remainder of reading recital to think about other things; for instance, racing his Shetland pony alongside Stuart's down the long avenue once class was dismissed!

Gathering a wide smile again while he set his gaze to that of Lucy's, Whit went striding up the aisle and planted himself at the front of the class. Quickly thumbing through the reader, he luckily found the lesson and began immediately to stumble over words which his eyes were seeing for the first time that day, while a dismayed Lucy listened and wondered. What would be the best course to take in persuading Whit to take more interest in his schoolbooks?

On this same afternoon, Elizabeth Drakston—having finally gathered the courage to seat herself in Frank's long vacant chair behind the desk she had seen him bent over often enough since that day he had brought her to Drakston Hall—sat submerged in memories, too. Some were happy and pleasant memories—some painful—others puzzling. And also, linked to all these things that had overloaded her mind was that ever prevailing question as to why Frank had been taken from her, taken at the very time their marriage had reached its highest point in mutual closeness and understanding. This had been particularly true relating to their physical relationship—a part of their marriage that had near ceased for them in recent months. Then, thought Elizabeth, there had come that soft April evening when she and Frank had found and embraced something that their marriage had always lacked even though she had liked to think it had been there all the time when; in truth, it had not. She had sensed a vast difference in

51

Frank. Although he had always been tender while making love to her, on that evening, it had seemed as though their mating was actually taking place for the first time with Frank being very much delighted with what he saw and keenly concerned with what he held. In those soft April shadows, all barriers had been cast aside as she and Frank had truly become one with the other in a joining of boundless giving Frank giving all of himself to her at last.

For months preceding that April evening, most the time, Frank had either snapped or not talked at all, shutting himself off from everybody for hours on end with no one being able to reach him. Then suddenly, Frank was himself again and even more, telling her how pretty she had looked in that yellow gown. Had it all come about because Eliza Heyward had come through the worst of her illness and had been on the road to recovery? And, where had Frank gone to on that evening when he was shot? Had he gone to green Sea? There were so many questions that had gone unanswered. She thought Frank had wanted to tell her what had happened in bringing on his death but had thought better of it, he had said to her in those last hours, "Elizabeth, always remember, dear, there was nothing you could have done to prevent this other than what I have already told you, to say more would serve no purpose at all." And, keenly wise to Frank's nature, she had refrained from going any further into it, and Frank had died without saying any more about it. What little else had been said between them had been about Stuart, with her promising Frank his wishes would be followed—seeing that Stuart was raised at Drakston Hall and also properly schooled and especially trained and instructed in respect to whatever vocation he chose when he reached the proper age.

Yes, at Frank's request, she planned to continue on with the school at Drakston Hall, too, keeping Lucy on as its instructor, if she would consent to stay, until all the present students had completed grammar school. That reminded her of something. She should see about the supplies and see about Lucy's salary also. She thought she should at least shoulder this one task, relieving Mr. Carson of the burden. So much had fallen on him since Frank's death. Yes, she would meet with the remaining members of the school board right away, Bruce, Dr. Seth, and Brent. She should not delay the meeting much longer even though she knew it was going to pain her dreadfully to preside in Frank's place.

There were so many things waiting that needed to be taken care of; for example, clearing out the drawers of this desk, something she came in here to do and supposed she should get on with it no matter how much she dreaded it mainly because of two things she knew it contained and had no desire to see again. That old yellowed deed of Early Cole's and the three concealed passports to Europe, one marked deceased.

Though she had nothing to go on save her own intuition, she had a feeling that business which had brought Early Cole to Drakston Hall that day, bringing that old worthless deed to Frank, had been an instrumental factor in leading up to the circumstance which had brought Frank's life to its end. She was certain of it because when she had come to the library to wait up for Frank the night he was shot, she had noticed the old Cole deed lying atop Frank's desk. From its appearance, it had looked as though Frank had been studying it and had, abruptly, thrown it aside. The Cole farm which Frank had acquired through foreclosure—something she had learned about when his estate had been probated at his death—bordered the lands of Green Sea, did it not?

Of course, she had not pursued this hunch of hers in any way. Neither had she revealed it. Nor did she think she would. The truth was, even if she were to start an investigation, it would matter little to her now what she may uncover. Frank was gone and anything she may do or might discover, was not going to bring him back to her. Besides, she must never forget that Frank had not been in favor of her knowing all the details, anyhow, or he would have told her himself. So, all things considered, she supposed she should try to put it out of her mind and began—at this very moment—to make an attempt to resume the duties that were her responsibility or this day, too, would go by seeing nothing accomplished once more by any effort on her part

Having somewhat reconciled herself to the inevitability of her situation, Elizabeth sighed resignedly and pulled the chair closer to the desk. She was starting to pull out the top drawer when she heard Frank's mother say, as she appeared in the open doorway, "Oh, there you are, dear! It's such a lovely afternoon, I thought perhaps you'd gone for a walk among those beautiful chrysanthemums in the garden."

Amy Drakston Carson's grief for her only blood son still persisted to inwardly sting her almost constantly. Though, true to form, she held on to her calm nature, allowing but very little of this pain to surface in the presence of others and none in the company of this sorrow-laden daughter-in-law if she could possibly get around it. Amy was too worried and concerned over those black-and-blue shadows under Elizabeth's eyes, to give way to any emotional grief in front of her. She was observing those marks now as Elizabeth looked up and said, "No, I haven't been out. I thought I'd tidy p this desk some and see about the school supplies."

Amy walked on across the room and laid a hand on Elizabeth's. "Don't worry about it dear. I'm sure Lucy will let us know when it's time to order more."

"I suppose so," said Elizabeth, pushing her chair back and rising to walk over to the window. Gazing forlornly at nothing for a moment or two, she suddenly went on, "Oh, Mother Drakston"—to please Frank, Elizabeth had continued to address Amy as a Drakston—"Will the hurt and loneliness ever cease?"

"Not entirely, dear. But, in time, yes, you will come to see the beauty of God's universe as you once did. It could be any time, perhaps tomorrow, or, as for that matter, it could even be today. That will happen though and when it does, you'll find that empty void you feel surrounds you now as having lessened considerably, and the pain of your hurt as well running lower in its intensity."

Elizabeth turned her head toward Amy, pondering her remark.

"I'd almost forgotten. You do know how it is, don't you, Mother Drakston?" She finally said.

"I must say, I do," Amy replied, "and, all too well, I fear. You see, when I lost Franklin, I felt as though the whole world had collapsed and was crushing me under it. Never having loved another man, I'd fallen in love with Franklin and married him at eighteen years of age. I could no more see myself enduring the days and nights without him, than I could see a newborn baby surviving without nourishment. I not only felt absolutely lost but helpless besides and, was to a certain degree, due to Franklin's safeguarding me too closely from the pitfalls of life. However, with Frank away at the time and Martha married and gone, too, I was forced to cope with problems that I'd never given the least thought to before simply because there was no one else here to shoulder them. I learned though and rather fast at that, I'd say, because the war was raging closer home day by day, bringing untold anxiety and problems, too, that one would've never thought would've come."

"And," said Elizabeth, "you faced them all alone. That in itself must've been a great burden for you."

"I'll say," agreed Amy. "But, looking back now, I can see all that heavy responsibility which had suddenly become mine alone, was the very thing that actually sustained me. Leastwise it occupied my mind, forcing my thoughts to center on something else besides the pain of my grief, even if it did exhaust me to no end, mentally and physically. Then, although I was beginning to wonder along with everybody else if it was ever going to end, that dreadful war was over and Frank had come home, bringing you and my grandson home, at last. And, soon after that, Matthew had walked straight into my heart. So, situations can and do change. You know, dear, this same thing could happen to you."

"What's that?" Asked Elizabeth, having allowed her wretched thoughts to lose Amy's prattle for a second or two.

"Love, Elizabeth dear, one can find love again." Stressed Amy.

"Oh—" murmured Elizabeth, turning back to gaze through the window which was giving her a direct view toward the one object that Amy was endeavoring to divert her attention away from the Drakston burial ground. "No, I don't think so, Mother Drakston."

"Of course, you don't, not now," replied Amy. "Neither did I when I found myself in your same position, and to be honest with you, had someone suggested it to me at the time and especially who it was likely to turn out to be. I would've thought they'd taken leave of their senses! Just as you do. I viewed marrying again as being totally out of the question, and Matthew Carson becoming my husband was a thought that had never entered my head until one day it suddenly came to me that I'd fallen deeply in love with him. I can tell you, dear, it does happen. Something else, too. It can be just as joyous and delightful as a first love. I've found supreme happiness with Matthew. We share a closeness that I would've never thought possible."

"Yes," murmured Elizabeth again. "it's obvious that you both adore one another, and I'm grateful that you found this wonderful gift to share with each other. Regarding myself though, I don't expect to find it again."

The finality of Elizabeth's passive manner induced Amy to say no more on the subject of love and marriage save, "Maybe not, dear, but I hope so," and she was turning to leave the room when, still not contented to leave Elizabeth at the window, she promptly decided to ask Elizabeth something she had wanted to bring up for some time but had declined to. She turned back, going on to ask, "Elizabeth dear, have you given any thought about going ahead with your visit abroad? Sometimes, a change of scenery will do wonders for one. Although I know I'd miss you and Stuart terribly, I'm willing to forget my feelings in suggesting this to you, because I want to help in every possible way that I can help."

Amy's sympathy touched Elizabeth. To Amy's delight, she turned from the window and walked back to the desk and took her seat, telling Amy, "You do help, Mother Drakston, in more ways than you're aware of, Uncle Matthew, too. As for going abroad, yes, I've thought about it. But, I'm sure for the present, anyway, that's as far as I'll venture with it, letting it cross my mind from time to time. I have no desire to be any place right now, except Drakston Hall. Perhaps next year or maybe when Stuart's a few years older, we'll go. I've written my parents and explained my feelings. They understand. You see, I still have a sense of feeling that Frank is close about me here, a sense of feeling safe and secure that I know only these walls of Drakston Hall can furnish me. I don't want to lose that, because I know if I were to part from this sense of closeness, I'd feel my loss as much again as I do now. Then, there's another important reason for my deciding to forego any trips abroad just yet. I want Stuart's roots to be firmly planted here at Drakston Hall while he's young in years, as all the Drakstons before him. To disrupt his growing years too much, would be unwise to my way of thinking. I know Frank would agree with me and I think you do, too, even though you did make this unselfish suggestion. I'm grateful to you, too, and I shall not forget it. I'm well aware of the deep devotion you hold for your grandson and can imagine what his leaving here for an indefinite period, would cost you. It was a most generous gesture on your part."

Amy was deeply moved, so much so, she did not trust her usual guarded emotion enough to make a verbal reply. Instead, she moved back to the desk and laid her hand atop Elizabeth's. In the close silence, Elizabeth stared for some few moments at her mother-in-law's hand. Then, she looked up at Amy and went on to say, "Don't worry about me, Mother Drakston, I think, from now on, I'm going to be all right."

Amy promptly weathered her flagging reserve, replying, "Yes, dear, I truly believe you will, at that."

The sudden sound of a horse's gallop coming up the drive caught the attention of both women, with Elizabeth's being instantly claimed by the manner the sound had affected in Amy. She suddenly appeared to have castoff all gloom, seeming as though her whole person had become swathed in a cloak of glowing radiance as she turned and looked toward the door, saying, "That's Matthew. He said he wouldn't be gone long. I'll see you later, dear," and she swept out of Elizabeth's sight as quickly as she had appeared, leaving Elizabeth wondering how Amy could have been so positive the rider was Matthew.

Elizabeth also thought about other things, past and future, as she sat and stared through the empty doorway for some few minutes, before she went on to do what she had started to do a good while before that.

Matthew Carson—still miraculously nimble for one nearing his sixty-fifth birthday—swing from the saddle and handed the reins of his blooded roan-colored mare to the stable groom. Yes, even though this year 1870 was far removed from what custom had been a decade prior, Drakston Hall still posed hardly any change whatever in its order of the day. Two stable grooms still continued to service the stables fulltime. And now, as the groom began to lead Matthew's mount away and he turned from the drive to proceed toward the front entrance— seeing the aged Albert opening the front door and standing aside as Amy stepped briskly through it onto the wide veranda—Matthew was started, halting in his steps. For a fleeting second, he had felt as though he were at another place, in another time, with no intervening years falling between, so alike the scene before him matched up with similar ones he had experienced in a bygone day.

Finding his steps again, Matthew also found Amy's face and returned her smile. At the same time, he was telling himself, 'steady there, Matthew Carson, don't allow your imagination to run wild. She may wear a striking resemblance to Anne, more as she grows older, but she is not Anne. She is Amy and you love her for herself alone. Likewise, neither is this Green Sea, its Drakston Hall. In a literal sense, nothing about the scene is the same but the faithful Albert, and it would serve you better to see it as such and brush all the other aside. One cannot relive the past, but, thankfully, one can live the present. Nevertheless, while Matthew was telling himself all these things— doling out a bit of his own philosophy to his over imaginative mind— he was also thinking that this had not been the first time he had sorta been thrown off his guard in the six months or more since he had become master of Drakston Hall to a position in his wildest imagination he would never have summoned to his mind, and he was thinking, too, that it probably would not be his last as he leaped up the steps and drew Amy to his side.

Those six months or so since the death of Frank Drakston, had not been easy months for Matthew Carson. Without any warning or planning for it, Matthew found his life at sixty-four years of age turned on a complete reverse course as he stepped into the duties that Frank's death thrust upon him, senior head and leader of Drakston Hall. Indeed, it was little wonder that Matthew found himself thinking in terms of his life then as being the same that it had been in former years, long past.

Once again, he had become master of a vast plantation. Once again, he had the same number in family members under his care and jurisdiction that he had had in his younger years. There was Amy, his wife. There was Elizabeth, his stepdaughter-in-law, who he had become very fond of. There were Stuart and Whit, two boy children, and this aspect was the part in the whole unbelievable circumstance which seemed the most awesome to Matthew. Though it was true, most often, Stuart tended to seek from his mother only what he had lost through the death of his father—appearing to become more attached to her than ever—the fact remained he spent a lot of time in the company of Matthew and Whit, too.

When the harvest had begun, Matthew had given Stuart and Whit permission a number of times to ride their ponies alongside him to the fields on his tours of inspection and, at those times, Matthew had found it was very hard for him to keep his thoughts from turning to the two sons who he had lost—near seeing Stuart and Whit as Phil and Nat when they had been small boys, too, riding their ponies alongside him over the fields of Green Sea. In Whit's case, the reflecting would become all the more vivid to Matthew as his gaze would catch Whit's profile.

Following Frank's burial, Amy Carson and Whit had remained at Drakston Hall while Matthew had gone back to Columbia alone to settle matters there. Although Matthew had been seriously considering to accept Frank's proposal that he, Amy, and Whit come back and reside at Drakston Hall, he had not fully made up his mind when he had brought Amy home to have a visit with her son before Frank sailed abroad. Even though Drakston Hall was a massive dwelling, Matthew had been giving some thought to the question of its being, big enough to house the two families together once Frank took the notion to return from abroad. To be more specific, what was mostly causing Matthew to hesitate was his wondering if he and his nephew could be contented under the same roof together.

However, once the tragedy had occurred, taking Frank's life, there had been no decision for Matthew to make. It appeared destiny and circumstances had made it for him. Besides Elizabeth and Stuart being left alone—neither capable of managing the operation of a plantation Elizabeth lacking the proper training to take over her husband's duties and Stuart too young in age—there was the question of Amy's vast holdings at Drakston Hall, too, a responsibility that Frank had chosen to handle for his mother. Thus, Matthew had gone back to Columbia and resigned his state senatorial duties, immediately. Then, with Albert's help he had packed the family's personal things and turned the rented house back over to its owner. After seeing Albert, along with the family possessions, safely aboard the train for home, Matthew had then taken a room at a nearby hotel and continued on with his senate duties until an appointee could be selected and voted in to take over his vacant seat, joining Amy at Drakston Hall a short while later.

Naturally, Albert—every much as awed by all the change of events as Matthew was if not more so, had been entrusted with the position of head butler at Drakston Hall. Though aged but still capable, he remained standing now in his spotless liveried whites just beyond the open door inside the hall as Matthew and Amy came through the doorway and Matthew—ever one to spark if he could—looked at him and quipped, "Albert, if we're to enjoy that delightful flavor of fresh pork sausage in our turkey dressing on Thanksgiving, maybe it wouldn't be a bad idea for us to mention this warm weather in our prayers."

"Been thinkin' the very same thing, Mister Matthew, grinned Albert his lined face crinkling up in additional furrows, "I'm prayin' this very night for frost."

"You do that, Albert. Now, don't you forget," jested Matthew again as he went walking on down the hallway with his arm still tucked around Amy's waist.

As they were settling down in their favorite chairs in the privacy of their sitting room, Matthew pulled out his pocket watch and giving it a quick glance said, as he replaced it, "I suppose the boys are still in class."

Louise Gore Sayre-David

Amy smiled, "Yes, dear, they are but don't fret, I fear we'll get the signal of their freedom loud enough in a short while form now."

"I'll go along with that," he told her and smiled back but his thoughts were far heavier than what his face was indicating, thinking to himself, "the boys. Here I go again. How many times have I repeated that same phrase in years past? Phil and Nat it was then. Now, Stuart and Whit. But I must, starting this very minute, make more effort to close my mind to the past and began to see and think of these children's individuality as being their own, identifying them with no other. My sons are gone. Nat lies in his eternal sleep at Green Sea, And Phil—where does Phil lie? What did happen to him? If I only knew. If I—" Suddenly, endeavoring to force his mind upon something else, Matthew reached toward a pile of newspapers, farm journals, and magazines stacked neatly on the end table beside his chair, searching through them. There was one newspaper, however, in the stack of current publications—the newspaper were mainly the Charleston Mercury—which was not a current issue. In fact, it was several weeks old and had been lying there all that time—carefully and neatly folded—bearing fact that its readers had felt a special affinity relative to it, understandably so because—bordered in black it paid numerous mourning tributes to the Confederate General Robert E. Lee who had passed away a month or more before that on October twelfth.

The paper's entire face was filled with esteemed editorials along with pictures of Lee, mostly features by the mercury's own editors paying homage to the highly acclaimed general, However, there was one or two which had been run through the curtesy of other publications, one in particular whose trade name was the "Pacesetter," a not too long established press in Lexington, Virginia—the place that General Lee had called home for a number of years due to his having accepted the post as president of Washington College, the position he was holding at his death.

This one feature; nevertheless, which had been taken from the Lexington paper had been editorialized by none other than the paper's own publisher-editor, John Fillmore-Lee and ironically as it was—as Matthew rummaged through the pile of current publications and reading material, this was the newspaper that he finally picked up and the one tribute that he was to come to discuss with Amy, saying to her now as he reached for his reading glasses, "I still find it hard to believe Lee is gone. He was truly a great man."

60

"Yes," agreed Amy, that's evident. But his eyes reveal such deep sadness, don't you think, Matthew?"

"I suppose, dear. No doubt he saw enough grief and destruction during the war years to leave them looking mournful," said Matthew, as his eyes fell to the feature that had been written by John Fillmore-Lee, beginning to read once again the article he had liked best of all.

So did yours my dear husband but one would never guess it from those alert blue depths which still sparkle so keenly in that handsome face of yours, thought Amy, as she regarded him with a deep tenderness while Matthew went on to say, "Listen at this, Amy, I think this write-up has summed Lee's qualities up best of all," going on to read the final passage of the article aloud, "—it is not this editor's aim to herald cries of thorough perfection regarding the deceased because likewise to all men, General Lee's superior qualities were not molded without some degree of defectiveness. However, and I am certain I am not alone in holding this opinion, I view this great leader as having been about as near perfect as the trials and glories of life will allow man to be. The most fundamental difference which existed between this remarkable gentleman and the majority of men—the fineness which made him unique in quality—were his everlasting humility and kindness that ever flowed from his heart in generous supply for all peoples, and his ability to effect an element of fitness in trying situations, namely—his surrender to general Grant at Appomattox Court House, an extremely agonizing circumstance for Lee and one which would have prostrated most men. But, where others would in all probability have appeared vanquished totally reduced in coming face to face with the conqueror—Lee seemed to become stronger and more imposing than ever, appearing to gain in strength and courage, too, over his adversary by easing the awkwardness and later seeming to emerge from the ordeal of the situation with more nobility than ever before. Humble but not meek, proud but not arrogant, majestic but not ostentatious—General Robert E. Lee was all this and more, too. Sleep peaceful, mighty man and warrior."

"I shall think he has, Matthew," agreed Amy, "how sublime. Who is this writer?"

"It says here, a John Fillmore-Lee," replied Matthew.

"Do you suppose he's one of General Lee's relatives?"

"Taking part of his name into account, he could very well be. Still, I'm inclined to think there's no family relationship. It's most likely he was associated with Lee's army during the war, becoming well acquainted with the general's make-up."

"Yes, I'm convinced, too, that's why he's able to define General Lee's character so vividly," said Amy. "His writing reveals the fact he knew the general personally."

"I'd like to meet this writer and I suppose I could through the paper, by letter, anyway. I like the way he deals with his subject, his desire to stick to fact and not paint a picture of illusion; for example, pointing out that Lee was not perfect before he went on to applaud the general's great virtues," said Matthew as he turned to the paper's second page and began to scan over it, continuing to say, "of course, all these features are most praiseworthy and seems to catch the true Lee. Listen, Amy, and tell me what you think of this—"

And Amy listened, most attentively, with them going on to discuss General Lee's life and death at length. Just the same, neither made any further reference to John Fillmore-Lee's feature, nor to the remark Matthew made concerning his desire to know the writer; the contact was never made.

Several weeks preceding this conversation between Amy and Matthew, in a rather modest two story brick building which they had rented and which housed the family upstairs and the Pacesetter's printing press and other business effects associated with it downstairs, John Fillmore-Lee turned to Rachelle who was working beside him at a huge copy desk and made the very same identical suggestion that Matthew had made to Amy—that she listen to the feature he had written—going on to read it aloud to her.

"Send it on to the pressroom as it is, John, it needs nothing more," said Rachelle, as he finished and looked at her questioningly. "I think the townspeople will like it."

"You mean that? You don't think it needs to be polished any at all?"

"No," she replied, "I think you've covered it all well enough—his illness and his death as well as his years here as president of Washington College and his brilliant achievements as leader of the Army of Northern Virginia. In fact, John, your writing sounds as though your memory of this honorable man goes way beyond the years since Gettysburg. It wouldn't surprise me one bit if we were to discover someday that you knew him personally."

John rose form his chair, saying nothing for a moment or two while he bent over the desk and sifted through more press notices which were being readied for the day's publication. Was Rachelle right? Was it possible he could have known General Lee in former years? The words had certainly seemed to flow through his mind easy enough. But no, that was too farfetched to start daydreaming about because when Lee had finally granted that interview to him, he had given no sign of recognizing him. Still, he must remember the general had looked upon hundreds of thousands of faces and even if they had met in some situation during the war, how could he expect to be recognized and especially after all this time? One's features and bearing changed and he was positive he was no exception to this inevitable again that he had not been the only one to be fated as such. If that tall striking officer shown in those pictures of Lee revealed the true likeness of Lee and told him anything at all, and no doubt the figure did because everyone was always saying what a handsome man Lee had been, he could ask for no better proof of what years and trouble could do to one's appearance. Not one single trace of that splendid good-looking soldier the stately general who had tried to lead the South to victory, had he seen in that stooped, white-haired man, who had granted him that interview a few months back.

If by chance Rachelle could be right, he wished to God Lee had remembered him—cost what it may! Sometimes for fleeting seconds, he became so awry, he felt as though he might be sitting on a barrel of gunpowder, watching an ignited fuse eating swiftly toward him. It was that dream that had started it all—the dream that had become so real that it was beginning to be very difficult for him to separate fact from illusion. Not only had it come to him in his sleep several times but had flashed across his mind even in waking hours once or twice, lately— an immense stately mansion with tall white columns gracing the entire structure setting at the end of a long avenue of live oaks. That was all. It made no difference how hard he struggled to link some part of his past life with it, nothing else had come through, so far. He had not told Rachelle. To imagine that he had been associated with something that grand, seemed too ridiculous to tell or think about. Had not Rachelle assured him many times over that he had been one among the thousands of wounded, dead and dying union soldiers who had come into Washington by the trainload from Gettysburg? Well, even so, and as absurd as that dream was, he had never kept any secrets from his wife, and he supposed he should not keep this from her. Though he hoped Rachelle would not attach too much importance to this one tiny glimpse which his mind's eye had refused to let go of.

Holding the gathered material in his hands, John sat back down, facing Rachelle who was still sitting idly searching him, and said, "Perhaps so, darling. But, if I've ever had any contact with General Lee in a former year, it refuses to come through. It's the same as that dream that's been bothering me, lately."

"Dream?" Rachelle quizzed anxiously, "What do you mean, John?"

"Well, it started out as a dream but now I'm not so sure that's all it is. It appears now to be a fleeting memory of something I've seen in the past, actually as preposterous as it is something I was a part of," he told her, going on to explain the scene which had become fixed in his mind, ending by asking her, "Rachelle, do you think it could possibly have some significance with those lost years, or is it some airy hope that I've imagined because I want to?"

She laid a tender hand on his withered arm.

"I'd near give my life, John, to be able to give you a positive answer. I will go so far as to say this though. Regardless of the circumstances in which I found you in, I've come to think you were, indeed, southern born. Darling, let me start with my letter inquiry again. Maybe if we were more open about it, somebody, somewhere, would come to recognize where you truly belong. Please, John," she gently implored.

He looked away, breaking their gaze, as he said, "No, dear, as much as I deplore to refuse you, I feel I have to."

"But why, John?"

He let a rather long moment pass before he finally said, "It's our little girl."

"Beth Anne?" Asked Rachelle, his unexpected remark disturbing her somewhat. "But, what does Beth Anne have to do with it, dear?"

"I don't want her hurt, Rachelle, and never so on my account. I don't think I could abide something like that."

"But, how could my starting an inquiry again harm Beth Anne, dear?" Rochelle pressed. "I don't quite follow you."

John's eyes turned back to Rachelle's face. "No, I can see you don't," he said. believe me, Rachelle, she would be. Eventually somebody would get around to taunting her about it."

"I don't see why," insisted Rachelle. "After living with you these number of years, I'm more positive than ever if we should be lucky enough to uncover any aspect of your past, would bring no shame upon us whatever."

Well, that's not exactly what I'm fearful about," he replied, suddenly laying the papers which he held aside and pressing his hands on either side of his head, "It's this, dear me! Don't you see if we were to spread word about my problem, it could lead to the populace as thinking and looking upon me as being, not all there? People can be very narrow minded, Rochelle, and all the more if there's some mystery involved. I don't want to run the risk of my child hearing whispers or worse still someone telling her, that her old man is so simple-minded he can't even remember who he is. She just started school here this fall and seems to be a very happy, well balanced little girl, so what do you say to our keeping it under our hat, dear, and go no further with it?"

Despite some validity in John's reasoning, Rachelle did not see, nor did she approve of his decision and was on the verge of telling him so as he began to gather up the notices which he had laid aside. She thought those who would look down on John's impairment were not worth one moment of their concern and was more than game to take on any other reaction she, John, or their child may encounter because of it. Deeply disappointed that he had taken the stand he had and in spite of his obvious desire to have the subject done with, she; nevertheless, did go further and inquire, "But, since we are on the subject, what about Beth Anne, John? What are your plans in regard to her concerning this matter? She's bound to ask of family and such when she's older. It's been easy enough for us to explain to others, the few times the occasion has called for it, that you lost your entire family during the war and have no desire to recount it, which luckless for us is the sad truth in a sense. Still, you don't plan to keep it from Beth Anne; also, do you?"

With papers in hand, John rose from his chair again, letting another long moment fall before he finally said, "No, I have no such intention. When I feel the time has approached that Beth Anne's self-possessed enough to absorb this unimaginable circumstance, I'll have a talk with her and explain everything. Who's to say? Maybe by that time I'll have something more to go on, I truly hope so." He pushed his chair aside. "Excuse me, dear, I'd better get this material to Sloan if I expect to see it featured in today's issue," he went on to tell her and hurriedly turned away, rushing on toward the adjoining room where his right-hand man and copy editor of the Pacesetter, Gilford Sloan—oblivious to everything else around him save the task which had him occupied, was busy making up the paper's edition for that day.

The gathering mist in Rochelle's eyes kept her idle for some few minutes longer.

John would have done well had he been less concerned with what the public may have thought or done and gone on and heeded Rachelle's wishes, for the man who sat in the next room and who John was now approaching, had his vague instinct been exposed to one tiny element of fact applying to John's problem, he might well have steered John on in the right direction, setting John back upon that course which he had unconsciously allowed his own instinct to guide him toward the fall before that—the course he so desired to follow till he reached what he unknowingly craved—Green Sea Plantation.

The man who called himself John Fillmore-Lee and Gilford Sloan were so much alike in some their personality traits it was almost as if they had been cast in the same mold. And yet, other traits belonging to these two men were a mile or more off from the other—so unmatched that it was indeed very strange they had related enough to one another in the beginning to even pass the time of day let alone having become working partners. Nevertheless, that was precisely what had ensured in spite of their chance meeting having been crowded with mistrust and suspicion on the part of both. Neither had been long sizing up the situation though and sensing the other's plight and had accepted one another in this principle, letting what may have been one's position or view in the past rest. And promptly, although they were strangers and for the most part remained that way regarding their previous years they were working together in a paralleled harmony—striving toward a common goal—to build the pacesetter's small circulation into a larger thriving business.

Success did seem apparent. Both men, appeared to be equal to the task before them besides that added endowment of an open and liberal nature—free-thinking and free tongued—a trait that hindered them none whatever in the type of work they were engaged in. Though, sometimes this asset did tend to make them appear as if they were somewhat snoopy. At any rate, each was highly emotional and sensitive, gifted with a keen intelligence even if it was subject to falter in despair every so often due to what the cruelty of war had inflicted upon their person—John's outwardly and inwardly—Sloan's all inside save what the torment of his grief made visible in his appearance through his weakness for strong drink. That ever-betraying sign of his overindulgence hardly ever left his face. Seldom were his smallish light-blue eyes free of that pinkish-watery sea they seemed to be swimming in and his florid complexion helped none at all to alleviate his weepy-looking gaze. Though the thin-cheeked face was unusually clean-shaven, and the pencil thin blond mustache neatly trimmed. His lank blond hair which he wore sorta long could have used a little more attention but would have been a problem to deal with in any case. And, if some mornings John saw Sloan's lean wiry frame quivering as though it may have been gripped by chill while his hand sailed an unsteady pencil back and forth writing down that endless flow of words which seemed to be stacked in Sloan's brain in boundless supply, he made all effort to ignore it because Sloan made few mistakes if any. Indeed, Sloan had demonstrated his competence many times over and now owned an interest in the newspaper—John's way of expressing his gratitude to Sloan.

This weakness of Gilford Sloan's was a trait belonging to the other side of his nature which bore no similarity to John's, actually effecting the main difference in their make-up. But, whereas John steadily struggled to remember the past, preferring to keep a clear head at all times, Sloan struggled to forget, constantly nipping the bottle when he was not on the "memory quencher" as Sloan had come to call it—the label he had attached to all alcoholic beverages.

From what little Gilford Sloan had revealed about his personal life, John doubted that he relished the taste of these spirits he indulged in as much as he did the fuddlement they affected. And now, as John neared the desk that Sloan was slumped over and saw his partner's obvious hang-over, John was reminded of the day they had met and recalled to his mind a remark Sloan had made then about wanting to forget. Still, by no means had the move to Lexington, Virginia thirteen months before—been an easy venture for John Fillmore-Lee either, but it had been a move he desired to make. The transfer would have demanded a full measure out of the strongest of arms not to mention the hardship it posed on a man who had only one arm that was whole in strength—an infirmity that had proven to be more of a problem than John had foreseen or counted on beforehand in the matter of setting up his residence and business in another location. By the time John had reached the final unloading and placing of the last of his household and newspaper effects which he prearranged to arrive in Lexington at the time of his own arrival, he felt as though every limb in his body had been disjointed—each separated from the other and was wondering which part was aching the worst.

The move had hardly been any easier on Rachelle. Still, she had readily gone along with John when he had suggested it. Even had there been any misgivings on her part—mainly the parting with her parents—It is doubtful she would have let one whisper pass her lips referring to it. John's wish was foremost with Rachelle and had ever been so. Yet, by the same token, even though her parents were sorrowful over the separation, they nor could anyone else deny the fact that John's devotion to Rachelle earned all the loyalty she was willing to give him.

Besides having long desired to have a place to themselves as well as feeling that he and Rachelle were way overdue in trying to make it on their own, John had fallen in love with the little sleeping mountain town some years before that when he and Rachelle and the baby had accompanied the Fillmore's to Lexington to visit the reverend's only sister and close relative who lived a short distance from the city. Though John had felt at the time that he needed to learn more about the newspaper business before giving in to the interest the place had stirred in him, there had been something about the homelike and comfortable mountain valley and its people that had touched off an exhilaration in John. The seemingly province setting, the lazy river with its scraggy, rocky bluffs winding through the picturesque laurel-laced low-lying hills which appeared to form a web of lacework around the easy-paced city, Lexington's historical Washington College and its military institute—all of this seemed to shed a light on something which gave John a new objective, urging him to settle there permanently. He felt as though he might have been following a beacon light that was guiding him toward some part of that intense urge each time he passed the Virginia Military Institute and saw its marching cadets.

John worked hard in trying to meet the bidding of this intuitional summons which had bred a new spirit in him. It had called for a lot of planning and looking ahead on his part. There had been a dwelling to find and rent which would accommodate both his family and his newspaper business. Then had come the task of crating and shipping the heavier and larger things first and getting them set up, such as the printing press. But, one colorful September day as John escorted Rachelle and his little five year old girl down the aisle toward their seats on a southbound train to Richmond where they changed trains for the final lap of their journey, while the voices of the Fillmore's were still ringing beside the coach with promises of visiting soon, he was to feel that he was finally headed in the right direction—gripped by a forefeeling that what he so desperately sought would someday truly materialize through his moving to Lexington.

Even so, the move taxed John's strength severely. And, added to his exasperating trial of trying to summon more power into his lame arm, as he tugged and pulled at a number of items which he should not have attempted to move by himself in the first place, was the knowledge that he had certainly overestimated September's promise of ideal weather. No hotter day had John thought he had ever experienced than the day he was carting the rest of his things from the station depot to the rented building. The full, pitiless September sun bore down as much as any sun of July that John could ever remember. Even the horse that came with the dray he had rented appeared to be endeavoring to persuade itself to an unconscious state so that it might be less aware of early afternoon's sun rays. John observed its drenched body and head, which was hanging as low as was possible for a horse's head to hang while in harness, as it stood motionlessly with its eyes closed.

Nevertheless, when it came to looking flagged, the scales were pretty much balanced between John and the horse he had began to pity. There was hardly a dry thread on him. His shirt was soaking wet, clinging to his back as he stood on the ground and leaned forward into the cart in attempting to get a firmer hold on the cask of printing paper which he had pulled and tugged at the edge of the open tailgate. As John strained with a dogged, unyielding will to move this last item from the cart without calling Rachelle for help, a voice drawled at his elbow "From the labeling on that cask and the name you have painted on your window, I take it you're in the newspaper business. I noticed it from across the street."

Startled, John let his hold on the cask of paper go and stepped back, swiftly running his eyes up and down his obviously unwearied company despite the sweltering day. A sudden flash of irritation gripped John. It nettled him plenty to think that his visitor who had suddenly dropped from out of nowhere and who stood there looking so collected and sound as a bell, with a cigar stuck in the corner of his mouth, could have been watching him labor so obstinately against the odds all alone without coming forth to give him a hand. John's irritation as well as for the sake of gaining more wind—he had no desire to reveal he had just about been done in because of his impairment, and caused him to be rather slow in coming up with his response. Swiftly, he let his hold on the cask of paper go and stepped back.

Finally, after he had pushed his hat back on his head which brought a mass of salt and pepper locks tumbling down on his flushed, beaded brow as he lifted his right arm and wiped his face on his shirtsleeve, John said, "Well, I guess one could say that's my trade. It happens to be my bread and butter, anyway. Though right at the present business is nil. I've got to get organized first."

Been in the business long?" The man asked, as he pulled his cigar from between his lips and let a puff of smoke whirl up through one eye which was cocked straight at John. His other eye, John noted, was free of smoke or anything else within its range since he had it completely closed.

"A few years," said John, somewhat snappish, telling himself that obviously holding back a helping hand which he was almost positive this man had done had not been enough to make him comfortable. Now it appeared he was ready to start probing.

However, John saw that if his visitor had been affected by his sharp reply or sensed his annoyance with him, he did not reveal it, "Should do all right with the college and institute both here in town offering things to report. There's always something going on at both places, even if some of it ain't worth the strain of reporting or reading. Of course, I want you to understand that remark doesn't hold, pertaining to anything General Lee does or anything he's involved in. No finer man or leader ever walked on the face of this earth than General Lee. I guess you know he's president of the college here even though I take it you're a newcomer to the region."

His irritation rapidly softening—the man's remarks had almost raised a smile on John's face, John told his visitor, while stepping into what little shade the building offered from the glare of the sun, "You're right on both accounts. I suppose I do fit that classification, though I hardly feel like a newcomer taking into account the number of trips I've made here in preparing for this move. Regarding the general, yes, I've kept track of his activities. I knew he was here."

Pushing back his own hat and finally opening both eyes as he followed John into the narrow strip of shade, John's visitor went on to volunteer, "I was in General Lee's Army of Northern Virginia. Except for two short furloughs, I gave four years of my life to Virginia. No complaint, mind you, I'd do it all over again. I felt honored to serve under General Lee, and stuck right there with him throughout the whole dame mess, right on up till the last order to fire was bellowed out. In fact, I was right there that day looking at the general when he rode up on Traveler and dismounted and walked straight through Mr. McLean's front door to discuss circumstances with Grant and his staff. I guess you know only Colonel Marshall was with General Lee while Grant was surrounded by a dozen or more of his men. Just another demonstration of Yankee yellowness. But I'll venture to tell you this much," he paused, offering his hand to John, his eyes questioning.

"John. John Fillmore-Lee," informed John, shaking the man's extended hand,

"Lee? Did you say Lee?" quizzed the man, his eyes concentrating deeply as their light blue color took on the look of glittering ice.

"Fillmore-Lee," corrected John. "It's two family names linked together by a dash."

"Oh, I see." Don't suppose you're related to the general?"

"No, I don't think so," said John.

The man's gleaming gaze faded instantly. Even his eyelids seemed to flop in disappointment as he resumed his story. "Well, as I was saying—oh, Gilford Sloan it is here. I almost forgot but Yankees seem to do that to me. Now, as I was saying or starting to say that would've been one bloody day for the history books, had not General Lee come out of that house just as whole as when he walked inside. You can take this as gospel there were many soldiers there that day, including yours truly, who were prepared to die in the last ditch, had the blue bellies harmed one hair on the general's head!"

Though Gilford Sloan's loyalty to his commander impressed John, Sloan's manner of expression had amused John, too. Finding his earlier irritation with his visitor all but gone. John said, "I can believe that. Also, I wouldn't be one bit surprised to learn that Grant and his staff gave plenty of thought to the very thing you're revealing, too. It's most likely they were greatly relieved when the meeting was adjourned, and General Lee was safely back among his own ranks without any incidents occurring."

"Could be, I wouldn't know, But, at any rate, they did have enough brains, that one time. to keep their dirty tricks up their sleeves," said Sloan rather scathingly, staring at John's lame arm and going on to add, "I take it you might have seen some of the fight yourself. Who did you serve under?"

John was thrown for a moment. Even though he had begun to enjoy Gilford Sloan's chatter, finding it fairly amusing, he was finding out something else, too. Gilford Sloan had a most assuming and direct approach. Well, John decided, since Sloan had dared to ask, he would make bold to tell him, "you're right again, Mr. Sloan, Gettysburg for one place, but I would as leave let my experiences lie, if you don't mind. Let's just say I served and let it go at that, shall we?"

Again, to John's surprise, if Gilford Sloan felt rebuffed or thought there had been anything amiss in his reply there was no trace of it on Sloan's behavior. Sloan seemed natural and unaffected as he said, "you bet. I'm with you all the way if that's your preference. There's some things connected with that war that I don't talk about, either. It's too painful. In fact, I wish I could blank out the whole damn mess and never think of it again. Unfortunately for me though I can't do that, even if I do try like hell the greater part of the time!"

It was at the fall of Sloan's last words when John saw the abrupt change of behavior. Gilford Sloan suddenly appeared to separate himself from everything, seeming to have fallen into a deep void as he set his tormented gaze unseeingly in the distance and began to puff rather fiercely away on his cigar.

Thinking it best to drop the subject where Sloan had stopped, going into it no further, John made no comment, letting the silence grow while he mused over the irony of their positions—Sloan wanting to blank everything out while he himself battled continuously to remember.

Granted, Gilford Sloan had been truthful when he had said he wanted to forget the war. Though what he failed to point out was he wanted to forget the last weeks of the Petersburg Campaign and what had followed it and not the entire four years. Those last weeks of war was the part that tormented Sloan, causing him to regret he had served through this period at all. Thus, he had not been quite truthful when he had told John he would do the same all over again relative to following his commander to the end. The truth was, Gilford Sloan had regretted a million times over he had not heeded the inevitable defeat which Lee's army had faced and gone home to his wife Lottie who was near giving birth to their first baby, when Lee had finally abandoned the siege of Petersburg in the face of a mammoth, well-equipped Federal army. He had chosen to remain though—trudging along with an army endeavoring to endure and stand despite the fact it bore not the slightest resemblance to an able and fighting army much less those once proud and polished troops who had made up the eminent army of Northern Virginia—the hope of the South.

Gilford Sloan had grown up on a small farm which lay within a two day's march northwest of Petersburg. At the onset of the Petersburg Campaign he had snatched a few days leave and gone home to visit his wife, Lottie and his parents. Sloan had not seen Lottie for near three years. Even so, their reunion was not only a happy one but fruitful as well. Lottie had conceived for the first time since their marriage. While the Confederate army had fought and waited out long months in the trenches at Petersburg, he had gone home once more; and instead of remaining at home when Lottie had asked him to, pointing out to him that he had given enough of himself to the cause, Sloan had still felt it was his duty to return to Lee's shrinking army—reasoning it was not as if he were leaving Lottie alone since she lived with his parents. But, what he had failed to see at the time and, this was the part that pained him so, even though his reasoning had been sound the fact remained, there had still been an element of frailty in it because he had put the cause first and his wife second.

In any event, he had marched on with Lee's rapidly crumbling forces, and, of course, the Confederates had been defeated and the surrender had gone hard with him—sticking in his throat like a bitter pill. All the same, once he had turned his face toward home—going every step of the way on soar bleeding feet—his spirits had risen once again as his active mind sorted, questioned, and made plans, coming to finally see and put things in the prospective. Gilford Sloan had done all he had been capable of doing for his country. Now, Gilford Sloan was going to do the same for his family. Yes, he was finally going home to Lottie. What did losing to the Yankees, sore feet, an all but empty stomach, or a ragged and wet shivering body amount to, anyway, compared to seeing Lottie slender as a reed once more running down the slope to meet him? And further, knowing by this time the family cradle was at last occupied with a little boy or girl? Nothing, he had told himself over and over again as he had more or less stumbled the miles away. Then, on one early flower-filled May Day, he had at last gained the bottom of the hill and had eagerly and joyously gazed and searched. But there had been no, Lottie—nothing—no sight or sound of any form of family had met his eyes or ears in the pressing ominous stillness except the warble of a lone yellowthroat sitting on the fence post near the house. He had forced his swiftly weakening legs to move on forward though and as he had closed in on the deserted grounds and seen the pronounced mark of some recent evil fortune, he had felt as though that Mini ball that he had escaped for four years had finally caught up with him, ripping his insides apart.

A neighbor man had imported the grim details. It seemed upon hearing of President Lincoln's assassination, a band of Union soldiers had become hysterical—Sloan ever thought that their concern had not been for the slain president at all but merely an excuse to give new life to their hate—and had taken it upon themselves to avenge the president's death by setting forth on an unauthorized raid, brutalizing every single Southerner and destroying his property that happened to fall within their revenging path—in some cases shooting the victim down in cold blood if they protested. This had been the Sloan's misfortune whose house had set in the raider's path. When the elder Sloan had raised a voice of objection at seeing his property destroyed, they had silenced him with a bullet. As his wife ran forth to aid him, she had become a victim. Even though the raiders did spare Lottie, their brutal deed indirectly cost her her life, anyway She had gone into shock and labor combined, immediately. When the neighbor had found her there had been very little he could do. The baby had already died, and Lottie was near death, but had lived long enough to inform him of most of what had taken place in addition to leaving a poignant message with him for her husband.

No need to say this lunatic and monstrous Yankee deed which had occurred after the war in Virginia had already ceased, resulting in the tragic deaths of his family and peculiarly in the case of his wife and baby, had been most too much for Gilford Sloan—a man already physically and emotionally drained by the trials of a harsh and anxious four year existence. He had never lived at his home another day or night. Having rented the small farm out, he had wandered aimlessly from place to place for five long years. Sometimes, he worked at odd jobs for short periods. Other times, he would hold up at some saloon for weeks, shooting craps or playing cards—having become so adept with cards he could have turned professional had he been so inclined, and no doubt could have made a profitable living. But, after so long at any one place, his interest would wave, and he would move on-ever nipping the bottle to ease his thoughts and restless nature. Thus, this was the state of Gilford Sloan's way of life when he had popped up at John's elbow without any warning.

Suddenly, Sloan removed his cigar and picked up the broken conversation, telling John, as he moved his gaze from the distance and planted it on John's front window, "I used to be in the newspaper business!"

"You were?" asked John, struck with surprise again. Gilford Sloan was certainly a difficult man to read. "Here in Lexington?"

"No, a little town down in the valley a few miles. As a matter of fact, before I got involved in that hellish war, I used to hold down two jobs, helping my daddy farm and working at the local newspaper office, too."

"I'm sure you know what it's all about then," said John. "What part of the operation did you mostly handle?"

"Anything that needed to be done. No particular part."

"Everything?" Questioned John, his interest rapidly building. The man could turn out to be a godsend. He was just before putting a notice for help on his window, anyway.

"Yep," Sloan was saying, "Any job that fell my way, from printing and setting type to writing editorials!"

Gilford Sloan possessing such versatile qualities was a little hard for John to absorb. He just stood and stared, waiting to see what else Gilford Sloan was going to come up with. He did not have a long wait. Sloan was staring him back and continuing to say, "Wondering why I'm not down there in the valley now, writing editorials, ain't you?"

Sloan's free approach had thrown John once again. He hesitated to reply, feeling somewhat concerned and embarrassed, too, in realizing that Gilford Sloan had read him so clearly. Finally, he managed a mere, "Well—" hesitating once more.

"It's all right," Sloan told him. "But, I could sorta read what you were thinking. It fell victim to that Yankee Hunter, everything,

75

printing press and all. Then he set fire to the building, in '64. The owner just did not have the means to start again from scratch."

"That's too bad. Though from what I've seen and heard since I've been engaged in this type of business, this publisher can take solace in the fact, for what little that may be, he's not alone in his dilemma. The war played havoc with numerous others, too," said John.

"I hope to tell," agreed Sloan. "You're looking at one of the unfortunates now."

"I'm sorry," John said. "I presume then that you're not with any other publishing firm at present."

"No, I've let others worry about spreading the news. Most of it has been too damn dismal to print, anyway."

"I won't argue that point with you. Still, has not it ever been the same over the centuries? All one has to do is open a history book. The evidence is there in bold print."

"I reckon so," Sloan nodded.

"Mr. Sloan—"

"No, none of that mister stuff," interrupted Sloan with a wave of his hand, "No point in putting a handle on it. Just plain Sloan will suffice. I never did go for Gilford too much."

"Of course," smiled John, "and you may refer to me likewise, John if you like, that's shorter. Anyhow, what I started to mention, and I hope you won't look at it as my taking too much liberty, but if you're interested in getting back into newspaper work, I could certainly use your talents and would be grateful for your help. I was just before advertising for more help on my window, anyway. If I'm to publish a daily paper which I hope to do, it's going to require my hiring more help than I've already hired."

"Well, I don't know," drawled Sloan, setting his gaze in the far distance once more. After a somewhat long pause and obvious busy mind, he went on, "Mind if I ask where you're from?"

"Not a bit, Washington, D.C." John replied, though he was wondering what that had to do with Sloan's decision. He soon found out.

Sloan's eyes shot back to his face, staring him down as he said, "One of them, aye? I might have known!"

"One of them what?" snapped John, stressing the word 'them', wondering now if he had made a mistake in offering to hire Sloan in the first place, considering this laxness in grammar.

"Yankees, that's what!" Sloan vehemently flared back. "I have you know I have no dealings with Yankees!"

A deep flush rose above John's bearded cheeks. "Then, I would advise you to remove yourself and be quick about it from what you obviously view as my contaminated presence and premises! I can see now that I was wrong to offer you employment on such short acquaintances, anyhow, but I'm withdrawing it as of this minute. With your biased views, you would be far more of a hindrance to my business than advantage. Further, before you go, I want you to understand I will not tolerate you or anyone else to stamp me as being anything but an American! The war is over, having ended five years ago Mr. Sloan! Good day!" John told him and pulling his hat down again he turned away from Gilford Sloan and stepped back out into the glaring Sun where the cask of printing paper still waited to be removed from the bed of the dray.

Resetting his own hat and yanking its brim down over a heavy expression of disdain Sloan retorted, "By all means! I take much pleasure in bidding you the same with an added goodbye!" He shrugged his shoulders and staying no longer in the narrow strip of shade, he quickly went shuffling his way on down the dusty sunbaked street.

As his steps began to build the distance; however, between himself and the man who he had so contemptuously rejected, Sloan was surprised to find that the satisfaction which he had ever loved to feel by letting a Yankee know his true sentiments, verbally, was missing. There seemed to be no feeling of triumph whatsoever in him. And, there was something else that shocked him, too. He became aware his conflicting thoughts were making an attempt to recount his whole conversation with John Fillmore-Lee, actually battling on the defensive in an effort to find justification for his heated renouncement of the man.

Suddenly, Sloan found his slowing steps had brought him to a complete stop. He felt confused, compelled to look back as he asked himself which of the two was it that was urging him to know if the Yankee had been successful in moving the cask of paper—his ever curiosity to know the outcome of a situation or concern for the Yankee's impairment? Moreover, there had been something about the man that he had become unable to identify—something he had been unable to put his finger on. And why in the world he felt this way in the matter of any one Yankee, let alone one who had kept pace with every heated remark he had uttered, was way passed Gilford Sloan's depth of reasoning.

At any rate, whatever it was that was prompting him, Sloan gave to its force and made a sudden about-face and when he did, he was to make no further effort to reason out his actions. The same instant he turned his head, he saw the cask of paper go tumbling form the arms of John Fillmore-Lee, bouncing forward in a rolling cloud of dust until it finally settled itself in a street rut a good distance from where the Yankee stood. Despite all he had endured at the hands of Yankee's, the incident was one Gilford Sloan took no pleasure in seeing. Before he even realized what, he was doing or giving any thought to what he was going to say, he went lumbering back to the scene. As he neared the lathered and clearly impassive horse and an obviously dashed John Fillmore-Lee, Sloan tossed his cigar away and said, "Take comfort if you can in learning you're not the first to lose out to those damnable, cumbersome things. I've met the same experience a number of times myself when I was engaged in newspaper work. If you'll allow me, I'd feel privileged to give you a hand with it."

John turned, examining Sloan with a somewhat surprised eye. Having said nothing after a long pause, he then took another long minute to wipe his face again on his shirtsleeve, finally saying—just when Sloan had concluded his offer of help was going to be ignored, "If you think you might escape the possibility of stigmatizing your person, Mr. Sloan. On no condition would I want that!"

Goddamn! The man had spunk, thought Sloan, even more than he had guessed when he had been watching him try to handle that miserable bulk from across the street! Well, Yankee or not, he had to admire him for that.

"I'm willing to chance it," he replied. "Be my guest, then," said John, gesturing toward the cask.

Once the barrel of paper had reached the spot where John had selected for it to set, Sloan stood back and slowly eyed the lower floor of the building, saying, "Looks like you're about ready for business. I like the way you're arranging things. It's convenient and should make for comfortable working."

"I hope so and profitable, too," replied John, "because I don't anticipate making any more business moves if I can possibly help it. It's hard enough on the sound, to say nothing of one who's at a disadvantage. My wife would attest to this. She's the one who's carried the greater part of this moving burden. I've been forced to have to subject her to the ordeal of tugging a lot of those things around but never again."

"Setting up something like this does present a problem," agreed Sloan, as he started to make a move toward the door. He paused; however, finding himself drawn to the place. Suddenly, eyeing an inkwell and a container of pens nearby, he knew he had stumbled onto something he had been searching for even though he had not been aware of his readiness to seek it. And, as astonishing as it seemed he heard himself asking if the job offer was still open, going on to point out to John, in a somewhat sportive manner while a smile began to lighten his somber expression, "you just told me you don't want your wife tugging at these things anymore and since I can see there's a few pieces that still remains to be set up in the right place, I thought—"

John met Sloan's growing grin with one of his own.

"I applaud your cleverness, Mr. Sloan. Now, I could hardly refuse you since you put it that way, could I?"

"Then, you'll reconsider and tell me it's a deal?" Sloan asked, more sober now, his eagerness to hold a pen again shining in his eyes.

"Yes, it's a deal, Mr. Sloan, providing you don't mind my attaching a very important stipulation."

"What's that? And remember, Sloan if you will, without the handle."

"All right. Sloan it is this," John said. "The stipulation is, that you stick to the proprieties of publishing and don't be persuaded too often, if at all, to separate the sheep from the goats! The readers I acquire, I want to hold on to them."

"Oh, that," laughed Sloan. "If you say so. You're the lieutenant."

"Lieutenant?" Quizzed John.

"Just a matter of speech," Sloan told him, giving no more thought to it 'til month's later although he continued to ever address John in this manner. Everything in Sloan's mind had become sidetracked at the time—trapped by the little girl who suddenly came bounding recklessly down the stairway. Sloan's attention became riveted to nothing else, seeing the child's extraordinary beauty as she ran on forward where he and John were standing and John was telling her, as he took her by the hand and rested an adoring gaze upon her, "Pet, you must use a little more caution in coming down those stairs. Besides all the pain and bother you'd endure, you wouldn't want to be hampered for several weeks by a broken arm or leg, would you?"

"No, Papa," the little girl chirped. "I'd miss skipping the rope!" Sloan noted how enchanting her long brown lashes curled upward, exposing her deep-violet eyes to the fullest as she looked up at her father.

"Indeed, you would, darling," John was telling her, "and doing lots of other things, too. Dear, this is Mr. Sloan. He'll be helping papa with the newspaper. Sloan, may I present my daughter, Beth Anne."

Quite ladylike and somewhat prim, Beth Anne bobbed a slight curtsy, murmured Gilford Sloan's name and extended her hand.

Gently—his every action effecting a near reverent air—Gilford Sloan took the small dainty hand in his and returned the child's greeting, all the while being painfully reminded of what might have been. Yet, despite the pain, something else was happening to him, too. He thought from that moment on it was going to be a lot easier for him to leave off drawing distinctions perhaps in time come to look upon all the populace as John Filmore-Lee himself—Americans and nothing more.

Now some thirteen months later, Sloan was scanning his eyes over the notice that John had handed him, saying, "So, you were at the surrender, too?"

"No," replied John, "I didn't quite make it."

"Well, one would think so. From the wording of this article. I'd sworn you'd been right there, observing the whole show."

"No, quite the contrary. Unfortunately, Gettysburg ended it all for me."

"Well, I'm sorry about your misfortune, but you can take my word for it, you sure didn't miss too much."

"I wonder about that," said John. "Enough said on that subject though. Do you think you can run that feature today?"

"If I stop chattering and get busy, I think I can."

"Thanks, Sloan" John said, turning to leave.

"Right on, Lieutenant." Sloan called after him, it finally dawned on Sloan, while his eyes followed John leaving the room, why he had been induced to call John "Lieutenant." There was something about the Yankee—his carriage and his manner mostly that reminded him of that wealthy dashing lieutenant form South Carolina who he had vaguely known—actually having seen him only once or twice before having begun that fatal march to Gettysburg.

In spite of the rush to run the feature on Lee, Sloan sat and pondered over it a few minutes, telling himself that it sure was a damn curious thing that he could remember the name of that vast plantation it was said the lieutenant was heir to and not his name! Yes, it was damn strange that Green Sea Plantation had stuck in his mind all these years! Green Sea. Had the lieutenant made it back to Green Sea? Maybe so, maybe not, but Gilford Sloan hoped so.

Sloan let his head fall back to his work.

Chapter Three

Winter swept in to pay its annual visit, spreading its drab and bleak oversized cloak about, snuffing out autumn's radiant attire, before this dreary visitor could scarcely settle down through and take a breath a live spring was walking through the doorway in an elegant flower-splashed apple-green dress. Shortly after, summer arrived, splattering its hot breath and radiating warmth over everything—oftentimes near spoiling springs graceful habit. Still, for all that, barely had these seasons come and made their mark on the land autumn was making its appearance again, turning all eyes upon its brilliant, flowing colors. And, so it went, one season dropping in after another to pay a call until time had counted many and the year was 1876 and the country was celebrating its centennial.

Yes, despite its having raised its arms once more in defending itself against its mother country for a second time and all the other blows and wounds and tortuous deeds of an additional war its own people had inflicted upon it—almost breaking it in half—the nation had held together and reached its hundredth birthday. However, to say it was radiantly hale and hearty, having healed entirely from all it had suffered, would be contrary to fact—a false claim. But the important part was it was still standing and standing whole; nevertheless. And further, one of its worst wounds—the raw and bleeding South, was mending at last.

Granted, this was to be the year that the South was to finally gain its foothold, and in a manner of speaking, come into its own again. The South fell to its good fortune through the new president. Although he himself was a Republican, undoubtedly President Rutherford B. Hayes viewed the South as having atoned for its "sin" long enough. When the last three Southern states of the former Confederacy, South Carolina, Florida and Louisiana—all of who remained to be under the stinging lash of the Radical Republicans—their sister states having already grasped political power, were to claim victory in this year's elections, the President backed their claiming success at the polls and within months had removed all federal troop and given the Democrats control again. Therefore, Sheriff Walt Hawkins and the likes of him rode in the driver's seat no longer, finding almost overnight they were now at the mercy of those who they had opposed for more than a decade. Of course, waking up to the fact that he was now helpless when it came to the matter of commanding the situation and having so many at his beck and call, the sheriff and a numerous number like him soon chose to drift to other whereabouts and were seen no more—their absence being nothing but a source of comfort to the majority of native Southerners.

Just as most these Northerners had come South after the war to take advantage of the kill such as Walt Hawkins—a good many of these same drifters and political adventurers now headed for the western territories, lured there by the notoriety, and most often finding refuge, of such famous outlaws as the James brothers and the youngers and Butch Cassidy and the Sundance kid all of who headed outlaw bands which were waging a war of prey on private and governmental properties alike that stretched across the entire western plains and as far south as the Rio Grande.

Among the many events which were to occur and draw considerable attention in this centennial year, there were two that were slated to have a lasting impact upon the nation—one was an invention—the other a tragedy. On June 22, 1876 the Seventh Cavalry under the command of General George Custer—the young, fiery yellow-haired general who had tangled with Jeb Stuart at Brandy Station and yellow Tavern some twelve years earlier, broke camp on the Yellowstone to march toward the Little Big Horn in pursuit of the warring Sioux Indians. For Custer though and a contingent of the Seventh's cavalrymen, it was to be their last march and fight. Three days later near the banks of the Little Big Horn, having become covered and hopelessly outnumbered by the Sioux and a number of other warring tribes, the general and every last man in the body of troops were massacred—a slaughter that stirred the nation. The other evnt occurred on March 10th, 1876 when a device invented by Alexander Graham Bell and called a telephone, transmitted the first words ever to be sent through one, a happening that was shortly to open to the country and other countries around the world as well as a whole new way of communicating

Indeed, at all events, even though the nation had had its share of shocks and ills—some of its more recent attacks being a financial panic in 1873 caused when the far-famed banking business of Jay Cooke and Company ceased all trade and the severe depression which followed this money panic in addition to gross political scandals in Congress and the president's cabinet along with the continuation of rising taxes—all having occurred during both Grant's administrations, as a whole the outlook for the country still appeared to be promising with the nation's birthday celebration of 1876 closing on a note of ringing optimism.

To be sure, this was the general feeling in the South as far as government was concerned. Regardless of high taxes, depression, or whatever, when it came to the political situation, the majority of Southerners were feeling every much as having been freed from bondage as the slaves had in meeting Sherman's army over a decade prior. Certainly, this was the case regarding the greater number of South Carolinians now that South Carolina's Radical government, the carpetbaggers, the scalawags, the federal troops, and all other Republican evils had been removed; and none other reigned as governor of their sovereign state than one of its own Civil War Heroes, the Celebrated and popular former cavalryman, General Wade Hampton!

And, what had these years brought to Green Sea? The depression for one thing, but Luke and Eliza had weathered it. It had not been easy. Still, on the other hand, they had not been burdened to desperation by it, either. Of Course, what accounted for their having survived it as well as they had was their ability to manage against the odds, the giving of their unceasing labors, and to each other their steadfast support and trust.

There had been bountiful harvests and there had been skimpy ones but none as meager as the harvest of 1870 when Luke was forced to borrow money, having run out way before Christmastide, against the next year's crop. All in all; however, as these seasons had fallen into the length of six years, no serious setbacks had occurred at Green Sea. The truth was, even with the crop disappointments and their continual struggle in keeping the lands of Green Sea from being snatched up by eager-eyed carpetbaggers, the Heywards felt these last years had been fruitful enough—feeling few ill winds had found their path and there had been rewards and more to counterbalance each and every sacrifice they had made. Though they had had the burdens of a depression and all the other trials of a Radical government, they had coped fairly well and without too much fear at that simply because there had been something else holding precedence over all those difficulties—their joy of seeing their two babies bloom into childhood and all being together as a family unit.

If Eliza adored her children in a limitless degree, which she did. Then, Luke idolized them. Eliza thought his overwhelming idolatry stemmed from the fact he had not been blessed with a brother or sister along with being deprived of a family relationship too early in life. Never did he raise his voice to either child. It was not necessary. Both children eagerly returned their father's devotion with nothing pleasing them more than to do "Papa's" bidding as they forever followed on his heels, if at all possible, wherever he went. "Mother", of course, was quite another matter with them. To be sure, they loved her but was well aware, too, she was not above snatching a hickory switch and stinging their legs and "bottom" if she thought their behavior warranted it.

Naturally, with the flow of time, the run of the familiar had changed—In some cases passed from being altogether. No longer did Eliza see that tall thin all black clad figure—save the white shirt—of Reverend Johnson's sweeping down the walkway with its long frock coat flagging jauntily behind while a stove pipe hat clung on at a haphazardly angle—no doubt whatever about the reverend's fidgety hands having pulled the hat off and slapped it back on his head at least three or four times since he had set out. No longer did the rafters of the Baptist Church near vibrate from the blooming voice. It had been stilled now way over a year.

One hot, humid, Sunday morning in August, or to be more exact it happened as the clock hand was marching on near one o'clock in the afternoon, without one fraction of warning and while the reverend had been still drumming away on the subject of Cain along with reminding his tired congregation for the umpteenth time that it stood a good chance of falling into the pits of Hades if it did not choose to mend its ways and soon at that, the reverend suddenly flailed his arms higher towards the heavens and toppled over the pulpit and on to the floor. Luke and Doctor Seth Roalf had sprung forth immediately to give the prostrated man assistance, being the first to reach his side and while doing so never dreaming the poor man had delivered his last sermon. The congregation, for the most part, was thinking likewise, reasoning that the high-strung minister had merely fainted from overdoing himself that time and, at the same time too, was feeling something near relief—mixed with a little guilt—that the fiery sermon had finally ceased. After all, by this late hour, most stomachs and in some cases other bodily organs as well had begun to send urgent messages. However, when Doctor Seth Roalf—visibly shaken—rose a short few minutes later and announced Reverend Johnson had passed on to his reward and asked the congregation to clear the church before they attempted to remove the body, everybody continued to sit on in stunned disbelief forgetting all about Sunday dinner and the outhouses, too. Finally, when it became apparent no one was thinking about moving, Luke took it upon himself to step forward and announce that he would give the benediction—saying a prayer in behalf of the departed minister before he blessed the others and finally got them filing down the aisle toward the door.

Reverend Johnson was laid to rest in the church cemetery only a few yards from the grave of Doctor Davis late in the afternoon of the next day. The Reverend Marsh Reed had been quickly summoned to preside at the last rites. He had held several revivals at the church besides having relieved the deceased from his duties a number of times. In addition, among the several visiting pastors who had preached at the church, Marsh Reed was the fancier with the majority and to a certain degree had already been selected to fill the late pastor's position. Just the same; however, as Eliza listened to what Marsh Reed had to say in regard to the passing of Reverend Johnson, she listened with misgivings and let some of it sank in with a grain of salt, especially when Marsh Reed said the Lord had destined Reverend Johnson to be taken in the precise place, time, and manner he had departed from them in. Eliza did not believe that. She firmly believed Reverend Johnson himself had had a hand in bringing on his sudden death simply by overstraining his heart and strength in general—reasoning that to shout and scream for a period of two hours or more in the sultry, stifling church where not a breath of a breeze circulated had without a doubt rushed him into his final sleep. She was positive to exert oneself in this manner under such humid conditions would have overstrained even the prime, young and hearty to say nothing of a man who had reached the age of Reverend Johnson. Actually, the minister's behavior had disappointed her. She had given him credit for having more sense, feeling he should have dismissed church early that day due to the heat wave.

Nevertheless, relative to her long-time minister, there was also something else that Eliza believed. She was certain if anyone's way could be paved to Heaven by screaming and shouting passages from the Bible, Reverend Johnson had done just that and had had a most easy journey and entry, besides. At any rate, though he did tend to be somewhat less stormy, it was Marsh Reed's voice singing from the pulpit nowadays rather than Reverend Johnson's.

The Heyward's social life was still kept at a minimum—the circle having grown no wider than it had been at the close of the war. There were visits to Elms with Caroline and Seth and Martha and Bruce at Oak Grove. And, of course, there were the family gatherings on holidays, the annual outing to Sandy Cove Beach in the fall, and a short visit with Tom and Betsy Green the spring before had even been managed. Even though it had stretched Luke and Eliza's budget rather thin and they had been pressed for time, too, because of spring planting, they had not been able to bring themselves to decline Tom and Betsy Green's housewarming invitation. They knew the Greens were counting on them to be there as their quest of honor and would be awfully disappointed if they failed them.

Tom Green had prospered and well at that in these postwar years. Even so, and for all Tom's competence, it was not too inconsequent of one to reason that as like as not North Carolina having won its government back from the Radicals as early as 1870 had had a great deal to do with Tom's prosperity. In any event, since he could afford to build one, Tom had decided that Betsy deserved a new house and though he had not built one that matched the low country mansions in grandeur, his house nevertheless was one to be proud of and certainly was worthy of the merry housewarming he threw to celebrate.

Tom had timed his celebration to fall in apple blossom time, pointing out that he wanted Luke and Eliza to see the orchards while they were in bloom. Now, Luke and Eliza knew what a blooming apple tree looked like. As far as that went, there was a small apple orchard at Green Sea. All the same, once they arrived at the Greens, they were to see what Tom had tried to convey to them. To see acres upon acres of swelling blooms clustered together in such divine profusion had been a sight to behold. As Eliza had stood atop a hillside and looked out over the blooming fields with a backdrop of the Blue Ridge Mountain range curtaining the far horizon she became caught up in a beauty of holiness, seeing the setting as holding an entity of godliness and feeling as though she was truly looking upon Eden and was certain she had never been any more closer to the hand of her Maker than she had been at that moment.

Even though she attended church on a regular basis, this aspect had little to do with these spontaneous moments of spiritualism which would flow through Eliza at any given time. The keeper of her own empathy and spiritual beliefs regarding her Maker, she required no prompting form Marsh Reed or anyone else in moving her to seek him. She reached out in her own way and on that spring day in Tom Green's apple orchards, she had done just that. While Luke, Tom and Betsy Green had chattered gayly around her, Eliza had silently humbled herself in prayer, thanking her Lord for granting her the joy of knowing and seeing this world which he had created with so much graceful beauty.

Seldom did Eliza's pathway cross with that of Bill Clarendon's anymore. Bill and his sister, Charlotte had come to circle among an entirely new group of people—mostly Bill's business associates in addition, of course, to the Coopers and Camden's the fact was, in spite of South Carolina's dire political situation in recent years, Bill Clarendon had become an enormously wealthy man—achieved mainly through the great quantity of lumber his sawmills produced. He had long back acquired another sawmill. In addition, there was the huge income from the vast Clarendon acreage. It seemed his success in business; however, had not held true as far as marriage went. Though he was widely known and popular among both sexes, Bill remained to stay single—so did Charlotte. Luke saw Bill fairly often, but this was through Luke's slow but positive effort in building the mansion he had promised Eliza. The lumber was still being produced at Bill's sawmills from timber cut at Green Sea.

In these years following the death of Frank Drakston, the visits that Eliza had made to Drakston Hall could have been counted on her hands with fingers to spare. Of course, even before frank's death, her visits to the grand plantation had dwindled till it was quite a rare happening for her to call there at all. Even so, now that Matthew Carson had become head of Drakston Hall and Frank was not around anymore, one would have thought that Eliza had come to view her visiting at the plantation in a totally different manner. This was not the case though. Although their relationship still continued to be closer than the average father and daughter relationship, most often if Matthew Carson saw his daughter, he journeyed to Green Sea to see her. Not once, since that day Eliza had taken her tearful leave of Frank's deathbed, had she gone back to Drakston Hall on a visit merely for the sake of visiting socially and nothing more. The only time she visited at the plantation was when she went there for a family get-together. It had now become a practice to rotate these family gatherings between three plantations, Drakston Hall, Green Sea, and Oak Grove—a custom that had begun after Matthew and Amy had settled permanently at Drakston Hall.

Just the same, for all Eliza's reluctance to call at Drakston Hall, neither had Elizabeth Drakston been overly anxious to call at Green Sea. Likewise, to Eliza regarding Drakston Hall, Elizabeth only went to Green Sea when a family gathering called for her presence there. As a matter of fact, if Elizabeth and Eliza's relationship had been sorta cool from the beginning having been doomed because of Frank's infatuation for Eliza, Frank's death had certainly done nothing in the way of altering the situation; that is, in the matter of warmth. Actually, their relationship had grown colder—a rather peculiar consequence considering that Frank was no longer a part of the scene and quite an ironical circumstance, too, taking into account not one word of reproof had they ever passed with one another. Nor had anyone else ever heard either utter one word of criticism about the other. None the less, the coldness was there, and the irony again was the fact that neither party could in all honesty put their finger on any one thing that the other had done or to who—If that had been the case—to have caused this state of cold politeness between them. Still, how was Eliza to know or understand the extent of Elizabeth's pain and mortification when she had seen her husband's open desire for his first cousin? By the same token, how was Elizabeth to know the trials that Eliza had been put to, which she normally would never have suffered, had it not been for Frank Drakston's baseness and self-interest besides the mental pain that she was still forced to fight with at times?

At any rate, both continued on with their cool politeness towards one another—very near an indifference, doing what each saw as one's duty, attending the family gatherings and going about one's own business and keeping one's mouth shut in regard to any ill remarks concerning the other. There was no question of doing otherwise. It simply was not their way.

Matthew Carson, aware of this distance between his daughter and step-daughter-in-law, made no effort to interfere, reasoning that time itself would no doubt mend the situation. He made allowances on the part of both, reasoning again that it surely could not have been no picnic for Elizabeth when she had had to endure the humiliation of Frank's open affection for another woman—namely Eliza, and regarding his beloved daughter he could think of a dozen reasons why she would shrink away from Drakston Hall and also be somewhat skitter around Elizabeth.

Actually, even though he did not know the worst of it, Matthew mourned the burdens Frank had put on his daughter.

Assuredly, Amy Carson also was well aware of this off-key harmony between Elizabeth and Eliza. But, for the sake of harmony itself, she pretended she wasn't. Behaving as though everything around her was in fine fettle when actually it was otherwise, was not too difficult a task for Amy Carson to carry off. She was not too easily prompted, anyway, to stir unpleasant things or stick her nose in a matter which she felt did not concern her. She accepted it as a matter of fact and went about her own business in her usual composed way— letting her wifely duties come first with her and helping Matthew raise Whit. And, in this one situation, Matthew Carson could not have been more thankful for Amy's seemingly lacking interest. Above all, he never wanted Amy to learn that Frank's tragic death and the burning of the Mansion at Green Sea and all those other disturbances at Green Sea had stemmed from Frank's desire to break up Eliza's marriage to Luke.

When Luke noticed how uneager Eliza seemed to call at Drakston Hall, including the year Elizabeth had taken her little son and gone to England to visit her parents, like Matthew, he sensed why and was to make no further suggestion that they visit there. In truth, since that night at Sandy Cove Beach, these years were the happier times for him and Eliza, anyhow. He very seldom let the late Frank Drakston and all those evil deeds which Frank had brought about cross his mind. That day standing at Frank Drakston's graveside—supporting Frank's widow on his arm—Luke had promised himself that he was going to make every effort to lay it all aside and forget it. As Frank was being laid to rest, Luke was silently praying to be granted the will power to bury all of it with Frank and also praying that he and Eliza may once again be as they had been before Frank had violated their relationship with his wayward conduct. And, it seemed his prayers had been answered. He and Eliza never mentioned the subject. On Luke's part it was as though it had never happened and he had come to believe that on the whole Eliza felt the same; that is, aside from this apparent phobia of hers associated with Drakston Hall. For all Luke's trust; however, that all was well with Eliza regarding Frank Drakston's deeds, to his dismay he was soon to begin gathering his doubts that she had buried anything.

Eliza did fear Drakston Hall. And, more than Luke, her father or anyone else could imagine, it pained her intensely that she had come to fear it. The many happy visits that she had made there in former years were not too obscured in her memory for her not to mourn them. Especially the beautiful gardens which had posed nothing for her but a cheering of heart. But, there was no joy now in walking the flower-laced flagstone paths. No joy in sitting upon the stone benches. No joy in sitting or walking anywhere as for that matter at the elegant plantation. The knowledge of Frank lying under a grassy mound not too far in the distance was too penetrating—a haunting threat that seemed to hang over her constantly when she was there. No, for all the ill will that had existed between them and all the hot retorts they had exchanged with one another, Eliza did not feel that it was Frank's ghost. The intimacy of their last few moments together had been too open and too tender to fret about that. On the other hand, it did seem to be something near a menacing phantom; nevertheless, a feeling which had induced her to believe she was far better off to stay away from the plantation as much as was possible.

With the exception of experiencing this jumpy feeling at Drakston Hall; and some despairing moments from time to time over the senselessness of Frank's tragic death, Eliza wanted to believe and had near convinced herself that she had laid all that trouble aside, too. The nightmares had stopped long back. Those dark engulfing storm clouds which had depressed her so had ceased sweeping towards her. At last, Eliza felt as though she had emerged from the darkness and gained the peace of light and asked for nothing more than to keep this contentment which she had found with Luke and her children. Thus, she was almost as disturbed as Luke was when she realized how heatedly and unjustly, she had reacted in the matter of an innocent accident which was to take place in this fall of 1876.

Jane Anne Heyward some eight years of age now, let one shrill scream—a frightening sound pass he lips as she swiftly went tumbling over and over down the tall sand dune. No question but what she would have come forth with one or two more at the very least had not the impact of the blow which had sent her sailing head over heels on her way, coupled with the fall itself, knocked the breath out of her. Though she was healthy, Jane Anne was not a robust child. She was still very thin and gangling as she had been at birth. But, in spite of her bony frame she bore an unusual prettiness with her deep-grey eyes and coal-black hair. Taking her thinness into consideration it would have not taken a severe blow to have rendered her breath short anyhow, let alone having a big strapping teenager like Luke Green who was more than double her size, sailing into her. Or at least, Jane Anne thought it had been Luke Green. As most accidents go, it had all happened so quickly she was not completely sure which of the two, Luke Green or Stuart Drakston, had sailed into her, hurling her down the steep sand hill. All she had been aware of at the moment as she and the rest had finally gained the summit of the hill, was standing with the others— Laura, Maggie, Whit, Carr, and Seth Roalf Junior—and watching the sudden tussle and chase which had begun between Luke Green and Stuart. Then, slap-bang, on the spot, someone had plowed into her and she was whirling in somersaults down the tall sand dune.

Gasping to catch her breath, if Jane Anne had had every reason to scream in having been hurled into her unexpected flight, now she had a far more cause to make an outcry. In addition to having had the unfortune of landing smack into a dense clump of sandbur weeds, finding herself virtually a prisoner of countless stinging needles pricking her face and hands and even her body through her clothing, there was the sudden presence of an intense throbbing pain in the wrist of her right hand, also. She did not cry out though. Instead she clamped her lips tightly together and let no other sign of her pain and misery come through save the brimming tears which had already plastered her lower long black eyelashes to her delicate cheeks. She made an attempt to get to her feet but found at once that any movement she made to free herself was going to do nothing except make the sandbur needles sting worse. Thus, perceiving that it was going to take someone else's assistance to aid with her escape, Jane Anne gave up and eased back down into her thorny prison, waiting for help to come.

Even though the pain in her wrist was growing worse and the sandbur weeds with their piercing thorns seeming to close farther in upon her—causing a wave of fear on the top of everything else as she became near hidden in their midst, Jane Anne was still determined she would not give way to the sobs contracting in her throat and cry out. For her, it was worrisome enough to be tagged the "baby" of the group—a label she loathed—besides taking any chances on what her playmates may think of her if she started wailing. They just might label her as being a "cry baby" to boot, she thought, and above everything she did not want that and especially on the part of Stuart Drakston!

Yes, regarding Stuart, the risk was just too great to take, She thought if Stuart Drakston were ever to give any indication that he was thinking of her as a "cry baby" that would be the worst day of her life and one of the worst things that could possibly happen. That would even be far worse than all the agony she was enduring now, and her wrist and the sandbur needles were certainly hurting her plenty enough. The fact was, she had had no wish to be called a baby of any sort for some time now, or be reminded of her young years, as far as that went. Not since that day in Sunday school when she had looked over her shoulder to see who had given her hair braids a tug and Stuart Drakston's inviting smile had met her gaze. Did Stuart suspect how much she liked him? She hoped so, but then taking into account the fact she had never told him or anybody else, not even her best friend, Laura, how she felt he probably did not. That was silly thinking. How could Stuart know when it was her best kept secret?

Lying there waiting and enduring while two big tears plunged off her cheeks, Jane Anne continued to muse and wonder, asking herself why in the world was it that everybody insisted on calling her the "baby", anyway. Why, she was already as tall as Carr and only Twelve months younger. What were a mere twelve months? Not much in her eye. But nobody else seemed to think so. It was the same with Laura. She was just as tall as Laura, plus the fact that Laura was the baby of her family, too, but no one ever mentioned anything about Laura being a baby whereas she herself was called a baby rather often—anyway far too much to suit her. She sure hoped her "baby label" had not drawn Stuart's attention to their age difference too often. Oh, if she were only as old as Stuart. Well, she wasn't! But, if she kept on growing and Stuart did not grow too fast it just might be that she would catch up with him in height, too, as she had Carr and Laura. No use in worrying about the age difference. Nothing could be done about that. Suddenly, voices were ringing in on Jane Anne's thoughts.

"I didn't push her," Luke Green was Yelling, "I didn't see her!"

Then, calm but forceful, to Jane Anne's delight, Stuart Drakston was replying, "Well, where were your eyes? She was standing right in front of you. You surely should've seen her, but no, you went plowing headlong right into her, pushed her clear down that steep sand hill, that is what you did!"

"So, help me, Stuart Drakston, if you say that once more, I'm going to sock you one!"

"If that's what you want," Stuart said, "Come on, because I still say you pushed her down!"

At this point, in spite of the stinging needles hindering her every move, Jane Anne could not resist rising to a sitting position any longer, cautiously parting the thorny weeds a bit with her left hand and peering out through her tear-drenched, blurred vision. Thorns or no thorns, it was not every day that a girl was granted the thrilling privilege of watching two vigorous, handsome boys—one her secret idol and the other a good friend, about to lock horns over her. Peering at them, she thought if the day were ever to come, though she doubted it would, that Stuart was no longer her secret idol that in all likelihood Luke Green would be the boy she would select to take Stuart's place. Though she sure hoped Luke would have stop giggling so much by the time. Luke seemed to think everything was funny, from tying his shoelaces to hearing jailor bark.

"It's what I want all right, Stuart Drakston!" Luke was yelling again, "And I think I could punch you to the sand with the first sock, too, but on second thought I'd better not. In the first place my parents disapprove of fighting, not to mention the fact they would be awfully disappointed with me if I were to have a fight with anyone while we're visiting here as guests of Mr. and Mrs. Heyward. If I did do what you're accusing me of, it surely wasn't intentional as you seem to want to imply, something I can't understand to begin with. I'm sorry Janie got hit in our scuffle, but I still say I didn't see her. It was an accident."

"Oh, me," Jane Anne groaned, briefly put out with Luke Green which was not uncommon for her because of Luke's way of addressing her. Who Luke picked up the "Janie" from she would never know, she was thinking. Everybody she knew called her Jane Anne, her full name. But Luke Green never did. To her vexation, it was always "Janie" with him. Further, somewhat crestfallen because it appeared now that Stuart and Luke Green's clash was not going to get beyond the stage of passing a few shouts and yells, she thought it was about time they stopped their bickering and gave some thought as to where she might be since she sure was not standing before them then.

Promptly however, Jane Anne was noting that before Stuart could seem to make up his mind as to how he wanted to comment upon Luke Green's remarks or do anything as for that matter, the other children were gathering around and Whit was looking about and asking in his usual unexcitable and calm nature, "Where is Jane Anne? I don't even see her."

Jane Anne liked Whit and Seth Roalf Junior, also. In fact, Jane Anne could not think of one boy she did not like, and it seemed the opposite sex was not lost to this attraction she held for them. In addition to being very protective of her, there was not a single boy in the group who did not look upon her with a fond eye.

Instantly, at Whit's having raised the all-important question, Jane Anne saw Stuart and Luke both stop their glaring at one another and anxiously look about them. Silly boys, she thought, Whit had used his head more than either of them. Now put out with both her favorites, Stuart and Luke, she suddenly called out from the patch of sandburs, "Here I am, Whit, will you please come and help me!"

However, no sooner than she had signaled form where she was all but hidden and the children had spotted her and came rushing forward, Jane Anne saw the grownups hastening towards her also from the campground where the preparation of starting supper had just gotten under way. Bruce Randolph and Tom Green were out in the woods gathering firewood but Luke Heyward having heard his daughter scream was in the lead, with the women following close behind. Immediately, Jane Anne's heart lifted and even the needles and the pain in her wrist were seeming to sting less severe, for regardless of how much she liked each of the boys gathering around her—Stuart Drakston included—she was certain she would never love any of them as much as she did the man falling upon his knees in the sand before her—her beloved "Papa."

"Kitten! What in the world happened, dear?" Luke was exclaiming as he took in the tear drenched eyes and bloodstained scratches on the face of his little girl, going on to tell her, while he was hastily reaching for his heavy gauntlets which were stuck in his hip pocket and jerking them on, "No, be quiet, darling, and don't move around, the thorns will scratch much worse if you do. Let papa get his gloves on and he'll have you unfastened in no time."

Now with the women rushing up to join the group, Eliza was crying, as she squatted down beside Luke, "Good heavens, Jane Anne! What have you gotten yourself into? Luke, is she all right? Why, even

95

your braids, dear, are full of sandbur thorns! Where on earth is your bonnet, anyway? Did you lose it or take it off as you usually do?"

"Not—this time, Mother," Jane Anne managed to croak through a tight throat, "The wind blew it off."

"Don't get upset, dear," Luke said. "I think she's all right, except for a few scratches and possibly a few bruises. I'll have her freed from this mess in a moment."

"I'm sorry, Mr. and Mrs. Heyward," Stuart Drakston was suddenly volunteering, having decided to stall no longer, "Jane Anne came by this accident on account of Luke and me. We were chasing one another and before we hardly knew what had taken place, she had already tumbled down the sand hill. We didn't notice that she was standing direct in our path. We should've been more careful. Is there anything we can help you with, sir?"

It had taken those few fleeting seconds to make Stuart Drakston a big man in the eye of Luke Green. Not one trace of his earlier anger with Stuart could Luke Green feel. Admiration had washed it all away and, with his feelings written plainly on his face as he met Stuart's gaze, he joined in, "Yes, Mr. and Mrs. Heyward, what Stuart says is true and I'm sorry, too. Perhaps I could hold those branches aside for you, sir, and give you more room. I'd be glad to."

"It's all right, boys, accidents will happen," said Luke, "and thanks for offering to help, but I think it may be better that you don't unless you have gloves on. Sandbur needles can be rather painful if they become embedded in one's flesh. I'll have her out in another few seconds. Though I can tell you this wool dress she's wearing isn't helping my effort any. It couldn't have made a more suitable pin cushion for these sharp thorns."

As usual, taking her father's word as being no less than law, Jane Anne had done as suggested. She had not made one move or let one whimper pass her lips outside of making the effort to answer her mother's questions about her bonnet. Her fortitude to bear with her paining hand, however, had finally runout. Though she was still trying to hold back the tears from her playmates, one or two rolled through the bloodstained scratches nonetheless as she held back no longer and brought a rapidly swelling, discolored hand up from the far side of her, cracking again, "Papa—my hand hurts."

Showing surprise, both parent's eyes flew to the injured hand.

"Good heavens, Luke!" Eliza cried, "Look at this child's hand!"

The Turbulence and the Struggle

Having finally gotten Jane Anne's long braids and clothing freed form the prickly clinging sandbur weeds, Luke picked her up and sat her upon the soft, comfortable sand, saying, as he gently took the small delicate-boned hand in his, "Let papa see darling," tenderly examining it.

Anxiously, Eliza cried again, "Luke, is it broken?"

"No, dear, but she does have a severe sprain in her wrist."

Luke looked at his daughter, lavishing a smile of admiration upon her with no less restraint than what Luke Green had shown in sending Stuart Drakston's way. "Come with, papa, kitten," he said as he rose with her in his arms. "You're one remarkable little girl to bear with your misfortune so splendidly. Once we get to the wagon, we'll see what we can do when Doctor Seth arrives to be with us, we'll let him take a look at your hand and your scratches, too. And, if I know Doctor Seth as well as I think I do, once he's finished treating you, he's going to reach back into that black medical bag of his and present you with a stick of candy. So, you see in spite of your mishap today, you still have something to look forward to."

All of a sudden, with the prospect of a candy treat in the making as well as finding the security of her father's arms very delightful, Jane Anne was not too concerned anymore about being the baby. Nor did she care any longer about what Stuart Drakston or the others may think of her behavior. In fact, she was thinking it was going to be rather nice to be carted around in her father's arms and; finally snuggling her head contentedly against his chest as he turned to take her to the campground, she said, through those long repressed sobs which had been locked in her throat, "Mother—please—find my bonnet."

"I will, dear, and be there shortly to help papa care for you, darling," Eliza promised, as she set her eyes fondly upon Luke's back and marveled as she had done many times before that at this easy nearness that he ever maintained with their two children—other children also and animals, too, as far as that went.

Nevertheless, regardless of those loving thoughts which were swelling Eliza's heart, not one single one stopped her form turning abruptly to Stuart Drakston and flaring, "Stuart Drakston! I would think a boy your age would find his own size to plow in to, not a child much younger than your years and a little girl at that!" totally ignoring Luke Green's involvement in the accident.

Crushed, and while the full rawness of his mortification weighed heavy upon him, Stuart replied, "I'm truly sorry, Mrs. Heyward, I truly am."

"Well," Eliza flared once more, "From this day forward, you'd do well to choose your playmates from your own age group! I don't want anything like this to happen anymore! Once is enough, you understand!"

"Yes, Ma'am," Stuart said, finally dropping his head.

Luke had not covered so much ground that Eliza's taking down of Stuart Drakston did not reach his ears. He stopped, puzzled as to why she was spending all her distress and wrath, too, upon Stuart Drakston alone. In the first place he disapproved of her holding anyone at fault for the accident not to mention holding one particular one responsible. He turned back a few steps and with his disapproval showing plainly on his face he said, "Eliza dear, I realize you're distressed, but don't you think it might be better for all concerned if we refrain from holding anyone responsible. Besides, if she never comes by any worse harm than having a sprained wrist before we get her raised, we'll all be lucky. Come on with me, boys, maybe after we see to Kitten's wrist, you can also help me finish making camp."

Luke said no more and turned back toward camp, with not only all the boys following behind him but Maggie and Laura as well. As they moved along, Stuart Drakston felt Luke Green's arm drop across his shoulder. Even so, when it came to buoying Stuarts spirit, Luke Green's sympathetic gesture helped little. For Stuart, despite any sympathy he may have received or anything else, the holiday outing had suddenly been wiped clean of all fun.

The incident was far from closed, however. Martha saw to that even if Betsy Green was part of her audience. She waited until the children were out of earshot. Then, with her face flaming in fury she turned on Eliza and blazed, "And, I would think, Eliza, you'd have been more stable and mature than to have picked Stuart out of the whole group to have spent your frustration on, accusing him alone for the accident when you know good and well others were involved besides him! I'm surprised at you to say the least!"

"Stay out of it, Martha, it's not your affair," retorted Eliza.

"Pooh!" Martha blazed back, "In your hat that may be but not mine! I'm making it my affair. Stuart is my nephew and, if I do say so, he bears a remarkable personality for a young teenager, one that certainly does not deserve the kind of lashing that you just spilled form your mouth! Elizabeth has done very well by him!"

"I won't dispute that, Martha, but it was my daughter who was injured, not yours."

"Oh, you're impossible today," Martha said, "You're refusing to even acknowledge anyone else has a point, much less make any effort to see it."

Well aware that her son had been involved and that was what Martha was trying to get across to Eliza—though in all truth she thought Martha might have been tamer about it—Betsy Green had become slightly uncomfortable by this time. She didn't know what to do. She felt she should say something. Still, she knew anything she might say would no doubt make it appear that she was siding with one against the other. In a sense, she did side with Martha. On the other hand, she could see how the accident would upset Eliza. She need not have worried though, for at this point Caroline was to save her from saying anything by suddenly laughing, "Mrs. Green, when you've spent as much time around these two as I have, something like this won't be any surprise at all to you. You see this sort of thing has been going on from time to time between Eliza and Martha ever since I can remember. In the end it never means a thing."

"Caroline's right, Betsy," Eliza agreed, "Martha and I do have our disagreements, and I think it's time we ended this one. I have to look for Jane Anne's bonnet anyway and also hurry back to help Luke care of her. I don't have time to carry this argument any further."

"Well, neither do I!" Martha flared back. "I'm going to start supper! I'm sorry Jane Anne was hurt, but I still say, Eliza, you were wrong and I'm not sorry I called your attention to it!" And, with that said Martha flounced on off through the spilling sand towards the wagons while Eliza, with the help of Betsy and Carolina, began to look for Jane Anne's bonnet.

By dusk as everybody were gathering their plates and eating utensils in making ready to partake of the savory smelling fried fish, stewed fish, roasted oysters and clams, steamed rice, baked sweet potatoes and fried cornbread, besides an array of other tempting dishes which had been prepared and brought from home, dark storm clouds were swiftly sweeping within close range, covering the hues of sunset from view altogether. And, one could also see streaks of lightning flashing on the ocean's far rim. Now, although it was not expressed aloud the thought was coming to a number in the group that it looked as though the elements were not going to let the day pass without spending some degree of fury, also. For the most part though things had settled down and camp had become pleasant enough. Doctor Seth had finally arrived and after seeing to his waiting patient's hand was seated quite contentedly beside Caroline, eating somewhat greedily from his overflowing plate which he had perched on his knees. Caroline, an ever sparse and dainty eater, merely smiled and took Seth's gluttony for this one time in stride. Taking into account that Seth had been called out to one of his ailing patients' way before daylight and in all probability had not eaten all day because he had lost the gravely ill man after all, she reasoned Seth's behavior was quite in order.

Actually, Caroline was not showering the doctor with too much of her attention, anyhow. Something else had caught her interest. And, while she gazed and mused over it, she wondered if anybody else among the grownups were observing that Seth Junior and Maggie Randolph had taken their plates and gathered off to themselves some distance from everybody else and were looking at one another with a glow of starry-eyed wonder.

Though her marriage to Doctor Seth Roalf had produced no children; in a sense, Caroline had not been overly aware of the fact because young Seth had always been there to fill this void in her life. Caroline had been ready and willing to give Seth's son the affection and attention he craved and, through this need of a motherless little boy, Caroline in turn had satisfied her maternal instinct that otherwise would have gone unnourished. Young Seth adored his stepmother and Caroline's feelings for her stepson were plain to be seen as she sat there and sent her smiling approval upon the young couple. Even though her acceptance of the fact that Seth Junior and Maggie both were on the threshold of leaving their youth forever and from all appearances ready to venture into an adult world together, this did not stop Caroline from wondering what Martha's view over the seemingly match would be. Caroline knew that Martha and the entire Randolph family, as a matter of fact, were banking on Maggie to keep a certain family tradition alive enrolling in the University of Virginia when her studies were terminated at Drakston Hall, which, of course, would be the current semester.

A Randolph attending any college other than the college that was founded by Thomas Jefferson was simply unthinkable. The

Randolph's had been among the first to contribute to the educational institution and the Randolph's of the low country could still boost and prove their close association with the college. Bruce's father not only held a sheepskin from the college himself, but his two children, Bruce and Lucy both had degrees as well. Further, it was no secret that the Randolph's still made contributions from time to time to the institution.

Whatever Martha or anyone else may come to think of the young couple's obvious attraction for one another, Caroline could see no cause for alarm just yet. Besides Seth Junior being too young, only sixteen, to think of taking a wife, there was also his own education to consider, she was thinking as she continued to let her attention be drawn towards the glowing teenagers. And, as she gazed and wished the youngsters well—in any case—and as much a she was devoted to Doctor Seth Roalf, Caroline could not any more stop her heart from faltering in poignancy than she could stop breathing. She had found on this night that she would never be truly able to lay aside those evenings of long ago when she, too, had had the glow of starlight in her own eyes—a glow that the battle of Gettysburg had so suddenly snuffed out.

At long last though the active and somewhat disorderly day had drawn to a close. The food had been relished. The tales had been told. The campfire had been banked and the goodnights said, and Caroline Roalf had departed for the Roalf wagon with her husband and her memories, too—memories that she was to find not even Seth Roalf's arms could quell on this one night.

It appeared however that doing battle with restless thoughts was more widespread than in the area of the Roalf wagon alone. It prevailed in others, too, the Heyward wagon in particular. Even when the rain finally came later on in the night, lashing against the wagon's heavy canvas with the intensity of a summer storm, it did not disturb Eliza's sleep at all because she still had not slept one wink. The day's events had been too trying for her to brush aside. She had lain for hours, trying to find a solid excuse she could offer in defense of her behavior toward Stuart Drakston. But, in the end she had come to recognize she had none. As much as she had had cause to have been alarmed and was still worried over Jane Anne's hand, she had come to see that in this one incident Martha had been right and she had been wrong, regretting her behavior so deeply that not only did she feel she had spoiled the holiday for herself but had ruined it for others as well, especially Stuart Drakston.

Even so, and as real and keen as Eliza's regret was, this still did not prevent her from clashing with Martha again, some months later, over the same subject matter and in a place that neither would have guessed or chosen to have an argument—the church yard!

Whether it was the lure of the honeysuckle—scented landscape which was splashed in glossy-white radiance with full-blooming dogwoods that was enticing him outside on this flowery spring day, or the fact he had become plain tired from his having emphasized his sermon more than usual by battering upon the pulpit at the end of every other statement he had uttered, the Reverend Marsh Reed astonished his congregation by suddenly bringing his drifting gaze away from the window and closing his open Bible. With only a few more words of warning falling form his lips, he said the benediction, wrapping up the Sunday worship service way short of its usual mark.

Taking advantage of the reverend's benevolence, if one would dare to chance such a thought, it had not taken the congregation very long to sift out into the balmy weather. Nor was it hurrying as it normally did to clear the church grounds. Even after a good half hour had gone by, the churchyard still echoed with shouts and laughter as the children played and chased one another around the church and in and out among the many groups of grownups who were continuing to chatter away the reverend's reprieve for this one Sunday.

Leaving out the length of time they had already spent chattering, there was nothing unusual about the gathering of one small group or the flow of subject matter passing back and forth between its members except for the frequent turning of Eliza's head in the direction of the Heyward children wherever their voices indicated their presence. In fact, Eliza's attention had become so drawn elsewhere that she might as well have excused herself altogether and joined the children rather than have tried to continue participating in a conversation that she had already lost track of once or twice. And, to make matters worse, Eliza's disinterest and what Martha was pretty sure was causing it, had not escaped Martha's eye. Likewise, Martha had also seen Jane Anne run up to Stuart Drakston and playfully slap at him and Stuart playfully return the slap. Then, when Jane Anne was to repeat her frolicsome act for a second time and Stuart caught hold of her hand and both were laughing as Jane Anne tried to pull away, Martha became outraged at seeing both their faces freeze in bewilderment and their hands drop down beside their sides, too, when Eliza suddenly filled the air with a demanding and rather irritant shriek, "Jane Anne, go on and get in the buggy, Mother and papa will be along in a moment or two."

Promptly, all the others in the small circle were to turn their heads also and were to see Jane Anne, obviously lost as to why she had been told to stop playing, pull her pink bonnet lower over her face and turn away in pronounced timidity, while Stuart Drakston wearing an expression of precise understanding first looked long at Eliza and then back to Jane Anne before he, too, walked away in the other direction.

Just as Luke was taking his eyes from his daughter's back to stare in question at his wife, Martha was fervently asking, "Why did you do that, Eliza?"

"Do what, for heavens sakes?" Eliza said.

"Let's not play games, Eliza, you know what I'm talking about." Retorted Martha.

"Play Games? What on earth do you mean?"

"You know what I mean," flared Martha. "You're just hedging!"

"I'm doing nothing of the sort!" Eliza hotly denied, her face growing red as a beet, while Luke, Bruce, Seth and Caroline Roalf all were stretching their eyes in surprise, thinking that Martha and Eliza were certainly not too particular about where they clashed and wondered just how far they would carry it. Now, Eliza was asking, "If you're referring to what I just told Jane Anne to do, am I not to make any decision regarding my child without first consulting you?"

"Oh, so you're finally acknowledging that you do know what I'm talking about!" Martha tossed back, her brown eyes snapping with the fury of leaping flames. "Though in doing so, you think you were smart enough to put me on the defensive at the same time. Well, it's not going to work, Eliza. You know better than to have put it that way. Of course, you know any standard you may set for your children or any disciplinary move you may take with them, is your affair not mine. However, I would appreciate it if you'd inform me as to why you behave as though the mere presence of Stuart is injurious to Jane Anne when she's in his company?"

"That's unfair, Martha, you're making much ado about nothing. I don't behave that way. But, since you've opened the subject, I don't mind telling you that I can't see them as being suitable playmates for each other. I think Stuart's a little too grown up for that!"

"Don't be silly, Eliza! You know they aren't playmates. That's just your excuse for not wanting him anywhere near her. Besides, will you tell me what possible harm could come from Stuart merely holding her hand as he was doing when you called to her? I can't understand what's come over you. Ever since last fall when we all were at the beach, you've behaved as if you think Stuart were some kind of monster!"

Now it was Eliza's eyes taking on the look of fire. "That's not true, Martha, and you may be certain that I don't take kindly to such an accusation as that!

"Girls!" Luke suddenly exclaimed, feeling it was time to call a halt to their bickering. "I fear if you don't get your tempers under control, Seth may have to minister to you right here on the church grounds."

Joining in, Bruce was agreeing, "I'll go along with you, Luke, on that score. Come on, Martha, it's time we were moving on, anyway. I see sis is already in the coach waiting on us. So long, everybody!"

"Might as well I suppose," Martha was flaring again, "I can see I'm getting nowhere with her!" She took a step to follow Bruce who was turning away but stopped short and turned back to Eliza, going on to say, "After all this, I don't reckon you'll let Jane Anne and Carr go on home with us as the children had planned. I don't mind telling you, Laura will be greatly disappointed if you don't!"

Hearing his wife's remarks, Bruce had also stopped and was looking back. Plans for the Heyward Children to accompany the Randolph's home from church was news to Bruce and Luke both. Of course, their not knowing about every little visit the children were planning to either plantation was not unusual. Still, since present matters between their wives were anything but pleasant, both men were feeling somewhat tense, wondering what Eliza was going to say. Forthwith; however, their tenseness was disappearing, and they were standing once again all agog shaking their heads at one another as Eliza told Martha, "I'm sorry, I forgot about that. Certainly, they may go, and I'll also be expecting you and Bruce to bring them home and everybody stay for supper!"

"Why, of Course!" Martha snapped, "What made you think we wouldn't?"

"It's settled then," Eliza said, ignoring Martha's last remark. Then, she turned to Caroline, adding, "Caroline, won't you and Seth come, too? We'll all miss you both if you aren't there."

Even though Caroline was used to Eliza's and Martha's fights with the results of this one being no surprise to her in the least, that did not make her wonder about Seth and how he felt, so she looked questioningly at him to make the decision.

"Sure, we'll be there" Seth laughed. "Wouldn't miss your fried chicken for anything, Eliza."

"What about my apple pie, Seth?" Eliza asked and smiled.

"Can it be?" Exclaimed Seth, turning to Caroline and going on, "Caroline, what do you say we don't wait till supper and go on to Green Sea now?"

"Oh, come on, Seth, and let's go home," laughed Caroline, breaking up the circle at last for that one Sunday.

On their way home from church, the Heywards had not had as much to say to one another as they normally did when they were alone. Further, in what they had had to say, the subject of Martha's quarrel with Eliza had been avoided altogether. Thus, Luke came in for another surprise when Eliza suddenly said, "Luke, what do you think about our transferring the children to one of Charleston's public schools in the fall?"

What was this? Luke was asking himself, as he turned his head to stare at his wife. Had Martha had more grounds for her heated accusation than he had realized? "Why would you want to do that," he finally asked. "Lucy's an excellent teacher. To my way of thinking they're much better off where they're at, receiving her undivided attention than they would be with some other teacher who's saddled with too many pupils to do that."

"You're right I suppose, but—"

"What is it, dear? Are you that much concerned over our little girl's passing fancy for Stuart Drakston?"

"Then, you have noticed, Luke," Eliza said, relief spreading over her face. "I was wondering if I was seeing something that didn't exist at all."

"No, you aren't, but I think you're making more out of it, dear, than you should. It's mere puppy love and nothing more, a perfectly normal process that all children go through. Take Carr; for instance. Right now, he visions Laura as the only girl for him, ever. Children go through these stages, only sometimes they fall in love with an adult rather than someone near their own age group. Besides, where Stuart's concerned, have you forgotten that he's already gone as far as he can go in his studies at Drakston Hall and won't even be there when school resumes in the fall, or didn't I tell you?"

"Tell me what?"

"No, I guess I didn't. It must've slipped my mind. Well, as a matter of fact, it seems that we won't be seeing much of Stuart, for the next several years except at vacation time. Your father was telling me the other day that Elizabeth's plans are to enroll Stuart in military school in the fall, the one that Frank attended, and then after his military training, she will enroll him at Oxford University in England. Elizabeth and Stuart both will live in England until he completes his schooling there."

"Military school? England?" Repeated Eliza. "No, I didn't know that, Luke. In fact, I haven't given one thought to anything like that. I didn't realize so many years have already gone by."

"Well, they have, dear. In a few more years Whit's studies will have been finished at Drakston Hall, also. Then, I suppose it'll be the Virginia Military Institute for him, too, if your father doesn't change his mind or Whit changes it for him. By then, the class at Drakston Hall will be thinned down to only five students I guess, Laura, Bill and Grace Cooper, and our two children. But, I've talked it over with Brent and Bruce and we'll continue to finance the school ourselves till all the children have completed their studies, which Lucy says she can arrange to fall within the same year by giving our two children a few extra studies along the way that she says they are capable of handling. Then, from what I can gather Lucy has plans to teach in the Charleston school system, after that."

It was obvious Eliza had only half-heard what Luke had said when she again repeated, "England. I wonder why she's going back to England after all these years."

"Who, Elizabeth?" Asked Luke, seeing that the news had stirred Eliza. "Well, I can see lots of reasons why she would. In the first place, England's her former home and her parents are still living there, and in the second place, Oxford's one of the highest-ranking universities in the world and she has the money to give her son the best. Actually, I think it's a wise decision on her part. Elizabeth's become almost a recluse in these later years. The change will do her good."

"But she does plan to come back, I mean when Stuart's schooling is over, doesn't she?"

"Oh, yes, Mr. Carson, says she's most assuring about that. She's

106

assured Aunt Amy that Stuart will come back to his birthright." Luke turned and smiled, "So, you see, dear, for several years anyway, our small daughter's infatuation for Stuart Drakston is going to present no problem for you at all, unless you find yourself trying to console her and can't because of his absence."

"We, love," Eliza said, smiling back at Luke.

And thus, a future happening and one with a staying impact which the Heywards would come to meet with in this Hampton Period or the South Carolina Bourbon era—two labels among the several that the forthcoming years would eventually come to be known as—had already begun to take form.

Chapter Four

Indeed, the years seemed to spin faster than ever in this so labeled, "Hampton Age." Time had now spun to the year 1880 and having turned over the final pages of his textbooks and handed in the last of his exam papers, sixteen year old Whit Carson—only a few days passed—had achieved and concluded an excellent school record under the tutelage of "Miss Lucy."

To be sure, the bond between Whit and his teacher had remained to be close throughout his school years. Though Lucy Randolph had seen to it that the striking, handsome teenager who was standing before her now with his deep-set brown eyes as bright as the spring day and his light-brown hair more rumpled than usual from his fast gallop up the drive on an offspring of Blossom's—a skittish dapple-grey mare by the name of Fancy, had never had reason to suspect that the close bond they shared was anything other than the fact that they just simply related to one another and that was all. Certainly, Lucy had betrayed no sign or word of their direct blood ties, ever.

Officially, school had been terminated for this term. Only a day or two preceding this day, Lucy had held final classes and closed school for spring and summer vacation, having watched Whit walk through the door of her classroom for the last time as one of her students with pensive thoughts and longings. Lucy had tried to steel herself for this inevitable encounter with change. She had reminded herself over and over that as sure as there is a beginning with everything there is always an end and, that this phase in Whit's life was only one of many that he must meet and also leave, if he was to embrace in full what the future held in store for him. Despite all her wishes though that Whit go forward, Lucy had found that she had constructed her resolve with more faulty material than anticipated. She had become aware of this as she had set out for Drakston Hall early that morning, coming to realize that she had left part of the conglomeration that had filled the drawers of her desk at Drakston Hall for no other reason whatever except to have a good excuse for going back so soon after school had been closed. She knew full well that she could have cleared out all the articles in the desk and taken everything home with her at one time if she had desired to. And, once she had arrived at Drakston Hall and gone on to the classroom where she took a seat behind her desk and began to sort out what papers and other things she had left, the fact of her purpose for having left them there and her weakly constructed resolve, too, came home to her more than ever as Whit bounded through the doorway and approached the desk, obviously hiding something behind him as he cheerfully greeted her.

While Whit's amiable, lopsided grin tugged at her heart more deeply than she had ever thought possible, Lucy, endeavoring to sound as unsentimental and natural as ever, looked up and smiled, "Why, Hello, Whit. It appears that you and Fancy, too, are making the most of your school freedom. I saw you giving her full rein through the window and couldn't make my mind up whether it was rider or horse who looked more exhilarated. I finally concluded it seemed about equal."

"Yes, Ma'am, I suppose we were," Agreed Whit, still grinning. "Fancy loves a loose rein as much as I enjoy letting her have one, especially coming up the drive. But I guess I was overdoing it a bit this time."

"Oh, I didn't mean to suggest that," Lucy quickly amended.

"I know that, ma'am," drawled Whit. "But, to tell you the truth, it was reckless of me. I could've been scalped or knocked senseless by one of those low-hanging branches had I not been watching out for them, or worse still gotten my neck broken by being thrown into a tree trunk had she taken a sudden notion to stop."

"Goodness Gracious! Let's save those kinds of possibilities, Whit. Though it is good that you're aware of these perils which fast riding can result in sometimes."

"Yes, ma'am, I'm aware of the danger involved all right, Dad and Mother have seen to that. I don't normally let Fancy run that fast though even if we do like racing up the drive, but I saw your mare and buggy parked at the hitching post and thought maybe you'd come back to gather up some of your things. I wanted to give you this before you left," Whit said, looking somewhat shy now as he brought a colorful, beribboned package out from behind him and held it out to Lucy, going on to tell her, "I didn't get the chance to give it to you the other day with the others around and all."

It surprised Lucy.

Actually, since Whit had kept her desk well-bedecked with the latest blooms from the formal gardens throughout his school years,

Lucy had thought that he was hiding a spring bouquet of flowers that he had quickly snatched for her form the numerous blooming flower beds. His gesture pleased her though and even more so because she had bought him a gift, too, some weeks before in anticipating his finishing school but had been waiting for the right moment to present it to him—a moment when there was no one else around but Whit and herself. Thinking that the occasion warranted it with nobody being wise to her move except perhaps the few who did know the circumstances, this was the first time that Lucy had allowed herself to be persuaded in buying Whit anything since she had granted Matthew and Amy Carson the right of sole custody.

Wanting to make the best of this one privilege which, in a sense, had been denied her and would continue to do so, Lucy's wish had been to give Whit something that would be durable and lasting. She had shopped for quite a long spell before she had finally settled on the gift—a small penknife whose handle was gold-inlaid and which she had had the jeweler to carve Whit's Initials (W.C) upon. The gift was inside her handbag and had been there from the day of its purchase. As she had set out to Drakston Hall that morning, she had hoped that she would have the opportunity to give it to Whit before she returned home.

Now, it looked as though the opportunity had arrived, Lucy was thinking as she smiled at Whit and reached for the pretty package, saying, "Oh, Whit, what a pleasant surprise and so beautifully wrapped!"

Agreeing with her again, Whit said, "Yes, Ma'am, it is. Mother wrapped it for me. But, I'm the one who selected it for you," he hurriedly explained with a chuckle.

Lucy laughed with him, her eyes brightening in happiness as she began to untie the big frilly bow. Then, while Whit anxiously watched, waiting for her reaction, she slipped the box from the paper and lifted its lid and when she did she was to instantly part with all the present and everything it held—including any laugher that her face may have revealed

Gazing down into the box at a delicately made light-grey silken shawl which was edged in pale-yellow tassels—the silken shinning threads looked identical to the one that was still in the locket which she seldom removed from her person, nothing existed for Lucy—no real anything nothing at all except that tender time when Nat Carson had cut a yellow tassel form his uniform and tied it around her finger. Even Whit—the innocent of that short and wonderful interlude, had been forgotten until from somewhere in that world she had left Lucy heard a voice telling her, "I'm sorry, Miss Lucy, I can see I should've left the selecting of the gift with Mother. I'll know better next time. I'd be most happy to exchange the shawl for something else, if you'd like."

The drift of Whit's remarks was not long in reaching Lucy even if she had allowed the past to capture her once more, holding her captive. Hugging the gift to her bosom, she was instantly leaping to her feet, crying, as she leaned forward over the desk, "Oh, no, please don't think that way, Whit. I'm so sorry I've given you that kind of impression. I love the gift. It's—it's—" She dropped her head, unable to continue for the moment, leaving Whit to wait and hope that she would go on and enlighten him further, while he puzzled over her behavior.

Just as a tear suddenly splashed on the desk, causing Whit to become more baffled than ever and uneasy, too, in wondering if he should make some kind of move, Lucy lifted her anguished face and forced herself to go on, telling him, "Please forgive me. You see, when I first saw the shawl it sorta shocked me, because there is something about it that reminds me so much of something else that was given to me a good many years ago by someone who was very dear to me. He— he was killed in the late war and, for a moment there, it seemed as though there had been no years at all, so vivid that time came back to me. Anyway, you couldn't have selected anything that would've pleased me any more than the shawl and I shall treasure it forever as I've always treasured this one other article, though unlike the shawl its size and material is near nothing. Its significance though is what's most precious to me and your beautiful shawl will be likewise with me. Thank you, Whit, ever so much, I'm most grateful that you look upon me so kindly."

Now knowing the reason for her behavior, Whit was feeling much better, quickly replying, "Be assured, ma'am, it's my pleasure and you're most welcome, though I am sorry that the gift brought back the grief of your loss."

As Whit's reply had fallen form his lips he had wondered if by any chance this person of who Miss Lucy had spoken of could be his dad's own younger son, Nat Carson who had rode off to the war with his older brother Phil—the latter whose fate was still unknown, and was to lose his life at yellow Tavern fighting alongside that great cavalry leader, General Jeb Stuart who had also been mortally wounded in the same battle. Over the years, Whit had heard a few rumors to the effect that Miss Lucy had liked the late Captain Carson very much and that had been the main reason she had chosen to become a spinster. Whit had never been overly concerned about the rumor until now though that Miss Lucy had awakened his interest, even if he had ever thought that she certainly was pretty enough to have attracted most any man that she possible could have desired.

Whit had begun to think hard about the matter, becoming almost as lost as Lucy had been moments before that. But, suddenly, he was to find he would have to pick another place for his musing owing to the fact that Miss Lucy had already reached inside her handbag and was bringing forth a neatly wrapped package of her own, saying to him, "Here, Whit, I have a gift for you, too. When I saw you through the window, I was hoping you'd find your way in here because like you, I've been waiting for an opportune time to give it to you." She laughed, "Go ahead and take it and don't look so startled. It's just a little something to show my appreciation for having such a capable student over the years, forgetting about the first year, of course!"

"By all means, Miss Lucy, let's forget that year," Laughed Whit. "If I remember correctly, I don't think I did one solitary thing but sit and stare at you!" Then, as he began to tear into the small package, he went on to tell her, more soberly but quite graciously, "If I were capable, Miss Lucy, that's because I was most fortunate in having you for my teacher."

"Well, maybe to recognize if your interest were to be aroused it was going to require a little urging on my part, that's all. You did the rest, Whit, but thanks for the kind words, anyhow," Lucy told him, seeing that besides Whit's capabilities regarding his studies, somewhere along the way he had also acquired a rather courtly charm, too, leaving her doubting little that there would be few hindrances for him where the future fairer sex would be involved.

Now, seeing what the small package had contained, Whit was exclaiming, "A penknife! And, what a handsome one at that!" Then, looking up at Lucy he went on to say, "How did you know, Miss Lucy?"

"Know what?" She asked, smiling at him.

"That I've always wanted a penknife with my initials engraved on it."

"Well, I didn't, but it makes me happy to know that I did select something you've wished for and didn't already have," said Lucy.

"No, I don't have one. Of course, I'm sure I would've had one or been given a sound reason why not, had I made mention of it to dad or mother, even if they do believe that those of us who make up the younger generation shouldn't be humored to every little wish or whim we may have."

"Yes, considering their generosity not only with you but toward others as well, I certainly can believe that," smiled Lucy, feeling overjoyed that she had been the one who had given Whit the penknife. But, all of a sudden, as she was continuing to watch Whit examine the gift, obviously admiring it, she saw his light expression change to one of gloom. Now, as Whit had puzzled over her behavior moments before that, Lucy likewise was puzzling over his.

As Lucy waited and wondered what was wrong, it seemed to her an eternity was falling. Still, when Whit was to finally clear the matter up, murmuring, "W.C., oh, how I wish those were my real initials," his words cut her so profoundly that she was wishing she were back in the dark as to what was troubling him causing her to yearn to tell him the truth so much that she found herself also wishing that she had foregone the gift idea altogether.

"But they are your initials, Whit," she cried, careful not to use the word, true.

Whit took his eyes from the elegantly engraved letters to stare at Lucy. A long, fearful moment fell before he was to reply, "I'm sorry, ma'am, you misunderstood me. What I meant was I wish I had come by those initials from being a true blood Carson and not one by adoption."

Lucy was crushed. At that moment, never had she yearned for anything as much as she was yearning to shout out the truth to Whit. But, of course, she did not. She was well aware that if she yielded to the urging of her heart that it would not only be a selfish move on her part, but she—in all probability—would be bringing a disruption to Whit's life that would be far more harmful than any anxiety he was feeling then or may feel from time to time over his adoption, to say nothing of destroying her whole purpose for having given him up in the first place, as well as abusing all the faith and trust that Matthew and Amy Carson had credited her with besides.

Thus, after taking a moment to think, weighing all the harm her disclosure could bring as she sat back down in her chair. Lucy went as far as she dared in revealing the truth to Whit, saying, at last, "I'm sorry, I guess I did fail to grasp the meaning of your remark. Still, I think that's because I've always tended to think of you and also see you as being no one else but a true Carson, and I'm certain the majority of your friends and family members think likewise. The truth is, I've yet to hear anyone mention your adoption. So, to me, that is proof itself that you, in all likelihood, is the only one who gives any thought to the matter."

"Do you really mean that, Miss Lucy, or are you just trying to ease my mind about it?" Whit asked, a spark of lightness returning to his face.

"Well, before I answer that, would you mind answering a question for me?" Lucy asked.

"I'll try," said Whit.

"Good enough" replied Lucy. "The question is, through the years of our friendship, can you recall my ever making any attempt to mislead you about anything, here in this classroom or otherwise?"

"That's easy. Certainly not!" Whit exclaimed.

"Well then," Lucy smiled, "you've answered your own question."

Now, looking surprised, Whit chuckled, "I guess I have at that." And, with his light mood much in evidence again, he studied Lucy for a moment and then continued to tell her, "As a matter of fact, Miss Lucy, even though I've known from the first that I was an adopted child, I've never given too much thought to my background before this and, come to think of it, it surely must be as you say because I can't remember having heard anyone else mention it, either. I did question dad about it once, a few years back, and although I could sense he had no wish to talk about it, it seemed there was little he could tell me, anyway. He did explain that he and mother adopted me through a young woman whose jurisdiction I was under at the time he and mother moved to Columbia and who they resided close to at the time. Most of the records were confidential, of course, even to him. But he did reveal to me what information he was able to gain. It seems I came under the jurisdiction of the court because my father had been killed in the war, leaving my mother alone and without help with no one to turn to. It appears when she learned the Carson's had come to love me and wanted to adopt me, knowing that they could give me every advantage in life which she couldn't, she willingly consented to give me up for all time and, in a very short while it seems I was a Carson by name, if not by blood."

Having been dealt about all she thought she was capable of coping with at any one time, Lucy rose from her chair once more and quickly began piling all the clutter which was lying atop her desk together, saying, as she wondered if she was going to have the strength to keep the conversation going at a normal pace till she was through and on her way home, "Well, since it's obvious the Carson's couldn't be more devoted to you, not to mention their vast wealth which will allow them to continue on with any assistance you may desire of them or through their securities throughout your lifetime, I think your mother was not only an unselfish and courageous person but a wise one as well."

"You know something, Miss Lucy, I'm going along with you again."

"You see, then," Lucy said, "adopted or otherwise, you really have no problem to speak of, because, in any case, those letters on that knife are valid and do stand for your legal name. Now, I wonder if I can persuade you to help me carry all this mess to the buggy. With your help, I think one trip will suffice. I have to hurry on home."

"Sure thing, ma'am, just show me what you want me to handle," Whit eagerly replied, quickly shoving Lucy's gift to him inside his trouser pocket.

She showed Whit the articles he could carry and then taking up the rest of the clutter along with the box that held the pretty shawl, she said, "I think this winds it up for this term, let's go." Walking through the doorway, she went on in a voice as normal as ever, "Whit, would you come back and pull all the window shades down and close the door?"

"Sure, Miss Lucy, anything else?"

She turned her head toward him and though her heart was heavy, she forced a smile through her words as she said, "No, I think that's all for this time unless you'd be good enough to make a suggestion as to who you think, among my remaining students would be the most eager to do all these little tasks that you've been doing over the years when school resumes again."

Taxing the gloom of her heart that much more with Nat Carson's identical smile, Whit grinned, "you really don't expect me to be that disloyal to my friends, do you?" Then, never giving her a chance to comment upon his jest or wonder about it, either, as for that matter, he continued "No, seriously, Miss Lucy, I've enjoyed doing these little errands for you, and I'm certain when fall rolls around again, you won't be lacking a helper in either Carr Heyward or Bill Cooper. They'll be more than glad to keep the blackboard washed off, carry books and sweep the floor, or do anything else you may ask of them."

But, unknown to you Whit there is going to be a vast difference, Lucy was thinking, as she merely kept smiling at him and let it rest.

They walked on down a short hallway and through an outside door which faced the long drive and the grove of pecan trees where the hitching post was located. This route isolated the comings and goings of the school from the other part of the huge mansion and was the route that Lucy used regularly except for those occasions when she called at Drakston Hall on a social basis. Descending the stone steps which were graced with stone pillars on either side and a grilled trellis of running rose vines—the rose vines boasting a profusion of bright color and bouquet aroma on this spring day—and taking the flagstone path that wound gracefully through the wide lawn, Lucy was now saying, "Speaking of fall reminds me of something. Have you made any definite decision yet about college?"

"Well, not college," Whit replied, "though I imagine to a great extent it will be similar to college in the beginning. If I'm accepted, I'll be entering the Naval Academy at Annapolis in the near future!"

Hardly expecting this kind of news, Lucy stopped short, though she strove to keep her voice level as she inquired, "Annapolis? The United States Naval Academy? You want to train for a career in the Navy?" Her heart was beating a wild rhythm.

Whit was not blind to her astonishment, however, saying, as he also stopped and smiled at her, "It does sound a little odd coming from someone who's grown up surrounded by cotton, tobacco, and rice fields not to mention all the fields of sweet potatoes and corn, too, doesn't it?"'

"Well, I won't say odd," she replied resuming her steps, "But I am surprised. The thought of your seeking a military career is something that just never entered my mind."

"Nor mine either," confessed Whit, "until I made my last journey to Sandy Cove Beach. It was then that I decided I wanted to explore that vast space of blueness beyond those roaring waves someday as a

116

navy man." Then, he laughed and went on to say, "Who knows, it could be that all those stories MR. Green recounted over and over through the years around the campfire at night about Bluebeard and his hidden treasure lying somewhere up there around the outer banks of North Carolina, had more of an impact on me at the time than I realized. Or perhaps somewhere among those unknown relatives of mine there was a roving seaman I took after!"

This last remark of Whit's brought Lucy's head around once more to look at him, recognizing on the spot something she had never before detected about Whit; that being, as much as he reminded her of Nat Carson, he had also inherited some of Phil Carson's light humor, too. Right at that moment, she felt it would be wiser of her to save any comment she might make regarding relatives and change the subject to another topic. Thus, she said instead, "I take it that Mr. and Mrs. Carson have given their approval."

By this time they had reached the buggy and as Whit shifted the load of books and papers in his arms to the inside of the vehicle, he told Lucy, "I wouldn't say approve exactly but if you mean are they going along with my wishes, the answer is yes, after three or four long discussions, of course. They both would've preferred that I'd gone the usual route, enrolled in college and then after graduation came home and helped with overseeing the plantation. They finally gave in though, and dad said he'd see what he could do about helping me submit my application, see that it falls into the right hands, so to speak."

While Whit, unhesitating, went on to perform the same little courtesy for Lucy that he had done for her many times before that—untying her mare—Lucy, silently, laid the articles she had been carrying on the buggy seat and climbed aboard. Now, as she took the reins from Whit's hands, she said, "Don't fret about your application, I'm certain it'll be approved and also just as certain that you'll go on and have a rewarding career in this vocation you've chosen."

"Thanks, Miss Lucy, but I'd be more optimistic about that if I knew you'd be there to encourage me when the going gets rough."

"See there, Whit Carson," said Lucy, "With that kind of flattery there's not a doubt in my mind that with or without me, you'll make it. Let me know as soon as you hear from your application." And, speaking to the mare, Lucy pulled on the reins and the buggy began to move.

117

She heard Whit's laughter peal after her.

"You bet, Miss Lucy, I'll ride to Oak Grove the moment I hear and thanks again for the knife," he hollered.

"The same here, Whit," Lucy hollered back, hoping that her words had not sounded too choked because she could not even see the drive for the flowing tears which had blinded her vision. She was not concerned about the aspect though and let them flow as they would. She knew her mare was too familiar with the routine of their journeys to Drakston Hall to get off course. What did concern her was the fact that it looked as though she was going to be separated from her son a lot more than she had ever counted on, regardless of the circumstances.

With her head bent low and her shoulders shaking as if she were gripped by chill under the heartbreaking sobs, she cried aloud, over the rumble of the buggy wheels as the mare made a fast turn into the road toward Oak Grove, "Oh, Nat, who on earth did he inherit that sailor notion from!"

Whit Carson's sailor notion was to hold firm; however, and as Lucy Randolph had predicted his application for admission to the Annapolis naval training post ran the processing channels as smoothly as clockwork, hardly giving Lucy or Matthew and Amy Carson any time at all for pondering and dwelling upon irrevocable factors in his decision relative to their hearts, so short the weeks were before his leave-taking. All the same, there was no escaping it any longer the day of Whit's departure. Everything was to lay bare before them, hitting hard at the hearts of all three as they spied the approaching northbound train in the distance where they waited with Whit on the railroad station platform.

Realizing that she deserved to be there and recognizing, too, that her presence would arouse no questioning thoughts in Whit's mind, or as far as that went in the minds of others either since the deep friendship between Whit and his teacher was common knowledge, Matthew and Amy had invited Lucy to accompany them to the train station to see Whit off.

Everybody had made an endeavor to let it be a cheerful leave-taking and; in truth, Whit's heart was cheerful. He was highly excited over embarking upon a career that was so vastly different and unlike the lifework of his family and friends—promising to write home often, to Lucy as well as his foster parents as the train swiftly covered the distant tracks. Still, for all his exuberance over venturing into this novel profession, when the final seconds came with the conductor calling a last warning "All aboard" and Whit was forced to make a grab for the valise setting at his feet, which held Amy's chicken sandwiches and other choice edibles along with a few personal things, and make a jump for the already moving train, he was to feel his heart skip in uncertainty for an instant or two. And, of the three people who had received his hasty warm goodbye, it would have been difficult; indeed, to have determined whose heart had dipped the lowest and which face following Whit's at the window of the moving train looked the most heavy-laden as he kept his hand going in a constant wave till he had faded from view.

Whit kept his promise though, succoring the loneliness of the three people who missed him most. His letters were soon flowing to Drakston Hall and Oak Grove too—the correspondence to Oak Grove resulting in Lucy Randolph, to her surprise and pleasure, finding herself still in the position of teacher to Whit as she tried to discuss and also take a stab at answering many questions—almost as many had Whit still been in her classroom at Drakston Hall, that naturally concerned this new pursuit that he had become engaged in and which, of course, her knowledge in was rather vague to say the least. Aware of this, Lucy decided she was not going to be outdone. She read and studied every book and manual she could find on the subject of Whit's chosen vacation and, in so doing, not only did she find another interest to help fill her days but was soon to discover that she was holding on to that closeness which was shared with Whit—keeping it alive— almost as avidly bad there been no miles between them at all.

Assuredly, to Matthew and Amy, the halls and rooms of Drakston Hall seemed lonely and empty without Whit's vibrant presence. The fact was, as devoted as they had become to Lucy Randolph's son— actually after all these years having come to think of Whit as being their own flesh and blood, in a certain sense, they had been dealt a far worse blow through the turn of circumstances than Lucy Randolph had. In Lucy's case, even if she had suffered in giving up her son and did miss her near daily contact with Whit, the fact remained she had somehow muddled through her ordeal and had achieved the one purpose she had yearned so desperately for. It was not a little thing with her to know that Whit had come by his legal name in spite of all.

It was her heart's greatest comfort even if she had been forced to work it out in secret. But, in Matthew and Amy's case there had been no purpose to gain; that is, none save their keen desire to help Lucy Randolph attain what had appeared to her to be an impossible something to carry off. Yet, by opening their hearts to Lucy, taking on the responsibility of raising her baby so that he could legally come by his rightful name, they had made themselves vulnerable for the very thing that Whit's absence had effected—heartache. Still again, regardless of what Whit's absence was costing them in loneliness for him, neither Matthew nor Amy had no regrets about coming to the aid of Lucy Randolph. Both would have done the same all over again, even if they had known in the beginning that Whit's interest in life would take him far beyond the lands of Drakston Hall, because in addition to their sincere desire to help Lucy they both had ever viewed the situation as being a divine working, thinking of Whit as having come to them as a blessed gift—sent to help alleviate the loss of Matthew Carson's two sons.

For all that; however, Whit Carson's choosing to embark upon a career that had already separated him from Drakston Hall, except for his letters and anticipated vacations, had not been the only distress that Matthew and Amy Carson was to be fronted within this year of 1880. That coming summer, Stuart Drakston, looking more like his late father every added year—something that Elizabeth took much pensive pride in—was to finish his military training in Virginia and return home only to leave once again with his mother for England just before school was to resume in September.

This second family parting, only a short time from the other and one that was to be for a long period of four years besides, had gone hard with Amy. She, too, took much pride in this only grandson, heir to Drakston Hall. In Stuart, Amy saw the Drakston lineage continuing on. She was deeply attached to him and held him most dear to her heart, with Matthew Carson not fully realizing how intense or how much this long pending separation from Stuart was paining Amy till he became aware she had finally dropped that ironclad reserve of hers and was weeping openly as the huge ocean liner, which Elizabeth and Stuart had boarded some moments earlier, begin to inch its way from dock side. But, as Amy wept, her tears washing right on through her dainty lace handkerchief, she had not become so heart-stricken that she was mindless to Matthew's comforting arms. Silently, she felt the strength of him drawing her closer to his side as he reached inside his pocket and handed her a handkerchief that was more absorbent to water. And, they remained silent with Amy continuing to weep, standing there on the wharf watching the huge ship sweep out to sea until it had become nothing but a blurry spot on the ocean's horizon.

Thus, as alone once again as they had been in the first year of their marriage when they had lived in the nation's capital, Matthew having begun to tenderly coax Amy away from the all but indistinct liner, was now adding, "Have you forgotten, dear, you still have me. In fact, after all the unheard-of Whit's decision, choosing sailing around on that water out there over farming, and then these last hectic weeks as well, I think we both could do with things settling down a bit. Come on dear, let's try finding our way through this mob to the coach and get on home." Still spry and belaying his age at least a full dozen years or more and with his outlook to the future sunny as ever, he laughed, "At our age and that goes double for me, I promise you, before we've hardly turned around twice the four years will have gone by and they'll be back home."

Immediately, Amy cut out all sorrowing thoughts, promptly regaining her stately bearing as she gave her eyes a final dab with Matthew's handkerchief and handed it back to him, telling him, "No, Matthew dear, I haven't forgotten I still have you. How could I, when I know that you and only you, make up the very best in my life?"

Sending her that ever devilish wink of his, Matthew grinned, "Now, that's what I call an appreciative girl. Thank you, dear," and giving Amy his arm, they turned their backs on the now vanished passenger ship and started making their way through the crowded wharf towards the waiting coach.

Despite Matthew's lightness, he could appreciate Amy's feelings over parting from Elizabeth and Stuart for such a prolonged duration. They both had long become his family, also. In truth, when it came to devotion and concern, Matthew had come to view this second family that he shared with Amy and his first family that he had had with Anne as being all one. If there were any distinguishable difference left at all it lay with his only beloved daughter, Mary Eliza who he still visited as often as two and three times a week.

Still and all though, there had come to be something else that was having a great deal to do with Matthew's numerous visits to Green Sea, even if he was ever ready to see Eliza and Luke and his grandchildren and visit with them. It was the mansion that Luke was building for Eliza. In this more prosperous South Carolina Bourbon era—a period that would have been deemed more successful and comfortable regardless of whether it was or not since Reconstruction was over with and state politics were mostly under the control of former Confederate leaders, Luke was progressing along rather rapidly with the mansion. The huge structure had indeed begun to take shape and Matthew Carson had started eying it with keen interest. In fact, Matthew had become so excited over the building of the mansion and its rapid change in recent months, actually becoming involved now to the extent of giving advice because Luke and Eliza both turned to him quite often in seeking his opinion about different matters regarding its construction, that he had begun to think of his visits to Green Sea as scoring a double hand—seeing what else Luke had completed about the mansion as well as visiting his loved ones there.

However, the building of the mansion at Green Sea nor any other everyday activity absorbed Matthew's mind so fully that it deterred him from knowing the presence of Amy and forever embracing this realization with gratitude. Oftentimes in the evenings, Matthew would lower his newspaper or perhaps lift his eyes from one of those endless farm journals he was forever reading to look at Amy, who would be as equally engrossed in some work of biography most likely, sitting in her chair opposite him. For some minutes, Matthew would observe her, hug Amy's elegant, quiet charm to him as he applauded himself over and over for having come to his senses that day and asking her to marry him. Sometimes, looking at Amy, he would find himself pondering over man's destiny—how one's general course could be totally altered in a way that it would induce one to move in an entirely different direction from what one would ever contemplate or vision in the wildest of imaginations. Certainly, Matthew told himself, he would never have envisioned himself and Amy Drakston sharing a deep and abiding love as man and wife in the huge Drakston mansion alone together in their older years. And, while he would reflect over this inconceivable wonder that fate had destined for him and Amy, Matthew would also be wondering at the same time if fortune had any more incredible happenings in store for him before he made his earthly departure.

The country's most momentous event in this year of 1880 had been the presidential election. Though when it came to vehement and passionate causes, this election had lacked in measuring up to the offerings of former presidential elections. Since Reconstruction had ended and the more prosperous days under President Hayes had done wonders for the nation's painful war wounds, the politicians had been hard put to come up with a topic that made for zestful shouting and stirring impacts—affecting the voter to the polls on their behalf. Thus, another Republican, James A. Garfield winning the election with ease had come as no surprise. But, unfortunately, Garfield had hardly had time to even realize his victory let alone demonstrate his potential before an assassin had cut him down, forcing him to relinquish his office to Chester A. Arthur—finally succumbing to his wounds on September 19, 1881. This same year, an international humanitarian institution, the American Red Cross, was founded by Clara Barton.

By the year 1884, politics had revived and was breathing vigorously once again, sweeping the country during the year's presidential campaign with the roaring fury of tornado winds. When the storm had finally subsided, the nation saw its first Democrat for many a long day, and a bachelor at that—the tall, stocky Grover Cleveland, ensconced in the White House. While in office though Cleveland was to yield to his bachelorhood, taking pretty Frances Folsom as his bride in a White House wedding on June 2, 1886. And, not only was Cleveland the first president to be married in the White House, but his potential as a chief executive proved to be as strong and sturdy as his build. Yet, for all the nation's interest in politics and the romance of its newly-elected president, the people's thoughts were also with a former president and Civil War hero, Ulysses S. Grant, who in addition to suffering from throat cancer which had taken his voice was also hovering near the brink of poverty from personal business failure. Grant was to die in 1885, with a number of famed Confederate leaders attending his last rites—his ill success as president as well as the bitterness of the war years having been forgotten in the grievous circumstances of his final days.

At all events; however, in this spring of 1884, that all important schoolroom that had been so prominent for such a long time at Drakston Hall was at last abandoned for good. On one rose-filled May day, Lucy Randolph—after having held a small informal graduation ceremony and little party for the last of her remaining students to finish school there—presenting their diplomas and then partaking of the cake and punch with them and exchanging well-wishes and goodbyes and sending them on their way, had pulled the window shades and closed the door herself this time. And, in deep nostalgia and alone—her young, energetic students had been long departed-she had stepped into the bright May sunshine and taken the gay-throned flagstone path to her waiting buggy thinking of Whit and all the others she had taught and prepared for college, or as in Whit's case some other vocation, in that one room at Drakston Hall.

Still, in spite of all the sentimental thoughts that had swamped Lucy when she had headed her mare down the drive for the last time as the schoolmarm of Drakston Hall, she had felt a tingle of triumph as well surging through her. Confident and self-assured, Lucy did not have to rely on hearing words of praise from the parents of her students, which, of course, she heard often enough, before she could indulge in feeling victorious. She knew she had done well by each and every student that had ever sat in her classroom at Drakston Hall and asked for nothing more than to be able to do the same by those of who she would be assigned to teach that coming fall in Charleston's public school system—have the satisfaction of indulging once again in having come through with success regarding her profession; because as Lucy's mare had pattered on home in a somewhat lazy gait in the warmth of that May afternoon, Lucy had thought that only she and the good Lord knew how much she had fretted over the muddle she had made out of her personal life—a life that had offered so precious little to exult in.

Still and all though Lucy Randolph had finally adjusted to what she now had come to believe had been the unavoidable from the very beginning. Even had she not come round to that way of thinking, certainly after twenty long years she would have become familiar with the way of things anyhow—attuned to all of it, even if she did continue to miss seeing Whit and the image of Nat Carson was still vivid in her thoughts.

During this four-year separation from Whit, there had been a few rewards for Lucy, giving her something that she had taken a lot of pleasure in. Daring to scorn caution because their hearts were always touched by her plight, Matthew and Amy Carson had invited Lucy not only once but twice to accompany them to Annapolis to see Whit— once while he had been a cadet and then again at the Naval Academy's graduation exercises when Whit had been commissioned a naval officer. Out of all the many young, handsome cadets, Lucy had been positive that when it came to good looks and splendor, Whit had outshone the entire class. Nor had Lucy's mind let Nat Carson slip from the scene, either. Nat's image had been right there, sharing the event with her. There had also been those brief periods, too, when Whit had vacationed at home—leaves that had brought Lucy and Whit to be in each other's company quite often, with the two of them falling into a lengthy discussion about Whit's chosen career while the others mostly sat and listened.

Nowadays; however, with Whit having been commissioned and assigned to a naval cruiser, there were no chances for visits. Neither did Lucy have any idea when there would be. Naturally, the letters that she had always treasured so much still came. Though, sometimes, the letters made Lucy feel all that more separated from Whit; in that, the postmark was so often from such a remote faraway place—Thailand, Cape town, South Africa, or some distant exotic island in the far Pacific. Still, eventually, Lucy was to overcome this consciousness of distance, too, and come to read the letters—which were often months old when they arrived, in a new light, dreaming of the day when perhaps Whit's ship would drop its anchor in the harbor of Charleston instead of those other strange, remote places that it forever seemed to find its way to.

In this same year, another of the younger generations had completed his studies, also. Having just gotten out of medical school, Seth Roalf Junior had come home in midwinter and married Maggie Randolph in a lavish home wedding. Laura Randolph and Jane Anne Heyward, both of whom were in full bloom of maturity now, and two or three more distant blooming cousins from New Orleans—whose families never made an appearance in the Carolina low country except to attend weddings or funerals, were the brides attendants. Promptly following the ceremony, young Seth lingered only long enough to shake a few hands—actually what few minutes it had taken Maggie to step out of her bridal gown and into her traveling clothes, before he had taken his bride and departed for Richmond, Virginia where he was slated to begin his internship immediately.

That star-spangled gaze that had kindled between Maggie and Seth Junior on that starry night at Sandy Cove had stayed permanently fixed, maintaining its same steady glow all these years—needless to say to the pique of Martha Randolph when one year began to add to another and her elder daughter, besides having lost interest in college and quit, was still waiting and talking about a wedding that appeared to be nowhere in sight. It had taken all the will power that Martha could possibly muster to keep from publicly flaring her indignation over the whole matter. She would actually bite her tongue in order to hold back her wrath from the explosion that it was forever bordering on, every time the subject of the couple's long drawn out courtship came up. And, she had gone ahead and spilled out her irritation to Caroline Roalf, not once but several times about how young Seth was dragging his feet toward the altar!

"Heavens and earth, Caroline!" Martha had stormed just a short while before Maggie and Caroline's stepson were to finally set a wedding date. "Have you forgotten that Maggie is nearing her twenty-fourth birthday? Why, besides having already become an old maid, if they wait much longer, she'll be ready to qualify for grandmother instead of the mother she should be!"

"Oh, that's nonsense, Martha," said Caroline, "Maggie's not that old. They'll have plenty of time to start a family. Seth Junior longs to be married, but it takes a long time for the study of medicine."

"Don't remind me," Snapped Martha, "and for crying out loud, would you pray tell me what studying has to do with business of that sort?"

Suppressing the laugh that had rushed to her throat, because Caroline was well aware that Martha saw nothing amusing about the situation, Caroline managed to croak, "Well, I would think a lot—" Then, swallowing the laugh altogether, she went on to say, "Martha, you have no idea how limited Seth Junior's personal time is. He studies way into the night, not just one night but every night to the week and has for a good long while, so he can finish before the usual graduation date. He loves Maggie dearly. He told me he hoped they could be married this winter, that he had no intention of waiting on till he finished serving his internship, even though it would be as much if not more confining than his studies had been,"

"Well, I was married at sixteen! I knew what I wanted, and I didn't drag my feet in going after it!" Martha retorted, regretting her quick tongue instantly as her face flamed blood-red.

To Martha's relief, though, her tongue bloomer raised only a faint smile from Caroline, who was far too modest to do more, letting that part of the subject drop as she went ahead and tactfully suggested to Martha that it would not be a bad idea to start thinking about wedding preparations instead of worrying over Maggie's age.

And Martha had heeded Caroline's advice, though the extreme

that Martha had gone to had not been at Caroline's suggestion. That had been Martha's own doings. She had thrown herself headlong into wedding preparations at once—so hell-bent in putting on a wedding that would not be forgotten the day after, that no sooner had the last grain of rice fallen on the happy couple, Martha took to her bed and after spending more than two days there would have stayed even longer had Bruce not threatened to send for Doctor Seth Roalf.

However much though that Martha had given of herself to Maggie's wedding, which indeed had fatigued her, this had not been the lone cause for her collapse. There was more to it than that. Her younger daughter's lack of interest in the several eligible young men, who had been among the guests, had simply been too much for Martha. Martha had begun to think that Laura favored books over boys, anyhow. Now, Maggie's wedding had convinced her. It made Martha shudder to think that Laura might follow in the footsteps of her Aunt Lucy. She knew that both her daughters had been born more Randolph than Drakston and silently wailed that it had not been enough to see one daughter grow into an old maid before she was married, now it looked as though Laura was headed down the same road and, as ill luck would have it—the road of an old maid schoolteacher at that! Then, on top of being disappointed in the way things seemed to be shaping up regarding Laura, this business about Elizabeth and Stuart being nowhere in sight when Maggie had gotten married had vexed Martha plenty. In the first place, Martha had never been able to see why Elizabeth had thought it necessary to take Stuart to England to complete his education, anyhow, To Martha's way of thinking, America's schools and colleges were up to any country's educating level and would have been adequate enough for Stuart's schooling. And, secondly, Martha had thought—even if she had sorely wanted to see Maggie married that since Maggie and Seth Junior's dillydallying had already made Maggie an old maid that it should not have bothered them in the least to have waited a little longer—spring, the given time when Elizabeth and Stuart were scheduled to return from England.

"No, let Seth Roalf go on about his business with others, Bruce, I'll be all right," sighed Martha, resigning at last to the plain fact that Maggie's wedding had done naught in the way of bringing her secret hopes into viewing range—an eligible suitor for Laura.

"Are you sure?" Bruce pressed, "You've been in bed now for over two days. I'm well aware, Martha, you won't be falling on your knees in my behalf for some time to come for telling you this, but the truth is, you look ghastly!"

Bruce was right. Martha sent him a look black as thunder, a look that plainly told him he had loused up any further attempt at making conversation with her; that is, not until she wiped that pout off her face and pulled her lower lip up, which, of course, he did not expect her to do immediately. Nonetheless, he was relieved to see that she was not too indisposed to pout even if it had taken his dim view of her looks to disclose the fact. Just the same, he went ahead and warned her of his intention before he made his exit. "Then, if the state of your health is all right, Martha, your way of putting it, not mine, mind you, I'll expect to see you out of that bed in a short while from now, or I shall see if Seth Roalf can find the reason for your lingering there!"

"Men," Martha inwardly seethed, as she set her pouting gaze upon the door that Bruce had just walked through. 'No way would they ever come to understand the trials of woman! Nor did it seem they even wanted to. Why, Bruce would laugh her off the entire premises, to some hiding place, if he really knew her main trouble. That time she had tried to talk to him about Maggie being an old maid was an example. He had looked at her as if she had suddenly gone batty or something. Then, he had given a snorting hee-hee and walked away from her. The Randolph's had never been people to hurry to the altar, anyway, and Bruce still looked on Laura as being nothing but a mere child. The truth was, Bruce himself would have dragged his own feet down the path to matrimony longer than he had, had not it been that she had given Bruce's hands more liberty with her that early Sunday evening behind those gardenia bushes in the garden. After that little sweet privileged session, Bruce had hardly been able to wait. As a matter of fact, neither had she!

Suddenly, recalling that Sunday evening of long ago was like having a soothing syrupy tonic flowing down her throat when it was raw, causing her worries—or what Martha deemed was worry, to matter no longer as a warm, rosy blush stole its way across her cheeks, hiding every trace of her scowl under it. And, instantly, Martha knew the kind of tonic it would take to revive her spirit and it most certainly could not be found in Doctor Seth Roalf's medical bag!

Now in the glowing tameness of her yearning, Martha was sorry that she had scowled at Bruce and were wishing that he had not been in such a hurry to depart from her company, even if she had looked at him with a long face. But, since he was not there, she decided there was nothing she could do but go ahead and get up as he had more or less demanded she do, or she would surely be finding herself—and soon at that—trying to answer Seth Roalf's probing questions—questions that certainly would have no bearing whatever on her needs right then!

Martha gave the bedclothes a swift push and sprang to the floor, taking heart again as something else popped in her mind aside form finding Bruce and charming him into retracing his steps. She thought of Jane Anne Heyward and was certain from all appearances she was not going to be alone in her mortification of seeing Laura grow into an old maid, because Eliza was going to be enduring the same, if the sedate and prim Jane Anne did not mend her ways, also.

Those silly girls! Nothing like their mothers, thought Martha, as she donned her last piece of clothes and banged the bedroom door after her.

Martha had put her finger on a true fact of both girl's personalities. Neither could not have been any different form their mothers. They both, Laura and Jane Anne as well, had inherited all the poise and queenly nature that their grandmothers, the Goodyear sisters, had been endowed with and then some. But, in Jane Anne's case, what Martha was in no position to see nor would she ever be, was the fact that there was plenty of warmth under Jane Anne's cool exterior just waiting to catch flame.

Louise Gore Sayre-David

Chapter Five

Exactly two weeks to the day that Lucy Randolph had held her small commencement party at Drakston Hall—terminating school there for all time—Elizabeth Drakston and her twenty two year old son, Stuart, who was ever most attentive by her side, were to sail back into the harbor of Charleston after a long absence of four years. Elizabeth had done what she had set out to do and what she felt Frank would have approved of her doing.

Now she was coming home. She had given their son the advantage of attending one of the world's most famed universities, telling Stuart all he was to gain by this opportunity, the chance of it lay with him and him alone.

Apparently, Elizabeth's son had not disappointed her because Stuart's academic record bore witness to that. Not only had he graduated at the head of his class in two chosen vocations law and agriculture but held doctorate degrees in both fields as well. In short, Stuart was a son to be proud of and Elizabeth Drakston was and a lot more, too. Even though she desired Stuart to be his own man, which he was in spite of his close relationship with his mother, this did not stop Elizabeth's life from centering round him.

The parting with her parents once again had gone hard with Elizabeth Drakston, due to her having felt it had been the final parting with her father because of his rapidly failing health. Still, she had felt that she should not delay any longer in seeing that Stuart came back to his rightful heirship, Drakston Hall. In truth, now that Stuart had completed his schooling, Elizabeth had had the feeling that if both she and Stuart had not set sail for Drakston Hall immediately, that Frank Drakston's ghost just might have been walking beside her in protest. Thus, paralleled both ways in what she deemed as duty, Elizabeth had been deeply burdened, but by promising she and Stuart would return to England for a visit in a year or perhaps no longer than two years, she had been able to bring an element of lightness into the parting with her parents after all.

The cable announcing Elizabeth's and Stuart's imminent arrival at Drakston Hall had indeed been a joyful piece of news to Amy and Matthew. Though neither had made mention of it in these intervening days since school had closed, Matthew and Amy both had felt—at

130

times—as though the huge mansion was actually being smothered from existence by the heavy hush of its walls. Then, the cable had arrived and, immediately, the old but sturdy house seemed to take a deep breath and breathe freely once again.

All the same, Amy's house cleaning spree had had a lot to do with the mansion's seemingly revival. In fact, by the time the servants had carried through with Amy's instructions, the entire house looked almost as if it had reverted back to the days of its fresh newness. There was not a rug in the whole house that had not been taken outside and draped across the clothesline in order to beat the dust and dirt out. There was not a window that had not been washed and its curtains or draperies laundered and cleaned. Not one inch of furniture had missed the wax and polish and the floors and wainscoting had been gone over, too. Even the walls had been dusted. In addition, the kitchen had suddenly taken on the looks of a beehive and smelled as though it may have been one—literally dripping with honey, so savory pleasing the fragrance of its cuisine filled the house. It was doubtful if Amy had eliminated one solitary dish from her menu that she had ever heard Elizabeth or Stuart utter the slightest preference for.

Since time had been limited before Elizabeth's and Stuart's arrival—not even two full days left to make ready for the homecoming when the cable had reached Drakston Hall, Matthew had feared that Amy had bitten off more than she could possibly chew in her thorough house cleaning bang not to mention all the baking and cooking she was also supervising. But, in mid-afternoon of the second day as he was leaving the library to go in search of Amy to warn her that it was about time to leave for Charleston to meet the docking liner, he was amazed once again at Amy's power to achieve the ultimate result in any undertaking she ventured upon. There she was already coming down the hall looking like a spring daisy all locked out in an up-to-the-minute brand-new flowery outfit, apparently on her way to remind him of the same thing he had started to remind her of.

Matthew stopped; his eyes busy running over her. Even though Amy had her head lowered pulling on her white kid gloves, which prevented Matthew from seeing a full view of her face, he knew every contour that it held anyway and was taking much pride in the fact that she still bore a striking figure—one that paralleled most handsomely with her elegant features, which betrayed her sixty-five years at least a minus fifteen or twenty.

Their minds could have been one as Amy finally settled the last of her fingers into her gloves and looked up to see Matthew stopped, staring at her. She smiled, takin in the fact that he was already dressed, too, and also marveled at how erect he stood despite his seventy-eight years, still very handsome in his grey and white pin-striped trousers which were topped with a solid grey cutaway coat over a white shirt and grey stock—remaining still to belie his own age by a dozen years or more.

She crossed on to where he stood and said, "You'd started after me. As anxious to see them as I am, I believe, aren't you, Matthew?"

"I guess I am, dear," he smiled, "since it's apparent our minds are running together. I've already sent for the coach. It should be here shortly." He reached for her gloved hand, going on to suggest, "Come on, let's wait on the porch." He turned his head again to look at her as they moved on down the hall. "I like your new outfit."

"Do you really, Matthew?"

"Delighted with it," he smiled, "but not as much with it as I am with the girl whose showing it off."

"Now, no flattering, Matthew." She teased, smilingly,

"Not for the world, Madam, would I be guilty of that!" He laughed.

"You know, I believe you, Matthew."

"You'd better," he told her and winked "Because regarding the fairer sex, I've always thought a man would be some dolt not to play it straight!"

"And, that wise philosophy is no doubt one the reasons you're so popular with us," she told him, looking at him fondly as they stepped through the doorway.

"Now, who's flattering who, if I may ask," he said, and laughed.

While they took their seats in their favorite rockers, which were placed side by side, Amy blithely went on to another subject, astonishing Matthew once again by asking, "Matthew dear, do you think there's any possible way we could gather the family and our close friends, those who live near us, for a dinner party tonight? Wouldn't that be fun?

"Fun?" Matthew quizzed, shaking his head in disbelief. "No, dear, I don't. I don't think it would be very amusing to me at all, to see your legs buckling under you!

"Oh, I haven't done that much, Matthew," Amy dissented,

somewhat disappointed that Matthew had finally raised an objection to something she had suggested.

"That's the whole problem, dear, you don't realize just how much you have done, but I do. Aside from those few restless winks you stole last night, you haven't stopped since that cable came. What do you say we let the dinner party's rest for a while? Besides, Luke and Bruce both are very busy with their crops right now and, although I'm positive Stuart and all the rest of the younger set would love your idea, I'm not all that sure Elizabeth would. I would imagine after that long ocean voyage; Elizabeth would want nothing more than to spend a few quiet hours with us and then retire. Come on, dear, here comes the coach. I promise, there's going to be a big evening ahead of you, anyway," Matthew said, rising from his rocker and giving Amy his hand.

Though Amy still felt put out somewhat, actually feeling a little peevish with Matthew, she went ahead and took his hand, gracefully making her way to the coach beside him and settling down upon its seat. But they were well on their way toward Charleston before she spoke again, finally melting the little chill that had crept between them by confessing, "Matthew dear, I must admit you know exactly what you were talking about. I really am more fatigued than I realized. I think I started to become aware of this the longer I sat in that porch rocker."

"I know, dear, and like I said, we'll have the family gathering when things settle down some. Anyway, what about that box supper that's planned for tomorrow night at the church? We've forgotten all about that," said Matthew.

"That's right, Matthew!" Amy exclaimed; the church social having become lost in the cable's exciting news. "I haven't even thought about that and wouldn't have if you hadn't reminded me!"

"Well, I repeat, dear, we're in for excitement enough without the wear and tear of having a dinner party thrown into the bargain as well."

"I fully agree with you, Matthew, and—well—I'm sorry for pouting with you that little while back there."

Matthew turned to look at Amy and jested, as he tried to keep a sober face, "What's that? You pout? Why, never in a hundred years, would you do that! Not my Amy, never in a hundred years!" He leaned over and gave her a peck on the cheek.

"Oh, Matthew," she laughed, "don't think for one second that I don't see right through that fairer sex philosophy of yours this time."

It did turn out to be a big evening as Matthew had assured—plenty big enough for Matthew and Amy Carson and especially in Matthew's case where the last steps of time's life ladder were already vibrating from his approaching feet. First of all, there had been those electrifying moments when Matthew and Amy's eyes had darted from head to head in search of the two faces who they had not set their eyes upon for four years—searching eagerly among that swarming mob making its way towards the great liner's gangplank. Then, after what had seemed like the length of a day to them, there had been the chilling excitement of finally spying Elizabeth's fair coloring—her shining tresses still reminding one of gold dust as they were caught in the rays of evening's sinking sunlight. And, at the same time, that quivering incredulity regarding the tall, handsome man whose arm Elizabeth had her own arm linked through.

Never, at that far a distance, would Matthew and Amy have recognized the man as being Stuart, had they not been expecting his attentive presence by Elizabeth's side. Stuart had only been eighteen, mature then they had thought, when he had left for England. But, they were quickly to observe they had been wrong. It was the returning Stuart who had grown into a man and a most striking one at that.

The truth was, to those who had swarmed around the reuniting family, that is, those of whom had not known the late Frank Drakston—whose facial likeness had been planted on the face of his son, had taken Stuart Drakston and Matthew Carson as being father and son meeting, even though they did not share one drop of common genetic blood between them. The cause for this was the fact that Stuart, passing his own father's height which had been average, had taken back after Elizabeth's side of the family—her father and uncles were tall men—and had grown well over six feet in height, the same height as Matthew Carson. In addition, Stuart's broad shoulders, tapering down to his brawny, slender middle, were near identical to the still muscular looking build which were those of Matthew Carson's. So, because of their similar physique, one could see why strangers would take them as being blood related.

Once those first overwhelming moments of meeting again had simmered down somewhat, Matthew and Stuart had shepherded Amy and Elizabeth to the coach and after seeing them settled down had gone back to check on the Drakston baggage, which had grown into an enormous bulk in this four-year duration. Plus, more than a dozen trunks of clothing and personal items there were boxes and boxes of Stuart's law books as well along with many other volumes on different subjects. The entire Drakston clan, those before Stuart and the present had always been avid readers and it appeared Stuart was going to be no different if all the books, he had lugged clear across the Atlantic Ocean meant anything. Outside of the one or two personal valises which were taken to the fancy late-model coach that Matthew and Amy were driving—one so elegantly embellished with extra details that it hardly provided room for all its passengers once they climbed aboard let alone the traveling bags, it had been necessary to check the rest of the baggage in storage till it could be picked up at a more convenient time. At any rate, before everything had been taken care of, it was way past sunset when Matthew and Amy and their returning family members had finally set out in the direction of home and; at last, were having the opportunity to seek that first-hand informative news of the other in addition to all those other things—what not and what had taken place that they had been deprived of doing for such a long time.

"I trust all's well at Green Sea," said Stuart, as he turned his head and peered through the darkened window of the coach as it rolled by the arch of the oak-lined avenue at Green Sea.

"Yes, and busy as usual," Matthew replied. "Luke has the mansion almost completed now. You would've noted had dark not overtaken us. I think their plans are to move in this coming fall, if the harvest turns out to their expectation."

"Well, I certainly wish them a productive one. I'm sure the loss of that other great Mansion has posed many trying ordeals for Mr. and Mrs. Heyward that otherwise they would've been spared. And, seeing something that splendor go up in flames besides all the other things that went with it must've been a harrowing experience for them. I wasn't very old at the time, perhaps four or a little older, but I can still remember how I was always awed by its many stately columns," Stuart said and instantly realized that he had no doubt stirred some unhappy memories for Matthew Carson, going on to beg an apology, "I'm sorry, Grandfather Carson, I hope you'll forgive my lack of delicacy in recalling a tragedy that I'm sure brought a great deal of suffering upon you, too."

"Yes, it did, but don't you fret about that now. To be honest with you, I've gotten so used to looking at the mansion that Luke and Mary Eliza have been in the progress of building all these years, actually taking part in many discussions with them concerning its construction, that it's becoming easier and easier for me to think of the other one as never having been there to begin with," Matthew told him and also made it a point to change the subject immediately as he went on and inquired of Elizabeth's parents. As to the health of her besides having no desire to even think of that senseless tragedy much less discuss it, Matthew Carson—at this late date—was not taking any chances on letting something slip that just might scar that cherished memory of Frank Drakston that these three people had steadfast and dear in their hearts.

His conscience was free, he was thinking—had forever been so, and he wanted it to stay that way. Better to let bygones remain in oblivion than run the risk of loading the minds of the blameless with the shady doings of the defenseless dead.

By having earned two doctorate degrees in two fields was evidence enough that Stuart Drakston had had other things to do with his mind, during that schooling period in England, besides letting it busy itself too often with those nostalgic thoughts of Drakston Hall that had had a way of slipping into his studies every now and then. Nonetheless, his refusal for having allowed this yearning to triumph over the objective his mind had been set upon was not to say his feelings had become bereft of caring one way or another about anything but his studies. Far from it. It was that stayable trait—to endure and never flinch away from carrying through with whatever confronted one to carry out that Stuart had inherited from his grandmother, Amy Drakston Carson and to a certain degree from his own mother; also, that had kept any wistful thought that may have come his way regarding Drakston Hall from having turned into acute homesickness.

Still, for all that singleness of purpose which Stuart had let reign over everything else while he had been away, the moment his eyes had glimpsed the century old Drakston mansion setting there in the glow of an early rising moon looking as though it may have been some great galaxy in all its quaint beauty, a flood of deep tenderness for all the things its stood for something more keenly felt than anything he had ever experience before washed over him. He was to recognize then how much he had truly yearned to come home and was suddenly regretting that their homecoming was being shadowed by the darkness of night. He could hardly wait for the next day's dawn when—in its light—his eyes could take in more of what he knew to be there. He wanted to explore it all to know that feel of its country soil cushioning his feet again. He wanted to ride through the lush, green cornfields and experience that exquisite touch of live corn silk and feast in the gladness of knowing that Drakston Hall's land had given origin to its being. He wanted to bask in the June sweetness of its jasmine and magnolias and feel once again that caressing breath of its dew—damp roses upon his face. Yes, he was more than eager to feed on all this pure and sweet natural wonderwork, which had not been his to delight in for such a longtime nourishment that London's fog and reeking vapors would have soiled in one day.

Having barely been able to hold his impatience until the light of day would give him an unobstructed view to all Drakston Hall's unsoiled beauty, Stuart was already out of bed and reaching for his trousers and shirt the next morning before the first pinkish hue had hardly glowed upon the eastern horizon. Reasoning that the homecoming had no doubt sapped everybody's energy; that is, everybody's but his own and, that all must be still sound asleep since he did not hear one single stir in the whole house, he slipped on his socks and taking his shoes in his hand he crept down the stairway and on down through the hall and out the back door of Drakston Hall, which had several of these smaller halls that usually led to side entrances that opened onto another, smaller hall which led to an outside door where promptly he set his feet upon a flagstone stoop. He sat down on the stoop and slipped on his shoes, looking out over the huge formal gardens that graced this side of the mansion and taking a deep gulp of its clean earthly freshness as he absentmindedly tied his shoelaces.

He rose and started following the flagstone path at the bottom of the stoop and was promptly in the garden. He walked slowly, stopping every now and then to absorb all the dewy loveliness around him, becoming so affirm with its nearness that he felt compelled once or twice to reach and touch some elegant bloom near his hand its graceful exquisiteness giving him something that he knew now only Drakston Hall was capable of bestowing to him and causing him to wonder how he had gotten through those long four years without coming home once.

He left the garden and walked on through the orchard and on through the adjoining grape arbor, taking care not to venture on down a little way farther into the unfrequented demise where nothing was lord or master save the bees who inhabited it. He walked on and came to one of the many broad whitewashed fences that enclosed Drakston Hall's closer fields. He leapt the fence and found his feet sinking in knee deep meadow grass, feeling much at home again with the doves and the quails and the meadow larks who made it their haven. As he continued to wade on through the knee high vegetation at an animated gait, having come to feel that he was so much in harmony with the land again that he and it had become one with the other singing in chorus, he plucked off one or two of the taller blades of grass and chewed upon its green freshness—walking on and on—turning and striding forth again, heading nowhere in particular until he became aware his feet had unconsciously led him back to the Drakston burial ground.

Stuart was not in the habit of making pilgrimages to the family's resting place. Nor had he ever been. He left that to the ones who desired to go; for example, his mother, Elizabeth and his cousin, Eliza Heyward who was known to have the habit of making many treks to the Carson burial ground in any given time. Nevertheless, since he found himself there, he walked on around the brick-walled enclosure and opening the lacy Iron Gate, he stepped inside and made his way to the marble tomb where his father lay.

Standing there, instinctively, reading the engraved letters of his father's name and the date of his birth and death which had been elaborately imprinted on the costly headstone. Stuart's mind—in a literal sense—became much more absorbed with the events that had surrounded that long-ago tragedy than the actual fact of the tragedy itself. True, he had adored his father, could still remember him. But, with the passing of time, the vividness of that adoration had gone— gone like that raw pain that had swollen his six-year-old heart to the point of feeling as if it would burst inside him. Yet, that inundated tension, the grief, the doctors, the milling people, his mother's tears, his own, and then the hearing of the final message of his father's death falling form the drawn and quivering lips of his grandmother, Amy. All of those things seemed almost as vivid as if it had been yesterday. Stuart wondered why that was.

Had he adored his father so intensely that he had willed that adoration to fade so that the pain would disappear, too, he was asking himself. Had the hurt and shock been so severe that it had caused him to lock that heroic worshipful picture of his father inside his heart—closed the door upon it for all time for fear of transferring it to some other man? Was that why he had drawn away from building a closer and deeper relationship with Matthew Carson at the time, turning to his mother instead to relieve the loss of that father-son comradeship that had been taken form him so suddenly? Yes, in all likelihood, because had not he and Whit gone off alone by themselves and cried together after grandmother had told them of his father's death, not only out of grief and pain, but because they had misinterpreted some of what she had tried to explain and had formed the opinion that it was only man who died? Woman never. He could not remember just how long they had clung to this theory. It must have been sometime though. How innocent and vulnerable they had been? Just went to show that grown-ups have no way of knowing what goes through a child's mind. Though in spite of this distorted view regarding men and death, he had come to hold Grandfather Matthew Carson in high esteem anyway.

However, that had not been the only time he and Whit had cried alone together. They had shared their sorrow and disappointments several times. Another time was the day they had found out they had not been born brothers. Then, for some time they had carried the notion they were close relatives anyhow. Just what degree of relation, he could not remember. But what he could recall was that devastating blow to both of them when they had been told that they were not related at all due to Whit's adoption. Thus, they had wept and wept hard about that. Moreover, they had shared their sorrow with one another again the day they had learned that it was himself and himself alone who was heir to Drakston Hall. Whit was not to share the heirship with him. Well, that had been another great disappointment to both of them. Grandmother had explained to Whit that he could live there at Drakston Hall as long as he chose to; and also, that she and Grandfather Carson had money in trust to meet his needs that he would not be forced to be dependent on anyone. But Whit had wanted land—part of Drakston Hall's land, and naturally being told that it was not to be, the tears had flowed again from both their eyes.

Whit's entry into the family circle had always been something of a mystery to him, anyhow. One Christmas, all of a sudden, Whit had appeared on the scene as a family member, seeming almost as if he had arrived via Santa's sleigh and been slipped in someone's Christmas stocking. After that Christmas, Whit had come to Drakston Hall often to visit, had been visiting the night his father was shot and continued to stay on following that tragedy. It had been sometime after his father's death, he could not remember just when or why, that he and Whit had gotten the idea they were brothers. Of Course, when they had grown older, they never discussed Whit's adoption. They had come to understand the situation and had gotten along fine with one another; in fact, hit it off with each other as well as any brothers ever had, he supposed.

For all that; however, and the fact that neither he or Whit had spoken of land sharing or anything of the like for several years, he could not help wondering if all that business had not played more of a part in Whit's choosing to follow a naval career than what had manifested on the surface. One thing for certain, Whit could not have chosen a profession any more separated from the land than what he had. On the other hand, many things could have prompted Whit in his decision to separate himself from all he had ever known. A desire to broaden his mind in more fields of work than the one field he had been exposed to all his life, perhaps? Or could it have been a hankering to explore other cultures of the world that to some extent he would most likely be privileged to do every time that ship, he had been assigned to docked in some foreign part? Excitement maybe? Or, putting it another way more than what a rural plantation had to offer? Well, if excitement and deriving unusual kicks had been the reason, it appeared Whit's naval career was not letting him down if all that merry making that he filled his letters with was grounds for belief. He would have to stress that fact to Whit when he wrote to him again because one thing was for certain, of all the things Drakston Hall would have provided Whit with had he chosen it over a naval career, that kind of amusement would positively have not been included among them!

Now, why—all of a sudden—did he feel induced to tell Whit that? Despite his devotion to Drakston Hall could it be he was a fraction envious of all that open freedom of Whits and Whit's—well, putting it mildly, frolicsome games? No, that kind of thinking was absurd. He couldn't be, even if he did have to stick to fact and admit the few romps and tumbles, he had engaged in had been spaced a long way apart. However, taking a look at the other side of the coin, had he really had a choice when it came to choosing his life's work as Whit had done?

Even had his father not met with an untimely death would not his own position have remained the same. Actually, in a way, the pattern had been cut the moment he was born. Yet, had it been otherwise, he thought the omission of Drakston Hall in his life in the past years would have been lesson enough in teaching him where his roots should be firmly imbedded, in any case. So, let Whit have his freedom—make the dizzy rounds in his exotic ports with all their opportunities for gay-living, or so it sounded from Whit's letters, he'd take Drakston Hall even if a yearly ball and a church social or two were about the limit of what he could expect in the way of diversion from his duties.

Come to think of it, Grandfather Carson said there was going to be a box supper social at the Baptist Church tomorrow night, a charity affair to help some young farmer, who was new to the region, replace all those tools and farm equipment which he had lost last week when his barn had burned. Everything required to make a crop had gone up in smoke save his one horse—the only thing that had been rescued. He would wait and write to Whit after the church social, tell him how it turned out. Some joke that was. He could just see that lopsided grin of Whit's taking on a twist of smugness as his eyes scanned the telling of such a dull activity. Church social indeed, compared to Whit's kind of amusement!

Well, he supposed he would be far better off to let Whit's high jinx go no further with him than the paper which Whit spelled it all out on and get on with his own day's doings. Besides, his stomach had already risen its hunger flag at least a half dozen times. He hoped the cooks were up by this time and on their way to the smoke house. He couldn't wait to sink his teeth in that hickory-cured ham. English muffin was one thing, but fried country ham and gravy were quite another. Further, he should go by the stables first and leave word for Fancy to be saddled up. Had to keep his promise to Whit that Fancy would get the chance to stretch those legs of hers, like she champed at the bit to do, the moment he arrived home. It had been too late last night so he reckoned that would serve as a well-spent starter for what the day's activities should happen to bring him—give Fancy the workout her energy deserved.

Stuart suddenly put an end to his self-counsel and turned away, abruptly leaving the headstone that marked his father's grave and making his way back to the gate which he had left ajar. Making certain the gate was firmly closed, he cut across the wide velvet green terrace that stretched to an acre or more between the cemetery and that of another flower-terraced mound which bordered it and also which tapered on down into the perfumed pathways of the formal garden that he had already walked at dawn. Threading his way back through the tree-lined flowery elegance, he aimed his direction toward the back yard, crossed it and was soon hitting the lane that led the way to the stables.

Sure enough, as he had suspected and was ravenously awaiting, the smell of frying ham was sifting through the back yard as Stuart had crossed it, causing him to quicken his step and take note, too, that he had spent more time than he had realized in familiarizing himself again with what was Drakston Hall—seeing, touching, tasting, smelling all those things that bonded him so indivisible to it. And, if the frying ham had not been enough to signal the time, there was nothing that would have convinced him more than the sight of the field hands hitching the work horses and mules to the plows and wagons as he neared the stable yards. Though none the hand's faces were too familiar to him now because it had been many years since he and Whit had rode the fields alongside Matthew Carson on their ponies—actually many he did not recognize at all, Stuart called out a cheerful good morning to everybody as he came into their midst, something his father before him had never done once in his entire lifetime—young or old, familiar or unfamiliar.

But Josh, who had begun his working years as a slave stable boy long before the war came that freed him and who still remained working at the stables in his freedom even though he now was white-haired and bent, Stuart did recognize and most genially at that as he stopped and slapped his arm across the stableman's shoulders and said, "From the looks of the stable yards, Josh, I take it you're still on the job. It's good to see you again. How's things going with you?"

Josh's shriveled face crinkled into one big smile as he looked up to gaze into Stuart's out of eyes that were hardly visible in the deep furrow that surrounded the toothless smiling scrutiny, he had no trouble at all in seeing that this son of Frank Drakston was nothing like Frank Drakston had been in character even if he did carry Frank Drakston's vivid features.

"Ah's right heah, Master Stuart," he finally said, still grinning, "Sho' nough Ah's right heah an' Ah's fine, too, as long as Ah keep des ole bones limbered up, an' it sho is good to see you too. It sho'nough is!"

"Well, it's good to be home, Josh, I can tell you," Stuart smiled back. "I've been up since dawn walking all over the place I couldn't wait to have a look at everything again. Thought I'd come by the stables to peek at Fancy, too, before I ate breakfast and leave word to have her saddled up and brought to the steps shortly. I promised Whit she would get the chance to really stretch her legs the minute I got home." With Josh beside him, he started walking on towards the back compartments of the huge stables to where the riding and carriage horses were housed—for the convenience of the field hands and to save time, too, Matthew Carson had shifted the work horses and mules to the front stalls long back, going on to inquire, "How is she, frisky as ever?"

Josh guffawed, "Ah say she is! Dat mare sho' nough is wild. Nothin' lak her mother Blossom wus. Bout two weeks back, she sailed right over dat high board fence out dere, makin' us chase her fer a mile, I do know. She ain't ben as frisky since den, dough."

Stuart had not been able to keep form wincing at the mention of his father's faithful mare's name. When he had outgrown his pony, he himself had taken to Blossom's back many times; that is, when he had not wanted to gallop very fast because Blossom had been getting on up in years by the time, he began to handle the riding horses. Still, because he was deeply attached to the mare, and he had not been alone in this since Blossom had been the most loved horse on the whole plantation, he had not turned her down too often, always riding her at a gentle pace and leaving Whit to win six races to his one all through the years. But, his tender regard for the aged mare saved him from having one regret over Whit's carrying the day the greater part of the time. During his first school year in England, Blossom had died in the ripe old age of her early thirties.

Willing the pain of Blossom's absence; however, to stay inert, Stuart was going on to say, as he and Josh were approaching Fancy's stall, "I should think that would be enough to calm her. But, it's a wonder she hadn't injured herself taking all those boards," suddenly letting forth with a shrill whistle—his and Whit's old standard in calling their mounts, and adding, as his eyes fell upon Fancy, "You'll learn one of these days, Fancy Girl, how are you?"

To Stuart's astonishment though instead of the high-strung, madcap sorrel mare lifting her perky ears higher and throwing her magnificent head back—letting that splendid reddish mane flow over

143

her shoulders in its full luxurious beauty while her big liquid brown eyes rolled in excited curiosity as one of her splitting nickers filled the stables in answering response, which he was expecting from her, Fancy barely lifted her drooped head that she had hanging over the gate to her stall or appeared to move her seemingly listless body from the spot she stood in.

Started, Stuart's brows began to knit closer together as he stopped and studied her. Why, for all the spirit this was, Fancy might have been some old worn out plug, he thought. Questioningly, he looked at Josh but saw that Josh seemed to be as surprised at the mare's appearance and behavior as he was. He walked on up to the gate of the stall, saying as he began to stroke the mare on the head, "Josh, what's happened to her? Her spirit's gone, seems to have vanished all together."

Josh squinted at the mare more closely, his own knitted brows adding additional furrows to his lined forehead while he said, "She do seem a might pecked fer her dis mornin', Master Stuart, dat she do."

"I think there's more to it than just being peaked, Josh. Are you sure she didn't hurt herself when she jumped that fence?"

"Nothin' we's see, Master Stuart. She just ain't ben as frisky since den, dat's all."

Stuart opened the gate and stepped inside Fancy's stall, giving the mare's leaden movement a mere minutely inspection when she moved aside at his entrance. Presently, he said, "I don't see anything either; that is, anything that's visible to the eye. But, don't bother to saddle her, Josh, not right away, anyhow. I'll wait and see what Grandfather Carson thinks about her behavior when I go to breakfast."

"As you say, Master Stuart," said Josh, as Stuart was stepping form Fancy's stall and turning to leave. But, suddenly, that splitting nicker that Stuart had been expecting was filling the air, starting him in his tracks, though the nicker had not come from Fancy. It had come from the back corral behind the stables.

"Wow!" Stuart exclaimed, turning to look towards the back of the building, "Who let go with that?"

Josh, hesitating to reply, looked down at his feet and began to toy at a pile of hay which was forever strewed over the inside stable yard with the toes of his dung-coated brogans. Some few seconds passed before he finally replied, "Dat's just de Gener'l sayin' good mornin' I reckin."

"The General?" Questioned Stuart.

"Uh-huh" murmured Josh, his sheepish expression pronouncing his sudden unwillingness to respond in his natural manner and give a straight-out answer. Though he did just go on and add, after pausing somewhat, "De new stallion," but his reluctance in having said so had been manifested in his faint and toneless voice—actually causing Stuart to strain his ears in order to pick the words up. And then, he was not certain that he had.

"A new stallion, aye?" Stuart said, taking a stab at chancing he had guessed right. Josh nodded with downcast eyes.

"Well, I think I'll have a look," Stuart told him, wondering why the stableman was shillyshallying at making conversation with him all of a sudden.

He turned away; however, walking on through the passageway of the stables in the direction of the back fenced enclosure, mentally noting that Josh was silently scuffling on his heels. Momentarily though his thoughts were suddenly turned form Josh's changed of manner to one of the most handsome bay-colored blooded stallions his eyes had ever set upon. Stuart stopped, overwhelmed at the horses' sleek form and well-proportioned facial features which were set off with a perfect white star that stretched in points from the end of his broad nose to the exact center of the upper bridge between his alert impressive eyes—eyes that Stuart would have sworn were more green in color than anything else, as he began walking on to cover the short distance between him and where the stallion stood eyeing Stuart in animated curiosity with his unusual green-flaked gaze.

Although the stallion's lofty head and tail bore evidence of his spirit and vivacity, something about his manner had told Stuart immediately that he had been plenty used to people and would not shun away from him and his hunch was proved out, for when he did reach the stallion's side, the horse hardly shifted from his tracks. And, when Stuart started to reach out and lay his hand on the powerfully built shoulders, the stallion stretched his neck round and playfully nudged at him; Stuart knew for certain then that he had made a friend.

Still forgetting Josh's sudden withdrawal, Stuart turned and said, while he attempted to stroke the horse through his playful nudges, "Josh, I've never seen his equal. Where did he come from?"

"Verginny," Josh mumbled and then pursed his lips so tightly together that Stuart decided to press him no further with questions there was Grandfather Carson to give him the details, anyway. But he did go on and tell him, "Well, one thing for certain, wherever he came from, he does their stables proud, Saddle him, Josh. After breakfast, he's going to take me for that ride that I was looking forward to delighting in on Fancy's back."

Having the dining room all to themselves since Amy and Elizabeth both had chosen to rest awhile longer, having only coffee and fruit juice for breakfast in their bedrooms, Matthew having played it somewhat cool while Stuart had been raving about the new stallion between his hasty gulps of grits, eggs, and fried ham and a few words about Josh's sudden change of manner to boot, suddenly saw no point in trying to keep the surprise hanging any longer. Scooping up the last mouthful of breakfast from his own plate, he reached for his coffee cup and leaning back in his chair, he took a gulp of coffee and chuckled, "Poor Josh, you had him in a tight spot."

"A tight spot?" Quizzed Stuart, letting his overloaded fork pause for the first time since he had sat down to breakfast.

"I'll say you did," smiled Matthew. "As a matter of fact, between you and the stallion your eagerness to have a look at him and him feeling he had to sound off with that loud whinny you've upset the applecart, so to speak. You see, he was supposed to be a surprise. That's why Josh had put him in the back lot. He's yours, Stuart, a coming home gift from your grandmother and me. We had planned to present him to you later this morning."

"Mine! A coming home gift! Oh gosh, Grandfather Carson, I feel rotten! I've spoiled everything!" Stuart exclaimed, laying his fork of ham back down on his plate and slumping down somewhat in his chair.

"Oh, think no more about it on our part and go ahead and finish your breakfast. The main thing, you are pleased with him, I gather?"

"Pleased!" Stuart suddenly beamed, his pangs of self-reproach quieting to some extent. "It's a lot more than being pleased, Grandfather Carson. I really can't express how I do feel I think he's superb and I'm truly grateful to you and grandmother both." He picked up his fork again. "I'm so sorry thought that I threw a monkey wrench into the works. No wonder Josh acted hesitant and sorta put out."

"I'll speak to Josh, don't fret over that. Your grandmother and I wanted to give you something and once we saw the stallion, we knew he was it. We know you like Fancy, but since Whit claims ownership to her, it's not quite the same as having your own. You've really never had a full-grown riding horse to call your own, so we thought it was way past time you did. If you don't like his name, we can change it to something else."

Matthew had purposely evaded pointing out that Blossom had truly never belonged to him either, since she had been Frank Drakston's riding horse, but Stuart had gotten the message, nevertheless.

"Oh no, I wouldn't think of changing his name," Stuart was saying, as he resumed his eating. "General suits him just fine. With his magnificent looks, he deserves a high-ranking name. Thanks again, Grandfather Carson, and grandmother, too, for your thoughtfulness."

"Well, you're quite welcome, and I'm sure you're going to like him even more when you take to that saddle shortly."

"You bet I will," Stuart assured, between his ravenous mouthfuls once more, though my wanting to go for an early morning ride is what's brought about my blowing the surprise like I have. I promised Whit the minute I got home; I'd see that Fancy was taken for a fast whirl again before she gets lazy. I went to tell Josh to have her readied and waiting by the time I finished breakfast." Stuart suddenly laid down his fork again. "But, something's wrong with Fancy, Grandfather Carson, or do you already know about it? That's when the General decided to announce his presence, at the very moment I'd started to leave the stables and was telling Josh not to saddle her until I discussed her condition with you."

"Fancy?" Questioned Matthew. "What seems to be the trouble?"

"I really have no idea. She's so droopy, nothing like the mare I last saw four years ago. Her spirit seems to have vanished altogether."

"Well, there was certainly nothing lacking about her spirit two weeks ago. She jumped that back fence, and I fear she gave the stable hands one of the hardest chases they've been engaged in for quite a while before they caught up with her. No, I didn't know there was anything wrong. I was out to the stables yesterday afternoon but didn't notice Fancy in particular. She was in her stall. I would've thought Josh would've mentioned it. Still, I guess he's so thankful to have her quiet, he's decided to let well enough alone.

"He was telling me about that chase she gave them and did mention that she hadn't been so frisky since then, though he seemed to be as shocked at her appearance this morning as I was. Maybe it sorta came on overnight with her."

"It's possible, yet, at the same time, I'll have to admit we could've overlooked it." Matthew smiled, "Remember for the last couple days, our minds and attention around this place, have been on something else other than the livestock. Four years is a long time, you know."

"Indeed, I do," replied Stuart and smiled back.

"I'll tell you what," suggested Matthew, "Finish your breakfast and we'll take another look at her. Perhaps it wouldn't hurt to ask Luke to take a look at her, too—" Matthew suddenly paused obviously thinking. "Luke's so busy now though with his crop, I hate to ask him to come all the way to Drakston Hall," he went on to add. "Wait a minute, I have a suggestion. I don't think she should be burdened with a rider though, maybe led but not ridden that far."

"I could take her, Grandfather Carson," Stuart volunteered.

"And forego your ride on General? Fancy will require one of the slower paced horses going to Green Sea, you know," reminded Matthew

"I don't mind," said Stuart. "I'm anxious to know what's wrong with her. I'll try out General some other time. I'm all finished with breakfast and ready to go see about her now, Grandfather Carson if you are."

"Let's go then," said Matthew, rising from his chair rather abruptly.

Chapter Six

She saw him before he saw her. And, even though this element of fortuity gave her time to wrestle with those strange sensations that the sight of him had awakened in her, instinctively repel them—drive them back to that core of flesh where they seeded as she intuitively reasoned that it was not the time or place for her to meet with these delicious unearthing's of womanly maturity, it also gave her adequate time, too, for taking stock of her appearance and have a few qualms as to what he may think when he did sight her.

She deeply regretted that her new grey riding habit was hanging in her clothes closet instead of gracing the full-grown lines and curves of her body where it should have been. So much was she regretting it, that she actually felt a twinge of resentment run through her, irritated with herself for having taken so little interest in her personal grooming that morning—having hastily donned her old riding habit which was way, way too short for her along with its soiled spots and tatters and frays, too, not to mention the fact that she was letting her hair flow freely in truth the way she preferred to wear it, rather than in the becoming pompadour style that she had begun to wear, lately.

Jane Anne Heyward's frets were all for nothing, though, even if she were unaware of it. For, when her father suddenly looked up and called out, "your timing is great, kitten. Not only have you come back in time to help me, but you've arrived in time to welcome back our long absent cousin as well," and Stuart Drakston turned his head to see her slip from the sidesaddle of her mount and come walking towards them with a feline gracefulness that one seldom saw transported so fully in one's carriage—no less stately steps than had she been a queen all decked out in majestic regalia—there was not one thought of outdated clothes or coiffure styles in his head. Nothing was he aware of but her unusual tall, sensuous attractiveness. He saw wideset eyes that were a true deep grey, so much so they reminded him of a winter-laden sky, though they glinted as luminous as the spring sunlight that encased the day of their meeting again. He saw coal-black flowing hair flaming a velvety soft-featured face and as it had been with her eyes was struck by the charming quaintness that was highlighted, but, even so, it was her mouth curving with full ripe lips parting in a flashing smile that he was carried away with most of all.

In fact, the countenance of the grown-up Jane Anne had awed Stuart so completely that for a few seconds he had felt confused and found himself wondering if some distant cousin from New Orleans who went by the name of kitten—as whacky as it sounded—could have appeared on the scene while he had been away, leaving the gangling and flat chested Jane Anne who he last remembered to be someplace else.

But, as she came on up to where he stood discussing Fancy's languor with Luke Heyward in the stable yard at Green Sea, saying to her father, "Certainly, Papa, just tell me what you'd like me to do," in that still soft, low toned voice that he also last remembered but not the obvious shyness that edged its way in too, when she paused long enough to let her eyes meet his before adding, "Hello, Stuart, welcome back. It'll be so nice to have you home again, we all missed you," Stuart—odd though it was to him—found a grateful gladness flowing through every fiber of his whole person that the girl before him was indeed Jane Anne and no other—Jane Anne the one person he himself had shed away from since that day on the church grounds when Jane Anne's mother had made it so obviously clear to him that their childhood play days had come to an end.

That was then though, and this was now. They both had grown up. Jane Anne was a young woman. He was a young man. Surely, Mrs. Heyward would see no cause for objecting to their keeping company now, Stuart was happily telling himself as he disregarded the presence of Luke Heyward and with his own smile beaming back at Jane Anne, told her, "Had I known you missed me, I would've left England sooner. I won't be leaving you again though. It's wonderful to see you, Jane Anne. I'm already finding out how truly nice it is to be home again." And, it was. Oh, it truly was. He secretly rejoiced.

Though she did possess an unusual loveliness, it was still that demure docility in Jane Anne Heyward's makeup that stood out as her most subtle charm. And, what made it so was the fact that it came through in a true light and not as an outside simulation of beguiled cunning to make a first impression, or to obtain some want that she may have desired. Her whole person spoke of its trueness—every word—every movement, motivating most anyone who happened to be in her company to its invulnerability, especially men, It made no difference who they were, her father, her brother, Luke Green, Stuart

Drakston, or whoever, most often they fell prey to this gentle, retiring veracity in Jane Anne's nature immediately. It moved them instantly to feel a desire to protect and shield her—keep any rough spots which may happen to occur in her walk of life's roadway as smooth as possible.

Of course, it had always been this way between Jane Anne and the male sex, from her toddler days on throughout her childhood. Now though upon reaching young womanhood she induced them to feel even a greater cause to shield her from all harm—safeguard the blossomed flower in all its soft, unspoiled beauty. Nonetheless, while Stuart Drakston looked at her and secretly rejoiced that he was home again, to his astonishment, and glory too, he found this interplaying affinity that he and other men had ever held toward Jane Anne, turning to something else on his part. There was an instant desire not only to protect this blooming flower before him, but to pluck it, too—smell it—taste it—savor it in all its tempting ripeness; and, at the same time, preserve its chaste freshness as well.

Stuart was hard put to understand his feeling, silently asking himself that in his awakening to Jane Anne's maturity, was he falling in love with her? Then, he mentally, in a sense, settled his own question for the time being by telling himself that if the feeling he was experiencing was what loving a woman set afloat in man, he was all for it. And, so it was, though his awakening to it was infused with some doubt; in that very moment, Stuart Drakston had truly and helplessly fallen in love with the fair and gentle Jane Anne Heyward.

If Eliza Heyward had shared an unusually close and devoted relationship with her own father while growing up to young womanhood, which she had and which the two of them still maintained with a fierce loyalty, then one had to view the devotion between Jane Anne Heyward and her father as being more than that—actually something coming near to a worshipful level. On Jane Anne's part, she had unconsciously disclosed this fact when she had responded to her father's statement before saying one word to Stuart Drakston, even though she had been deeply moved and thrilled to see Stuart besides the fact that he was long absent company of a four year duration. But that was Jane Anne's way where her father was concerned. In short, he came first with her.

On Luke Heyward's part, it went without saying that he had looked upon his daughter with almost reverent eye ever since that awesome moment when Seth Roalf had laid the helpless infant Jane Anne in his arms. One factor that played a big part in Luke's feelings for his daughter was the fact that; to him, she was his own mother over and then some in looks and personality, too. Another factor that bound Luke and daughter in such close amity was due to Jane Anne's love for animals. She adored them. Never mind the fleas, the lice, the gruffness, the sometimes-appalling condition of the animal, the blood; she never backed off, having a tender way with them that even exceeded that of her father's hand and which the animals seemed to recognize and respond to instantly—making it easier to administer to them with less difficulty. Forever on Luke's heels, even before her school years, she was always there helping "Papa doctor the animals" as she would put it, all those who were ailing at Green Sea in addition to those who were brought from neighboring plantations and farms to Green Sea for treatment; that is, those who were still able to make the journey, otherwise Luke went to them without her. Whereas Carr had no taste for veterinary work in any degree—the sight of blood or anything on that order always turned him a little green—nothing seemed to be too gruesome for Jane Anne's eyes. Thus, in a manner of speaking, she had become Luke's veterinarian nurse and a capable one at that, assisting him in all his aiding the animals unless it was circumstances Luke thought she should not be exposed to.

On no account had this close rapport between father and daughter hindered the same common spirit from growing between Jane Anne and her mother and her brother as well. As a matter of fact, Jane Anne had been blessed with such a loving nature—a nature so filled with kindness and love for everybody and everything that she could very well afford to distribute it around, which, of course, she did in loving abundance.

This unique and unaffected nature which her daughter had been born with had not been lost on Eliza. Earlier on this same day, Eliza had made mention of it in a conversation that she was having with Jane Anne as they were tidying up the house together. No, save Pete who had helped in the kitchen since he was big enough to reach the tabletops, actually having become chef at Green Sea by now, Eliza had never had servants in the small house. Having reached the bedrooms, Eliza was saying, as she began to tidy up the bedroom that she shared with Luke while Jane Anne had started to go on to her own room which adjoined that of her parents, "Well, if the tobacco and cotton crop turns out to what we foresee that it will this year, it shouldn't be too long, dear, before we all will have more accommodating sleeping quarters. Only the Lord knows how cramped those rooms have always seemed to me, though I've never complained of it to your father, bless him. No doubt they've seemed overstuffed to him, too."

Jane Anne stopped at her bedroom door and turned back, telling her mother, "But, I've never looked on these rooms as putting up with something unpleasant, Mother. I love my bedroom with its white and pink organdy curtains, bedspread, and canopy. I think it's every much as pretty and nice as Laura's is at Oak Grove."

Eliza smiled, "Prettier, dear, if you ask me, even though you don't have a separate dressing and powder room. But, that's because your taste in colors far excels that of Laura's. Why on earth Martha gave in to that child and allowed her to splash that purple and orange flowered chintzy around in her bedroom is above me to understand. It reminds me of walking into the entrance of a circus enclosure or maybe a showboat's saloon."

"Oh, Mother," laughed Jane Anne, "that's funny because Laura and Aunt Martha, too, Eliza's and Martha's children called the other's parents aunt and uncle—think that chintzy is simply beautiful."

"Well, I'm glad," said Eliza, her face showing not one tiny fraction of humor, "for I'm sure they're the only ones who do." She suddenly sat down on her unmade bed, going on to say, as she gazed at the far enter wall between the bedroom and the living room where a good portion of the wall's space was taken up with the canvas-wrapped family portraits which were stacked one upon the other from the floor up, you know, dear, I think one of the nicest things the move to the new mansion will furnish us, one of the things I know that'll make me the happiest, will be that I'll finally have adequate space and the right kind of walls to hang the family portraits on. I suppose I could've hung one or two of the smaller ones somewhere in this house, but I just couldn't bring myself to hang one or two, unless I put up every last one, which, of course, was unthinkable in this small house. I started to hang Mother's one day in the living room, anyway. But, when I got it unwrapped and took it out there, I immediately saw there was no place to hang fathers. Although mother has been gone for such a long time and father is still with us, and I pray will be for many years to come, I felt I didn't want to put up one without the other."

Jane Anne stepped nearer to where Eliza sat and took her seat on the edge of the bed beside her, saying, "What was Grandmother Anne like, Mother? She was so beautiful."

Eliza brought her gaze from the stack of portraits and settled it on her daughter, replying, after a few brief seconds, "An awfully lot like you, darling, though you resemble your Grandmother Jane Heyward more in looks, but you're every much as beautiful as my mother was and without question she was lovely. Luke says you don't only look like his mother but have her personality, too. Still, I think you have a lot of my own mother in you. What was she like? Well, she was very composed and self-controlled with a stately carriage, but these traits were affected with such warmth and serenity that everything seemed to radiate in a more peaceful light when she was near, something like your step-grandmother Amy and yourself. She had excellent taste in her personal dress. I cannot recall ever seeing her, that she was not attractively groomed."

"Sometimes, Mother, when I think about it, I find it sorta strange though that Grandfather married her sister."

"You wouldn't, dear, had you seen his loneliness as I did. I think he mourned my mother every day until he did marry Aunt Amy."

"Which of the two sisters, Mother, do you suppose he has loved the more?"

"Well, speaking of something out of the ordinary!" Eliza said, a frown arching her brows. "What on earth made you think of that?" Her gaze drifted back to the portraits, obviously thoughtful. "Come to think of it, I've never given that any thought. I guess the reason, is because Father and Mother seemed to have such a happy marriage. He adored my mother. I'll never forget her sudden death that day in New Orleans. Father was totally devastated by it. In answer to your question, all I know is, my father would adore any woman who became his wife. That's the way he is. I don't think it's a question of loving one more than the other. It's a matter of him giving his wife his complete devotion which he did give my mother and now is giving to Aunt Amy" Eliza paused and then went on to add rather headedly, her eyes still set on the far wall, "He's not like some men. No matter how much some pretend to love their wife that still doesn't stop them from desiring some other woman and even taking her if they can!" She swiftly brought her eyes back to her daughter. "How did I become involved in such a ridiculous subject, anyhow? Scoot now and let's get these beds made." She sprang to her feet and endeavoring to conceal the flush that she felt on her face she quickly bent over and began to straighten the bed covers.

Smiling at her mother, Jane Anne got up from the bed, but she did not hurry away, she hesitated and said, "Mother, there's no cause to blush, I know about the birds and the bees!"

Still somewhat flustered by where the conversation had carried her mind to, Eliza straightened up and with her hands on her hips said, a little sharpness edging her voice, "Well, I should think so, and all the more, too, why your father and I expect you to conduct yourself in the proper manner, young lady."

"The proper manner?" Questioned Jane Anne, as she wondered how she could improve on her behavior.

"Now, don't start probing, Jane Anne, not on that subject, you know good and well what I mean."

"No, not quite, mother," insisted Jane Anne.

"Not quite? Well, I thought you just said—" Eliza stopped, scrutinizing Jane Anne for a moment. Perhaps it might be best if she did go into the subject a little more deeply with this virtuous, timid daughter. "Never mind, now you listen and listen carefully," she began once more, endeavoring to lose the sharpness in her voice. "In courting, the girl always sets the pace. Men are made up of a different nature than women. As a rule, a man will go as far as a woman will allow and that means, if she's too free and easy in her behavior, there's no restraining the man once things reach a certain point. It's a must, a girl be on her guard against that sort of thing."

Eliza had told her daughter a lot in this brief lecture yet, she had told her nothing. Unlike Martha, Eliza and Luke both had discouraged this only daughter of theirs from courting too soon. Thus, Jane Anne's social life had been kept at the minimum—mostly in a crowd. Seldom had she been paired with a boy alone and then there had been no physical attraction involved, only a harmonious feeling of friendship and high regard on the part of both. Therefore, Jane Anne simply could not comprehend why it was a must she be on her guard since, so far, nothing had occurred to guard against, relative to her or the boy involved.

Completely baffled over this vague side of human nature that her mother had endeavored to enlighten her to but had only confused her, Jane Anne, further questioned "On her guard? I don't think I'm following you very well, Mother."

"Well, for heaven's sakes, Jane Anne," declared Eliza once more in exasperation, "I don't know how else to explain it—" she paused again, her weighty subject sending one of her hands to her head for it to rest against in her moment of trial. Finally, after a long taxing moment, she decided that it might be better if she abandoned the sex subject altogether, suddenly going on to tell Jane Anne, as she let her hand fall back down to her hip, "Besides, I don't like discussing things of that nature, no how. Now, scram, young lady, and get your room tidied up, if you still want to go riding this morning. It's getting on up in the day. But you remember what I've told you. I repeat when it comes to courting, your father and I expect you to always be in control of the situation and conduct yourself most properly." She abruptly turned back to the bed and once again started the task of getting it made up, indicating that she was indeed closing the subject of sex then and there.

Deeply disappointed, Jane Anne said, "of course, Mother, and turned away to her own task, feeling as though her mother had put a blindfold on her when she was already in a dark room. It was true, she did know about the birds and the bees but only to the extent that they did mate and that was all. Having sighted the mating of the farm animals many times, Jane Anne had ever looked on it as an ordinary run of things between male and female in order to produce their offspring and nothing more. Never had she dreamed that a need or want was also involved in the act that the fulfilling of a biological physical urge was also being assuaged at the time, too. And, when it came to the humanistic side of the picture, Jane Anne's vision of imagination in what occurred was so dense that it was left short of being ridiculous.

However, as fate should work it, it was to be only a few hours from then before some of the mystery that shrouded her mother's lecture began to come in focus to Jane Anne, anyway, despite Eliza's timidity at discussing the sex subject with her daughter. Since Jane Anne was a highly sensitive and deep-thinking young woman when she put her mind to the task, it had only taken that first awakening physical response that had run the length of her whole body upon sighting Stuart Drakston—actually having prickled and lingered somewhat in certain nerve cores to let her see to some degree into the meaning of what her mother had tried to convey to her but unfortunately had merely stirred and brushed over.

And now, as she gazed back into Stuarts Drakston's eyes, hearing his chivalrous reply to her getting and taking in his handsome looks, feeling another delicious thrill much more violent than the first coursing itself through her again—one that to her astonishment made her yearn to go into his arms and feel his mouth upon hers, a whole new light was suddenly thrown on the birds and bees business. And, sensing, too, that Stuart Drakston was also yearning to do precisely what she found herself desiring of him, her mother's words finally made an impact, in that, she instantly saw how vulnerable man and woman were to this dark side of human nature that a mere few hours earlier had been such a deep mystery but now appeared to be something no less than awe inspiring to her.

Though it was a moment she could have held forever and not let go of or changed not one single thing about it, unless their meeting again might have taken place in private where she was certain had that been the case Stuart Drakston would have taken her in his arms and was just as certain she would not have resisted, Jane Anne—not forgetting proprieties—took it upon herself to break this captivating moment that had her gaze so firmly planted to that of Stuart Drakston's, she had not forgotten her father's presence as Stuart seemed to have done, although her father did appear to be giving his attention more too Fancy than anything else.

Even so, there was not the least doubt in Jane Anne's mind that Luke Heyward was plenty aware of all the ogling that was going on— no doubt thinking that she and Stuart were certainly holding their moment of greeting for an unusually long time. Thus, somewhat timorous, she turned from Stuart to her father and said, "What's wrong with Fancy, Papa? She looks so droopy and lifeless, not like herself at all."

"I'm not certain, dear, just yet," said Luke as he stepped three or four paces away from where they all stood, stopping to peer at Fancy from a side view. He walked to the other side of the mare and made the same observation. Then, he walked several more paces away from Fancy and scrutinized her from a straight direct angle, went on to inquire of Stuart, "you say she jumped that back corral at Drakston Hall about three weeks ago?"

With his eyes still lingering more on Jane Anne than the ailing mare or the actions of Luke Heyward, Stuart brought his head up fast, replying, "That's the report form Josh, Mr. Heyward." Stepping back to where Fancy continued to stand perfectly motionless in her phlegmatic state, Luke took his hand and tenderly examined the area just above the mare's breastbone, which caused her to tremble and shift her position somewhat.

"I'm not sure, or I should say as sure as I'd like to be, but I think her trouble lies right here," Luke finally said, "In this cavity here above her breastbone! She's so fleshy and has such a long coat, it's difficult to tell, but to me, this area looks puffed out more than what's normal. I think there's something there. You see how tender the place is by her sudden change of behavior."

"Then, you're going to operate, aren't you Papa?" Jane Anne said as she stepped closer and began to stroke Fancy on the head. Typical of Jane Anne, something else had suddenly become more important than those enlightening thrills that were still creeping over her each time those corner glances that she and Stuart Drakston were continuing to steal toward the other came together.

"That depends, dear, on what I find when I get some of that hair cut off and sheared away. Her languor gives every indication of being feverish, possibly caused by infection from an injury she received when she jumped that high fence, maybe even an abscess, if that swelling above her breastbone tells me anything. Stuart, would you lead her on over there to that first fence post where it's shady and tether her closely to it while I get my things from the barn. I won't be too long. I keep everything I usually need handy and ready," Luke said, as he quickly turned away, hurrying toward the barn with the aged jailor—tongue lolling—straggling along beside him.

"Certainly, Mr. Heyward and if I can help you with something else, don't hesitate to holler," Stuart called out to Luke's back.

Luke turned his head and hollered back, "I won't", striding on toward the barn.

Though Stuart began to carry out Luke's instructions immediately, he also began to take advantage of every single second of his absence as well to pay court to his grownup daughter by inquiring of her, as she continued to stay close beside the mare and stroke her on the head, "Are you all prepared for the box supper tonight, Jane Anne?"

A box supper was one social that always brought an air of excitement to the neighborhood—the one event that lured the whole community, young and old alike, to come happily flocking together. The main draw of the occasion was due to the surprises and, sometimes disappointments too, that it furnished. This was owing to the fact that the women or as for that matter, neither the men, never knew who they were going to end up eating supper with. The colorful, decorated boxes which were individually prepared and stacked full of delicious edibles by the women and which were to be auctioned off and purchased by the men bore no outside identification. It was only when the man opened his purchased box and saw a name inside that he knew who he was going to be sharing the box with for supper. Thus, there were a lot of laughs, surprises, and dashed hopes, too. But any letdowns were taken in a good-natured spirit and everybody, as a rule, had a delightful evening.

Overjoyed that Stuart was obviously interested as ever in low country box suppers despite all that worldly wisdom he had acquired, not to mention London's more sophisticated entertainments which he had been exposed to all those years, Jane Anne smiled and questioned back, "you mean you've already heard about that?" From the moment she had sighted him, she had hoped that he had heard and would mention it.

"Yes, I have," he said, "that was one of the first things I did hear about. Grandfather Carson told me about its last night. I do gather that you'll be there?"

"Oh, yes," she happily assured her heart giving a sudden flutter, "we all will. Papa's to auction off the boxes."

"Mind telling me what color of paper yours will be wrapped in or some other definite clue?" He asked, his pleasing smile growing wider while his eyes met hers in a merry glow.

Though his suggestion delighted her, she blushingly demurred, "I can't do that, Stuart. It wouldn't be fair to the others, you know."

"Regarding your lovely charm, I couldn't agree more," he was quick to compliment his gladsome features set most attentive on her face. "But I was hoping you'd take pity on me since I've been deprived of your company for such a long time."

His gallant appeal was playing hard on her resistance, causing her to truthfully confess, "I'd really like to, Stuart, but I feel I shouldn't break the rules."

"But, no one would know but us," he pressed, in a more serious and anxious manner now because their privacy would be gone shortly. He had seen Luke emerging from the barn with his medical supplies.

She still demurred, lowering her eyes from his face. But finally, his debonair air had broken her down in spite of some guilt that was working its way to her conscience. "I suppose not—" she said but paused as she lifted her eyes back to his. She saw that she had resisted his plea a little too long. Her father was too near them to go any further with it, and the disappointment on Stuart's face did not escape her attention, either.

"That's fine, Stuart," Luke was saying, as he came on with his supplies and set them down on the ground near the ailing mare. "Stand right there where you are and keep your hands ready to grab her bridle in case she gets in a bucking mood, and, dear, you keep to this side of her where you can easily reach these supplies for me and also be more safe from those front feet of hers if she does begin to put up a fight."

Among the things that Luke had brought back stacked in a large dishpan—Luke being ever staunch when it came to cleanliness regardless of what it involved always kept these supplies thoroughly sterilized and wrapped in clean cloths, were shears, pliers, scissors, a knife with a fairly long blade that was kept razor-sharp, some cotton and a few clean rags, and two antiseptic powders, Sulphur and a white antiseptic which contained boric acid among some other lesser compounds.

While Stuart made an effort to heed Luke's instructions and become more mindful of what was taking place at the moment rather than fretting over his failure to find out the identity to the supper box which Jane Anne had prepared, and Jane Anne took her place as her father had advised—both looking on—Luke, hurriedly reaching for the shears first, was now addressing his next words to the mare, saying, "Fancy girl, I'm going to mark up your pretty coat quite a bit but, in time, it'll be back as attractive as ever. Now, you bear with me and this shouldn't take long."

As Luke was hoping, Fancy put up little protest. She was plenty used to shears and currycombs, too. Even so, as her long chest hair began to fall under his feet, he was soon to see that her condition would have justified her shifting her feet a little more than what she had suddenly started to do once again when his shears made direct contact with the edema that he had been certain about and which he could now see was puffed out more than he had realized because of its location and the mare's long, thick coat.

Luke stopped shearing, saying to the mare again, "Stay girl," as he peered closer at the swollen mass, noting that it was a deep angry looking red in the center where something had obviously struck her leaving a long and ugly jagged mark, though the torn flesh had knitted back together. "Just as I thought," he went on saying, "It's a bad injury that's turned into an abscess. There's no doubt a big splinter on one of those boards had to do this." He palpated the edema slightly with a fingertip, suddenly dropping the shears upon the ground and asking Jane Anne to hand him the knife.

With Stuart holding fast to Fancy's bridle and Jane Anne, too, making an all-out effort to keep the mare as calm as possible by continuing to stroke her on her side and keep up a flow of soothing words to her, Luke eased the tip end of the knife's blade into the center of the inflamed mark and when he did the swollen mass burst instantly with a gush of blood and pus spurting everywhere. And, at the same time, something else was startlingly noticeable also. Fancy had quieted the shifting of her feet altogether.

The infection was running out in such a heavy stream that Luke grabbed the dishpan and tumbling the rest of the supplies out on the ground, held it up close against Fancy's chest so as to keep the fulsome mess contained as best he could form streaming over the mare and everywhere else, too.

When the flow of infection had slacked-off somewhat, Luke said, "Here, dear, would you keep the pan in place, I want to get as much of that infection out of there as possible." And, as Stuart Drakston stood and marveled at the way Jane Anne took the dishpan, which was over one third full of the reeking matter, and never flinched once in doing what her father had asked of her, Luke took his fingertips and slightly palpated the huge abscess once again, causing more infection to flow out.

The fact was, Jane Anne's matter of fact manner, regarding her fulsome task, was suddenly making Stuart a little self-conscious and especially now since Fancy did not require his hands restraining her by the bridle. Thus, in spite of the squeamishness that was already gathering in his stomach, he heard himself saying, "Jane Anne, I'll hold the pan if you'd like," because being Stuart, he thought a gentleman would offer to do no less.

Even so, Stuart was greatly relieved to hear Jane Anne tell him as she looked up and met his eyes again, "Oh no, Stuart, you'd surely soil your white linen shirt, but thanks anyway. It doesn't matter about these old clothes I have on."

However, despite her declining his considerateness—something that had impressed her further with him, Stuart was suddenly busying his hands anyway for Luke was exclaiming, "Good Lord! It was a splinter and it's still in there. Quick, somebody hand me the pliers!"

None of the three people—yes, Luke included—could hardly believe the size of the splinter that Luke was quick to seize with the pliers and pull from the ulcerated flesh. It looked to be near two inches wide and over six inches long. Of course, the imbedded splinter had left an ugly gaping hole and, for a few tense seconds, Luke was not so sure he had done the right thing fearful that he had done the mare more harm than he had good by removing the splinter at all; because, from the looks of things, it appeared as though his cure was going to do as much damage as the kill, so to speak.

But then, an amazing thing happened, or it was no less than that to the three people who had their eyes fastened on the mare. Notwithstanding the poisonous load of wood that she had carried around for over three weeks, in addition to all the trial and shock she had just undergone treatment that certainly so far had not been of much benefit when it came to the question of appearance, Fancy suddenly seemed to do a complete about-face. No longer did her head hang in that seemingly dreamy state. It came up to its normal lofty high in a flash of spirit that bore a lot of resemblance to that haughty air which she was noted for. And, on top of that, her long, bushy tail lifted from its flagged state, too, and suddenly swept up over her back like a beautiful spreading fan.

"Oh, look! Papa!" Cried Jane Anne, as she still stood holding the dishpan as likewise with her father continuing to hold the pliers with the splinter while Stuart just stood silent through all of it and gaped in wonder, "She's going to be all right!"

"I think you're right, kitten!" Luke exclaimed, springing back in action now that the mare's sudden change of behavior had buoyed him to say nothing of his daughter's added optimism. "But I must admit I was beginning to have my doubts." He threw the pliers with the decayed contents aside and grabbed up some cotton, one or two rags, and the antiseptic. Then, while Stuart held Fancy by the bridle again and Jane Anne helped him with the drying up of the poisonous mucus and applying the medicine—thoroughly knowledgeable with her father's order of treatment Jane Anne had already set the dishpan with the nasty infection aside, Luke continued to say as he worked, "It's a good thing the infection formed around the splinter and stayed out of her bloodstream, or I fear Whit would've been looking for another riding horse when he comes home again. You've heard the expression, 'enough to kill a horse.' Well, in this case, that splinter could've very well done that had things not progressed along as they did. And, I'm not so sure that the infection wouldn't have killed her anyway had it stayed here in her chest cavity a few more days."

"Do you think the abscess would've finally burst on its own, Mr. Heyward?" Asked Stuart.

"That's hard to say, Stuart, it may have. Still, at that point, she'd no doubt been at the critical stage then. The infection's taken its toll on her as it is. Listen, why not leave her here for a few days? I'll need to apply this medicine fairly often for the first few days anyway. You can come back after her when she's started healing some. Right now, I don't think she's up to tracking all that distance back to Drakston Hall."

"Sure, Mr. Heyward, whatever you think is best," agreed Stuart.

"Well then, that does it for now. Dear, you may go on inside if you wish, you've been a great help to me and you, too, Stuart. Let me gather up these things and we'll take her on inside the stables. I'll only be a jiffy. I'll take care of that mess later. I want to bury it in a hole somewhere," Luke said, indicating the dishpan by looking at it and giving a revolted shrug as he began to pick up his other supplies, adding when his hand reached the pliers, "but, I think I'll keep this splinter as a memento."

"I was glad to help Papa." Jane Anne hastily put in to her father's back, and to Stuart's surprise and delight too, took full advantage of the moment by stepping closer to him and whispering, "It's blue with a yellow bow," going on to call out as she turned rapidly on her heels toward the house, "Again, welcome home, Stuart, and give my regards to your mother."

"Thanks, Jane Anne, I'll be sure to," Stuart hollered back, elated at how things seemed to be going on his first day home. Moreover, it looked as though that box supper was going to make for lighter news when he did pen that letter to Whit. Yes, indeed, he thought again when he suddenly saw Jane Anne—gliding gracefully on across the lane and on toward the little grey house that she was born in, look back over her shoulder and give him a rather meek but lovable little wave. He managed to return it before Luke, now having gathered up everything but the dishpan, turned and said, "Come on, and I'll show you what stall to put her in."

Later, in recounting the experience with Matthew, Stuart added, "And, Grandfather Carson, you should've been there and seen how Jane Anne pitched right in and helped. I can't get over it. Most girls would've run the other way or either swooned over in a faint." He left his own squeamishness out of the subject.

Matthew smiled, "I know, but not my granddaughter. She's a remarkable young woman in more ways than one."

"I must say she is," said Stuart. "But, why didn't you tell me, Grandfather Carson, well sorta prepare me?"

"Prepare you? For what, pray tell," asked Matthew, arching his brows. Somewhere along the line he had lost this young man!"

"That she's so grown up and beautiful. I hardly recognized her." Stuart told him.

"Oh, that," said Matthew, suddenly amused and relieved, too, that he hadn't lost Stuart through any failing of his own.

Trying to keep a straight face, he went on, "Well, to be honest, I would have, had I known it was going to be so important to you."

Stuarts head came around fast to meet Matthew Carson's twinkling stare and, all of a sudden, step grandfather and step grandson burst out laughing together.

Matthew and Stuart's conversation had taken place in the stable yard. Matthew happened to be there, talking with Josh about Fancy, when Stuart had rode in from Green Sea without her. After learning that Fancy had indeed not become food for worms since he had last seen her something that was bothering Josh quite a lot because deep in his heart he knew he had not been as observant of the mare as he should have been, Josh had taken Stuart's mount and long disappeared, leaving the two men alone with their conversation.

Now, with the echo of their laughter falling upon the stillness of the June afternoon, they started moving on towards the mansion together, with Stuart bringing up another subject that was to make Matthew ponder if his gist to Stuart, a moment earlier, had not had a more firmer foundation than what he had taken into consideration at the time he had been making it.

His laughter having subsided altogether at this point, Stuart was saying, "Grandfather Carson, I came to a final decision about an important matter on my way home from Green Sea a while ago."

"You did?" Asked Matthew, cocking an attentive glance in Stuart's direction. "Care to share it?"

"Not at all," replied Stuart, "because I think it's not only something you and grandmother will approve of, or at least I hope so, but something I'm sure that'll make mother very happy also."

Well, come on out with it. I've never liked suspense in any degree."

Stuart laughed. "All right. You see that west wing on the mansion there?" Matthew looked up. "Yes, what about it?"

"Well that's going to become my law office, Grandfather Carson. Actually, the idea popped in my head this morning while I was strolling over the ground. Then, coming home from Green Sea, I got to thinking a lot about the future and concluded for certain that's what I want to do. I'm going to make Drakston Hall the permanent base for everything that concerns my life from here on out. Aside from taking a vacation every now and then, I don't plan on leaving here anymore. I want to do all my work here, live with the wife of my choice here and raise our children here. The west wing will no longer be in use since school has been terminated for good. I see no reason why I couldn't use the space for my law practice instead of renting some building in Charleston where I'd be forced to travel back and forth each workday in all kinds of weather. There's plenty of space here. My clients will be able to come and go without causing any irregularity in the family's living pattern, just as it was with the school Besides, when I'm not busy with clients or working on some case, that'll give me more time to help you shoulder some of the load you've been carrying for too long now. What do you think about it?" Stuart finally asked, halting his steps.

Matthew stopped too, taking in the serious anxiousness reflected on Stuart's face as he told him, "I think my granddaughter isn't the only remarkable young member of this family. You're wise and remarkable as well, and I feel blessed and much honored to be able to share things of this nature with you. Let me say again, welcome home, Stuart Drakston!" and with that said, Matthew extended him a strong hand.

Be that as it may, Stuart Drakston was soon to sense—much to his letdown—that Eliza Heyward was not going to be singing one single word of praise in his behalf, let alone paying him the laudatory compliment her father had paid him, no matter how many doctorate degrees he was the holder of, any other accomplishments he may achieve, wise decisions he may make and carry out, or anything else he did worthy of a lauding word or nod. His hope that she had changed her attitude, relating to her obvious discomfort over his being in Jane Anne's company, was to fall despairingly low no later than that very same night at the box supper social.

Still overwhelmed in thrilling wonder by his first sight of the grown-up Jane Anne, and the memory of her friendly little wave tucked secretly in his heart, Stuart, accompanied by Matthew, Amy, and his mother, could not have set out for the church social in a gayer mood. Even so, before the evening's social function had hardly gotten underway, a good portion of this cheer had already taken leave of him, though others were not aware of it because he strove not to let it show and did manage to carry the evening off rather well despite his disappointment.

It had all started during the auctioning of the colorful array of supper boxes which had begun as soon as Marsh Reed concluded the last word of the short church service. Yes, there were times when the Reverend Marsh Reed did allow his stomach to overrule his head no matter how devout his intentions were in going a little further with the Lord's words, and especially in a case such as this where so many pretty supper boxes were displayed just below the pulpit—boxes that he knew were loaded to the brim with all kinds of tasty edibles— delicacies that the Reverend could literally vision and taste through their crepe paper wrappings. At any rate, when Luke came to his daughter's pretty, blue box with its yellow bow and held it up asking for an opening bid, which Stuart was promptly to make, and a fervent contest for the box was to begin between him and Bill Cooper—over many loud shouts, laughs, and smiling nods from the majority present encouraging them on, Stuart's crushing blow came when he turned his head and happened to see Eliza Heyward' s cold expression directed straight at him. So uncordial was her fixed stare in all that sea of smiles that surrounded her, Stuart knew there could be no mistaking of Eliza Heyward's disapproval, and to make matters worse as far as Stuart was concerned, was the fact that he was not getting as much out of the contest as he pretended he was, anyway, for the reason that he was not the type to flaunt his family's wealth.

The fact was, though Eliza's cold expression had taken the wind out of his sails and chilled the evening for him, Stuart shared her viewpoint to a certain degree, understanding why she would disapprove of the over average bidding for the supper box. In no circumstance had Stuart ever flaunted the Drakston dollars and never once regarding this event had he thought he would become involved in a situation that would even hint at his family's wealthy position let alone publicize it so boldly, or at least Stuart felt as though he was doing just that. However, for all his shriveling over what he was doing, since Stuart knew the supper box did indeed belong to Jane Anne, he was determined he would not give in and allow Bill Cooper to walk away with it, if he was forced to stand there and exhibit the weight of his wallet all evening long.

Moreover, if all that was not enough to daunt the occasion for Stuart, knowledge that Bill Cooper did not give one total damn who the supper box belonged to one way or another and actually had no wish to purchase it for any amount—low or high—was certainly another added dissatisfaction and enough to rub the best of natures. Stuart knew Bill Cooper—the Coopers had equal dollars to flaunt thanks to the late Frank Drakston—was running the bidding way out of line just for the hell of it.

Finally, when the rival bidding between the two had reached the point that it had carried the price of the supper box to a ridiculous amount, Bill Cooper, his grin spreading from ear-to-ear, shouted, "I yield the battle, Stuart, the box is yours! I hope it's full of cracklings or pickled pig's feet, because if that's the case, we've surely run the price of hogs up for this year's market!" And, Luke, not even taking time to draw a long breath he was so relieved they had called it quits was instantly following the rules of the auction and bellowing out, though he felt like a fool for doing so when the average price for the boxes seldom exceeded four dollars, "Do I hear a higher bid, gentlemen? Fifty-five dollars once, fifty-five dollars twice, fifty-five dollars three times! Sold to Stuart Drakston!"

By this time, aside from the one or two slight cackles that Bill Cooper's just had drawn out, all encouraging jeers has ceased, turning to silent astonishment over Stuart Drakston paying out fifty-five dollars for a lone supper box, for the entire pile of boxes had not been expected to sell for much more than that amount.

Stuart was no less astonished, and he was embarrassed, too, over the way things had gone. He felt that Eliza Heyward had a lot of company now in her obvious dislike of him, feeling that everyone was looking on him as being no less than a pompous ass. But, still trying to be a good sport on the outside even if he didn't feel like much on the inside, he promptly waved Bill Cooper aside and with his own grin firmly planted on, he strode forward in the midst of the quietness and taking out his wallet he counted out fifty-five dollars—every dollar that he had on him as ironical as it was—and claimed his purchase from no other than Matthew, who was handling that part of the proceedings and the one person there who Stuart felt knew he was pretending his gleeful manner. The message had been clear in his stepfather's handshake.

All the same; however, Stuart felt that he and he alone had shattered the whole affair by being aware that the blue and yellow box had belonged to Jane Anne. Since she had told him, he had felt compelled to continue on bidding against Bill Cooper. He was not down over the money he had paid out, by no means. Besides being more than glad that he was able to contribute fifty-five dollars towards the farmer's needs, he would have gladly paid out even more to have the pleasure of sharing the supper box with Jane Anne and enjoying her company—the way he had come to feel about her in this short time. What he was down over, most of all, was the fact that he knew he had—along with Bill Cooper's help of course—put the other men present in an awkward situation regarding the purchasing of the remaining supper boxes.

But, at last, the last box had been auctioned off and Stuart was feeling a lot easier as he was making his way through the crowd to seek his supper partner, even if he did feel that on top of everything else he had caused several women present to start wearing a sour face—not because he had paid out fifty-five dollars for Jane Anne Heyward's supper box he was certain, but because their partners had not shelled out fifty-five dollars, too, for the pleasure of their food and company!

Nonetheless, Stuart saw that despite the sour face it was beginning to be a busy time with the couples pairing up together and selecting some place where they could partake of the picnic style supper— picked at random amid the church pews, noting in some cases they had already settled down and started eating in a lively, harmonious accord together. Apparently, nothing like a new face and the novelty of hearing someone else's chatter for a change, Stuart thought and took another brighter view of the situation.

Even so, it was not an easy thing with Stuart to be going in the seeking of his own supper partner, because Jane Anne was seated right beside her mother who Stuart observed was still wearing her same expression of displeasure, bringing him to start wondering if it was his behavior regarding the auction that she disfavored so much or simply himself in general. But, gathering all the tact that one was capable of gathering, Stuart proceeded on and after addressing Eliza Heyward in the most unobtrusively and decorous manner possible, he then smilingly told Jane Anne that he believed he had come by the honor of having her company for supper and offered her his arm. At the same instant, Doctor Seth Roalf came bounding through the crowd in search of Eliza to claim her for his supper partner, with both she and Jane Anne accepting the invitations most graciously. Forthwith, in their endeavor to find someplace where they could eat, the two couples were to part company and go their separate way—something else that brought another fraction of east to Stuart.

Desiring a place that was about as inconspicuous as he could find in a public gathering without making it appear as if he wanted to hide, Stuart, in pursuance of his wish, was having a rather busy moment casting his eyes about the crowded church. He was becoming down again and was almost to the point of giving up and flopping down most any place when he spotted just what he was looking for—the vacant end of one of the church benches over near the outside wall. Hoping some other couple had not spotted it, too, and were on their way to take possession of it, Stuart swiftly glided Jane Anne in that direction and presently they were seating themselves.

A window nearby was giving them a full glow of a new moon rising. They both had taken notice of it as they had taken their seats and placed the supper box on the bench between them, though neither made mention of it. All the same, both were plenty aware of the embodying romanticism it was adding to the moment and their near sequestered spot.

All cheer now, Stuart undone the box's crepe paper wrappings and lifted off the lid, exclaiming, "Fried chicken, and my favorite cake and pie both! How lucky can I get?"

Jane Anne smiled, "It isn't all luck, Stuart. You see, they're all my favorites, too!" They both laughed and while Stuart reached inside and handed her one of the two white linen napkins that she thoughtfully placed with the food, she told him, her laughter subsiding to all seriousness, "Stuart, I hate so much that things have gone the way they have, and on your first day home at that. I feel most of it is all my fault, too. Had I not told you the colors of this box, you wouldn't have felt compelled to have kept on bidding against Bill Cooper's exorbitant bids. I'm so sorry you were forced to pay such an unreasonable amount for hardly nothing."

So, she saw, too, that he had not planned on becoming the bigwig of the doings and had derived no pleasure from it. "Nothing," he echoed, taking the liberty of laying his hand upon hers. "Listen, dear, don't give another thought to that. Bill had his fun, and I'm sure our new neighbor will put the money to good use. I'm grateful I was able to help out. Besides, to me, it's worth every penny I paid to have the pleasure of sitting here with you tonight. You know, I've been gone a long time." He smiled. "And, who says fried chicken, apple pie and chocolate cake are hardly nothing? Not Stuart Drakston. Now, let's eat and while we do, I want you to fill me in on everything that's happened since I've been away."

"That's a big order, Stuart," she said, her pretty smile coming in view again, "but I'll try."

As Jane Anne began to talk in that whispery—throated voice of hers—bringing Stuart up to date with happenings that had mostly occurred among the younger set, while the glow of moonlight shining through the window helped in lighting the rarity of her attractive features, it was no hard matter at all for him to forget everything outside of what he was seeing and hearing at the moment.

The certainty that he was still far from standing in Eliza Heyward's good graces and had indeed, on this very occasion, pushed himself farther into that dark comer where apparently she viewed hm, seemed to matter less and less to him each minute he stayed in the company of her daughter. In fact, the softness of Jane Anne's voice and her natural simplicity had so enraptured Stuart that he had become completely relaxed, forgetting about Jane Anne's mother's coldness and the whole affair. Even when the social had broken up and he and Jane Anne had rejoined her and escorted Jane Anne to the Heyward coach as if there was no chill on Eliza's part nor had ever been. The truth was, he was seeing nothing save what he wanted to see and feeling nothing save what he wanted to feel—his sense awakened to only his joyful gladness in seeing Jane Anne Heyward's face light up every time she looked at him.

The Turbulence and the Struggle

It was only when Stuart, surrounded by his own family, was inside his own coach and well on his way back towards Drakston Hall that he emerged enough from his charm-struck state to rationalize some the facts. Looking back on the events of the evening, he saw there was no question of his having—once again—gotten off to a bad start with Eliza Heyward. Musing over it as the carriage bumped along over the clay-hardened ruts in the late spring night, he finally concluded that regardless of how much he had enjoyed Jane Anne's company, it might be better—for all concerned—if he kept a low profile for a while. It had been plain to him on this day that Jane Anne was unusually close to her parents and her brother, too, and also their sheltering of her was an undeniable fact; therefore, making it a must that he not rush things. Besides, that would not be the honorable way, anyhow, Stuart was telling himself, even if he had had to restrain himself in keeping his arms glued to his sides when he had said good night to Jane Anne!

But, how long should he wait? That was the important question. He wanted to go rushing right back to Green Sea tomorrow but since that was out—when? One week? Two weeks? The week following? Well, one thing for sure, it appeared if he sought the company of Jane Anne Heyward in the way that his better judgement was guiding him, it most assuredly was going to be a difficult way.

Having become fairly disarmed by his vexed question, Stuart sighed and settled further down in the soft-cushioned seat with his problem, unaware that those who rode along with him were keenly cognizant to his mood—especially Elizabeth. But since she never intruded upon her son's thoughts unless invited to do so she kept silent. Though his unusually long silence and obvious restlessness this time had made her a little more eager than normal to know what had brought it all about. Elizabeth had attached no real significance to the staggering amount that Stuart had paid for the supper box. She looked on it as having been an unplanned sort of devilish confrontation between friends and nothing more, never dreaming there had been more to it than that on Stuart's part.

At any rate, as Stuart continued to mull over the fact that he was not going to be seeing much of Jane Anne Heyward, at any given time, if his instincts regarding how to deal with Jane Anne's mother's behavior were on the right track, he fell back to reviewing the day's events and that first unbelievable moment of seeing the mature Jane

171

Anne. And, suddenly, the impact of realizing he did not have to ransack his mind another second as when he should call to Green Sea again, brought him fidgeting to the edge of the seat once more in anticipation. Fancy! What better excuse could he have for going right back to Green Sea tomorrow, the next day, and the next day, too, as far as that went! Yes, first thing in the morning, he would be bound for Green Sea on General and Eliza Heyward shouldn't be none the wiser to the real reason for his frequent calling there. Though he truly did hope that Whit's mare would recover! Still, he must not forget that being granted the best of excuses for going back to Green Sea so soon, would be a guarantee that he would see Jane Anne. And further, if he were going to guard his intentions and keep everything on the quiet as his mind was telling him to do, when in the world would he ever have the opportunity to be alone with Jane Anne—really alone—just the two of them as if they were courting? That was the big question and one that appeared to be about hopeless as far as materializing any time soon.

Discouraged again, Stuart resettled himself in the seat once more while his mother watched and remained to wonder.

On the second Sunday following that week; however, things were to start turning more in Stuart's favor when Jane Anne—upon entering the huge dining room at Drakston Hall—was to exclaim, "Oh, Grandmother Amy, you always set such a lovely table! Your centerpiece of pink roses in that silver dish is simply beautiful!" An innocent remark that was to bring the couple quite a reward.

Jane Anne was there because Matthew had prevailed upon Amy to forget about having a large ball in celebration of Elizabeth's and Stuart's homecoming and hold only a Sunday dinner affair instead for family and a few close friends, since it was such a busy season for most people. Elizabeth and Stuart both had fully agreed with Matthew. Thus, Amy had given in and among those who were present were Mollie and Brent Cooper and their two grown children, Bill and Grace. Martha, Bruce, and Laura. The reverend Marsh Reed, who had always sent a rather eager eye in the way of Elizabeth Drakston and especially since the day she became a widow, though Elizbeth had never encouraged his interest in her nor did it appear that she ever would—the reverend or anyone else as for that matter. Caroline and Doctor Seth, and, of course, the Heyward family.

"Almost as pretty as you are, darling, in that lovely pink voile dress," Jane Anne's step grandmother smilingly replied as she and Matthew, with her on his arm, were proceeding to lead their dinner guests on towards the bountiful, elegantly set table.

"And, I'll second that," Matthew put in, smiling at his granddaughter, too, whose rosy cheeks were suddenly flushing a deeper pink from the attention as she and all the rest—following Martha's lead—were settling in their places. "In fact, I'd be willing to bet that this dinner table has never been graced by lovelier girls and prettier women at any one time. Every last one of you look no less beautiful than a full-blooming rose yourselves in your pretty summer dresses."

"Oh, Uncle Matthew," scoffed Martha flouncing down in her chair, "you're so chivalrous you would include us, too, when you know perfectly well that a rose is the last thing that we older women would come near resembling!"

"I know no such thing," Matthew solemnly declared, but there was no mistaking the roguish look dancing in his eyes. Matthew always got a kick out of Martha's no-nonsense approach to everything.

"Well, you should," she smarted right back, "or at least have put us in that last rose of summer group where we all belong!"

Luke, for another, had never failed to be amused by Martha's straight-shooting tongue, either. Still a lean and handsome man, though his shoulders were a little bent from all the burdens he had carried and the coal-black temples were now mostly white, he threw back his head and giving that same hearty, deep laugh of his, said, "Mr. Carson, though you haven't asked for it, but I'd advise you to change the subject before Martha leads you into water that you'll find difficult to swim out of."

"I agree, Luke," said Bruce. "My wife has just proven once again how unpredictable she is by pursuing a subject that most women would not only never mention let alone drawing people's attention to!"

Everybody laughed.

"Well, I'm going to agree with Matthew though," said Amy, tenderly touching her husband on the arm from where she sat to the right of him. "I think no time of year brings out nature's best like June does and that goes for the roses and all our guests, too, including you, Martha dear, in spite of your inferior view." She looked on down to the opposite end of the table where Marsh Reed was seated and giving him a slight nod went on, "Reverend Reed, would you pay us the honor of saying the blessing?"

173

"Surely, Mrs. Carson," Marsh Reed replied, abruptly hanging his head and letting a long and drawn out prayer spill forth that consisted of naming separately most every person seated at the table, in addition to the butler and also his assistants who were standing nearby, before he finally ended it.

As the servants began to serve the attractive and tasty dishes from the great rosewood Sheraton sideboard, Amy piped in again, "Speaking of the centerpiece, Jane Anne dear, you'd really have to tour the garden to appreciate the roses. I do believe I've never seen lovelier blooms than we have this year. They're all so pretty, I started to mix the bouquet, then on second thought I decided to use only those delicate pinks, and I must agree they do look irresistible."

"They are lovely, Grandmother Amy," Jane Anne said. "I think the pink roses are my favorite anyway. We have some pretty roses in the garden at Green Sea, but I don't believe we have any that particular color."

"No, I'm sure we don't, dear," Eliza said, "but I wish we did. Come to think of it, I guess I'd take the rose first if I were forced to make a choice, next to the violets, of course." She found Luke's eyes across the table and smiled.

"Well, in that case, Eliza dear," said Amy, "you and Jane Anne both must see all of Drakston Hall's lovely roses in their natural state before you take your leave today." And then, to Stuart's amazement and something he could have thrown both his arms around his grandmother for in gratitude, she turned to him where he was seated on her right and sweetly prattled on,

"Stuart dear, after we've finished with dinner and everybody's had time to freshen up a bit, would you see that Jane Anne and all the rest of our younger guests are taken on a tour of the garden. Make sure you show them all the other blooming flowers and shrubs as well as the roses. Actually, it's so pleasant out there, I'd think that all of you would prefer it over the parlor, anyway."

Stuart hastened so in hopes of settling what Amy had so miraculously suggested before any objections might be risen and possibly the whole idea was done away with, that the mouthful of food he had just pushed in his mouth all went down in one gulp, almost choking him and much to his chagrin caused him to only half-croak, "Surely, Grandmother," when he had wanted to say more. But, despite his embarrassment over his guttural, unenthusiastic reply, he could not help letting his eyes find Jane Anne's across the table and could not only have hugged her, too, and Laura and ·Grace as well when they all saved his bad moment by exclaiming in unison, "Oh, We'd love to."

"Well then," Amy blithely continued to babble, "It's settled I suppose, but you girls stick to the shady pathways out of the sun. We wouldn't want those lovely complexions sunburned." Then, she was telling Eliza, "Eliza dear, when it cools off a bit outside, the rest of us will go for our stroll, if you don't mind waiting."

And, once more, Stuart was marveling at how well his grandmother seemed to be handling things when Eliza, wearing an elfish smile much to his relief, looked up from her plate and replied, "Certainly not, Aunt Amy. Regarding me and all your other fading guests, as Martha insisted on grouping us, I think that might be best, anyway!"

Everybody guffawed again but Martha. She saw no amusement in being outsmarted by Eliza. In truth, at age forty-one-years old, Eliza Heyward was still far from looking like a faded out rose, and especially on this day all decked out in her new blue and lavender sprigged summer voile. There was not a grey hair in her head or one that was visible, anyway, and one had to look hard to detect the one or two thin lines her face held. Her figure was still slender and firm; in fact, her waistline had barely expanded more than an inch, if that much. In short, fortunately for her,' her excessive driving energy combined with her genetic make-up which she had inherited from Matthew Carson, had made it rather difficult for the ravages of time to leave what few marks were there. She remained to be a beautiful woman and, when it came to being attractive and holding her own, her Cousin Martha did not lag too many feet behind her—a fact that still contented Bruce Randolph as much as Eliza's beauty contented Luke.

Whether their move was by choice, or whether an intuitive supposition had caused them to think that properness called for no less, or had sensed that Stuart Drakston desired to look at the roses with Jane Anne and ·only Jane Anne—since neither couple had ever paired off together before this day—no sooner than Stuart and his guests entered the garden, Carr and Grace Cooper took off down one pathway and Brent Cooper took Laura by the hand and headed down another, leaving Stuart and Jane Anne standing alone together at last.

Though Stuart had gone back to Green Sea not just one day, two days, or three days in this intervening period since the church social, he had gone back most everyday—making good use of Whit's mare's impairment for calling there in his hopes of seeing more of Jane Anne. Even so, all his journeying there and all his efforts had amounted to no more than passing the time of day with her once or twice. The truth was—most the time—he had not even seen her, let alone be in her company any length of time. Whether, or not his defeat had been incidental or Jane Anne herself had purposely avoided the stables altogether when he was there, or, as for that matter, Eliza Heyward had had a helping hand in his thwarted effort, Stuart had no idea.

In any event, as things had turned out, checking on Fancy and finally bringing her back to her own stable at Drakston Hall in the latter part of this same week, had been the pith of Stuart's entire journeying to Green Sea so far. When it came to any hope he may have held in making contact with Jane Anne, he had hardly been any more successful than had he been journeying to some other neighboring plantation and had come to think that maybe he was going about the whole business in the wrong way. In fact, he had even gone so far as to wonder if he had over exaggerated Eliza Heyward's behavior toward him out of plain fear on his part of confronting her with his honorable intentions toward her daughter; that is, seek her permission to call on Jane Anne. At any rate, outside of managing to sit beside Jane Anne in church on the Sunday following the box supper and again on this Sunday, exchanging a word or two of pleasantries with her, nothing else had materialized.

So, it was no small wonder that Stuart was suddenly feeling as if he were walking on the light perfumed air of the garden instead of the ground—awed at finally finding himself alone with Jane Anne and amid the full-blooming flowers and the deep lush greenery of the garden to boot! He instantly knew the place he desired to take her to in this flower-scented haven and it, most assuredly, was not the rose garden! That one particular spot that had become his refuge lately— that one stone bench among the many which were placed here and there throughout the gardens—that lone bench which in addition to being sheltered by a giant red oak with trailing wisteria vines growing through its branches and the soothing sound of a fountain nearby playing on lily pads, was also near hidden from all view by the crape myrtle and mimosa trees, that crowded the area around it, with their red and purple and pink blooms hanging in profusion.

Several times in the past few days, Stuart had sought the place out—going there to mediate in hopes of gaining some insight into the matter of that disaccord that ever seemed to hang between himself and Eliza Heyward—questioning himself over and over as to why this disharmony was there in the first place and why he was unable to break through her aloofness towards him. And, even though his peaceful sanctuary had provided him with not one degree of understanding this complex problem dealing with Eliza Heyward, in no way did this stop him from yearning to have a few minutes of privacy in the very same spot with her daughter.

But first, being Stuart, he had no wish to rush Jane Anne and especially until he had some idea how she felt about him. In short, he wanted first to make sure that those impression she had been carrying of her behavior towards him were true and sound and not just some foolish fantasy on his part, there because he had allowed his imagination to see something that was not there because he desired it no other way.

Now, having made certain that the others were well out of earshot and with his smile belying his fearfulness of how she may respond, Stuart waited no longer, plunging headlong into the matter, "It's seemed like months to me since we shared supper the other night at church. I've been wondering if you could possibly feel the same way."

Shyly, averting Stuart's gaze, Jane Anne looked down at her hands which she had crossed together somewhat primly in front of her. But, nonetheless, if Stuart's grandmother had awed him earlier with her suggestions, Jane Anne—true to her nature, rendered him almost speechless by telling him, "I don't think you've been out of my thoughts hardly a moment since then."

Though her reply had been far more than what he had expected, actually near taking his breath, Stuart's feet had no trouble gaining Jane Anne's side. Nor did his hands meet with any clumsiness, either. Still, while one instantly covered hers and his other found its way around her slender waist, he did have some difficulty in trying to come up with a fitting reply—words that would match hers in all their sincerity without sounding as though they were being spoken with a continental sleekness.

All the same, he didn't linger too long, presently telling her, "I was praying you'd say something like that," and now having heard even more than what he had hoped for, he went on to add, his smile now widening in gladness, "Since most the roses are on further down toward the road, do you mind if I first show you another spot out here that I've grown most fond of, lately?"

"N—o—o, I suppose not," she said, looking up at him with a rather searching expression, and then going on to inquire, as she anxiously transferred her gaze over the gardens, "But where is it?"

"No need for any fear," he laughed, "you'll be safe with me."

She blushed. "I know that, I was only—" she stopped. How could she tell Stuart about that pace business her mother had spoken of?"

"And, I was only teasing you," he laughed again. "Come on and I'll show you, it's just a little way from right where we're standing, but you can't see it due to the way the garden has changed over the years. I rather like it this way though with many of the shrubs having grown into trees. It makes for more of that shade that Grandmother was talking about and I wholeheartedly agree with her. Your complexion is much too pretty to be harmed by the sun."

Stuart saw her cheeks flush slightly again as she smiled at him and trustingly let him guide her on down the flagstone pathway that wound through tall boxwoods and lilacs and blooming gardenia bushes and flower beds. Then, he was saying, as he stopped to lift a huge cluster of draping Crape Myrtle blooms that was blocking their way higher above his bent head "Here it is. Looks almost like an enclosed room doesn't it?"

She stepped by him, uttering a cry of exclamation as he let the Crape Myrtle branch fall back in place and she was to see all the unusual quaintness that time had framed—her lovely grey eyes growing wider m surprise as she took in the fountain and the stone bench that her own mother had sat upon as a sixteen year old girl, admiring the same spot. Though she or Stuart were never to know.

"Oh, Stuart, no wonder you've grown fond of it! It's such a lovely and charming place. I've noticed this big oak, loaded down with the blooming wisteria in early spring many times, but I didn't know the bench, or the fountain were here; in fact, none of this," she indicated, with a spread of her hands.

"I knew you'd love it," he said. "That's why I wanted you to see it."

"Oh, I do!" She cried, suddenly fastening her eyes on a blue jay that came wheeling into light on a lily pad at the fountain and was instantly having some trouble in trying to balance itself. "Oh, look, Stuart!"

"Yes, I've noticed that the birds appear to like this place as much as I do, and they're so tame. One's presence doesn't seem to bother them in the least. Look, here comes another one," he said, as the second blue jay came wheeling in and seemed quite determined to light on the same lily pad that the first blue jay was still trying to settle upon, causing a rather loud clamor to start ringing out.

"Oh, look at that, Stuart! I think they're actually quarreling with one another," she laughed, turning to look at Stuart. Their eyes met and held. Her laughter drifted away. And, suddenly, Stuart was saying, as he reached for her, "No, darling, I'd rather look at you," and the instant he touched her—even before she was to feel and savor his hungering lips planting kisses on her face, her ear lobes, and on down her neck, Jane Anne Heyward knew that Stuart Drakston was indeed that first love that she had waited for. And, when she felt his mouth on hers at last, them clinging together in all the burning ripeness of young passion, she was certain this first love with Stuart Drakston would be her last—so solid in its trueness, that it would be enough to sustain her for all time.

Now, there was no shyness with her. In Stuart's arms, nothing mattered but Stuart. Yes, handsome Stuart Drakston was setting the pace and she was finding herself most willing to follow it. Stuart had now become the actual being of her spirit—her wants—her needs. She had gone into his arms as natural and unpretending as if he had reached for her dozens of times before this day and, at that moment, never wanted Stuart to take his mouth from hers.

Still, when he finally did, the words she heard falling from his lips were to thrill her even more. "I've fallen in love with you, Jane Anne," Stuart was telling her. "In fact, I think I've always loved you. But this, darling, the way I feel now, it's—it's. How can I say it?" He paused, drawing her closer. "Well, all of it, everything, is so much more than I'd ever hoped to experience with any girl."

"I know, Stuart," she whispered, "I know." Then, she slightly pulled away, her earnest features turned up to his. "Loving you as I do, how can I but not know?"

He eagerly pulled her back to him, suddenly exclaiming, before his mouth found hers again, "Oh, God, darling, how I'll ever be grateful for pink roses!" and he was.

But, as much as Stuart yearned for her and wanted that very minute to ask Jane Anne Heyward to be his wife, he was well aware it was not going to be that simple. To begin with, falling in love almost overnight and being married, was certainly, far from following the conventional standards that both of them had had instilled in them since birth. Stuart could just imagine the uproar and fury he would set in motion, especially on Eliza Heyward' s part, if he were to coax the sixteen year old Jane Anne into marrying him in less than three weeks after his return from England when; in truth, he had never called on her socially. Further, besides conventions and discords to think about, there was something else to consider—to Stuart the most important part of all, leaving out of course the love he felt for the girl he held in his arms. He was well aware that if he were ever to gain that harmony which he craved with Eliza Heyward—to his way of thinking a necessary element for the kind of future happiness he wanted to have with her daughter—it was going to be essential that he curb his passion for a while and take it all step by step and easy steps at that, regardless of what the torture may cost him.

Thus, with all these thoughts spinning through his mind, Stuart forced himself to remove his mouth from Jane Anne's inviting lips and said, as he smiled down at her, "We'd better make tracks toward those pink roses, darling, before our absence attracts attention."

Chapter Seven

The land had given. Luke and Eliza had given. In some measure each and every last person who dwelled at Green Sea—from tenant or sharecropper to the landlord, had given. And, there it stood at last gracing that same knoll where the other stately mansion had set and all the other main homesteads of Green Sea before it—beaming a new dazzling white through the long avenue of live oaks—a great handiwork of majestic beauty that caught every eye that happened to pass or go through the huge ornate archway leading to the plantation.

The effort had been one long toilsome task, actually taking a whole fifteen years to bring it to its completion. Be that as it may, though, Luke Heyward had finally made good his long ago promise to his wife. Green Sea could boost another elegant mansion worthy of its lands. Even though Luke would have been the first to admit fifteen years was a might overlong for the carrying through with any project, at the same time, when he or anyone else who was familiar with the situation stopped to consider all the factors which had been involved, fifteen years did not seem to be such an unreasonable duration of time after all. Even had there been no hindrances and setbacks by the late Frank Drakston's hand, no depressions or crop failures, either, the building of the mansion would have required a good many years, anyhow, considering that it was a frame structure with every plank and board being used having been cut from Green Sea's own timberlands and undergoing a drying out period of two years or more before going into the mansion's construction.

Yes, aside from the ornamental trimmings and the solid mahogany engraved panel work in the library, the fine, ornate woodwork, doors and carved mantels and the parquet floor in the entrance foyer, Green Sea's own timber had built the mansion. Even the brick which had been required for the building of its numerous chimneys, its ground— foundation and outside doorsteps, and those which formed the base for the supporting of its huge front columns that towered the length of two full stories, had been handmade at Green Sea. The mansions sills, resting atop the brick foundation, were hand-hewn cypress. For the most part, its exterior and interior both were longleaf white pine. The grand, curving staircase and its floors, with the exception of the foyer, were white oak, its rich golden hues striking a handsome contrast with the mansion's darker mahogany trimmings—the same white oak that Luke had marked that day on the ridge.

Quite the contrary to what one would have assumed that Luke would be prompted to do he had on no account attempted to copy the grand, unique mansion that had gone to ashes and dust—the mansion that Matthew Carson had more or less built at Green Sea, and the one that Luke had promised Eliza he would try to replace someday. To a certain degree, the mansion that Luke had built with its eight front-porch ionic columns and fine basic lines of old Greek revival, resembled Drakston Hall more in appearance than what one would have expected it to.

If Luke Heyward had been conscious of this fact when he had sought the help of professional architects, working with them in order to achieve the floor plan and outside lines he had desired, nobody knew of it but Luke Heyward. Nor did anyone ever know. Taking the fineness of Luke's character and nature into account, it is almost safe to assume—human behavior being such as it is—that if Luke had been persuaded by anything regarding his preference for Drakston Hall's architectural style it was his subconscious that had done the inducing rather than his knowledgeable sense. Perhaps Luke's subconscious was still more disturbed over the late Frank Drakston's deeds than he was aware of. Even to the extent—as preposterous as it was—that he was trying to tell that spectral image of the late Frank Drakston that used to visit his mind too often something—perhaps trying to prove to it that he was indeed worthy of Eliza Carson after all and not that no-good worthless white trash who Frank Drakston had ever labeled him to be. Then again, maybe lying somewhere submerged in Luke's mind had been only a keen desire to want to demonstrate his own likes—his own abilities.

In any case, leaving out his constant concern for his family, Luke had finally fulfilled his life's ambition. And, if that spectral image of Frank had indeed paid a few visits upon his subconscious, inducing his moves to any degree, while he had been in the process of carrying through with this desire, his all abiding love for Eliza had surely persuaded him to also make some moves that otherwise he would not have bothered with—causing him to add a few sentimental extras here and there. For instance, the beautiful chandeliers in both the formal parlor and dining room were suspended from plaster medallions in the ceilings which were molded in the design of violets. Also, the long full-length etched glass panes on either side of the mahogany front door were etched in the violet design. Moreover, the front door carried further proof of how deep Luke's love and devotion run for his wife and the whole Carson family. Not only did the door carry an engraved Heyward coat of arms but the Carson crest as well right beside it. When Eliza saw this additional sentimental touch, tears of gratitude for Luke's love and thoughtfulness washed down her cheeks.

With his arm circling her waist, Luke had smiled down at Eliza and told her as they had stood admiring the handsome door, "You really didn't think I'd forget about all that Carson sweat that's gone into the makings of this plantation and this house as well, did you?" Then, before she could reply and with his smile continuing to grow, he had teasingly added, "Besides, doll, in case there's someone out there who may not know that we're a team, I couldn't think of a better way or place to emphasize the fact than have it engraved in our front door."

Surprising Luke not one bit, Eliza, somewhat defiantly, had swiftly brushed at the tears on her cheeks with the back of her hand and said, "Well, if there is anyone out there who holds that kind of notion in their head after all this time, they're a fool, Luke, and wouldn't understand the meaning of your gesture anyhow, despite all the trouble and expense you've gone to!"

By late summer of that year, the rich harvest that Luke and Eliza had been hoping for seemed almost assured. From all signs it appeared that both of Green Sea's two main money crops, cotton and tobacco, were going to yield far above what a normal year produced, especially the tobacco crop, bringing in that needed cash for the move to the new mansion. Even though a good many poundage of the flue-cured tobacco had yet to be readied for market, by the first week in September, this crop had already brought in enough cash money from the thousands of pounds which had been prepared and sold to put a sizable down payment on the new furnishings that had been purchased for the new mansion.

Though she was ever wary of debts and mortgages, Eliza had gone ahead and agreed with Luke's decision to order the new furnishings earlier in the summer when the crops had looked promising. Now she was glad she had, because it looked as though the tobacco crop alone would almost cover the expense they had gone to, leaving the greater

183

portion of the earnings from the cotton to help carry them through the burdens of making another crop. However, Eliza had not ordered new furnishings for all the rooms in the new mansion. She and Luke were using a lot of the same pieces of furniture they had already lived with for eighteen years. Some of the bedrooms were outfitted with the same furniture they had used in the little grey house. Jane Anne had her same bedroom furniture. So did Carr. But these furnishings were only a few years old, having been bought when the children had reached their teens. Besides, the furniture had been the best money could buy. Regarding their two children, the Heywards were unstinting in nothingness. Nonetheless, even with some of their used furniture helping to outfit the new mansion, its size and elegance had still required Luke and Eliza to be most liberal with their purse strings before family could move into all the new grandeur and conveniences that awaited them.

The new furnishings had been purchased through one of Charleston's chief mercantile stores, and the day the store's wagons came rumbling up the drive with all the brightly, handsome pieces were indeed an exciting day at Green Sea. Yet, it was doubtful if anyone at the plantation was any more excited and jubilant than the aged Doss, though he had only a few short months to live from the dropsy that had begun to plague him. And, aside from going back to spend his nights at the small grey house, which Doss had moved into with Hannah and Pete when Luke and Eliza had vacated it, Doss would mostly live these few months left to him plumped down somewhere on the new mansion's two verandas—the front or the back— whichever suited him at the time. Luke and Eliza never uttered one word of protest. They would not have anyway, even if they had not been thoroughly knowledgeable of Doss' condition through Seth Roalf, because they both thought that Doss had more than earned his leisure. They had not forgotten the many times he had helped Luke rebuild the mansions foundation, to say nothing of all the puttering he had put in over the fifteen-year period on its construction.

All the same, the day the new furnishings were delivered, Doss was right there clumping in and out the mansion to see where each piece was to rest at as it was carried inside from the store's wagons and placed. Finally, when everything had been set up and put in its location, again nobody seemed any prouder and more pleased with the delightful results than Doss. While his face beamed with obvious pleasure, he took a good look at each room, nodded his approval to Eliza and Luke and then clumped back outside. And granted, Doss' nods of approval were only the beginnings of many. There were quite a few more from Eliza's and Luke's family and friends, with not the first single one spent unduly because the final results were indeed deserving of every approving nod that was given.

Knowing that Luke preferred bright pastels to the darker colors and that he also loved the color blue in all shades, Eliza had chosen blue to dominate the color scheme in the new mansion along with creams, yellows and greens. But, from the deeper tones of the blue and cream imperial Brussels rugs to the lighter blue velvet over draperies that dressed the huge ornate corniced windows in the living room and dining room, blue was the color that reigned throughout the first-floor rooms. And, it did strike a pleasing accent with the other pretty colors, not to mention how well all this lively glow blended with the rich dark tones of the lovely rosewood and mahogany furniture that the Heywards had purchased.

Among the several pieces of the newly arrived furniture were not only one but two beautiful Empire sofas. While a lovely light-green brocade graced the formal parlor another one of the same lines and materials in a sunny yellow rested against one of the walls in the over-large entrance hall—its colorful presence giving the mansion a quaint and charming inviting air, with both sofas complimenting the dining room chairs and several smaller straight chairs as well whose seats were identical in color and fabric to that of the lovely blue window hangings.

Still, the one thing that seemed to give the mansion its finishing touch and bring a complete harmonious sense of balance to the pleasingly blended decor of the mansion's rooms, were the numerous family portraits that at last had suitable wall space to hang upon. But Eliza did not choose to hang all the portraits together—one following another on the stairway wall as they had hung in the other mansion. She chose instead to hang most of them on separate walls. The beautiful portrait of Anne Carson with her light-rose gown was placed over the green sofa in the living room. The portrait of Matthew Carson accompanied it on an opposite wall. The two smaller portraits of Joshua and Jane Heyward were placed side by side over the yellow sofa in the huge foyer. Jane Heyward's blue gown blended as perfect with the yellow sofa as the pink gown that Anne Carson was wearing

185

in her portrait did with the green sofa.

The day this job was finally getting underway was a day and a task that Eliza had awaited in anticipation. Yet, in spite of the joy she felt over having enough wall space and then some to accommodate all the family portraits at last, the task had its poignant moments for her and Luke both. Still, not one portrait did they hang of those long absent faces that it did not make them feel as though the loved ones were truly aware of the event, actually emerging from the Canvas to help them share in their good fortune. Having moved into the new mansion the first week of September, Luke and Eliza had been moved only a few days when this task was being seen to.

Luke and Eliza had rushed in making the move to the new mansion—even before half the crops had been gathered—for several reasons. In addition to feeling that September was their lucky month since it was the month they had been married and also had seen their two children into the world—marking three occasions in the month to celebrate, they had wanted to make the move and celebrate all these dates together combined with a housewarming before Carr and Jane Anne left for college in Virginia on the twentieth of the month. Jane Anne and Laura both were to enroll at the University of Virginia. But, unlike her brother who was looking forward to following the male traditions of the family by attending the Virginia Military Institute at Lexington, Jane Anne's heart was not in it. Though her parents, or anyone else as for that matter, were aware of it, Jane Anne's most aspiring ambition was to be nothing more than Stuart Drakston's wife. From the second their mouths had come together; she had yearned for little else.

At any rate, in order to celebrate all the month's events, their children's birthdays, their own twenty-fourth wedding anniversary and the move to the new mansion before the college leave-taking was to take place, Luke and Eliza had settled on the fifteenth of September, which fell on a Saturday, for the celebration ball. Yes, Green Sea was holding its first ball for many a year and, with all the chores of moving and starting to make preparations for the ball, plus being in the middle of a harvest, it was not too surprising that Luke and Eliza were sparing very much of their time for musing over the everyday activities of their children.

Ever striving to make Carr's and Jane Anne's young years a time of life that they could think of in later years being a free and laughter-loving time, Luke and Eliza both were not opposed to sound, wholesome entertainment. Nor had they ever been, even if they were somewhat oversensitive pertaining to their children's whereabouts and welfare. In fact, they were all for the younger set having parties on Saturday nights at Green Sea or some other neighboring plantation, going for horseback rides, and hayrides, too, if the hayrides were chaperoned by an older adult. Rather than objecting to any one of these activities, they had encouraged Carr and Jane Anne both to participate in them and also to feel free to bring their friends to Green Sea. And, in recent months, if Eliza had found herself holding a degree of compunction form time to time over the fact that Stuart Drakston with his overeager eye towards her daughter—a fact that she had strained every nerve to ignore and make nothing of—was ever present and taking part in all this wholesome fun and had been since his return from England she still had not the foggiest idea that he and Jane Anne were madly in love with one another.

Of course, neither Eliza nor Luke had ever taken it upon themselves to crowd the younger set too closely when they gathered at Green Sea. The space of their small house had not required much supervision from them, anyhow. Besides, they trusted both their children to know right from wrong and, so far, this trust had paid off with the Heyward family's relationship going as smooth as velvet.

The day that Luke and Eliza were seeing to the hanging of the family portraits, though, a glimmer of what had been going on between Stuart and Jane Anne came through to both of them as bright as a ray of sunshine. Luke seeing what truly dwelled in his daughter's heart, silently accepted it and said nothing. But, profoundly shaken and disappointed, Eliza verbally denounced it on the spot, and even though she did try to the understanding and remain calm while airing her view, it was to be the beginning of many discords that would continue to affect the family's melodious harmony until it was to finally erupt in one of the worst kinds of ways and near destroy Eliza in the process.

"Place it just a wee bit farther to the right, Pete," Luke said, as he took back the portrait, which was that of Eliza painted with her two brothers, from Pete's hands and stepped aside while Pete refastened the last of the many wall brackets that he had been called upon to help with that morning.

Pete, the abandoned baby, was a full-grown man now. He was tall, at least six feet, with classical features that set him apart from the race of who he lived and dwelled with. Though his mahogany-colored skin was as dark in hue as Hannah's, who had become mother to Pete in every sense of the word but blood, his other characteristic traits reminded Eliza more and more of Julia with each passing day. Eliza was certain that in the slenderness of Pete's lips and nose, his lean jaw line and high-cheek bones, she was seeing the mark of no one but Julia. In addition, there were other signs, too, that confirmed the soundness of her belief—his regal dignity—the quiet manner—causing her to give devout thanks many times over that she and Luke and, yes, Jailer too, had found Pete and saved him from what would have been his sure death. With Pete having become almost as much a part of the Heyward household at Green Sea as anyone else since he had long back become its chef, in some strange way his presence there made Eliza feel as if she were still keeping in touch with the slave girl, Julia, who she had grown up with. No, Pete had never worked in the fields a day in his life. Having spent so many hours in the kitchen watching Eliza and Hannah, too, prepare the food when Hannah had helped Eliza out so much in those years when Carr and Jane Anne were still babies, Pete had stepped into the role of Chef as natural as if he had been born and raised for that purpose. Seldom did he leave the kitchen to help with some other work in the house. Those times he was called upon to help was usually a chore that was not commonplace routine; most often, requiring either a man's strength or height, such as the handling of the portraits.

Having fastened the bracket to the stairway wall, Pete turned and took the portrait from Luke and hanging it with the same painstaking care that all his other duties were performed with, he stared at it a moment and then said, as he followed Luke on down the three or four steps of the stairway, "Miss Eliza, Carr favors you and that brother you called Phil. He sure is a Carson over." Likewise, to Julia, Pete's dialect hardly varied form that of Carr's who he had played with countless of hours while growing up.

"You have a sharp eye, Pete," said Luke, crossing the hall to where Eliza was standing helping them position the portraits. "Those were my very words the day our son was born." His arm circled Eliza's waist as he, too, gazed at the likeness of Phil Carson.

"Yes, one doesn't have to look long at that before Carr comes to mind," agreed Eliza, staring wistfully at the portrait. "After all these years, I still get the feeling that perhaps someday—" she stopped. The memories had suddenly become too vivid. Her throat too tight.

Trying to break the rising flood that he was certain was rushing to Eliza's eyes, Luke hastily put in, "That'll be all, Pete, and you've been a lot of help. I think you'll still have time to put your touch to that delicious beef stew I smell cooking before dinner."

"As good as already done, Mr. Luke," Pete smiled, turning away toward the hall's back doorway.

Luke's reminder that the dinner hour was fast approaching had helped. Quickly swallowing down the tightness, Eliza called out to Pete's back, "And, make sure there's plenty of biscuits, Pete, to eat with the stewed fruit."

Flashing another smile, Pete turned his head, "I'll make certain, Miss Eliza," he assured and was whistling as he disappeared through the door.

Giving the walls around them one more quick look, Luke said, "Well, I guess as far as this job's concerned this does i!,darling. They're finally up again and I pray this time they'll be there for keeps."

"Amen to that, Luke," Eliza solemnly declared, going on to add after pausing briefly, "Luke, we have come a long way together, haven't we?"

"Yes, dear, a long way," he told her, gathering her closer.

Suddenly, the sound of heels hurrying across the front veranda was turning their heads, both knowing the familiar clack belonged to no other than their daughter, even before she breezed through the door in a bubbling state of blitheness.

"Well, hello, kitten," her father smilingly greeted, "I suspected you'd deserted us, but we've been so busy, I hadn't gotten around to inquiring of your whereabouts."

"Oh, Papa," Jane Anne laughed, her dancing gaze circling the newly adorned walls, "don't you remember last night at supper?"

"Last night at supper?" Luke questioned soberly, dropping his head. "Yes, now that you've reminded me," he went on as he appeared to be studying the floor pattern at his feet, "it does seem I recall a little something about you trying to convince your mother that all the chores had been seen to and you'd be idle this morning."

"Now, Papa, stop your pretending you didn't know where I was at, and you're teasing, too. You know perfectly well that housework goes on forever and, that when I said I'd like to go riding this morning that mother and I hardly mentioned it, or all the other things we'll need to do before the ball on Saturday night." Her merry gaze continued to dance from portrait to portrait.

"Don't fret, dear, he remembered all right," Scoffed Eliza, "or he would've been asking of your whereabouts the very first thing. Did you have a nice ride?"

"I had a wonderful time, Mother. I met Stuart and we rode awhile together, almost to Elms. Oh, Mother, the portraits look so nice. They've really dressed up our beautiful home." She dashed over to the sofa. "And, look how you've arranged Grandfather and Grandmother Heywards! You have such excellent taste, Mother. Never would I have thought of placing them above the sofa, side by side."

"Yes, you would too, but come on into the parlor and see what you think of it," said Eliza, as she moved from the circle of Luke's arm and taking his hand, led the way into the parlor.

"And, you've put Grandmother Anne's above the sofa in here!" Jane Anne cried and then ran on to where Matthew Carson's was placed, crying again, "And Grandfather's over here! Oh, everything's just perfect! Don't you think so, Papa?"

"Well, I suppose about as perfect as we Heywards have the power and means to make it," quipped Luke with a relaxed, pleasing smile, "That is, if we can be excused for getting the cart ahead of the horse somewhat regarding the question of the means."

Jane Anne giggled. "I can see, Papa, you're set on having the last word today, so I'm going to run. Besides, there's all that pretty new crystal to wash and place. I'd better change my clothes and get busy." She started to make a dart for the doorway, but her mother's voice stopped her.

"Wait just a moment, dear, I'd like a word with you," Eliza was saying. "It's too near dinner, anyway, to start on the glassware."

As Jane Anne whirled back to face her mother, her apology was already falling, "I'm so sorry, Mother, I shouldn't have stayed this long. I didn't realize it's so late."

"Never mind about that," said Eliza, waving her daughter's apology aside. "It's Stuart, dear. You failed to mention that he would be riding along with you when you asked for my permission to go riding this morning."

The merry dance in Jane Anne's deep-grey eyes halted to an instant stop, as she set her gaze on her mother's face in puzzlement. A rather tense hush fell over the room before she finally said, "It's true,

Mother, I didn't mention Stuart because I didn't know that he would be along."

"You didn't know?" Eliza flared, unable to hold her composure any longer.

''No, Ma'am. I had only rode a short distance when I met Stuart, riding General, coming toward Green Sea"

"I see," Eliza tartly retorted. "But you were riding in the direction of Drakston Hall, were you not? Why not some other direction besides that way? And, for the life of me I can't see why the company of Stuart Drakston appears to overwhelm you so, here lately. You've never appeared to be that excited or interested regarding Bill Cooper's company, or; for instance, the prospect of a visit from Luke Green."

The growing coldness in her mother's voice had cut Jane Anne severely, sending her slipping down on the edge of the straight chair that she was standing near. Still, with her eyes resting on her folded hands in her lap, she made no effort to disclaim one word of her mother's remarks.

"What you've pointed out is true, Mother," she said softly. "Even though I do enjoy Bill's company and Luke's, too, I've never enjoyed being with them as I do being with Stuart. It's not the same—" she hesitated on the last word, wondering if she should go ahead and confess her love for Stuart. No, perhaps it would be better to wait, she thought, since it was obvious her mother was already displeased with her. She would try to put her feelings for Stuart in another way. "Stuart's so interesting to be with. He knows so many wonderful things to talk about. He can talk endlessly about England—" She let her last word trail off again, realizing that every word she was uttering in the way of trying to explain how she felt, was sounding more sillier and foolish as she went along and telling her parents nothing about her true emotions, either.

"Well," Eliza retorted again, "maybe when you've completed four years of college, you won't think Stuart Drakston is so informed and worldly after all and will also realize that he isn't near as interesting as you think he is now!"

Four years! Four years of being away from Stuart, months at the time! Surely her mother did not disapprove of Stuart so much that she would insist on her attending college for four long years, when she had no desire to even attend one semester. Why this sudden stand against Stuart, anyway?

"Mother, I don't understand any of this," Jane Anne murmured. "I though you liked Stuart and had no objecting of my being in his company."

"Only through the family—connected relationship with no romantic notions involved," Eliza declared, "do I approve of your being together."

The incredulous severity of her mother's remark brought Jane Anne's head up fast. Dumbfounded, her anxious grey eyes beseechingly sought the face of her father. But, to her further dismay she saw that in addition to all light seeming to have vanished from his face, he appeared as though he had vanished in person, too—totally lost to both her and her mother, as well as everything else around him.

Knowing that her beloved father had always spoken well of Stuart and had still chosen not to intervene in Stuart's behalf, and appearing, also, to have removed himself from the scene, besides, had completely bewildered and crushed Jane Anne. Her eyes danced no longer. They appeared passive. Her bearing appeared to be the same as she slowly rose from her chair and started to turn away—wanting to do nothing right at that moment but to escape, if she could, from this first shadow that had fallen so suddenly on her well-ordered life. Yet, even though she was far from assertive by nature from somewhere within her she gained the courage to press a little further into the matter.

"But, why Mother?" She implored, turning back, her love for Stuart buoying her courage, "Stuart's such a fine person."

Eliza knew all too well the blow she had dealt her daughter. She could plainly see that all the sunniness Jane Anne had swept into the house with, was gone. Still, she could not any more help trying to shield Jane Anne from Stuart Drakston's eyes, ring down the curtain on their obvious attraction for one another, than she could stop breathing. Just the same, she wanted and did try to soften the sting of her biting retorts.

"For one thing, dear, there's your formal schooling to consider. But, most of all, you're too young in years yet to become emotionally involved with any young man, and particularly in Stuart's case, with him being so many years older than you are."

Had it not been a subject of such paramount concern to Jane Anne, she could have seen a lot of amusement in her mother's reply, taking into account that she instantly thought of the eight years age difference between her parents. Nonetheless, she was greatly heartened anyway, because it appeared her mother's statement regarding age had not been lost on her father either, seeming to jerk him out of that dreamy state he appeared to be in. Though he did not comment on the remark, Jane Anne saw that it had indeed brought his mind back from wherever it had strayed to.

With her father now appearing to be intently engrossed on what was being said, Jane Anne felt strengthened and took it upon herself to defend the age matter. As a faint light began to appear on her face again, she said, "Oh, Mother, I'm not that young, and Stuart certainly isn t that old."

"Maybe in your estimation, dear. But, to the best of my belief, I see it otherwise and hope you'll see it my way, too, or I will have to speak to Start about the matter," Eliza warned.

"Oh, no, Mother, please don't do that," Jane Anne pied, her new-found strength rapidly slipping away again.

"Very well, then, not unless I'm forced to. You may run on and change from your riding habit. Pete will be calling dinner shortly," Eliza told her rather calmly though she was far from feeling calm as she stepped to the doorway and fastened her eyes on her daughter' back, keeping them there til Jane Anne had covered every long foot of the winding stairs and disappeared from her sight.

Not more than a mere few hours before the ball on Saturday night Eliza was to come by another generous helping of anxiety. For all the pleasure and good she had gotten out of eating that week, as well as her feelings in general—both physical and mental—that was the way Eliza had come to think of herself as having been served an everlasting dish of anxiousness every day and nothing more. As a rule, it had always been Luke with the quivery stomach if things were not going just right. But now, with her concern over her daughter's infatuation— she refused to call it anything else—for Stuart Drakston, along with the added burden of the ball, it seemed this week had been Eliza's turn to have the inside jitters.

However, even though this latest jolt to come Eliza's way was of a totally different nature from anything that had fronted her thus far that week, actually more amusing than anything else, the startling surprise of it left her feeling somewhat winded, nevertheless.

On that Saturday afternoon, there was hardly a person at Green Sea who was not engaged in some task or other in the last-minute preparations for that night's ball. Bessie and Ruth, assisted by their grown daughters, were busy fluttering from one bedroom to the other dressing out each room and the dressing room that joined it in fresh, clean linens for the invited guests who would be staying over. Pete, Prudence, Daisy and Hannah—though Hannah like Doss was mostly sitting—were submerged in the kitchen's stacks of roast meats, cakes, pies, and other delicacies. Sam was busy chopping and preserving ice for the iced drinks to be served. Luke and Charlie had set out for the Charleston depot with the carriage to meet the Greens, who were coming for the celebration and to get in a little surf fishing on the side, too, while they were there. Jane Anne was busy arranging fresh cut flowers from the garden—mostly late summer roses—throughout the rooms and thinking about all the dilemma her love for Stuart Drakston had stirred. And, Eliza was busy placing the polished silver and new gleaming crystal on the table, when, suddenly, the loud chatter of the front door's chimes almost made her drop the Waterford wine glass she held in her hand.

Having long been without a butler for a good many years—the aged Albert from Drakston Hall was to do the honors that night, with both Matthew Carson and Albert, too, thinking it a wonderful idea when Eliza and Luke had suggested it—Eliza looked around and seeing that no one else was on their way to answer the ring, which was getting to have a more impatient sound to it by the second, she set the piece of crystal down and went hurrying to the door herself.

Hoping that some disaster had not fallen to spoil this first celebration that she and Luke had waited for and planned on so long, Eliza, in her mounting apprehension because no guests were expected this early, jerked at the doorknob a lot harder than she had meant to and besides almost causing her caller to come toppling inside over her, was nearly startled out of her skin to see that the visitor was a stranger and a woman at that—very stylishly—clad in fashions that had clearly come at heavy cost—Eliza thought almost too rich and expensive for afternoon travel.

It was obvious the woman, who had her fashionable handbag looped over one arm, had been peering rather closely at the handsome front door—doubtless inspecting the double coat of arms. It was also obvious she had no qualms about giving herself away because as she instantly made a grab for her gold-rimmed spectacles with one hand and caught at the doorjamb with the other to keep her balance, she was merrily chuckling away, "Perhaps someday I'll learn that doors do open!"

"Oh, I'm so sorry," Eliza cried, noticing while she did that it did not seem to take the woman an instant to go about slipping her spectacles inside her handbag out of sight as well as pulling herself up to her rather stately height, though it was plain she was getting to be well on into the years. "I shouldn't have jerked at the door in such haste, but you see I was—"

"Hello, Eliza," the woman was saying, letting Eliza get no further with her apology, "You've hardly changed at all. I would've known you any place," giving every appearance that she was an old bosom friend of Eliza's and that Eliza had actually been expecting her arrival.

Eliza was stumped, mentally crowding every second with questions relative to unraveling the woman's identity. And, seeing that her unexpected visitor had arrived in a hired hack from Charleston with it and its driver still waiting parked in the drive, helped none whatsoever.

Barely conscious of what she was saying, Eliza replied, "Thank you," studying the woman's face more closely as she continued to labor for her name. Eliza thought there was something vaguely familiar about her fixedly expression—the small poutish looking mouth that was curving with a rather bemused smile and that shrewish glint under wisps of grey-tumbling curls, which were set off most becomingly by her deep-rose, veil-draped velvet hat, were slowly but surely approaching the door of Eliza's memory.

But suddenly, the woman was saying again, distracting Eliza's light of recognition, "You don't recognize me, do you? Well, I'm not one bit shocked or surprised. That's why I warned him in advance what to expect!"

"Him—Luke?" Eliza questioned; her thoughts now turned completely around as she wondered why Luke hadn't prepared her for what seemed to be the woman's pending arrival at Green Sea. "I'm sorry but Luke isn't home right at the present. If you care to wait—"

With another merry chuckle bubbling in her throat, the woman cut in again, "No, no, dear, not Luke! Mr. Drexwell, dear. Mr. Anthony Drexwell of Louisiana!"

"Mrs. Wainwright!" Shrieked Eliza, that June night at Windsor suddenly flooding her mind as she grasped her caller's hands, "Oh, please forgive my awkwardness!"

"Oh, phew with that," laughed Rebecca, "time and my blundering way of going about things more than justified it. But, Rebecca if you please and none of that Mrs. Wainwright business, though God only knows how much I loved that man!"

Obviously, others, too, Eliza was thinking as she also laughed and said, "Rebecca then, and is Luke going to be surprised! Why, he just penned a letter to you a couple days ago."

"Not any more surprised than I am at being here," gushed Rebecca. "But things began to happen all of a sudden so here I am. You see, Mr. Drexwell—I mean Tony, wired me to come to Louisiana immediately, actually only two days following Mrs. Drexwell's funeral! Poor Tony, he was desolate and for good cause let me tell you—" Rebecca broke off with a long sigh and let her mouth go droopy all of a sudden as she silently shook her head back and forth a few times, giving her remark time to evoke the strongest possible effect even though she already had Eliza peering into her face most anxiously. Finally, she resumed, "would you believe that after all these years of sitting in that wheelchair, that poor woman came by her death from that very chair when it suddenly rolled down a slight incline and slammed into a tree?"

"No!" Eliza cried, "How terrible!"

"Well, she did," declared Rebecca. "It seems there were no servants within reach to overtake the chair and stop it, and Tony wasn't around either. Anyway, Tony thought I might reach New Orleans quicker if I took a ship into Charleston and then board a train for the rest of the journey. But no sooner than we docked in Charleston harbor this morning, I knew I wasn't going one foot farther toward Louisiana until I saw Luke Heyward again! Besides, since Tony and I have waited this long, I can't see where a few more days apart would matter that much, do you?"

She peered back at Eliza rather intently, her face still solemn.

How should I know, Eliza silently thought, sorta amused that Rebecca Wainwright would put such a question to her and did; indeed, seem to be asking it in all seriousness. Suppressing her urge to laugh, she murmured, hoping the words would qualify for what Rebecca apparently wanted to hear, "No, a day or two out of years isn't that long a time."

"Precisely the way I see it," Rebecca said, bobbing her head in approval. "I'll send him a wire though, explaining my delay since I've sent most of my things on. After all the trouble Tony's been through, I wouldn't want to cause him any additional alarm by having all that

196

baggage arriving without any Rebecca in sight." She drew another deep breath and pulled her mouth up, setting it in a rather determined line. "Tony has had many difficult years, but there was nothing I could do, the situation being as it was. I meant to see to it that whatever else Rebecca Wainwright can be accused of, stealing a husband from a wheelchair victim would never make the list!" Floored, Eliza was thankful that Jane Anne chose that very instant to emerge from the rose garden with her basket of cut roses and start racing across the yard for the front veranda, catching Rebecca Wainwright's eye and turning her head with rapt attention; and also, sparing herself the ordeal of having to comment any further on the subject of Tony Drexwell's and Rebecca Wainwright's obvious long alliance with one another.

Even so, as Jane Anne came bounding on up the steps and Eliza promptly plunged into making the introductions with Rebecca crying aloud, "Luke Heyward reincarnated! You divine angel!" before she could even cover the proper proprieties of presenting them to one another, Eliza wondered just what kind of explanation Rebecca had tucked away—other than stealing as she herself had put it—for explaining her continued relationship with Tony Drexwell all those years his wife had sat in her wheel chair—a relationship that Eliza was viewing as having, without question, been kindled most ordinately for it to endure and keep aflame over a period of twenty-five years!

"Mrs. Wainwright, what a pleasure it is to meet you at last!" Exclaimed Jane Anne, setting her rose-filled basket down on the floor at her feet and giving Rebecca her hand, "Papa has often spoken of you."

"Kindly, I dare say," Rebecca charmingly chirped back. "You divine child."

"Oh, yes, most kindly, Mrs. Wainwright," Jane Anne blithely assured. "Papa has told us many beautiful and wonderful stories about his life at Windsor."

"Really, child?" Rebecca quizzed, that pert glint returning to her eyes. "So, like myself, I gather Luke hasn't forgotten Windsor?"

"Oh, no, Mrs. Wainwright, Papa could never forget those days. His memories of Windsor are too dear for that."

"Yes—Yes—I can see that, Angel, in those divine grey eyes of yours that reminds me so much of your father's," murmured Rebecca, thinking to herself that the part about Windsor that she was unable to forget—the part that had always plagued her most and reminded her

197

over and over what a damn fool she had been, was the day that Luke Heyward could have been hers had she played her cards right instead of advising him to strike out for South Carolina into the arms of Eliza Carson!

And, that had not been all. Besides having the burden of this knowledge gnawing at her more often than she had ever thought possible through the years—something she had sensed when she and Luke had said goodbye at Windsor—knowing that Windsor could have remained hers for keeps, too, because Luke Heyward would have saved it for her just as he had saved Green Sea from those carpetbaggers for Eliza Carson, had actually given her migraine more times than she cared to remember! And now, if all that other had not been enough, here was something else that was far worse than anything she had suffered because of her stupidity regarding Luke Heyward; in that, the fact that she herself could have very well been this divine girl's mother instead of Eliza Carson was, surely coming home to her—pounding at her no less intense than had someone plopped her one with a sledgehammer right between the eyes!

Oh well—now, what was this that this child was saying? She must remember to stay more clearheaded and not dwell over her mistakes where she was prone to wallow far more often than was healthy for her and have to ask that questions be repeated while she was here at Green Sea, or it just might get back to Tony Drexwell's ears that Rebecca Wainwright was either going a little haywire in the upper story or losing her hearing—maybe both—and possibly cause her to miss out on another good opportunity to preside as mistress over a grand estate! She was not so much of a screwball that she did not realize, that at her age, a chance like that was not likely to come her way anymore. Furthermore, taking one thing with another, she meant she was not going to lose out in being compensated for all those years she had waited for Tony Drexwell, taking up all that time in pouring out trillions of consoling and encouraging words to him on paper when she might have put it to a better advantage; for example; using it to look over the field for another possible catch!

Letting her mental lecture whirl at the hub of each word as she tried to effect the best possible disguise that she was indeed asking Jane Anne to repeat her statement, Rebecca—keenly aware that Eliza had both eyes on her, smiled sweetly and said, "The Heywards, dear one?" Though she was not sure, Rebecca thought Jane Anne had said something about favoring someone.

"Yes, ma' am, I was just saying that Papa says I look just like my grandmother Jane Heyward," Jane Anne replied.

Lying, because her thoughts had certainly been running far beyond the girl before her, Rebecca said, "Well—yes, I can see that, too, after taking that long silent moment there to study those exquisite features of yours. Still, I'm going so far as to say I think your beauty is one of a kind, far exceeding that of your Grandmother Heywards. In fact, I'd say it looks no less perfect than those beautiful roses you're carrying in that basked." She suddenly batted her eyes somewhat coyly and gave a little giggle. "Fixing up the parlor for all those Saturday night beaus, aren't you?"

Caught short—she certainly had not expected the elderly, cosmopolitan Rebecca to be so pert and saucy, Jane Anne said nothing and felt even more vulnerable under Rebecca's peer because of the sudden blush flushing her face.

However, Eliza did say something, coming to her daughter's aid and telling Rebecca, "Not only in the parlor, Rebecca, but the entire house as well. We're giving our first ball tonight, and Jane Anne's taking care of the flower arrangements."

Rebecca's mouth fell open, the news silencing her as she stared back at Eliza.

"A ball? Did you say you're giving a ball here at Green Sea tonight?" She finally asked forgetting all about her earlier concern over making positive she had beard correctly—a trait with her that was more attributed to her habit of letting her mind thrash around in wild circles than become of the failing of her hearing or empty—headedness, either, as far as that went.

"That's what I said," smiled Eliza.

"Well—" Rebecca beamed and then paused, seeming as though she was momentarily in doubt about something. Then, just as quickly she was suddenly singing out again, 'So much the better! How lucky for Rebecca Wainwright!" And, without delaying one second longer, she whirled around and sent a rather loud and enthusiastic whoop to the cabman to fetch her overnight bag, which to Eliza's and Jane Anne's astonishment turned out to be no ordinary traveling bag at all but a trunk so huge and heavy that the thickset, burly driver could barely move it from the hack. He finally managed; however and waddled with it to the edge of the porch where he deposited it with somewhat noisy grunts and a look of impatient disgust, too, for Rebecca In the deep scowl he sent Rebecca, there was no mistaking his irritation.

All the same, when Rebecca—chipper as a child—immediately opened her handbag and swept to where he stood frowning at her, thrusting several pieces of gold in his hand, she won him over instantly. With the falling of each coin, the man's dark mood seemed to grow lighter until his face was shining as bright as the glittery gold he held. As a matter of fact, Rebecca made such a smash hit with him, that before he turned away toward his cab, he bowed so courtly over her hand that it caused her to wonder if she possibly could have overlooked something about the gent—moving her to lean toward him a little farther for a closer inspection—which told her curious mind nothing before he finally did turn from her scrutiny and was on his way again.

Frisking back across the porch to rejoin Eliza and Jane Anne, whose eyes were taking in the astounding fact that Rebecca Wainwright appeared to have dropped at least twenty years from her age in no time flat, she staggered Eliza again by saying, "Tell Me, Eliza dear, will that divine Matthew Carson be here tonight? I can hardly wait to set my eyes on him again. You know, when I heard that he had remarried, to your mother's sister I believe?" She paused and held an unwinking eye on Eliza waiting to be ascertained she was correct.

"Yes, he married Aunt Amy Drakston," Eliza finally volunteered, wondering if she was being sensible in assisting Rebecca's prattle one word farther.

"Oh, yes," Rebecca continued, "I recall the name now, dear Luke has made mention of her from time to time in his letters. Anyway, I truly regretted that three thousand miles of ocean had prevented me from having a try at catching the divine man myself1 I'm here now though and married or not, I simply refuse to leave until I see that handsome man and have another dance with him. After having him all to herself for twenty years or better, I would think Mrs. Carson wouldn't object too much at sparing him for a dance or two with an old friend, would you?" Her piercing gaze hung on Eliza's face again.

Eliza stared back, regarding Rebecca for a moment. It was hard for her to think that Rebecca would talk such nonsense and mean it. Seeing; however, that there was not one single crack of a smile nowhere on her face, Eliza—hardly able to take it all in—decided that it might be more wise to remind Rebecca Wainwright that those days at Windsor when she and her father had been guests there, had not occurred the week before or last year, either, as for that matter, but years and years before that. Moreover, Rebecca being an old friend of her father's was news to her; but, of course, she let that matter rest.

At last, she finally told Rebecca, "Father is seventy-nine years old, Rebecca, a little too old to be counting dances with anyone I should think."

"Oh, my, he's not well?" Rebecca cried. "How dreadful. I'm so sorry to hear that!"

"No, no, you've misunderstood me," Eliza hastily corrected, beginning to feel as though she was rapidly approaching her wit's end. "Father is well, I'm happy to say. I only meant—"

"What! Oh, my goodness, what a relief!" Rebecca was crying again, cutting Eliza off as one of her hands clasped the frothy piles of lace circling her throat. "For a moment there, I was feeling something awful, thinking I might not even get the chance to see him while I'm here, let alone dance with him!"

"Of course, you will," assured Eliza, feeling now as if she were assuring the desire of a child instead of a grown woman and quite a matronly one at that. "Father will be here tonight and Aunt Amy, too. I'm sorry I gave you the impression he wouldn't be, but I was just trying to say that it's been a long time and Father's not as young as he used to be."

"Time? Age? Oh, phew with that business," laughed Rebecca, her childish manner seeming to vanish in the wisdom of what she was saying. "Seventy-nine or ninety-nine, what's the difference as long as one is up and about, going ahead with one's business and the joy of living."

All but recovered now from Rebecca's brusqueness and rapidly warming to those other girls like, impish qualities that she was seeing in Rebecca Wainwright, Jane Anne smiled and said, "Well, Grandfather certainly hasn't failed to do that yet. Stuart says he's the youngest seventy-nine he'll ever hope to see."

"See there," Rebecca said, turning her attention back to Jane Anne with Eliza noting as she did how the small pouty mouth was setting in a smirk. "Somehow, I just knew that time had smiled most pleasantly on that divine man." But then, all of a sudden, it seemed Rebecca's shrewd eye had caught on to something else that would bring added flavor to what was being said, going on, "Stuart. Oh, yes, I can see now that he's the one. I'm positive of it. Why, I would almost bet that this ball tonight is to announce your engagement to that young man, isn't it, dear one?"

Before Jane Anne—blushing deeply again but this time around with a bemused smile, could comment on Rebecca's remark, Eliza— far from amused, was already saying, "Certainly not, Rebecca, nothing of the kind! It's a housewarming, combined with celebrating the children's birthdays and mine and Luke's twenty-fourth wedding anniversary. Jane Anne will be leaving for college in a few days. It'll be a long time before there's any engagement party held here at Green Sea."

"As beautiful as this child is? In a pig's eye!" hooted Rebecca, curling her button-hole mouth in mockery. "Don't you realize, Eliza dear, that you won't be any more successful in keeping those young blades from swarming around her than your father was in keeping them from flocking around you at Windsor?" She turned back to Jane Anne. "I do gather, angel child, that your mother has told you all about those days at Windsor when she not only had every young dandy there ogling for her attention but snatched your dear father right out from under the pretty nose of at least a dozen Virginia belles and, all this, in one afternoon outing at that, mind you!"

A dozen Virginia belles indeed! Angel child and also that word divine, too! Suddenly, Eliza had run out of patience. Guest or not, Never had she so desired to see a woman ensconced behind closed doors and out of her sigh as she did the zippy and nosey, Rebecca Wainwright, and stalling not one second longer, she could not have made it more plainer to Rebecca than had she come right out and said so.

"Yes, Rebecca, she has heard about Windsor but not the dandies or my conquest of Luke, either, and I'm afraid she's going to have to wait, too, because those roses should've already been put in water. Besides, you must be plenty fatigued from your long journey and would like to retire for a spell before the ball begins."

Seeing that she had pretty much stirred Eliza's blood, Rebecca, gathering one of the most innocent smiles that one was capable of mustering, said, "Of course, dear, you're absolutely right. Knowing that you must be awfully busy and the like and since I do want to look my very best for tonight and realize that every additional minute that I rest will certainly be beneficial to me on that score, I really should've suggested retiring myself."

Though Eliza's smile was rather thin, she nevertheless mustered one herself and replied, "Good, come on in. I'll have someone fetch your trunk upstairs shortly," and relenting somewhat because Rebecca was a guest and an old friend of Luke's to boot, she stepped aside and cordially gestured for Rebecca to precede her into the hallway.

Even so, Eliza had not relented so much that she wanted to subject herself to Rebecca's prattle while getting her settling in, so as Rebecca was taking in all the unique splendor of the grand foyer—uttering oh's to this and oh's to that—Eliza made a fast decision, saying to Jane—Anne who was following with the basket of roses, "I'll take the roses, dear, and see to them and you can show Mrs. Wainwright to her room the bedroom that is opposite yours across the hall."

However for all that, Eliza was instantly regretting that she had not settled the capricious Rebecca in herself, telling herself that she should have known that Rebecca Wainwright would stay a step ahead of her no matter what, when she heard Rebecca say—no sooner than her feet had found the first step of the stairway as she smiled—that catlike smile of hers in Jane Anne's face and dropped a snug arm around her waist "Now dear one, I want you to tell your Aunt Rebecca all about that young man Stuart Drakston and I mean everything, leaving nothing out. There's nothing I like better than listening to a true love story between lovers!"

Aunt Rebecca! True love! Lovers! Eliza stood, letting the roses continue to wilt as she fastened a flaming eye on Rebecca's departing back and, almost felt that she could strangle her when Rebecca upon reaching the upper hall stalled for a few seconds and looking back over her shoulder sent down a bold look of triumph plus a little wave!

Their eyes held for only a second, but it was long enough to bring a scorching flush to Eliza's face. Even after Rebecca had disappeared, she remained in the same spot for a long minute, feeling as though Rebecca Wainwright had taken a yardstick and measured every emotion and every thought that was running through her body.

Chapter Eight

Dusk, and the brightening beam of a full circle moon were rapidly eating the last rays of the weather—perfect twilight before Eliza could bring herself to feel easy and comfortable enough about the party's preparations—including her own reflection which was gazing back at her from the gilt framed mirror of her dressing table; to let well enough alone and precede to the entry hall on Luke's arm for the receiving of their guests.

By this hour, Eliza should not have harbored one fraction of fear that all was not in order relative to the party and its anticipated success. In each and every room it was evident the final effect served the new mansion's grandeur duly and was also plain for all to see that there had been a proficient "Paver of the way" to bring it all about.

In addition to the elegance of roses embellishing still the glowing richness of their silver and crystal containers, which bedecked all the first-floor rooms, there were many other baskets of late-blooming flowers and tall tubs of wood fern, magnolia, and boxwood setting amid the furnishings of the entry hall and along the walls of the ballroom, too. And added to this charming garden effect, were garlands and garlands of glossy green ivy trailing along the fireplace mantels and over and around the long, wide windows in the ballroom which gave one a full view of the moon-drenched formal garden. The windows in the ballroom had been left bare of any window dressing for those two purposes—to give one a free hand in decorating when told the window dressings had been ordered long back to suit the occasion as well as saving the garden's picturesque view which lay directly beyond the windows only a few feet—Anne Carson's garden which Doss had kept preserved through the years. There were two huge fireplaces at either end of the ballroom but, on this soft September night, they had been left unlighted. Even so, with silver candelabras bearing flaming tapers amid the lush green ivy on all the fireplace mantels as well as both ends of the dining room table, too, and some fifty more tapers glowing from the huge crystal chandelier in the ballroom, plus all the gleam that the chandeliers in the entry hall, the parlor, and the dining room were also radiating, the entire mansion seemed to be blanketed by the inviting warmth of glowing fireplaces, anyhow.

The massive sliding doors that separated the entry hall from the ballroom on its left had been opened and pushed far back inside the wall on either side from view, almost making those two sections on the first-floor appear as being one large room; and in addition to the entry hall's comfortable seating, more chairs had been added to it and along the walls of the ballroom, also.

It appeared that nothing had been overlooked in readying the festive setting. Even an ivy and flower decked dais had been erected in the ballroom and also outfitted with easy straight-backed chairs for the comfort of the professional musicians from Charleston, who had been engaged to furnish music for the affair. Likewise, with the windows, the floor in the ballroom had also been left bare of any covering. With the pleasure of their two children having been in mind more than anything else—visioning more social affairs for Green Sea in the future now that the mansion was completed and knowing that most often these affairs called for dancing aplenty, Luke and Eliza had chosen not to cover the oaken floor with rugs, leaving its wide gleaming boards instead ready and waiting for the lively "hooves" of anyone who wanted to take to them at any given time.

The gown that Eliza had just slipped into was new. Solely for this one event she had purchased it and also had pampered her likes in the doing, a luxury she had not allowed herself to indulge in for long years; that is, without viewing what the dress offered pertaining to its service—ability rather than pleasing her eye alone. And yet, in the long run, her final choice turned out to be no more sensational in lines, material, or style than had she been purchasing it for a Sunday afternoon visit with Martha!

Perhaps purchasing clothes with an eye directed more toward their usefulness instead of what actually pleased her, had been forced on Eliza far too long for her to lay down the habit all at once. Then again, taking the gown's color into account, a sapphire blue shimmery satin, one wonders in her deep concern for Luke's likes and dislikes could not have prompted her in her final selection more than she realized despite yielding to her own whims for the first time since the war, as a matter of fact.

At any rate. whatever the case, once the plain, simple gown with its straight long sleeves modified mandarin collar, and fully gored skirt along with a rhinestone-buckled belt clinching the waistline, was finally clinging ever so gently to Eliza's still subtle, girlish-like figure, proof that she had known what she was doing when she had made her selection was clearly manifested in the mirror before her. Never had she owned a gown that accentuated the violet-blue depths of her eyes so fully or complimented her comely person more attractively. She knew it, too, and felt good about it.

Even so, after giving her hair which was dressed in a fashionable deep-waved pompadour another last minute inspection, she still hesitated at the dressing table, unable to make her mind up as to whether she should wear any more jewelry other than the plain gold bracelet that circled her wrist.

Letting her hand pause at the neckline of her gown, she turned to Luke, who seemed preoccupied with his own dressing, and said, "Luke, do you think this dress would look better with some jewelry, perhaps Mother's pearls here around the collar?"

Luke turned to face her, slipping his arms into his shirt. Suddenly, his hands became idle. Presently, after having taken what had appeared to be time to study her question, he told her, "you know, sweet, your beauty tonight is an absolute mystery to me, considering all the burdens and toil that's come your way since you married me almost twenty-four years ago." Eliza was short on vanity. "Well, I'm pleased, Luke that you seem pleased with what you see, but that's not what I asked you." She smiled. "Besides, if there is any mystery connected with the way I look tonight in spite of those grueling years as you've put it, it's probably because there hasn't been a single day that I've spent with you that's seemed long. In fact, when I do call the years of our marriage to mind, they seem more like twenty-four days to me than twenty-four years."

"That they do, love," he said, the present seeming to be forgotten as his eyes still remained on her.

"The pearls, Luke," she laughed. "I asked, what do you think about my wearing pearls with this gown?"

"Oh, that," he murmured, swiftly arresting his thoughts and giving his attention to her question, his eyes falling to her gown. "No, I don't think so. I think maybe a pretty sapphire broach would do, but not pearls. In fact, I'm sure of it to pin on just where that collar divides at."

"Well, I don't have a sapphire broach, so I guess that takes care of that," she said with an air of total indifference, finally rising from the dressing table and turning her back to it. "Better hurry on with your own dressing, Luke, or our first guests will be arriving to find us absent from the front door. Here, let me give you a helping hand."

She stepped closer and started buttoning his shirt.

He stopped her, clasping his hands over hers as he smiled down at her and said, "No sapphire broach? Says who?" Then, he let her hands go and reached for his coat that was lying on the bed. He ran his hand inside an inner pocket and drawing forth a small, dainty package he reached for her hand again and laid it inside her palm.

It was too much like magic for Eliza to absorb all at once. She had to have time, because not since their wedding day when Luke had slipped a gold wedding band on her finger had he given her any jewelry. Of course, she knew that was owing to the fact that Luke had never had a spare cent to spend on jewelry or anything else that did not concern keeping Green Sea in operation or his family's daily needs. Certainly, baubles of worth or otherwise, had been totally out of the picture. Thus, she just stood and looked back at him, the tiny box resting in her palm.

Quickly going on with the buttoning of his shirt and stuffing his shirttail inside his trousers, Luke laughed, "I know I've shocked you, darling, but try to pull yourself together and take a look at it. I intended giving it to you on the twenty-fourth but blame your own self now that I've fouled up, for your wanting to wear pearls when in truth with your looks you really don't need pearls or that, either, as for that matter."

Of course, Eliza knew what the tiny box held before she went ahead and opened it; yet to see that the broach was indeed a real sapphire and one that was surrounded by genuine diamond chips at that, was more of a surprise to her than had she had no inkling at all of what Luke had brought her.

"Luke! It's so pretty, but we can't afford this not after buying all those other things. Why, this must've cost a fortune!" She cried, looking up at him.

Luke was slipping on his coat—yes, his coat and trousers, too, were new and Eliza almost forgot the broach when she looked at him. True, his shoulders were stooped a little and the jet-black hair was graying. Still to her, he had never looked more elegant or handsome, even counting their wedding day.

"Forget about the cost, dear, and pin it on your gown," he said. "I thought if we could afford all the other, and we must be able to since we bought it and it's all in our possession, that surely I could afford to buy you something special for our anniversary after twenty-four years of having been unable to spare even one cent for anything like that. Besides, we still have a lot of tobacco to sell. Our earnings from it should pretty well carry us to next summer's tobacco gathering. So, quit your worrying and let's count our blessings and make this an occasion to remember."

Eliza knew Luke was right and instantly regretted having said one word about their spending, or what they could or could not afford.

"Of course, Luke, you're right and we'll do just that," she smiled. And, stepping back to the dressing table with Luke watching her she unfastened the broach from its tiny velvet pillow and was pinning it on when a light tap sounded at the door.

"There's our daughter," Luke said, striding across the room. "I'd recognize that timed tap of hers anywhere."

Literally skipping through the doorway—the thought of Stuart Drakston being in attendance had put her feet on clouds—Jane Anne, whose own new gown was as flowing and bright as the blooming goldenrod blazing a golden-yellow along the ditch banks and roadways, stopped short, exclaiming, "Oh, Papa, you've given Mother the broach! I might've known you would, the minute you saw her in her new gown!"

"Not so, this time, kitten," her father smiled, "It was only when I saw that she was seriously thinking of donning pearls, which I couldn't see, that I broke down."

"And, I might've known that you were in on the whole deal," Eliza interjected and laughed, looking at her daughter's reflection in the mirror as she was taking another look at her

own reflection and liking what she saw. The sparkle of the diamonds against the blue of her gown had added that desired touch she had wanted.

"No, not until, Papa, had already made the selection himself and bought it," laughed Jane Anne. "So, it appears both of us are half-hitting at facts. But you look so lovely, Mother, none of it matters."

Eliza turned away from the mirror again.

"Thank you, darling, but I feel it's my happiness tonight over everything, including the fact that our two children couldn't be more handsome, that's played a big part with the way I look. You're so pretty, dear, with your beautiful black hair flowing over the collar of your yellow gown like that."

What Eliza did not know was the fact that Jane Anne had chosen to let her hair hang loose and free, save that which the yellow bow she had tied in the back was holding in place, only because Stuart Drakston preferred it that way. Stuart had made no secret of his preference to Jane Anne. He liked to see her hair long and loose, flowing in the wind, as he had seen it the day that he had taken Fancy to Green Sea and saw the grown-up Jane Anne for the first time. The irony of all this was that Eliza was not only telling Jane Anne the truth about her hair style but was pleased with it, too, because it tended to picture her daughter as being what she truly viewed Jane Anne as, a mere adolescent schoolgirl and nothing more—something she hoped Stuart Drakston would finally see, too, and get it through his head once and for all that Jane Anne was too young in years for him. There is no doubt that Eliza would have coiled every strand of Jane Anne's hair atop her head that very minute, had she known that this same "little girl" look was one of the things about Jane Anne that had captivated Stuart Drakston.

Pulling forth his pocket watch and checking the time, Luke was saying as he slipped the watch back in his waist pocket, "I must agree with your mother, kitten, you are most charming to look at. In fact, I see not one single thing about you or her that could be improved on. So, what do you both say we all get on downstairs before one of you, or maybe both, decides differently and take a run over there to that mirror again."

"Not me, Papa," said Jane Anne, "I've been finished with that or gave up I should say a good while ago and visited with Mrs. Wainwright. That's why I'm here." She looked at her mother. "Mother, Mrs. Wainwright asked me to tell you not to get alarmed if she didn't come downstairs for a while yet."

A flash of uneasiness crossed Eliza's face.

"What's wrong? Is she ill?"

"Oh, no, Mrs. Wainwright's fine. In fact, she's took it upon herself to put the finishing touch to my hair. She said since she lost a great deal of her beauty rest when Papa came home this afternoon, that it was most essential she make up for it now by lying down for at least one hour with a wet cloth applied to her eyes and face."

"Heaven!" Eliza sniffed with a pronounced sneer, "What vanity? I hope it works. Thank you, dear, you may run on. Your father and I will follow in a moment."

As Jane Anne smiled and made a dash through the doorway, Eliza, letting a bit of concern mix with the sneer, turned to Luke and asked, "What do you think, Luke, shall I look in on her before going on downstairs?"

Luke laughed, "Not unless you uncurl your lips beforehand, darling."

Eliza quickly dropped the sneer and smiled back at him.

"Is it that obvious, Luke?"

"A moment ago, yes," he replied.

"I'm sorry, Luke, I'll try to be more discreet from now on, where Rebecca's concerned. But she really stumps me. That woman is the biggest flirt I'll ever hope to see. Did you see how she was ogling and battering her eyes at Tom Green no sooner than you made the introductions? I was actually embarrassed."

Luke chuckled again. "And, Tom loved every second of it," he said.

"Well, that may be," Eliza scoffed, "but I don't think Betsy derived much joy from it. To tell you the truth, I think if Betsy were not the lady she is, Rebecca Wainwright would've heard a few high words from her, right then and there. And, that word divine. I think I'll scream if I hear it uttered one more time!"

"Oh, I don't think it was all that bad, darling."

"You don't? Well, how come your face was telling a complete different story, before she turned her attention from you to Tom Green?"

"I was just shocked at seeing her, that's all, surely not at her behavior. Rebecca's always been a flirt and will remain being one regardless of how many Tony Drexwell's she's involved with. You can't imagine how stunned I was when she suddenly came sailing down those stairs and threw herself in my arms, when, long ago, I'd given up the thought of ever seeing her again. Why, I was just penning a letter to her the other night, never dreaming she was already sailing the Atlantic on her way to Tony Drexwell. I tell you; it was almost like seeing someone rising from the grave."

"Poor Mr. Drexwell," said Eliza. "Yes, poor Mr. Drexwell," echoed Luke, chuckling slightly again. "Well, shall I look in on her?" Eliza added. "You never did say."

"No, she's all right. Let her drowse in peace and come on down whenever she wishes." Luke gave another chuckle. "In point of the fairer sex, if my hunch is right, she'll be down soon enough, anyway."

Eliza made a face at him and then was laughing with him as they moved from the s bedroom and on toward the staircase.

One hundred guests had been invited and even though no one made it a point to count heads, it would have been safe for one to betted that more than one hundred and twenty-five came. Though they had wondered at the time what Bill Clarendon and his stay-at-home sister, Charlotte would do regarding the invitation they were sending to Clarendon Plantation—since all ties between the Heywards and the Clarendon's had all but ceased to exist by this date, Eliza had headed their guest list with Bill and Charlotte's name anyway. And; in truth, surprising the Heywards, both Clarendon's came. In fact, the Clarendon coach was the first coach to swing into the circular drive and drop its two passengers at the steps before heading on to park at the stable yard.

Bill and Charlotte were already crossing the threshold as Luke and Eliza—both pleased and happy to see them, came hurrying along the wide, circular stairway. They barely made it to the center of the hallway—their chosen spot for the greeting of their guests, before the aged Albert in full white trappings finished announcing, in a thin but proud and distinct voice, "The honorable, Mr. William Clarendon and Miss Charlotte Clarendon."

Likewise, to Luke, Bill Clarendon had also grown white-temple and still remained to be lean and handsome, too. Possessing his same easy manner, he paused and exchanged a few cordial words with Albert before he moved on to grasp Luke's hand in a most hearty greeting and on to hold Eliza's long enough to plant a light caress upon it and tell her, as Luke was warmly welcoming the nearly white-headed Charlotte "I'm honored and proud, Eliza, to be here, sharing in all this tonight with you and Luke."

"And, we feel honored and happy too, Bill, to have this opportunity again to enjoy the company of you and Charlotte both," she smilingly told him and turned to embrace his sister as he smiled back at her and moved on into the ballroom where the musicians were already filling the house with the strains of a Strauss Waltz and the daughters of Bessie and Ruth, also outfitted in full-white dress, were waiting with attractive trays of hors d'oeuvers and Pete was offering frosted glasses of vintage wines—nothing any stronger in the way of alcohol was served in the Heyward household.

In addition to all the tempting appetizers that were awaiting the newly arrivals, there were mountains of ham steaks, roast beef, fried chicken, broiled duckling and quail, shad roe, fried shrimp and shrimp casserole, fresh oysters in the shell, corn dodgers, white bread, biscuits, rice, potato salad, candied yams, watercress salad, butter beans, canned summer squash, lemon pie, coconut pie, chess pie, marble cake, lady Baltimore cake, and topping all this off a frozen chocolate mousse, too—all waiting to be devoured later on in the evenings by incited appetites and danced—out ones as well.

Rapidly, following the Clarendon's they kept coming, one coach after another until the more than a hundred guests were milling around, visiting with one another and also warming up their stomachs from the continual offering of drinks and appetizers. Though Pete nor the two maids had had any previous experience in the line of work they were engaged in, Eliza took pride in the fact that they were carrying out her few instructions with the expertness of one seasoned to the task. She was noting with pleasure that all three appeared to be no less practiced than the masterly, know-how Albert doing the honors at the door, though unlike Albert they were being kept on a constant run—aside from the time they were serving—between the ballroom and the kitchen pantry carrying empty and loaded trays back and forth.

Finally, the last guest had been greeted and Luke was looking down at Eliza and saying, as he took her by the hand and started to move toward the ballroom, "Come on, dear, I think it's time for us to make a start at breaking in that oaken floor that we marked long ago, remember?"

"Indeed, I do, darling," Eliza smiled. "Everything you promised that day, you've made it all come true."

"We, dear," he corrected, entering the ballroom and signaling for the band to start a waltz.

The crowd moved back and gave them the floor which they gracefully circled once and then Luke was motioning for the others to join in and the ball had begun—a ball that had every appearance of continuing indefinitely as the evening wore on so jubilant it became. All the same, this was not to say that it joyfully continued on without having the usual amount of those little annoyances which forever pop up when that many people are assembled together, not to mention the one or two wet blankets that always seem to be at all gatherings along with another certain number whose going to be themselves regardless of whenever or wherever it is or no matter what. At any rate, it would be impossible for anybody to please more than a hundred guests in any situation, or, as for that matter, have the behavior of all that many guests pleasing a host, simply because people were people—namely, Rebecca Wainwright for one as well as the hostess herself, Eliza Heyward.

On the part of Rebecca, she let the ball get in full swing before she made her appearance, descending upon the crowded ballroom with the impact of a full-blown hurricane. From the second she alighted to the first floor, it seemed as though Rebecca had set her eye on this one night as being her last hurrah so to speak; that is, as far as feeling free to let herself go in living it up a bit before she settled down to more confined quarters in Louisiana!

Her outfit was sensational and, this description still did not do justice to its eye-opening originality. Further, how Rebecca came by such a unique style was another question, because it bore not one trace of similarity to current fashion or to the dress of many other women present who were sporting the fashionable bustle which had been popular for some time. The bustle was a framework worn under the skirt in the back below the waist for the purpose of giving one's skirt a more attractive drape—a ridiculous fashion that brought many laughs to the surface, and especially when some of the less fortunate who could not afford a store bought one reverted to making their own out of corn meal or sawdust and having it burst open in public, sifting all about! Eliza simply would have no part of the bustle and Luke supported her fully, saying it was absurd because as far as he could see most women were endowed enough in that certain spot without adding any addition bulging.

At any rate, Rebecca's gown sported neither the draped, protruding bustle in the back, or a pronounced waistline above a gored skirt like Eliza was wearing. Instead, more than anything else, it resembled a colorful, flimsy tent that a gust of wind might have set afloat. Yet, at the same time, its gauze material, its mauve color, and all its abundance of frilly rose point lace ruffles and fluffy feathered trimming weaving back and forth, plus the two elaborate plumes which Rebecca had fastened with diamond stick pins to the banked pile of snowy-white curls atop her head and which matched the plumage of her gown, brought one to wonder—for a split second—if a straying flamingo had not flown through the windows and lighted among them!

There was hardly a head in the ballroom that Rebecca had not turned in her direction—old and young alike, and also scarcely a one of these people who were not whispering to their companion or to the neighbor at their elbow, "Who's the pretty lady in all the feathers?"

However, Eliza was one who was not whispering. After a thoughtful few seconds upon spying Rebecca, thinking back to Rebecca's first reaction at hearing about the ball, Eliza was telling Luke, "That woman's wearing her dressing gown, Luke!"

Pausing their waltz somewhat, Luke turned his head to find Rebecca again, saying, "What are you talking about? She can't be. Rebecca wouldn't be that bold."

"You don't think? Well, take a closer look and then tell me if you're ever seen anybody else wearing an evening dress that came within a mile looking like what that woman has on. She hasn't been resting for a hour. That was her sly excuse for having enough time to get that preposterous outfit together and get it on and also for timing herself to make that grand entrance that she's making. In her scatterbrain way, she probably sent the wrong trunk on ahead to Louisiana, leaving herself short on dress clothes. Either that, or she didn't expect to do much of anything while she's here but get her beauty rest. Certainly, she didn't think she'd be attending a ball. I'd bet my life on that. Suitable clothes or not though, it's apparent she meant she was not going to miss anything."

"Could be you're right, dear," said Luke, still looking over his shoulder at Rebecca making a beeline toward Matthew Carson where he and Amy and several more couples were seated against the wall, "and if you are, I dare say she has one extraordinary imagination to come up with such an incredible creation on so short a notice. She looks sensational."

"If one's particular to peahens," Eliza jeered, pretending to be offended with his praise of Rebecca. Then, dumping the long face, she whispered excitedly, "Will you look at that, Luke! Of all the men who's here, she's headed straight for Father. Poor father!"

"I'm looking, love," laughed Luke, "and I would advise that you don't waste too much pity on him. I'd say he's rather flattered, from the looks of him!"

Matthew Carson was flattered. He had already been told of Rebecca's unexpected visit to Green Sea; and, in truth, was eagerly awaiting her arrival downstairs. Those amorous looks that Rebecca had sent him so openly long years back had come afresh in his mind again. He was most anxious to see her, mostly because he was wondering if the years had mellowed her any. One glance; however, and Matthew was wondering no more. Even if she had not signaled him gut among the more than three dozen men present and barely acknowledged his introductions of them before she had her hand in his and was gleefully pulling him from his chair to waltz with her— leaving the reserved Amy near gasping in horror for the first time in her life at her blatancy the flamboyant outfit had left no doubt in Matthew's mind that it would take something more than years to mellow the forward Rebecca.

Matthew Carson had always been a tireless dancer and a very able one; therefore, in spite of Eliza's fears the years had not taken so much out of him that he was greatly strained to carry through with what Rebecca demanded. In fact, he rather like waltzing with Rebecca again and not only waltzed her around the ballroom once but twice, before he gave her up to another gentleman who was vying for her attention and returned to the piqued Amy.

Jealousness had not nettled Amy. She felt very secure in Matthew's love. Loving him as dearly as she did, she was only concerned about his welfare, telling herself that if Matthew could not bring himself to hold aloof from the giddy, brazen Rebecca—which deep down she knew he was incapable of doing with anybody, that he should have cut their waltz shorter than he had. Once he had returned to her though and appeared to be none the worse for helping warm the floor with Rebecca—patting her hand reassuringly—Amy's staying charm surfaced once again and was to hold intact for the remainder of the night. Though she did have to endure the chattering Rebecca's presence time and time again. Maybe the reason Amy's calm was to hold a lot easier was the fact, not for one moment all evening long, was Rebecca to find herself lacking an escort, always having one hanging to her side every time she felt inclined to seek Matthew's company again. In any event, it was plain that by no means was Rebecca going to let Matthew rid himself of her company for good and, short of leaving early, there was little Amy could do about it had she had a mind to.

For all Rebecca's interest in Matthew, this did not seem to discourage other men from looking her way and bringing most of them to seek her out. She took the party by storm, flitting from one man's arms to another and leaving wives and sweethearts alike all in a twitter at her brazenness. As she had pointed out to Eliza earlier in the day, Rebecca was not concerned with the age factor, and no doubt this attitude on her part was a major element in the gaining of her popularity. All the same, the majority of Rebecca's admirers seemed to be near witch—charmed with her, appearing—unlike Matthew Carson—not to give one hoot whether their wives or sweethearts were ruffled or not as they bounded off to the dance floor to have a waltz with Rebecca. And, as the evening wore on, even Eliza was brought to admit—to herself of course—that the men's seemingly obsession with Rebecca was partly, if not all, justified because she had to agree with Luke, Rebecca did look sensational.

Scrutinizing Rebecca as she floated from arm to arm in the gleaming candlelight, Eliza was brought to reason that she looked nowhere near her age. With the betrayal of her middle age—the throat and the arms—well hidden in the laces and feathers of her flowing, flimsy pink gauze and with her little pouty mouth and cheeks, too, glowing a deep rosy-red under the banks and banks of snowy-white curls, plus her young in heart manner to boot, Eliza saw that Rebecca actually radiated an air of cherub-like youth that one was hard put to resist.

In any case, Rebecca became the life of the party, going on from the arms of Matthew Carson to make her conquest. Before the celebration ended, there was hardly a woman present who had escaped being victimized of their escort from time to time. She appeared tireless, never pausing or seeming to want to until she latched on to Bill Clarendon and learned he was a bachelor and a very affluent one at that. But, unfortunately for Rebecca, Bill happened to be one of the few men who seemed to be immune to that aura of intoxication surrounding her. True, she did amuse him, but that was as far as it went with Bill. Finally, when Rebecca saw, in her cunning way, that she was making no headway with Bill Clarendon, she latched on to Luke and—once she did—appeared to be in no hurry to turn him loose, either. At this point, Bill began to work his way through the crowd in search for Eliza. He saw his action as being only right and in justice, since Rebecca Wainwright had snagged her husband for what looked like an awfully long waltz.

Aside from the few words that Bill Clarendon had exchanged with Eliza earlier on his arrival, there had been no more conversation between them. Nonetheless, and even though their greeting had been short and mostly bordering on propriety, too, with no more words exchanged, the fact remained there had been a lot more involved at the time, than a mere few pleasantries being passed between host and guest.

First, there was the white-haired solemn-faced solitudinarian, Charlotte who had finally made it back to Green Sea after a period of twenty-four years; her appearance there making it seem to Eliza as if there was something almost holy about it. Then, there was Bill still a bachelor a fact that had brought him to reason—long back—that for the good of all concerned he would cut all social ties with Green Sea. There had been no pleasant way for him, Eliza, or Luke to go on trying to maintain close ties with one another, even if he and Luke did continue to do business together, with his sawmill producing near all the lumber that went into the building of the new mansion. All this unspoken reasoning though and carrying through with might just as well have been openly aired and settled upon by all three people, so visible it had lain between them through the years. Yet, agreed upon or not, it had worked and seemingly well at that; that is to say, until Bill saw Eliza turn her head and find his face as he was crossing the length of the room toward her. Then, in his case, he was not so sure because, instantly, as well as having an awareness of a deep loss of purpose for being there engulfed him in oversupply, there was also a feeling of coming off second best coupled with finding himself yearning for a little more than that, yearning hopelessly to see some signification or expression in this celebration that would hold some little something special for him, too.

Having not the remotest idea when he would be calling to Green Sea again—if ever any more—when he did take his leave on this night he yearned to leave there with some little something of time and the place and the girl he had loved and lost, no matter how inconsequential, all tucked inside him for keeps.

Thus, hoping and yearning, Bill approaching Eliza, opened his arms and said, "Will you do me the honor, Eliza, it's been a long time?"

"Too long, Bill," was her unexpected reply as she entered his arms without one second's hesitation, with the years suddenly spilling away for Bill Clarendon—spilling clear back to that time long ago at Drakston Hall when coming off second best with Eliza had never entered his mind. Round and round he and Eliza whirled, finally whirled passed Luke and Rebecca

Wainwright with Bill coming back to the present to say, "your guest, Mrs. Wainwright is most charming, in her unique way If I might add."

"Unique is the right word," quipped Eliza with a flash of wit. "Pertaining to the charming aspect though, I am curious as to which you're referring to, the plumes and the feathers or the peahen who's wearing them? Surely you can't mean both!"

Suddenly Bill was hilarious, almost doubling in stitches.

"Well—" he finally voiced. Then using discretion, he let the word falter and went no further, though his mirth remained very much alive.

Trying to cover her own humor, Eliza swallowed the giggle rising in her throat and quipped again, "Oh, don't mind me, go on and say what you think. I'm having a wonderful time and certainly wouldn't think of letting some remark about Marie Antoinette's reincarnation, praise or otherwise, spoil the evening for me!"

Thinking of the French queen who had lost her splendid, bedecked head by way of the guillotine as he instinctively turned his own head in the direction of Rebecca Wainwright, Bill, seeing that Eliza had a valid point, laughed so hard again that Eliza was unable to hold out any longer, laughing uproariously with him.

Quieting somewhat she said, "Well, go on and tell me." "Tell you what?" He laughed. "Oh, you know, Mrs. Wainwright, silly," she said still giggling.

"Oh, yes, Mrs. Wainwright," he repeated. Then trying to look serious through his smile as Eliza had tried to attempt moments earlier, he went on to tell her, "That's funny, seems I've completely forgotten what I meant to say about that." Not really had Bill forgotten. He just had no desire to take up one second of this open freeness that he had recaptured with Eliza, after so many long years, to discuss the cunning tactics of a woman who held no interest for him. For what little time it would last, he wanted to make the best of these moments with Eliza, ask of Elias's comfort—her well-being, and have her inquire of his. It was not much, but neither had he asked for much. Knowing who Eliza's heart centered in, he had known better than to do that. Moreover, neither would he let himself be deluded into seeing something that did not exist. The important part was, he had discovered that he and Eliza could laugh together again and laugh with a free heart and revel in it.

While Eliza and Bill Clarendon were having their mirthful Waltz and carrying on a much animated conversation as they shared unpunctual news of affairs and interest with one another, Eliza was not so absorbed that she was letting her problem—or what she was turning into a problem—with her daughter slip her mind. The fact was, she was slowly but surely beginning to see red over the whole affair, though she was managing somewhere to keep it well shrouded from Bill eyes as well as those of her other guests.

It was no mischance—so that Eliza had taken note that Stuart and Jane Anne were still waltzing together. In fact, she had not, for one moment, failed to keep one corner of her eye seeking their whereabouts ever since she had cornered Jane Anne off by herself and told her, as easygoing as possible—not more than a hour earlier, "Don't forget, dear, you have an obligation to see that more than one guest of the younger set is entertained." That was all she had said, and she had thought at the time that that was all there would be to it since Jane Anne, appearing willing and agreeable, had replied, "yes, mother," and had raced on off to have a dance with the blond and fairly heavy-set Luke Green immediately.

The one waltz with Luke, though, had been nothing but a short interim for Jane Anne before going right back into the arms of Stuart Drakston. Eliza could see that now and it infuriated her plenty. It seemed her daughter had not only turned a deaf ear when she had expressed her feelings about the matter a few days prior but had also not taken one word of her warning then as well as on this occasion, too, as being nothing but idle chatter.

Well, Eliza thought, as Bill Clarendon was whirling her through the final steps of their own waltz, if the showdown had to come tonight, so be it! Just as quickly as she could do so without drawing attention to her actions, she would ask Jane Anne and Stuart, too, to meet her in the library for a moment. Before she was through, they both would know how much she disapproved of them acting as if there were not another soul around them. Her daughter would finally realize that she had not just been talking through her hat! And, Stuart Drakston would at last learn of her true sentiments regarding his heated chase after her daughter! Yes, bare her mind she would and bare it in a few minutes to boot! It was soon going to be time to start serving supper to the guests; the quests; she certainly could not take up too much time with those foolish youngsters.

Unknown to Eliza, her daughter had been on to her constant scrutiny all along and was far more distressed over the whole situation—and aggrieved too—then what her gentle nature had revealed in the numerous waltz she and Stuart had engaged in. And, relative to the way things were stacking up, Stuart, too, was far more enlightened than Eliza thought he was when she

finally got her chance and commanded that they come with her to the library. Indeed, although they had not known when it would come or in what manner, they both were expecting some sort of raking-down and, in a way, were prepared for it and were also not too surprised to find themselves marching toward the library with Eliza hot on their heels.

Stuart had not seen Jane Anne for several days, not since the morning of their ride together and knew instantly, the moment he had seen her upon his arrival that something had gone amiss. "Darling, what's the matter? Even though you couldn't be more beautiful, I see you're very unhappy about something," he said, no sooner than they had waltzed half a dozen steps together.

Jane Anne's answer had been silence and Stuart had pressed no further for some time. But, noting that she kept looking in the direction of her mother was all the clue that he needed to know where the trouble lay. Having planned on this very night to ask Jane Anne Heyward to be his wife and also front her parents as well for their consent, if Jane Anne said yes which he knew she would, Stuart meant to get to the bottom of the trouble. He bid his time and the crowded ballroom was in his favor. He was soon waltzing Jane Anne into the hallway and on through the front door till they had gained the porch. But the porch was also crowded with other couples, leaving them with still no privacy to talk in. He looked around and spying the little vine-covered summerhouse in the moon-drenched garden where the morning glory vines still painted it a bright blue in the September mornings, he took Jane Anne by the hand and made a dash for it. Yes, this was the same summerhouse—Doss had kept replacing its decaying latticework— that Jane Anne's mother almost lost her virginity in and would have had it not been for Luke Heyward's self-discipline and commanding conscious. Though there was no question of Jane Anne losing hers, so short the stolen minutes would have to be and the fact their minds were too taken with their troubled thoughts.

"Now, darling," Stuart said, gently gathering her to him, "We can't stay out here too long, we'll be missed, so hurry and tell me what's bothering you.

She did as he had asked, telling him, most of what her mother had said in regard to their close friendship and of her mother's ruling that it was to end, finishing by saying through muffled sobs, "and I think I'll die, Stuart, if I can't be with you anymore."

Though Stuart had sensed that Eliza Heyward's feelings toward him left a lot to be desired, he still was shocked to learn that she demanded an end to his paying court to Jane Anne, and especially after he had called at Green Sea for several months. He saw that his plan to win Eliza Heyward over, before he openly discussed his love for Jane Anne with both her parents, had not worked at all. He wondered briefly if he had not made a mistake by going the route he had. Then he dismissed the thought by telling himself he would never have gained Eliza Heyward's permission to court her daughter no matter what.

Seeing the tears streak Jane Anne's face in the shafts of moonlight streaming through the latticework, Stuart, crestfallen, pulled his handkerchief from his pocket and said, "There, darling, please don't cry. Your pretty face will be all streaked, if you do." While Jane Anne wiped at her tears, he went on to question, "And she gave no other reasons except what you've told me?"

Jane Anne blew her nose and said, as she dabbed at her face a final time and handed Stuart his handkerchief back, "No, nothing else. Just my schooling and the age difference."

Feeble excuses thought Stuart.

"What about your father? How does he feel about all this?"

"I really don't know. Papa was present when Mother told me, but he never expressed himself one way or another. What are we going to do, Stuart?"

"I don't know, dear, let me think a minute," he said, pulling her closer, and while his heart thumped in his ears from the sheer delight of holding her, he suddenly exclaimed, never dreaming his proposal would come in such a manner, "We can get married, that's what! Leave right now and be married tonight!"

Young as she was and loving him deeply, too, she still pulled back and cried in astonishment, "No, Stuart, we can't do that! I do love you so, and feel I'd be happy living in your arms without leaving them ever, but I could never bring myself to do that to Papa and Mother. I love them, too. Besides, Mother has saved her wedding gown all these years for the day I'll be married in it, in a home wedding as she was."

In the pale moonlight, he studied her startled face for a moment before he pulled her back to him, kissing her long and hard on her warm returning mouth. Now, he forced himself to pull back from her.

"Well, I must confess, darling," he said, "as much as I love you, too, and want you, I don't hold much with the idea, either, of running off into the night like a pair of criminals, even if I don't know what I'll do when you do go away to school."

"I know, Stuart, and I promise you, we'll be married the minute we win my parents approval."

"Well, in that case, we'd better hurry and get back inside," he smiled, "having your mother find us out here surely won't help our effort to do that. We'll go back and behave as near our natural selves as we can and see what happens. Come on, darling."

See they had!

Rushing ahead of Jane Anne and Stuart as they all three approached the library, Eliza reaching for the doorknob flung the door aside and stopped, signifying that the stricken pair who she had in her charge were to precede her through the doorway. Jane Anne resolved not to let go of Stuart's hand, stepped into the room, taking Stuart with her which had resulted in a rather close squeeze through the door. Nevertheless, they found themselves inside, making it together and still standing together as they watched Eliza follow without ever once taking her eyes off them as she shoved the door closed with her foot.

Standing with her back against the door while her two hands gripped onto the doorknob as Jane Anne and Stuart stared fixedly back at her, Eliza spared not one single word, promptly making her attack, "I would've preferred this situation never coming to this not tonight of all times, but since your behavior has made a confrontation unavoidable despite the occasion, I'll try to deal with it in as little time and few words that I can because there are numerous guests here and I do owe them the courtesy of my presence as much as possible. Needless to tell you I'm very much annoyed, and especially disappointed with you, Jane Anne, for not abiding my wishes and putting me in this position—"

"Please, Mother," Jane Anne interrupted, "don't be this way, I—" Her voice broke and stopped.

Still observing Eliza Heyward and noting how she was bracing herself against the door, making it appear to him as if she were thinking she had two naughty children cornered who might try to make a dash for it, Stuart suddenly began to look on the whole matter as being equal to an amusing episode in a comedy drama. All of a sudden, he was seeing all of it as being nothing but a lot of crankiness on the part of Jane Anne's mother and was telling himself that it probably was not as serious as Jane Anne thought it was. So, with his usual levelheadedness and a great deal of new found confidence, he wasted no time, either, in taking up where Jane Anne left off, saying, before Eliza could resume her attack, "Mrs. Heyward, for my part, If I've displeased you in any degree, overstepped or failed to measure up to the decencies of convention here tonight, I'm not only truly sorry and beg your apology, but for the remainder of the time I am here, will be happy to comply with whatever rules of conduct you may propose."

Disarmed for a brief moment by Stuart's cool and oiled apology, Eliza, not thinking, hastily snapped, "No, it's not that—" and too late realized she had contradicted her own accusation which fused her annoyance that much more as she cut her remark, and Stuart's lifted brow fastened on her was surely no cooling agent. She bore down all the harder as she resumed, "I mean it's not that altogether. It's this ridiculous infatuation that you and Jane Anne appear to hold for one another. It's got to stop and stop this very minute, Stuart Drakston, do you understand!"

Stuart eyed Eliza for a moment, seeing now that there was more behind Jane Anne's tears than what he had concluded. He was hard put in his deciding what to say, asking himself if he should tell her then and there of his feelings for Jane Anne or wait. He chose the former, seeing no sense in hedging about the matter any longer even if he could see that Eliza Heyward was steeped to the fullest with vexation.

"No, Mrs. Heyward," he said, "I'm sorry to say I don't understand, even if it is obvious you've totally misconceived this whole matter. I can assure you my feelings for Jane Anne is no passing fancy, and I believe I'd be safe to say she feels likewise toward me. We love one another and would like you and Mr. Heyward's consent to be married."

Now, it was Eliza's eye hanging on Stuart and not a very tender-looking one at that. Finally, in a voice hard as steel, she said, "Do you mean to stand there, Stuart Drakston, and have the insolence to tell me that you and our daughter are in love and want to be married when you've never once approached me or her father with your intentions. I can't believe, not even you, would be so lacking in properness and honor."

"I deserve that lash, Mrs. Heyward, but the reason I didn't, is because of the very thing that's taking place in this room, right at this moment. Still, the fact remains, I haven't hidden my intentions from anybody, when Jane Anne and I have been in each other's company, here at Green Sea or any place else. Surely you could see we were falling in love with one another, despite your believing otherwise."

Literally hissing, Eliza flung back, "Of course, I could see how your roving eyes were following my daughters every step! I'm not blind, thank God! And, don't think for one moment have I approved of it, even though I've kept silent until this week, when I mentioned all this unpleasantness to Jane Anne and also told her it had to stop!"

Stuart did not comment on the coarseness Eliza had charged him with, telling her instead, "Then, what I sensed all along is true. Not have you only objected to my being in Jane Anne's presence, Mrs. Heyward, but you've rejected my visits to Green Sea, too, including my appearance here tonight even though on this occasion I am here by invitation."

"I didn't say that at all, but since you've been so brave as to open the subject—no, I can't deny that I've looked on your visits here with an unwelcoming eye, and fear I will continue on to view them no differently unless you're willing to give up those foolish notions about my daughter and do so immediately."

"You're asking the impossible of me, Mrs. Heyward. I love your daughter. I think I've loved her since the first day I ever remember seeing her and I shall always love her, whether you look on me with an agreeable eye or not."

"Well, in that case then," Eliza declared, "I shall go back to my guests and trust in the meantime, that you will gain enough civility to do what would be fitting and proper, without my having to point it out to you!"

"Oh please, both of you," Jane Anne cried again, feeling as though she might have been a ball being tossed back and forth, "I can't stand anymore! Please, I love you both!"

"I'm sorry, darling," said Stuart, turning to look at Jane Anne, and swiftly his love for her made him come to a rapid decision to try to compromise with her mother before all was lost. He turned back to Eliza. "Please, Mrs. Heyward, I'm pleading, too, because I don't want it this way between us. Although I love Jane Anne and would like for us to be married immediately, I can still sympathize with your position, too. I realize it's only natural for you to be protective and concerned about anything that involves your children, and I have no quarrel with that. If you feel Jane Anne is too young in years now to be my wife, I'm willing to wait for her, even two more years until she reaches eighteen, if that is what's bothering you. In the meantime, she could go ahead with her college education as you desire her to." He dared to send her a faint, warm smile. "I believe you were eighteen when you and Mr. Heyward were married, were you not?"

If Eliza heard Start's question, saw or sensed his endeavor to reach her, she gave no indication of it as she responded rather tensely, "I've already stated my wishes regarding this situation, and I shall not alter them, now or ever."

"Mother!" Jane Anne exclaimed once more, finally bursting into tears, you can't mean that. I love Stuart."

"I do mean it, dear, for your own good." Eliza said.

Feeling helpless, as he saw there was no compromising to be had with Eliza Heyward, Stuart, wondering when he would hold Jane Anne's hand again, tightened his grip on it and said, "Before I take my leave, Mrs. Heyward—" Stuart saw Eliza's brow make a sudden lift. "Yes, I'm leaving, so it won't be necessary for you to tell me to go. Anyway, before I do go, won't you tell me why you disapprove of me so? I feel I have a right to know and don't think I'm being unreasonable in asking it of you."

"Well, you may ask all you like," flared Eliza, "but I have no intention of prolonging this aggravating matter another second by going into any explanation for my actions. It would serve no purpose, whatever. I must get back to my guests. All I'm saying is this. I know what's best for my daughter, you don't. Now, if you'll excuse me, I'll go and be considerate enough to leave you both the freedom of a few minutes to say goodbye in private!" She whirled her back to them and had flung the door aside when Stuart's voice, calling her name, stopped her. She turned back, seeing for the first time through the whole discussion a deep flush streaking across Stuarts face.

There was no mistaking Stuart Drakston's anger and exasperation as he himself carried the matter a step or two farther by telling her,

"Very well, it will be as you wish but pertaining to the privacy, no thank you, Mrs. Heyward. I won't say goodbye to Jane Anne. And, I also think it's only the fair thing to do on my part to warn you, that I shall continue to go on with the endeavor of trying to win her for my wife. No, not in secret places, Mrs. Heyward, but at church and any other public place or otherwise that we may happen to meet." He dropped Jane Anne's hand and then looking at her longingly, Stuart inclined his head and lightly brushed her teary cheeks with his lips. "Good night, darling. I hope to see you tomorrow at church," and with that said and holding his head high as he turned it and looked straight ahead, Stuart strode forward and passed Eliza where she was standing beside the wide-flung door, revealing no sign of emotion about him that he was even aware she was present.

Amazed that Stuart Drakston had chosen to clear out so quickly and turn down those few brief minutes of privacy with Jane Anne that she had offered him, Eliza was feeling somewhat slapped-down as she stared at his departing back, and was suddenly having another blow rendered her, which she had not counted on, when Jane Anne sobbed despairingly through her tears, "Mother, how could you hurt us so?"

Having just finished a rather accelerated waltz with the light-footed and the jolly Tom Green, whose wife Betsy was starting to take a second turn around the dance floor with the Reverend Marsh Reed, Elizabeth Drakston had just begun to really fall into the swing of the party and enjoy herself—a rare thing for her to do at Green Sea, when she suddenly spied Stuart seeking her out. "Excuse me for a moment, Mr. Green, I believe my son wants a word with me."

"Surely, Mrs. Elizabeth, as long as it's your son because we have another number coming up when we catch our breath," hooted Tom as Elizabeth hurried through the crowd, meeting Stuart near the front door.

Now seeing, Stuart's flushed face, she cried with fear, lifting her hand to his brow, "You're ill, dear!"

His hand quickly caught hers, "No, mother, nothing like that," he assured. "It's just a personal matter that's boiled my blood a little too hot, I guess. Listen, I'm taking my leave now, but I want the rest of you to stay and enjoy yourselves. When I arrive home, I'll have the coachman to return with the coach. If Grandfather Carson or Grandmother should inquire of my whereabouts, just tell them that something came up, which required my attending to. I'll fill you in later on, but I'd prefer they not know the real reason I'm leaving. It may worry them."

Seeing the situation for what it was, more clearly by the second, Elizabeth said, "Let me get my wrap, son, I'll go with you. Mr. Green has already whirled my legs partly off, anyhow."

"Please, Mother, do as I ask and stay. I think its best."

"Well, all right, then. But, are you sure there's not something I can do?"

"I fear not, dear," he smiled, "not this time. Enjoy yourself, Mother, and have a good time. Mr. Greens waiting for that second dance, I see." He let go his mother's hand and strode on out, leaving Elizabeth looking after him as wistfully as Jane Anne had when he had strode from the library.

Of course, it was impossible for Elizabeth Drakston to regain even one degree of that zest which she undoubtedly had begun to catch from lighthearted Tom Green, when her son's anxious face had sent her hurrying to him. Though Elizabeth's person may have been at Green Sea, engaging in the festive occasion that was no sign her thoughts were taken with any of it. For the remainder of the evening, Elizabeth's mind was centered on one thing and that was her son back at Drakston Hall.

Elizabeth did take notice of one thing, though, and was not surprised in the least to see it. That was that subdued look that Jane Anne Heyward began to wear shortly after Stuart's departure. To Elizabeth, Jane Anne did not like much in having the makings of taking on the looks of a dazed puppet being dangled, as she was whirled from one set of arms to those of the next of the several young men who had promptly been at her elbow the moment they had noticed Stuart Drakston had left the scene. Indeed, Elizabeth was not one bit astonished to spot Jane Anne rapidly ascending the long-curved stairway during the buffet supper which Pete and the two maids had begun serving the guests about one hour later never to make it back downstairs another time for the rest of the ball. The circulating word soon got around that Jane Anne had fallen victim to a violent sick headache. If there were any doubters of the report, Elizabeth was not one of them. She believed the report.

Having been well aware of her son's growing affection for the grownup Jane Anne and the same affection for Stuart shining in Jane Anne's eyes, ever since she and her son had returned from England,

Elizabeth was positive that Jane Anne had indeed taken a headache and she also believed that Stuart's leave-taking and Jane Anne's indisposition were linked to something that Eliza Heyward had done. She did not know what, nor could she imagine. But she was positive that Eliza had done something.

All the same, Elizabeth Drakston finally made it through the evening, carrying her son's wishes out and very well at that, she thought with relief whereupon arriving home she saw a light burning in the window of Stuart's law office—giving credence to that ready explanation that she had had for Matthew and Amy when they had inquired of Stuart's whereabouts. She had told them that it was most likely someone had needed urgent legal help.

This happenstance of Stuart turning to his law books in his effort to deaden that blasting encounter between himself and Eliza Heyward that was still resounding in his ears when he had gotten home, could have had a lot more soundness to it than what Elizabeth was thinking as she sighted the lighted office. Unlike his late father Frank Drakston, Stuart was fast becoming one of the area's most well-liked and trusted young man. Besides that forever number of people who take advantage of every and any chance to obtain something for free, there were several clients as well tromping in and out of Stuart's law office daily and had been since the first day he had opened his law practice in Lucy Randolph's old schoolroom,

Still and all, though, in addition to Elizabeth and those three of whom the matter had involved and was tormenting at the time, it appeared the library episode was to have a profound impact on one or two others as well before the night was over. Doctor Seth Roalf and Caroline were to be led into a clash themselves over another subject— one they had thought they would never open by having discussed the matter. Yes, the doctor had been called upstairs and Jane Anne had told "Uncle Seth" what was making her head split, and the doctor in his endeavor to reassure his wife that no serious malady had struck had told Caroline. Rebecca Wainwright, because of her meddling way, was; also, to become so upset and agitated with Eliza over the affair that she did—for a change—listen to her brainy side telling her if she did not settle down and take it all more calmly that she just might fall with a stroke and lose out on those amorous delights that she was looking forward to experiencing with Tony Drexwell, and for once in her life too, bowed to defeat in trying to aid a love affair. And Luke, naturally, when he finally learned the full details form Eliza—later on in the early morning hours as she was cooing happily and contentedly in his arms following one of their most pleasurable and delightful coition for many months—he was torn between wife and child, a state of being that made any thought which popped in his head in the way of mending the situation seem not only disloyal to all parties involved but guideless to him besides. Hence, even though he was deeply disturbed, Luke kept his opinions to himself and tried to give a little encouragement and comfort to all and was later to much regret that he did not follow with a more urgent course of action.

In her clever and busybody manner, Rebecca was upstairs and quietly pushing open the door of Jane Anne's bedroom and softly calling "Angel Child" before Jane Anne had hardly gotten out of her ball gown and fallen on the bed, sobbing miserably.

Now with the lull of Rebecca's pitying voice coming through to Jane Anne, her sobs grew ever louder and when they did Rebecca did not wait any longer to be invited in, she rushed on over across the room to the bed and plumping down on the soft, giving feather mattresses she took Jane Anne in her arms and coaxed soothingly, "Now, nothing like a good cry, dear one, and telling everything to a sympathetic ear such as Aunt Rebecca's. The good Lord above knows I'm well-qualified, too, considering the experiences I've gone through in trying to help mend those ever so many lover's quarrels among my numerous acquaintances over the years, not to mention having to deal with a few of my own tender attachments, I dare say! Now, what is this all about? Why did that nice young man go stalking out of here so early this evening? Was it because—well that he became a little overanxious and frightened when you two slipped out to the summerhouse for a spell and you wouldn't listen to his apologies?"

"Oh, no, Aunt Rebecca, Stuart did nothing and he could never frighten me," sobbed Jane Anne. "I love him too much for that." Granted, being Jane Anne, she would not have called Rebecca anything but "Aunt" after Rebecca's first labeling herself that, for all the world, for fear of hurting Rebecca's feelings. Furthermore, lucky for Rebecca, Jane Anne was too upset to stop and wonder how did "Aunt Rebecca" Know that she and Stuart were in the summerhouse.

"Ah me, dear one," Rebecca went on almost crooning as she swayed back and forth with Jane Anne nestled against her, "if I've ever heard the word or know anything about its meaning, I would say your love for that young man is truly pure and sweet. But, why are you so distressed? Is it because he was called away on some lawyer business of some kind? If that's the case, can't say I'd do any differently, if I were sixteen again and he was my beau." She reached inside her bosom and drawing forth a dainty but serviceable handkerchief she put it in Jane Anne's hand. "But now it's time to dry your eyes, dear child, and powder your nose. We surely don't want that handsome blade, and a good catch too if I may add, see your face and eyes all red and swollen when he does rush back here tonight to have that last dance with you."

Jane Anne wailed that much harder, as she made an endeavor to catch her tears with the handkerchief, telling Rebecca between sobs, "Stuart won't ever be back, tonight or any other time! Mother might as well have told him he wasn't welcome here and to take his leave as quickly as possible! She thinks I'm too young for Stuart and says we must stop seeing one another—courting—I mean!"

Rebecca stopped swaying, staring down at the distraught girl in her arms in disbelief. Fleetingly, she wondered again if her ears were failing on her after all. Then, certain that she had heard Jane Anne correctly, she gasped, "But, why would your mother do a simple thing like that? Really! Just how old is that young man, child? He certainly didn't look as if his muscles and bones were ready to give way to me!"

"Stuart's twenty-two and I'm sixteen," Jane Anne weepingly informed.

"An ideal age! Simply ideal for the both of you! Why, surely your mother must have bubbles in her thinking tank tonight to have given that young man the boot because of that. Really! She should ask that fine Doctor Seth to give her a soothing tonic. It certainly wouldn't harm, if it did her no good," Rebecca, appalled that Eliza would hold such an idiotic notion, was firmly declaring just as Eliza rushed through the doorway.

Furious, not only because of what she had overheard but because of Rebecca's interference as well, and especially in a matter which Eliza considered was strictly none of Rebecca's business, Eliza retorted, rushing on over to the side of the bed, "I'll be the judge of that, Rebecca, and why are you up here, anyway?" But, taking in the fact that Jane Anne was no longer dressed, Eliza appeared to be surprised and more concerned with that aspect than she was in what Rebecca may have replied as she went on to inquire of her daughter,

"Dear, why have you undressed and the ball hardly half over?"

Plenty burned by Eliza's stinging insult, even though she was fully aware she more or less had it coming, because she certainly had not been paying Eliza the compliments of the season, Rebecca fired back—adding more fuel—before Jane Anne had a chance to reply, "You're surely minus some buttons to be asking your daughter that, after giving your boot to her sweetheart not less than an hour ago and a finer looking young man and a gentleman at that, I have yet to see! I should know, I had a most delightful dance and conversation with him while Jane Anne danced with that other man—Green, I believe."

"So, I noticed, Rebecca," Eliza shot right back. "Are there any left who you haven't danced with? Perhaps you should go back downstairs and run a tally to that effect and leave my daughter to me!"

Started, at her hostess power to sting when she had a mind to, for a moment, as Rebecca stared up at Eliza, she appeared to be as much beyond the ability to speak had she been wearing a muzzle. However, Eliza should have known her put down had not also, stopped Rebecca's mind from working, too. Though her tongue was idle her mind was working plenty, traveling clear back to those days at Windsor when the situation was reversed, and she had been hostess to the sixteen year old Eliza Carson, who she herself had seen returning twenty-four year old Luke Heyward's kisses with the burning passion of one experienced to the game.

The mere thought of it made Rebecca seethe with rage as she suddenly bristled and let her tongue explode back, "Perhaps that's not such a bad idea, since your male guests appear to enjoy my company so much. Maybe I'll liven up the dullness that my absence no doubt has affected. In the meantime, I would suggest that you open your eyes wide enough to see that Jane Anne isn't that little girl anymore that you're still visioning her to be. She is a mature woman. Her needs and wants are every much as deep and whole, maybe more who knows, as yours were at sixteen when I paired you and Luke Heyward off together that day at Windsor to enjoy a secluded trail ride, after I saw that both of you were itching to know one another better. You were delighted and fell head over heels in love with him that very afternoon, seeming not to mind one bit that there was an eight-year age gap between you! You'd do well to recall these facts to your mind, Eliza. Maybe it would bring you to see, before it's too late just how unreasonable you're being regarding this situation—"

231

No question about it, Rebecca had lost her muzzle and there is no telling how much farther she would have carried it, had not Jane Anne at that very instant chosen to sob, "Mother, my head is splitting," bringing both women to swiftly give her their whole attention, as each was suddenly moving a hand toward her brow. Both women were relieved to find that they felt no fever. Even so, that fact still did not stop either of them from thinking that no chances should be taken, and particularly in circumstances where a doctor was so near.

"I'm sorry, dear, I didn't know," Eliza said and started to ask Rebecca if she would be so kind as to ask Doctor Seth to come upstairs immediately when she did rejoin the party. Knowing well Rebecca's flare; however, for going into a long melodramatic oratory if the chance came her, Eliza, for fear that Rebecca would go downstairs and alarm the whole house, possibly ending the party right then, quickly changed her mind and told Jane Anne that she would go and get Doctor Seth to come and give her a sedative.

Promptly, Eliza was back, bringing the doctor with her. They found Rebecca still sitting on the bed continuing to soothe Jane Anne who had begun to sneeze periodically.

"So, I see you're coming down with the sniffles, young Lady," stated the doctor as he moved toward the bed to lay his hand on Jane Anne's brow as her mother and Rebecca had done. Though, he could see, too, that she had been crying buckets of tears, he made no mention of that not then.

"I don't believe it's a cold, Seth," Eliza filled in. "I think the sneezes are resulting from all those plumes and feathers she has her head buried in."

In the course of attending the Heyward family as their physician over the years, Doctor Seth Roalf had come to see through Eliza Heyward's temperament inside and out and understand it as much, if not more thoroughly, than Doctor John Davis ever had. He had already guessed that something had vexed Eliza sorely. Now, having heard her remark regarding feathers, Seth Roalf was getting a pretty fair picture of what had supplied some of Eliza's vexation anyway Rebecca.

The doctor smiled in his beard. "If you'll be so kind, Mrs. Wainwright—"

Rebecca let the glare that she had planted on Eliza's face go instantly, stammering, before the doctor was forced to go on asking her to move, "Why, yes—yes, of course, doctor," and as delicately as she could she eased away from Jane Anne, telling her, "I'll look in on you later, Angel Child," and rose to her feet—moving away quickly as to give Seth Roalf the opportunity to examine his patient.

Embarrassed and angry with herself, too, for letting this last insult from Eliza get at her so much that she had failed to notice that Seth Roalf had been waiting for her to move, Rebecca sent another glare Eliza's way, promising herself that—come morning—she was going to remove herself from Eliza Heyward's presence for good, as she pursed her mouth firmly and flitted out the door. Moreover, she was going to return to the party and take it by storm once more. Never mind about her best and newly purchased pink gauze dressing gown—the one that she had planned on donning on her wedding night to Tony being ruined with that child's tears—the beautiful feather trimming crushed and so soggy—wet that she looked something like a scaled chicken before its feathers were picked off, she was going to rejoin the crowd, anyway, and have herself a ball! Besides, who would have their eyes on her attire, anyhow, once the men were holding her a trifle too closely again!

And Rebecca Wainwright did as she had vowed. Though Luke, Tom Green, Matthew, Marsh Reed, yes; and Seth Roalf, too, as well as a number of others, were disappointed that Rebecca was removing her cheerful self from their midst and had prevailed upon her to extend her visit for at least a few days more, Rebecca remained firm in her decision to take her leave of Green Sea. She was saying her goodbyes and by eight o'clock the next morning. She would not listen to Luke's suggestion that he himself or someone else accompany her to the train depot, telling him that she had arrived alone, and she surely could find her way back alone. Besides, it was Sunday and she had no desire to stand in the way of keeping anyone from their church for even one Sunday! Thus, Luke did the next best thing. The Heyward's newest coach and most capable driver, Charlie, would take Rebecca to Charleston to make her train schedule.

Rebecca's farewell with Jane Anne had been warm and tender, with Jane Anne becoming sadden over her leaving, because she felt that she and Stuart were losing their most staunch ally even though they had not known Rebecca not even the length of one day. Jane Anne did not go downstairs to see Rebecca off. Instead, she was waiting and looking out from her bedroom window, so that she could wave and blow Rebecca a kiss in private. Jane Anne thought her goodbye to

Rebecca would be punctuated with a more personal feeling that way than had she been standing with the others on the porch.

The leave-taking took place immediately following breakfast, and a number of guests the Greens among them—who would not be taking their own leave for several more days, had also gone out to the porch with Luke and Eliza to see Rebecca off.

Rebecca wasted little time and few words with the women in the group—including Eliza, only sparing her hostess a simple "Thank you" and a slight peck on the cheek. The men presented a different story though and especially Luke and Tom Green when she came to them. Rebecca had purposely saved Tom Green for one of the last, because she had a feeling that Betsy Green was about as much fed up with her as Eliza was, simply for the reason that she and Tom, both being of a lively nature, had hit it off so well.

Now flaunting her airs, a bit and dangling her forthcoming position a little, Rebecca turned to a beaming Tom Green and told him, "Mr. Green, you are one delight to have around. If you're ever in the vicinity of New Orleans, do remember that I'm not too far away at, Hanging Moss. Oh, that's the name of my prospective husband's plantation. Tony and I both would be most happy to welcome you anytime, day or night." She deliberately excluded Betsy from the invitation. "Hanging Moss is well-known. Just mention the name and you won't have any trouble being set in its direction. Now, don't forget, Hanging Moss, is the name."

"You can count on my memory, Mrs. Wainwright. It will be my pleasure. You can count on it, I certainly won't let you or the name of that plantation slip in the background," grinned Tom Green, as he pumped Rebecca's hand rather long, appearing hesitate to turn it loose while Betsy was feeling—right at that moment—that she would also take a little pleasure, too, in seeing Tom with Rebecca Wainwright right beside him hanging from a limb at Hanging Moss!"

"How delightful," said Rebecca to Tom as she gave him a smiling nod and then turned to Luke, lifting her hand. "Dear Luke, do keep well and watch over that dear, beautiful daughter of yours who looks so much like you," again deliberately leaving Eliza out completely as she had Betsy, and chattering on continually as Tom on one side of her and Luke on the other escorted her to the waiting coach and saw that she was safely ensconced aboard.

Before the wheels of the coach had hardly turned once to start

Rebecca on her way, she noted that Eliza and Betsy Green had already sprinted inside. But did Rebecca mind? Not a smidge. She was too preoccupied with waving to the young girl in the window and the two men standing in the carriage way. And, though there was truly no thought in Rebecca's mind of never going back to Green Sea the ten or more years she was to dwell at Hanging Moss Plantation in Louisiana as Mrs. Anthony Drexwell that was the way it was to turn out. This was her first and last visit to Green Sea. Moreover, Rebecca did not see Jane Anne, Luke, or Tom Green ever again, even though she and Luke were to continue to carry on their correspondence until the day, some years later, a wire came from Tony Drexwell telling of Rebecca's death in a yellow fever epidemic.

Luke was grieved. But, even in his sorrow to learn that Rebecca was gone, and also in his awareness, too, that he was going to miss receiving her newsy and somewhat dizzy letters, he still could hardly think of her without experiencing a certain degree of light amusement, too. Yes, as Rebecca seemed disposed to lighten many situations in life with a little of her childlike humor—let's not leave out at the cost of others sometimes—likewise in death, it appeared it was not going to change.

As Rebecca had vowed to leave Green Sea the morning after the party and had kept her vow, similarly, Stuart Drakston was to remain firm in his stand. The very next day at church, he was to prove to Eliza that he had not been merely talking gibberish in the library when he had warned her of his intentions.

On this particular Sunday morning, whether it was fortune doing the timing or just the way things fell, the Heyward and Drakston carriages were to roll up on the churchyard at the same time. Most parishioners had a routine place they parked their vehicles. Even though the spots were not reserved by any distinct mark, as a rule, each family carriage was parked in the same spot at every church service with near precise accuracy. The two carriages—Luke was driving a much less pretentious surrey that had seen a few years use since he had insisted Rebecca leave in the best Green Sea could offer—preceded on to their customary places and parked side by side with only a few feet of ground separating them—a habit that had been going on since before Franklin Drakston Jr. and Matthew Carson had married the Goodyear sisters. The Randolph coach and the coach from Elms were parked close by, though their occupants had already vacated them and gone on inside the church.

Everything was to progress along at a normal pace, despite the airing of differences the night before between Stuart and Eliza. As soon as the Drakston's driver Luke was handling his own team—hopped down and swing the doors of the costly open-carriage aside, Stuart leapt out and was giving his mother and grandmother a hand and standing by until he saw that Matthew Carson had lighted safely on the ground, too. While Luke was tethering his team of horses to the sturdy oak that had ever served as the Heyward's hitching post, Carr likewise to Stuart was giving a hand to his mother and sister in stepping down from the surrey. Then, there were the usual "Good, mornings and what a fine day" as everybody bunched together and went on toward the church with the elders in the group pairing together and Stuart falling beside Carr and Jane Anne. Stuart went on to take his seat beside Jane Anne as he managed to do every Sunday morning since his return home. The fact that Eliza Heyward cut a rather cold eye his way as everybody was getting settled down, paused him none whatever. And, there was no change in his manner once the church service was over and the congregation was back outside upon the grounds, exchanging small talk, though what Stuart was saying to Jane Anne could not have been classified as such. What he was saying to her was coming from the heart as they were walking back slowly together toward the carriages.

Stuart was holding Jane Anne's hand, telling her, "I'm sorry, darling, about your headache last night. Mother told me that you were taken ill several hours before the party ended." Stuart like his mother believed, too, that Jane Anne, had truly been ill. The pallor of her face and the dark-violet pools under her eyes were evidence enough.

"Yes, I did have a terrible headache, but to tell you the truth, I guess it was rewarding in a way, because I was simply having a miserable time after you left."

"Well, I didn't leave of my own free will, you know. I had a miserable night, too." "I know, Stuart," she replied, as their feet paused, and they looked at one another.

Studying the longing and yearning that was stamped on her face so clearly, he went on, "you do realize there is a remedy for such misery, do you not?"

"Yes," she finally said and blushed.

"Well, marry me then," he pleaded, "right now, darling, today, and then nobody could keep us apart."

236

"I can't, Stuart, as much as I love you, I can't. I want everything pleasant and right when we do marry. I want a home wedding, with a white dress and Papa giving me away, and all the rest. You do understand, don't you?"

"I'm trying to. But, what will I have after you go away? There will be nothing, not even this much, like we are now. Nothing to look forward to."

Now, she was reading his face, seeing not a trace of light about his handsome features and, although she felt as down as he did if not more, she forced herself to smile as she said, "You mean to say my letters are going to affect so little consequence? I should think they'd mean something to you?"

He seemed surprised.

"Letters?" he said, his face brightening. "I haven't ever thought about letters. All I've had my mind on is your leaving and wondering when I'll see you again. You mean you'll write?"

"Every single day, Stuart," she said. "I haven't been forbidden to, so I don't see why not. Of course, the subject hasn't come up, nor will I bring it up. Still, I must be honest and tell you that regardless of what may come up, if anything, I plan to write to you, and I shall be expecting a reply to each letter I mail to Drakston Hall."

And "And, you'll get your reply," he promised. "There come our families, and I guess this is goodbye, and I can't even kiss you." His expression grew dark again.

"No, not goodbye, Stuart. Let's make it a pact to never say goodbye as long as we live. I promise, darling, we will marry the day I get my parent's consent. I believe Mother will view it all differently in time. I love each one of you dearly, and want us to be a family together, not one that's separated," she said, with both growing silent as they were now being overtaken and bypassed by the Heywards and Stuart's family, as well as Doctor Seth and Caroline and the Randolph's, too, all of who had been vising together on the church grounds, with Martha singing out as she passed, "Look at the lovebirds," which—naturally-caused Eliza to become even more ill-humored than she already was. But, for this one time, Eliza saved what she was thinking and did not spout off at Martha, who; in truth, was in the dark as to what had taken place in the library. Jane Anne and Stuart never resumed the topic they were discussing. Their hearts were too taken with the moment upon them. They had let the silence grow.

Now, both families were settled in their carriages and waiting, and Stuart's grip was growing tighter and tighter on Jane Anne's hand and she could not bring herself to use force in pulling away.

But, finally seeing that Eliza Heyward was turning fully around in her seat to stare at them, Jane Anne, said, "I have to go, Stuart, they're waiting."

"Yes, they're waiting, darling," he said, letting go of her hand. "But don't forget, so am I."

She forced another smile.

"As if I could," she said, and suddenly was running toward her father's surrey with half blinding tears which Stuart did not see.

But, having already turned his own team of horses around and hollering out a "Good day" to his friends as he headed the carriage toward home, Doctor Seth and also Caroline did see how unhappy Jane Anne had become over her parting with Stuart Drakston.

"Did you see that, Seth?" Caroline ventured to say, "I wish there were something I could do to help."

The doctor swiftly reached for his wife's hand. He was more than ready and happy to meet and accept what apparently was Caroline's way in letting him know that she had decided to dismiss their little tiff of the night before forming her thoughts. Yet, as much as Seth was glad his wife appeared to be ready to patch up their tiff in harmony— unquestionably regaining her usual even-tempered steadiness under the flow of March Reed's alarm cries, he was thinking—the doctor was still a mite wary over becoming engaged in another "affairs of the heart" discussion with Caroline, especially if it was going to bear upon anybody or any one thing connected with Green Sea.

So, while Seth lovingly patted his wife's hand with one hand and held onto the reins with the other, he gingerly told her, "But, there isn't dear, or I'm led to believe there isn't. Besides, if we're to maintain our close friendship with both families, which I'm positive you want to do and so do I, we can't afford to become involved. Maybe it'll all blow over, anyway." He turned his head and smiled at her. "Let's turn the team around and head for O'Henry's before we go home, and get us some ice cream. I think it'd taste mighty good. What do you say?"

"Dessert before dinner?" she smiled back.

"Before and after, too, if it's ice cream," he laughed.

Since Doctor Seth Roalf had not had many spare days over the years to visit with his friends and neighbors just for the simple joy of visiting and that alone—due to his busy practice his wife had made untold visits to Green Sea when Seth had not accompanied her. Besides those many times when Caroline had set out from Elms alone to call on Eliza—days when Seth had seen he could manage his office without her help—there had also been numerous occasions when Seth had dropped Caroline off at the archway to visit with Eliza while he had gone on to pay a call on some patient who was too ill to journey to his office for treatment, or to some other patient who did not have the money or the means to journey with, or perhaps to call on someone else at which nothing was at stake save Seth's own wish to have his curiosity satisfied regarding their welfare.

In any case, it seemed those numerous times when Eliza and Caroline had had the urge to view the family portraits and check them for possible harm, the doctor had never been present. Granted, Seth had heard Caroline make mention of this diverted pastime between herself and Eliza on several visits, but since he also had been deep-versed in the story of how Eliza had chanced her life to save the portraits as well as her shortage of suitable wall space to accommodate them in the small grey house, he had never held anything more than polite casual interest in the subject on those occasions when Caroline had been moved to talk about it. Once, Seth did go so far as to inquire why did Eliza not go ahead and hang one or two of the portraits in the small house, anyway.

"Eliza will never do that," Caroline had told him. "That's the way she is. Unless she can hang every last one, her deep-rooted loyalty and love for each of those family members will stop her from selecting any one or two among the group to display in her home. To her, only hanging one or two, would be a betrayal to the others."

Thus, well aware that Eliza Heyward was indeed fiercely emotional in the matter of her attachments and affections, sometimes to the point of near idolatry whether it concerned thing or person, Seth had understood and attached no more importance to the subject.

However, it was a totally different story with the doctor on the night of the housewarming ball. In addition to being shocked and surprised at the number of portraits—the majority of them life size—which the hall held alone, Seth was also to become strangely moved no sooner than he had entered the hallway with Caroline and gotten his first glimpse of the portrait-adorned walls, and especially as his eye caught the likeness of the sixteen year old Eliza painted with her two brothers on either side of her. Although Seth was drawn to all the portraits, and found himself going back to the hallway time and time again throughout the evening to study them, it was always that one certain one which was to intrigue him most, causing him to experience an unfathomable urge to stand and gaze at it. It was not the likeness of Eliza and the late Nat Carson whose faces the doctor was staring at so intently. It was the face of Eliza's older late brother, Phil Carson.

Seth Roalf was profoundly puzzled over his reaction. The doctor wanted to think and did think that his marriage to Caroline had been consummated and established on mutual solid basis, made out of whole cloth, so to speak—not so thinly fabricated that the mere likeness of the man who she had once loved and been engaged to marry, would lure him to stand and gaze in questioning disquietude. He pondered over the aspect of it for a good while, before his thoughts were suddenly coming together and making a comprehensible impact as to why the portrait was captivating his attention so. Seth Roalf was certain he had seen Phil Carson's face before this night!

Where and when Seth Roalf had seen the face, he had no idea and had just begun to make an attempt at trying to place the odd circumstance in his mind when he was called on to go upstairs. Of course, with the obvious discord between Eliza and Rebecca Wainwright attracting his attention, plus his regard for his patient and all the particulars she had imparted to him concerning her headache, Seth was forced to push his own personal thoughts aside until later. But, once he and Caroline were on their way home, conversing quietly about Eliza's disapproval of Stuart Drakston and the occasional pitfalls and entanglements which forever seems to surround the wooing act, with nothing to distract Seth's attention in the night's late stillness from the subject but that of the motion of the rolling buggy and the smooth clip-clop of the horse's hooves, he found himself reflecting once more over his stunning recognition of the face in the portrait. And, suddenly, without the slightest warning, Seth's thoughts were all merging together and forming a long-forgotten scene of an anxious Rachelle Fillmore bending over the stilled and bloody body of a combat trooper just arrived from Gettysburg! A soldier whose head upon first glance looked as though a bullet had gone tearing through its—dark brown wavy hair filled with blood, fragments of shell, and dirt plastered to a deathlike face—a mangled and torn left arm dangling helplessly from a filthy makeshift stretcher!

The September night was warm, but Doctor Seth Roalf had suddenly become ice-cold. He had not thought of the gentle pretty Rachelle Fillmore for years. Further, why his mind had come to link the likeness in the portrait with that gory scene and, that emaciated, silent soldier who had stared up at him and Rachelle so imploringly for days and days—never speaking no matter how much he was coaxed, was beyond any reasoning of Seth's to understand. Yes, to identify the likeness of the late Confederate officer Phil Carson with the mangled and mute Union private from Gettysburg as being the same person, was indeed too insane for Seth to grasp in one minute or even a number of additional minutes.

Continuing to feel as if his blood was actually curdling, the doctor had become so unusually silent and long absorbed in the possible absurdity of such a happening taking place, that finally Caroline was arousing herself from the curve of his arm to inquire of him, "What's the matter, Seth? You seem so tense in the last little while, and do you realize you didn't even answer me? Not only that but I'm positive you haven't spoken one word in the last half hour."

"I'm sorry, dear, would you repeat the question."

"See there, you didn't even hear me. I—well to tell you the truth, I've completely forgotten what it was, now. It was something regarding Stuart and Jane Anne. I'll think of it, and in the meantime, I want you to tell me what's wrong. I know there's something."

Should he tell Caroline? They had always shared everything or leastways he thought they had. He could be wrong in thinking the soldier was Phil Carson. No, as eerie as it was, that soldier's eyes, so much like Eliza's and the likeness of Phil Carson in the portrait, had stared up at him too many hours for him to forget the look. But, what about the Yankee uniform? Well, there could be many explanations regarding that reconnaissance assignment maybe? Still, if that were the answer, why would any man elevated to the personage and rank in life as that of Philipp Carson choose to continue to hide his true identity in the uniform of the enemy and remain permanently listed as a missing casualty of Gettysburg—giving up his family—the girl he was engaged to marry—his friends—his heirship to Green Sea? No, that was too senseless to fit. What then? Was it because the soldier who he thought was Philipp Carson, had been shell-shocked to permanent silence and was unable to talk or afraid to maybe? No, that didn't fit, either, had not Rachelle Fillmore finally induced the soldier to break his silence? Indeed, had not Rachelle Fillmore and the soldier become such fast and close friends that she offered him the comfort of her home for his convalescence? Further, was it possible that the soldier could indeed have been Philipp Carson, with Rachelle Fillmore's presence projecting for him the only transference open to his negative behavior, giving his emotional instability the strength it sought and, at the same time, causing his mind to block out everything else except that dreamlike peace that no doubt she was able to bring him? He certainly appeared to have no qualms about accepting her proposal, and people did do strange things—taking courses of action sometimes that were entirely without rhyme or reason.

Breaking in upon Seth's thoughts, Caroline said, her impatience revealed in every word, "Seth, I'm still waiting, in case you've forgotten."

"I know, dear, and I'm sorry," Seth quickly replied, and trying to approach the subject in a casual manner went on, "I guess I have been letting Eliza's late relatives and ancestors take up too much space in my thoughts tonight. But I'll have to say those portraits she finally dug from the pantry, don't only capture the eye at first glance but, in my opinion, also brings an instant changeless and abiding air to that new mansion that elsewise would take a hundred years of living to effect."

Rather hesitantly Caroline said, her thoughts had not bargained for his remark, "yes—what you say is true. Still, I must point out on Eliza's behalf, that being stashed in the pantry all those years as you've put it, didn't stop her from looking at those portraits often enough."

Without doubt you too, Seth was thinking as he went on, "Well, she certainly does have a number of distinguished-looking ancestors to display, not to mention those other splendid paintings of her own family."

Caroline let a marked silence drop before she ventured to tell him, "I'm sorry, Seth, I can see by staring at those portraits tonight like I did, that I've hurt you."

"Not really, dear. In fact, it's the other way around," he said. "You see, if they hadn't captured your attention, I'd be much more concerned about that aspect, than the fact that you did stare."

They let another silence drop. But, suddenly, Seth was saying before he even realized how far he was taking the subject, "Caroline, just how well did you know Philipp Carson?"

The question stumped Caroline. At once, she was making a wider space between her husband and herself on the buggy seat.

"I should think I knew him well enough," she snapped, "since we grew up together and were engaged to marry one another. Though I haven't the least idea what's under the surface of your question, or what might've prompted you to ask it. Surely not because I did stare at his portrait tonight perhaps a little more than I should have!"

Too late, Seth saw he had overplayed the hand he was contemplating on playing.

"I've offended you," he said, "but I didn't mean to. The question did lack a degree of fitness, I'm sorry."

Tempering somewhat to her husband's offered regrets, Caroline, reconsidering, replied, "Well, as long as we've been married and especially with my having come to our marriage holding no secrets from you, I should think I have every right to be insulted. However, I will offer this much concerning your sudden interest in the man I was once engaged to. Phil was full of life, gregarious, with a great sense of humor. Though he was highly emotional like Eliza, he was still a bit prankish. He liked to jest and cut jokes, a regular extrovert I would say."

"Makes everything all the more complex." Seth declared.

Now, thrown into a state of utter confusion that brought her voice rising to a rare pitch of highness, Caroline was flaring again, "What in the world are you talking about, if I may ask!"

With a tone of voice matching hers, Seth blared back, "Philipp Carson, that's what!" And, feeling as if he were being gored by the horns of the dilemma that his very own logic had affected, he went on blaring out, "I'm almost positive I dressed the wounds of that very same man, following the Battle of Gettysburg! If I didn't, he was surely Philipp Carson's twin or his reincarnation, I don't know which!"

So helplessly numb Seth's remark did Caroline in, she did not like much in toppling from the buggy, though she made an effort to conceal the impact of his divulgence form him. Even so, she found her hands gripping onto the buggy seat in order to steady herself, as she said in a trembling voice, "I'm aware, Seth, I'm repeating myself, but what on God's green earth, do you mean? Are you saying that you think Philipp Carson is alive? If you are holding to such a bizarre idea, do you realize you're talking about a man whose death has been grieved for a period of twenty-one years or more?"

Only then, as Caroline's trembling voice brought Seth's head turning in her direction, was the extremity of his explosive unbosoming revealed to him. Seeing her ghost-white face in the brightness of the moonlit night, he quickly made a grab for her hand, saying, "I can see my blabbering has shocked you half to death. I guess I should've kept my thoughts relating to that matter to myself. I would have, had I known you'd gotten so upset. Let's forget I even said it, shall we?"

"No, Seth, you've gone too far with the matter to suggest we stop now," she said, as she peered back at him with an unswerving look shining in her eyes. "I want to hear everything, any cause or occasion that would give support for you making such a statement!".

Aside from the fact that he had had high hopes of his own in respect to Rachelle Fillmore, Seth told her everything—leaving out nothing as Caroline's eyes never once strayed from his direction, though Seth had turned back to the business of keeping his horse headed the right way while he talked.

Finally, when Seth's story had played out, he heard Caroline mutter, "A Yankee—a Yankee in a private's uniform."

Seth's head shot around to face Caroline again.

"Yes, but as I've tried to explain, there could be lots of reasons for those circumstances and especially in battle." He said.

"I see," she muttered once more and turning her head away from him and much to Seth's surprise she continued on in a voice growing with indignation, "besides the absurdity of your story, what you're trying to say is that perhaps I didn't know Phil at all, that he could've used such a circumstance, if that was the case, to turn his back away from everything and everyone he even knew—Including me!"

"Now, Caroline, I didn't say no such thing! Oh, please what's the point of our bickering about it, anyway? I wish I'd never mentioned it! Like I said, let's forget it and not discuss it anymore. It has been a long time and I could be mistaken."

"I doubt I'll completely forget it, Seth, but I do agree with your suggestion, we say no more about it. Heaven forbid Eliza ever finding out that you think you saw her brother

fraternizing with the Yankees! Worse still, there's no telling what it would do to poor Mr. Matthew, after all these years. Really, I'm very much put out with you, Seth, for harboring such a staggering belief and particularly about someone you never knew at all. And further, for your information, I'm glad we've finally reached Elms, where I can take my leave of you and be alone for a while!" And, firing off that remark at her husband, Caroline was already jumping from the buggy and making a dash for the porch steps no sooner than Seth had pulled on the horse's reins to stop the buggy.

All the same, Seth was also beginning to feel put out—becoming every much as perturbed right at that moment with his wife as she appeared to be with him, because he was positive that it was more for vanity's sake than anything else that Caroline had taken the stand she had.

Sitting there, watching his wife go flipping into the house, Seth began to play with the idea of trying to make contact with Rachelle Fillmore once again and rapidly, began to gain ground toward convincing himself that he should not allow Caroline's irrational behavior to triumph over the strong and valid points he had made regarding the subject. Yes, Seth became persuaded to try to locate the whereabouts of Rachelle Fillmore in order to find out what did; indeed, ever happen to the Yankee soldier.

But now, with Caroline smiling at him as he turned the buggy to head for O'Henry's General Store, Seth decided to part from his idea of stirring into the past. Besides, he had found, long ago, that health-wise it was better not to. Still, in spite of any decision the doctor might have made about putting an end-all any plan or idea he may have held in an attempt to clear things, the outcome would have been changed little if any; in that, destiny itself had already lifted its hand to give the warning winds another stir—thrusting yesteryear with the here and now.